PRAISE FOR
BLOOD SECRETS

"Inherent Truth, the first in the Blood Secrets Trilogy--
and Ms. Anthony's debut!--is a stunner! Gripping and
engaging from the start, this book will take over your
life for a day or two and is the kind of book avid readers
will quickly devour."

— Kandy, Amazon

"Fabulous book! I could not put it down once I began
reading and can't wait for book two!"

— Cathy G., Goodreads

"Psychological thrillers with a bit of paranormal thrown
in are my favorite books to read and this one did not
disappoint! Not many books can keep you guessing and
piecing together clues right up until the end! This will
definitely be a series to follow! "

— Moms4Missions, Amazon

"An outstanding novel. It is a complex mystery, with
many twists and turns. It captivated me from the
beginning."

— Sondra H., Goodreads

INHERENT LIES

BLOOD SECRETS ✠ BOOK 2

ALICIA ANTHONY

ISBN: 978-1-7333624-3-6 (Print)

ISBN: 978-1-7333624-2-9 (Ebook)

Published by Drury Lane Books, USA.

Keep up with Alicia online for up-to-the-minute news and reader extras:

www.AliciaAnthonyBooks.com

Cover Art by Paper and Sage.

www.PaperandSage.com

For Doug,

*the plot twist behind my own
happily ever after.*

Thank you for cheering me on.

1

LIV

I should have been three thousand miles away that night, not standing in the drizzle watching recovery units unearth the remains of a twelve-year-old girl. I shivered as the piercing caw of a crow sounded from the church steeple behind me.

"Tis an omen, it is." Michael Donaghey's white hair lay plastered to his head, darkened by an afternoon spent in Irish mist. Although he now lived in Dublin, he'd grown up in County Cork and his accent was heavy even to native Irish. To an American like me, he sounded like what I'd always thought an Irish man should sound like, a mix between Darby O'Gill and a post-pubescent Lucky Charms leprechaun.

Michael had been with the Dublin Garda "since God was a young man," as he liked to say, and had taken me under his wing since the afternoon I'd mustered the courage to call the number on the scrap of paper I'd found under the floorboards in my grandmother's old cottage. That was almost six months ago. And despite my sister's urging, I'd never intended to stay this long.

The trip was planned. Head to Ireland, tie up some loose ends with my grandmother's estate, go home. I'd even factored in a little time with the sister I'd never known. Her offer to teach me more about my gifts growing more enticing with every misunderstood dream. After all that, it'd be time to go back to Cascade Hills. Time to pick up the pieces of my jigsaw puzzle of a life. But once I met Michael, it was easier to stay. Easier to claim that life had gotten in the way. When the truth was, death had other ideas.

Michael's arm blanketed my shoulder in warmth as he joined me at the rock wall. Below us, the countryside opened, revealing lush hills and valleys just outside Dublin City. Behind us, across a narrow road, stood Johnnie Fox's Pub, whose claim to fame was being the "highest" pub in all of Ireland.

I'd visited with Ashlyn my first night in Ireland. Beyond the quaint nooks and crannies of the pub, there'd been another draw. A sensation, far greater than the cozy warmth of Guinness, filtered through my veins, beckoning me with a sense of belonging.

Whispers of, *"Welcome home,"* wafted on the breeze. Maybe it was because I was with the sister I'd just recently learned existed, or the fact that I was in a country that held a special place in my grandmother's heart. Regardless, I felt safe and welcomed in the land of my ancestors, people who afforded magic and the unexplainable an air of importance I'd never before experienced.

Trust me, I know how cheesy that sounds. And now, as jacketed professionals sifted through a blanket of overgrown vegetation to haul the decomposing remains of an innocent little girl to the morgue, safe was the most remote emotion.

I pushed the memory of that first night at the pub away and

leaned into Michael's side, the rainproof fabric of our navy blue Garda jackets sliding noisily against each other.

"It's not fair," I heard myself say, realizing too late that I was more distraught over the role I was forced to play versus the death of someone's daughter. I took a breath and tried to cover, scuffing my tennis shoe over a loose rock at the base of the wall. "She didn't do anything to deserve this."

"Oh, Liv, thirty years I've been watching these things happen, and thirty years later I still don't understand the evils of man." Michael paused, his voice getting quiet. "You, though, just like your ma, you see it."

"What if I don't want to see it anymore?" For the first time I lent a voice to the frustration nagging at me.

Michael sighed, his broad shoulders rose and fell as he gave my shoulder a squeeze. "We aren't always afforded the opportunity to choose our destiny."

Since arriving in Dublin, Michael had become one of the few people I could confide in. Before the trip, I'd anticipated Ashlyn would have filled that role. I owed her a debt of gratitude for giving me reason enough to leave the heartache of Cascade Hills in my rear-view mirror. But since I'd been working with Michael, my relationship with my sister had changed.

We still got together for dinner and drinks at least once a week, but there was an air of inexplicable friction between us. I'd first felt it one morning at Grandma's cottage, the buzz of pent up energy humming between us. And now, the way my body buzzed with pinpricks of dissatisfaction when we were together proved she felt the rift as powerfully as I did. Even so, she never let on.

Ashlyn was busy with her own caseload for the Garda so our talks usually circled around the everyday minutiae of our jobs. Rarely did we allow our conversations to venture into the realm of our personal relationship. I was thankful for that. I had a feeling I wouldn't like what she had to say.

"Perhaps it's time to take a break, my love." Michael had started calling me that the first day I met him, and the nickname stuck.

I glanced over at him, grateful for a reason to stop watching as techs zipped what was left of the girl's blackened body into an oversized bag and lifted her onto a gurney.

Michael's blue eyes twinkled down at me, the skin crinkled at the corners above round rosy cheeks. His easy smile was what had first drawn me to him. Many officers in the Garda were so serious in their work. Michael tempered his professionalism with a good dose of Irish wit. It was obvious why my birthmother had chosen him as her partner some twenty years before.

No matter what case he was working, what horrific crime he was forced to solve, he never allowed the horrible parts of his job to cloud his psyche.

"The devil knocks on our door every day, lads. The key is, not to let him in." I'd heard that turn of phrase from Michael countless times. The younger generation of officers had taken to ignoring him. It was hard not to notice the sideways glances between them, the condescension toward an old man teetering on the edge of senility, spouting nonsense. But from the beginning, I knew he was different.

"Donaghey, Sullivan! Over here!" One of the crime scene investigators motioned for us from the bottom of the hill. I followed Michael over the low rock wall. Picking my way down the embankment with care, I worked to keep a firm grip on the wet foliage beneath the rubber soles of my tennis shoes. Michael, by contrast, trotted easily down the incline, ignoring any threat the rain-glazed vegetation posed to a man of his age.

I hurried to join him just as one of the investigators began to speak.

"Could be the murder weapon." The older of the two men pointed into the knee-high grass.

Michael glanced back at me, waiting for my input. I peered down into the weeds. A knife, about eight inches long with a curved blade glinted up at me. It was caked with mud, the ivory handle blackened by time and grime. I blew a silent stream of air through my lips as relief flooded me. The knife had nothing to do with the girl's death, sparing me from the impromptu vision that too often accompanied crime scene finds.

"It's not the murder weapon," I said. "She was strangled."

Two sets of eyes bored into me.

"Quite a coincidence, then, isn't it? How can you be sure?" The younger of the two crime scene investigators gave me a doubtful look, one eyebrow raised, voice ripe with skepticism.

"Has she been wrong before?" Michael shot back. "Give us a ring when the forensics come in. Sure, they'll be looking for ligatures."

And so it had been for the last several months, Michael cocooning me from skeptics while I re-opened cases long cold with ever intensifying visions. There was an obvious divide within the Garda. A good majority believed that psychic dreams held merit. Most still had grandmothers that swore by the call of the banshee. But not everyone was willing to admit those beliefs, at least not out loud.

Others asserted psychic mediums were nothing more than a spoof, a hoax meant to draw attention or money. I had a file full of newly closed cases to prove otherwise, so it didn't bother me, except when we were in the field and one of the investigators called me out.

Sometimes I think they just wanted me to go there, to tell them the gory details of the images that haunted me, rubbernecking their way into my own personal freak show. But there was only one person I wanted in the room when I was relaying a vision, and that was Michael.

I glanced up the hill toward Johnnie Fox's as we walked away from the scene. The setting sun peeked slowly from behind receding clouds, shooting rays of sunshine down onto the sheep field beyond the pub. In a moment, the weeping skies would clear and there would be a rainbow, a meteorological phenomenon marking the predictable shift of the Irish sky that never ceased to amaze me.

A crow called again from the church as Michael and I approached the car. The steeple drew my attention once more as the bird took flight, vacating the bell tower with a few strong flaps of blue-black wings. The girl had been found exactly where I'd said she would. Our job here was done.

The rain-streaked passenger window of the car brightened as the clouds drifted away. An arc of vibrant colors sliding down behind Johnnie Fox's. Michael pulled the car away from the side of the road, winding down the hill toward the city while the fear-widened eyes of a twelve-year-old girl shadowed my thoughts.

2

LIV

For the third time in as many weeks, Michael and I walked up the steep concrete stairs that flanked the façade of the once bustling St. Mary Home for Children. Located just outside of Dublin, the children's home had closed a handful of years ago after a devastating fire. The remaining children scattered to other institutions.

Father Kelly met us in the front hall and led us through catacombs of shadowy rooms frozen in time before we finally emerged in a bright sunlit courtyard. Each of my last few cases had led us here, and I was growing frustrated by the less than productive visits.

Until now, the cases I'd worked had ended with tragic confirmation for families that had long since succumbed to the knowledge that their child was dead. Now that we were dealing with orphans, I would have preferred to see those familiar streaks of agony on the face of a mother or father. Instead, I was forced to endure Father Kelly's high forehead and reddened cheeks drawn upward in a jovial grin as he accommodated questions about children he'd never met. Children who'd never known the love of a family.

My chest tightened at the thought as I shuffled along the brick pavers behind the two men. I should find comfort in the fact that I wasn't breaking the hearts of actual families, just informing a glorified caretaker of the deaths of former residents. But somehow, the unnatural absence of grief only made me feel worse.

"Her name was Saoirse," Michael started.

I'd written S-E-A-R-S-H-A at the top of my journal entry before learning how to properly spell the traditional Irish name. I could add that to the list of ways I'd failed her since this journey began.

"We aren't sure of a surname. We were hoping you might have access to records that could shed some light on that for us. She was aged twelve years upon death." Michael pulled a wrought iron chair away from a bistro table and waited for me to sit before settling himself, keeping his eyes locked on Father Kelly as he spoke. "Early reports gauge time of death at three years past."

"'Tis an awful thing, it is. The third child. Is that right?" Father Kelly shook his head and proceeded to write Saoirse's name in a leather-bound portfolio he carried. I couldn't help but notice he spelled it right. "I will do what I can, but as you know, all the files were lost in the fire. 'Tis not within my power to provide the information you seek."

"Is there anyone still working for the church today that may have known Saoirse personally, Mr. Kelly?" I asked.

Grey eyes lit on mine. His accommodating demeanor crumbled under my calculated lack of respect. "It's *Father* Kelly, Miss Sullivan."

Every hint of patience evaporated from his narrowed gaze. This man was as far from a father as I'd ever witnessed, but I nodded and corrected my error, noting the color that flooded his cheeks.

"As you well know, the home is not in operation any longer. The church has held onto the building for various purposes, but we no longer employ staff here." His cordiality returned.

Anger crept up through my core, caused in part by the indifference of a man who'd never met the young girls who haunted my dreams. We'd sat around this same table, had this same conversation regarding the disappearance and discovery of two other unknown girls before we'd finally found Saoirse. And now that we had, there was no way I was going to allow this man to dictate whether or not I could deliver peace.

I studied him as he spoke. His stiff white collar sank into the folds of skin around his neck as he tilted his head in what I knew to be feigned concern. The sudden urge to be a spectator as that collar squeezed tighter, cutting off his ability to breathe, just like the last moments of the girls in my dreams, washed over me like a tidal wave. His index finger moved up to tug at the collar as he cleared his throat.

I excused myself, pushing the bistro chair away from the table, metal legs scraping noisily on the flagstones beneath. The heat of frustration fueled my steps. The image of Saoirse, red hair fanned out on the floor, framing her freckled face as she gasped her last breaths haunted me now as it had since the first time she came, three nights after Ashlyn left Sullivan Farm.

"I assume the church can provide us with a list of employees from, say 1995 through the time the home closed?" Michael continued the questioning, and I knew I'd have to explain my departure later.

"I'll certainly see what I can do."

Their voices drifted into the background as I skirted the windows along the courtyard, peeking in through dust-darkened glass. A layer of grime coated the tile floors of the interior. Most of the rooms still had furniture. A twin-size cot or set of bunk beds occupied each one, paired with a mirrored four-drawer dresser on the wall opposite. In one room, a red hymnal had been left on one of the beds.

"Miss Sullivan?" I jerked to attention as Father Kelly approached from behind. "We seem to have gotten off on the wrong foot. I want to let you know that I think what you do is nothing short of amazing. The Garda is lucky to have your... expertise."

Although his words were kind, considerate even, my mind worked to read something else, something less sincere. I wanted to feel it, lurking just beneath the surface of that collar, but I couldn't pry it free.

I smiled, thanking him for his time and took his outstretched hand. I clenched my teeth against the gasp that gripped my lungs as our skin touched. My flesh singed as I pumped his arm once, dropping his hand like a hot pan fresh from the oven. If experience hadn't taught me otherwise, I would have sworn the man's dark energy had burned a scar into my palm. It was all I could do not to check to be sure.

Whoever Father Kelly was, he was certainly not an innocent party, but nothing I'd seen in my dreams could link him to any crime. In fact, he'd not even been employed by the church when the two older girls had disappeared, so whatever was clouding his energy today had less to do with the deaths of young girls and more to do with how he currently chose to live his life. Which, frankly, I had no interest in.

"What was that about?" Michael asked as we drove away from the home. His eyes didn't leave the gravel drive as he wove the Garda vehicle around potholes the size of small ponds.

"I couldn't take his flippancy."

"Flippancy, eh?" Michael laughed, a genuine chuckle that rose from deep in his chest. Just the sound of it curled the corner of my lip into a smile. I tucked my lip under my teeth like an insolent child refusing to be drawn out of sulkiness. "Ah, I like that word."

"There's something about him, Michael. He doesn't care. It's frustrating."

"Ah, Liv. The thing is, the whole world is filled with flippant arses like our dear friend *Father* Kelly." He threw me a wink as he stressed the salutation. "It's our job to figure out which arses are criminals, and which are not."

"What do you know about him?" I asked. Still trying to make sense of the darkness I'd felt when I took Father Kelly's hand.

"Father Kelly? Well, he's been at St. Mary since just before the fire. It was his first appointment out of seminary. Was a businessman of sorts, before then."

"What kind of business?"

"Owned several rental units, I believe. He's got a clean report, Liv. Came from just down the road, originally. Greystones, if you know the place." Michael paused. I could feel his eyes boring into me. "Not so much as a parking ticket."

I swallowed at the mention of Greystones. I'd only known one other person from that town, and it was an individual I'd be happy to forget.

The car filled with silence as we headed toward the Bridewell Garda Station. Winding hedge-lined roads became bustling city streets. The hum of traffic created a soundtrack between us. Michael knew I was hiding something from him, and I was at a loss about how to broach the subject. In all our months together, I'd never felt the need to hide anything from him. Why now?

We were back inside his office before I spoke. "She's why I came to Ireland."

"Saoirse, eh?" He spoke without looking at me, jotting notes from our meeting with Father Kelly. He kept his light blue eyes on the open case folder spread across his desk as we sat across from one another.

"She started coming to me after..." I swallowed the urge to mention Ridge. I'd only allowed the man who'd left me scarred and alone color conversation once since working with Michael. Today didn't need to be different. "Even before I knew who she was, I knew she needed me."

I picked at a thread dangling from the cuff of my Garda jacket, peeling it free and balling it between my fingers. The energy in the room spiked as I leaned forward, flicking the ball of renegade cotton into the wastebasket. Michael was watching me. I set my jaw against the surge. The invisible current in the air pricked at me, signaling what was to come.

"Why do you think she started coming to you then?" His eyes bored into mine. "After..." He let the word hang, teasing me.

I shrugged. "When Ridge left, everything changed. The visions. The psychometry. I just didn't know what to do with it all. I couldn't control it."

"So, you think if Ridge had never left, if you'd never been attacked, Saoirse never would've come?"

The possibility spun in my skull. It seemed unlikely. "Maybe."

Michael set his pen aside and rolled his chair toward the metal filing cabinet in the corner of his office.

"Your mother sketched what she saw. Quite an artist, she was. Likely where you get your eye for photography, I'd wager." He reached into the back of the top drawer, pulling out the final file without checking the tab.

Your mother, the words sounded foreign to my ears. The electrical swell in the room sent perspiration to my palms. I skimmed my hands along the tops of my thighs, replacing uncomfortable clamminess with the heat of friction. When Michael turned toward me, his face was solemn, eyes glued to the folder he grasped in front of his chest with both hands, like a treasure he was afraid to part with.

"These were the images that haunted her. The ghosts she was chasing, just like you've chased Saoirse."

Michael passed the manila folder to me. His fingers lingered on a corner until I pulled it away, the exchange calming the tide of energy in the room. Either he never intended to give this to me, or he'd been scared of my reaction. My heart thumped a rhythm in my chest, echoing a bodhrán, building to climax before I turned the cover aside.

Wide eyes stared back at me. The same eyes I saw when I closed my own at night. Saoirse's eyes. I thumbed through pages of rough-edged drawing paper, a collection of close-ups and vignettes, drawn in charcoal, with every minute detail accounted for. They were carbon copies of the images that played out in my own dreams.

"How could she know?" I felt my own question more than heard it. Breath escaping my lungs in an unsteady puff. The birthmother I'd never known had been dead for nearly six years, long before Saoirse met her fate.

"Can you explain how you know about the girls in your visions?" Michael's voice was calm, soothing.

Of course I couldn't. I'd been dealing with them since I was ten, and I still had no idea why or how they chose me.

I sunk into the chair, sighing through a mounting sense of despair. The circumstances surrounding my mother's death were sketchy, and not something I'd allowed myself to ponder since arriving in Ireland. Frankly, I wasn't sure I had the mental stamina to tackle those details in the midst of the Saoirse case.

Michael reached over and closed the file before I'd even made it halfway through the stack. A wisp of regret hung in the air around him.

"Some things are meant to be, Liv. But remember, our past is not a dictate of our future."

All I could do was nod, breath clinging tight in my chest.

"You don't have to do anything with that information. One of these days maybe it will help you find a sense of peace. Take it home and tuck it away. It's been molding away in that old cabinet far too long. Your mother would want you to have it."

I ran my hands over the front of the folder, hoping to pick up some remnant of energy from the mother I never knew. But there was nothing but smooth silence.

"I need to make it right for Saoirse, Michael. I need to find out how she ended up in that field all alone. If I can do that, I can go home." I shifted to the relative safety of the investigation. My birthmother may not have been able to prevent Saoirse's death, but I could sure as hell try to punish the person responsible.

"The lab will find something." Michael reached a weathered hand over to cover mine. "You've done all you can do."

This was the glitch in my system, in this ability I'd been granted. My visions allowed me to see the crime, hear the voices, feel the panic, but not once had I been able to see the face of the attacker. I'd never admitted it to anyone, but it was as if I saw the crime from the perpetrator's point of view. Expressions of terror on the faces of innocent victims were the wallpaper of my dreams.

I suppose it was my Achilles heel. Once I'd led the Garda

to the body, I was useless. It was up to forensics and a revisitation of case files to uncover the truth.

I'd been lucky at first. Almost as if the stars were aligning for the sole purpose of helping me build my confidence. Each case had been solvable. The attackers had gone on to escalate, kill again, and all but one had been incarcerated for other crimes by the time I led the Garda to the body. But the last few had tested my conviction.

I'd unearthed the bodies of the St. Mary's girls, but we had yet to uncover a lead on the perpetrators. Time had wiped away any trace of the girls' existence, including any evidence of their deaths. Until now. Now I had proof that even my mother had seen them. She'd known they were in trouble long before they'd ended up dead. And in spite of what I was sure were her best efforts, she couldn't save them.

Michael glanced at his watch, his drawn face erupting into a smile. He slammed Saoirse's case file closed and tossed it into the basket on the corner of the desk.

"Not much we can do until forensics comes back with their report, is there?" He rose from his chair and shrugged into a worn tweed jacket with patches on the elbows, a throwback to the seventies that only he could pull off.

"Does Ashlyn know about this? The sketches, I mean?" I thumbed the worn corner of the manila folder.

"Oh, Liv. You can't keep comparing yourself to your sister. I'm sure she knew about your mother's need to help the women in that folder. I don't know if she knew all the details."

Ashlyn had grown up with Aimee in Ireland. I was the one our mother had deemed expendable, the one she'd chosen to trade for a steady stream of checks and the possibility of a better life. I often wondered what that childhood had been like. Ashlyn claimed Aimee had been a loving mother, but instinct told me she'd been preoccupied. How could a person devote themselves to a child when ghosts ran amok in their mind?

"I never thought it would be like this. I thought that once I found Saoirse I'd be free. I thought it would be over."

Michael leaned down to kiss my forehead, the light scent of old leather and musk wrapping around me, lingering as he pulled away.

"Our past has a way of creeping up on us, doesn't it?" Michael nodded toward the folder still clutched in my lap. "It's up to us to decide when to cut the ties, love."

"Have you done that? Have you cut the ties to your past?" It was unfair of me to play that card, I knew. But I also needed advice from someone who'd been in my shoes, who'd spent time running from spirits of his own.

Michael reached for the brown fedora he wore nearly every day. He turned the brim in his hands, his fingers working along the edge until the hat performed two complete 360 degree turns.

"I thought I had. But the ghosts of those we love tend to return when we least expect them."

Michael looked at me, the usual glint of mischief absent from his gaze. I swallowed, the weight of guilt descending on my chest. I knew the ghost he was referring to was me.

3

RIDGE

Ridge McCaffrey leaned back in his chair, listening to the late afternoon drone of the Cascade Hills Police Station. Low voices mumbled from desks, one sided telephone conversations, and the occasional click of computer keyboards. It had taken some time after returning to Cascade Hills from D.C., but he'd readjusted since Sowards had sent him back, forced to face the low key, slow moving, small-town existence without Liv there to liven things up.

Maybe that's why when the local District Attorney's wife showed up in the station house with a blotchy complexion, runny mascara and disheveled ponytail, she'd garnered everyone's full attention. The worst part was, she'd asked for Ridge by name. That was his first red flag. Ridge wasn't friendly with Scott Roberts or his wife, so why she felt the need to hand pick him left a knot of suspicion in his gut.

Ridge had followed protocol, done what was expected of a detective in a fresh missing persons case. He'd searched the missing woman's apartment, conducted preliminary interviews with family and friends. On the surface, it looked like Mrs.

Roberts' sister had run off, maybe with a new man. Of course, that theory wasn't an acceptable explanation to the brass who was looking over his shoulder every step of the way. Just what he needed, one more set of eyes watching his every move.

He glanced again at the name on the back of the photograph in his hand, Jessica Garrison. It didn't ring any bells. She didn't have a record of any kind, not even a moving violation, which was somewhat odd for a twenty-four-year-old woman. No computers were found in her apartment, another oddity, and even her credit history was limited. But the give-away for Ridge was her lack of any social media footprint. Women in her age group didn't stay away from Instagram or Twitter unless there was a distinct reason. Ridge hoped his budding theory was wrong.

He shuffled some pages in her file, pulling a document from the back of the stack and skimming. Garrison's background check had turned out a clean report when she'd applied for a job with Avery Pharmaceuticals out of college. As a pharmaceutical rep, she was out of town on business every now and again, but according to Mrs. Roberts, she never went anywhere without telling her family. By all accounts, she'd lived in Cascade Hills ever since her parents moved here when she was a teenager. Except for four years spent at Ohio State, less than forty miles away, she was a local.

Ridge's chair squeaked as he leaned forward. A tiny crease worked its way between dark eyebrows as he studied the paperwork. He hated missing persons cases. The families were always so desperate for answers, and those answers often didn't come in nice neat little packages. At least the job would help keep his mind off his own mangled personal life.

"I've got a bad feeling about this one," Ridge said, as his partner, Adam Miller, lowered into the chair opposite him. "I wonder if we're looking at it the wrong way. There's no evidence she was taken from the house against her will. If she left the apartment with someone, it's possible she's been gone longer than we think."

Adam screwed his mouth to the side, considering. He blew a stream of air across a steaming cup of coffee before unwrapping his daily sausage, egg, and cheese muffin. He took a bite and shrugged before offering an answer.

"Work can account for her last Tuesday, right? So, we're looking at a three-day window between then and the time her sister reported her."

Ridge nodded, trying to mask disgust as Adam took another bite of the greasy breakfast sandwich.

"Somebody somewhere had to have seen her in the last few days. Let's canvas her neighborhood again. Check the stores. Send out some more feelers. She didn't just vanish into thin air." Adam lifted his weight from the chair and reached to grab his jacket.

"Finish your sandwich. You're not getting in my car with that heart attack in a wrapper. I won't be able to get the smell out for a week."

Adam rolled his eyes and stuffed the remaining half of the sandwich into his mouth, leaving Ridge to cringe.

"How you don't weigh 350 pounds and get winded walking to the john is beyond me." Ridge sighed as he stood.

"Good genes," Adam said with a laugh and a pat to his slender gut once he'd cleared his palate of breakfast.

"McCaffrey." Both detectives turned to see their superior, Captain Frank Wallace, glaring at them from his office doorway. "Got a minute?"

Adam raised an eyebrow at Ridge. "What'd you do now?"

"Hell if I know." Ridge wove his way through the maze of desks to Captain Wallace's office.

"Close the door behind you." A twinge of surprise

heightened Ridge's senses. Wallace was known for his open door policy. In fact, in the six years Ridge had been with the Cascade Hills PD, he could only remember closing the door once. And it hadn't been good news then.

"What's on your mind, Captain?"

Wallace blew out a steady breath through pursed lips. Time hadn't been a friend to Frank Wallace. Too many late nights, coupled with excessive sun, mapped leathery lines on his round face, giving him the appearance of a man far older than his fifty-two years. Wallace scratched the back of his head, smoothing what was left of his steely hair, before he perched his hands at his waist. He paced back and forth, studying the industrial carpet under his feet.

Ridge watched the clench and release of muscle in the captain's jaw. From the other side of the faux wood desk, he looked menacing, as if he were about to unleash some fury. Ridge knew better. Wallace could be formidable, but he was honest and fair, two attributes Ridge respected, and for the life of him he couldn't think of anything he'd done that would warrant a reprimand. So, here they were.

"CSU found something at Garrison's apartment."

Ridge lurched forward in the chair. There was no reason to hide his surprise with Captain Wallace.

"Miller should be here for this." He started to stand, but Wallace shook his head, settling into the high-backed office chair before signaling to Ridge to stay put. He pushed an evidence bag toward Ridge.

"It's been processed."

Ridge slid the newspaper clipping out of the plastic bag and unfolded it. It was from *The Irish Times*, published about two months ago. Ridge read the headline twice. *US Native Solves 15-Year-Old Cold Case.* His eyes skimmed the text, it was nothing earth shattering.

The write up was about a woman who'd led Dublin police to the remains of a girl who'd gone missing fifteen years ago. It was nothing more than a PR piece for the Garda, letting their community know that unsolved cases weren't forgotten.

Ridge's eyes settled on the grainy newspaper photograph. Two women in civilian clothes stood with two men dressed in Garda uniforms. All four smiled in the direction of the camera. His eyes lingered on the woman to the right whose smile didn't reach her eyes. His chest tightened.

"Interesting article," Ridge said, hoping he'd put up an appropriate wall when faced with the photo of Liv Sullivan. He scrubbed a hand down his face, the stubble from a day or two without shaving scratched at his palm. "Where'd they find it?"

"It was tucked between the mattress and box springs in Garrison's bedroom. With this." Ridge could read the words on the front of the envelope without extracting the evidence from the plastic bag.

Ridge's name, in care of Cascade Hills Police Department, addressed to the precinct. The words gripped his attention.

"Mrs. Roberts asked for you when she came in yesterday. What's the connection, McCaffrey? How do you know Garrison?"

"I never met her, Captain." Ridge studied the mid-size envelope, hesitating before lifting it from the desk. "May I?"

Wallace nodded. Ridge could feel the captain's grey-blue eyes scrutinizing his every move. Both men stayed silent as Ridge shook the contents of the envelope into his hand.

"When's the last time you spoke to Olivia Sullivan?"

The question jerked Ridge's attention away from the folded paper in his hand.

"Months," Ridge admitted. "Not since before she confronted Lyle Hunt." He didn't add that he'd been keeping close tabs on her in other ways. Wallace was on a need to know basis as far as Liv was concerned.

"Open it." His captain's voice was quiet, fatherly.

The silence of the room closed in on Ridge as he unfolded the blank piece of paper, revealing several photographs.

The ticking of the wall clock ricocheted like gunfire. *Liv.* The neurons in his brain spiked adrenalin through his system. *In trouble.* His heart thumped against his chest. *Pull it together, McCaffrey.* He shoved the paper and accompanying photographs onto the captain's desk, hoping his superior hadn't caught the tremble of his hand.

"Ridge," Wallace never called him by his first name. "Who's Garrison? Where did she get these pictures? How is she connected to Liv?"

A shiver ran down Ridge's spine, coercing the hairs on the back of his neck to attention as he put the pieces together. He knew there was more to the Garrison case, but he hadn't expected the small town missing persons case to turn into the break he'd been waiting on. If a connection between Garrison and Liv existed it wasn't something he could divulge to Wallace, or anyone else. Not yet.

Ridge refocused and shook his head, sliding a hand through the dark sorrel waves of his hair. Wallace leaned back in the chair, his own hands sweeping the smooth leather of the armrests as he spoke.

"What happened between you and Liv is hardly a secret, Ridge. I know things didn't end well. But maybe it's time Liv came back to Cascade Hills. Whatever her involvement is, we need to know. There's a reason Jessica Garrison was hanging onto a newspaper article and pictures of Liv. With the Hunt trial wrapping up, that's more than a coincidence, I'd say."

Wallace waited for a response. Ridge lifted his eyes to meet the captain's gaze, clenching his jaw to satisfy the anger coursing through his veins. He didn't want Liv involved in any of this. She was supposed to be safe in Dublin. That was Sowards' promise, and the sole reason he'd agreed to stay away. He pushed against the building knot of irritation and nodded.

"If this does have something to do with her, we need to make sure she's safe, somewhere we can keep tabs on her."

The words stung Ridge's eardrums. That had been his assignment from the beginning. Not that he'd performed his duties very well at times. His cobalt gaze searched the photographs now spread across the desk in front of him. There were three of them, each taken with a telephoto lens.

One depicted Liv sitting in a booth at a pub. She was with Ashlyn, Ridge could tell by the long strawberry blonde hair opposite Liv. Two other individuals, the same men from the newspaper clipping, were with them. One was Michael Donaghey, the Dublin Garda officer Liv was working with. The other was most likely Shane Leary, Ashlyn's co-worker turned boyfriend.

Liv was wearing a smile again, but this time it was real. Ridge swallowed hard. This should give him satisfaction after the way the newspaper photo had ripped through him. At least she looked happy. A weight descended on his chest as a twinge of jealousy joined the familiar pang of separation.

Six months she'd been gone. And for what? Because he couldn't get his shit together long enough to separate fact from fiction? Thoughts of the life that could have been plagued him. If only he'd been man enough to challenge his supervisor's dictate. Besides, he'd made up for it. He'd found Ashlyn. At least that's the story he told himself.

He turned his focus to the second photo. Liv was walking down a street...alone. Her auburn hair cascaded in soft curls down her back and out behind her. She was moving quickly, too quickly for a leisurely stroll, as streetlamps glowed in the background.

Every muscle in Ridge's core tightened. She was so far away. It was Garrison who was missing now, but Liv would be next if he didn't do something. Of that he was certain. Someone was watching her. Resting easy with the knowledge that she was protected was a charade he could no longer keep.

In the final picture, Liv stood in a darkened hallway, sliding a key into the door to her apartment. It was a profile view. An image that could only have been taken by someone occupying the same hall. Even with a telephoto lens, the photographer was likely no more than fifty feet from Liv's door. The fact that whoever took these photographs knew exactly where to find her sent a spiral of fury through Ridge. *What the hell was Donaghey doing over there?*

"What are you thinking, McCaffrey?" Crap, he'd been quiet for too long. Wallace was like a bloodhound when he thought someone was keeping something from him.

"I'm thinking she's an easy target. Whoever took these already knows how to get to her." Ridge fought the strain in his voice.

"I've already put a call in to the Dublin Garda. They gave me the cell number of the officer she's working with..." Wallace searched his desk for the scrap of paper he'd written the man's name on. "Michael...somebody..."

"Donaghey," Ridge supplied.

"Yes, that's it. Anyway, give him a call." Wallace continued to dig on the desk. "Ah! Here it is."

Ridge wondered how the man ever found anything on a desk so disorganized. It was a far cry from his own, which sported just two neat stacks. Wallace handed the number over to Ridge before scooping up the clipping and the photographs and depositing them in their assigned evidence bags.

INHERENT LIES | 25

"I'll scan everything for you, McCaffrey." Ridge nodded and headed toward the door, hesitating a moment as the captain added, "Don't even think about going over there yourself. We've got our hands full here with the Garrison case." Wallace knew him too well.

Ridge ignored Adam as he strode past their workstation, making it necessary for his partner to trot to catch up.

"McCaffrey! I thought we were going to hit the pavement."

"Sorry, Adam. I've got to take care of something first."

Ridge pushed open the glass door that separated the inner workings of the Cascade Hills Police Station from the rest of the world.

His black Shelby, parked on the far end of the asphalt lot, would offer the sanctuary Ridge needed to complete this call. Although Liv's departure from Cascade Hills may have seemed abrupt, it had been carefully orchestrated. And Ridge felt her absence with every ounce of his being. She'd nearly lost her life because of him, and he'd be damned if he let it happen again.

All he wanted to do was turn back the clock and start over. He'd change how he reacted when Liv's ex, Jason Abbott, transformed her from the woman he loved to a possible criminal. Deep down he'd known she wasn't involved. But the Bureau hadn't been so sure.

She'd begged him to believe the truth. But the integrity of his assignment had to come first. The Bureau couldn't risk the chance of her going rogue, not to mention the exposure a trial might bring. So, he'd followed orders and pushed her away. It had all been in the plan, but he hated himself for it.

The only positive was that Ridge was now privy to every detail of what Liv was doing in Ireland. He knew she was working with the Garda on cold cases, under the radar training for the Bureau's program that was long overdue. And she'd been very successful. Sowards told him he should feel a sense of pride in playing a small role in this part of her life. But he felt more like a puppeteer, keeping tabs from afar, and pulling strings when necessary. And it was not the role he wanted to play in Liv's life. But he'd done what he could, learned about her life through his overseas contacts. And worked in concert with them to eliminate any possible threats. At least, he thought he had.

A pang of guilt sliced through him as the wall of secrets he kept reared its ugly head. Secrets he'd hidden so long they now blended with reality. Some of which he'd be forced to share if Liv returned to Cascade Hills.

He could still see the hurt in her eyes their last night together. It was as painful now as it had been the night he checked her arms for track marks, searching for evidence of a lie he knew she wasn't capable of telling. Her voice had pleaded for him to understand...to trust. Even the scent of her hung heavy in his memory, a beachy sweetness he couldn't shake.

You had no choice, he reminded himself as he approached his car. He'd done what his assignment required him to do. Separated himself from a volatile asset and fulfilled his duties. But the result had been devastating, for both of them.

Ridge's skin crawled at the thought of the attack that almost ended Liv's life. She'd done exactly what the Bureau had hoped for. She'd confronted a madman in order to clear her name, a last ditch effort to help Ridge understand who she really was. She'd taken the route of honesty, and she'd done it all for him. All without realizing how the impact of her actions would affect the rest of her life.

Ridge, on the other hand, had chosen the coward's way out. Picked his profession over the woman he loved. He might as well admit it. At first, he'd been able to justify the choice. He told himself she was better off without him, better off in Ireland away from the lies he'd been forced to live. But the fact remained, she was the epicenter, both of his job and his heart, which was a dangerous place to be.

Ridge stood with his arms braced on the roof of the Shelby. The heat of sun-warmed metal collided with the cool October breeze. Assignment or not, he should have been there for her then, just like he should be there now.

He slid into the black leather of the coupe's driver seat and let out a soft groan. The warmth of the car's interior enveloped him as possibilities tumbled in his mind. How long would it take to get Liv on a plane and home again? Who would watch over her until she reached Ohio? That was Donaghey's job, but those photos proved he wasn't up to the task.

Ridge's stomach knotted. The realization that by pulling just a few more strings he could have Liv back in Cascade Hills within twenty-four hours. And that was all the incentive he needed.

He punched in a contact number and crumpled up Captain Wallace's paper scrap. Tossing the note into the console cup holder, he positioned the phone next to his ear, waiting for the line to click open.

Before the gruff voice at the other end could form a greeting, Ridge was already speaking.

"Sowards, it's McCaffrey. We need to talk about the Sullivan op."

When Ashlyn invited me to Ireland, she failed to mention the fact that much of my time would be spent with a rotund, agoraphobic, muumuu clad bald man who burned incense and claimed to play cards with dead writers (Oscar Wilde, specifically). On more than one occasion, I'd trotted up the steps into Herman Mayhew's third floor apartment to find him slamming his hand of cards down on the nineteenth century felt topped poker table, muttering, "One should always play fairly, my arse!" The first few times, it caught me off guard. Eventually, nothing Herman did surprised me.

"Liv! You're just in time, my love. Wilde here has beat me again." Herman rose from his chair to meet me in the entryway, leading me away from the spectral guest only he could see and into the sitting room of the flat.

I was fairly certain that every piece of furniture in the overcrowded room was as old as the building itself, which I'd judged to be early 1700s by its character and relative location to the River Liffey. A thin coating of century-old dust hid in every nook and cranny, giving the once royal red sofa a greyed burgundy hue. I no longer tried to brush it away.

"You know, Herman, I saw a posting at the university. You should take some poker classes. Beat him at his own game."

I smiled at the funny-looking man in front of me. I never would have thought I'd be taking life lessons from a man like Herman. He was about my height, five feet four inches at the most, and wore wire-rimmed glasses perched at the end of his pinched nose. His cheeks were always a rosy red, and I often wondered if the Jameson in the carafe on the wet bar was the cause, although in all our sessions, I'd never seen him drink.

"Ah, Liv. You didn't come here today to give me pointers in the game of poker." He settled into a vintage chair and waited for me to speak, tugging at the fabric of the muumuu so that it didn't gather, blimp-style, around his midsection.

"We found Saoirse."

"As I knew you would. She's been waiting for you."

I'd come here to ask the question that had been burning inside me since I'd worked my way through the file of my mother's sketches. Why I couldn't force the words through my lips was beyond me. I turned from the sofa I'd been using for support and made my way toward the window, squinting through the grime to the street below.

"Why didn't you tell me about my mother?" My words were so quiet I wasn't sure he'd be able to hear me. *Coward*, my inner voice shouted. I turned to face him. "Why didn't you tell me she'd seen Saoirse?" I hesitated, my voice dropping. "That she'd seen me."

"I see you've been doing some digging." He didn't show even the slightest hint of surprise. As if he knew what I'd come to ask, which, quite frankly, was a distinct possibility. "I didn't think you were ready. Evidently, Mr. Donaghey felt otherwise."

I hesitated, wondering at the purse of Herman's lips as he studied me.

"Ready or not." I pulled the manila file folder out of my messenger bag and tossed it onto the table between us.

Herman sucked in a deep breath and resituated his glasses, pulling the file closer. "'Tis been ages since I looked upon your mother's work."

"Was Aimee right? Was the fire at St. Mary's intentional?"

"She could never prove it, Liv. There was no evidence."

"Forget evidence!" My voice rose. My jaws ached from the continuous clench they'd been in since arriving at Herman's flat. I moved from my post behind the sofa, sitting across from the one man with the ability to explain the notes in my mother's file. "You and I both know that evidence is only part of the picture. It's not all about the girls at the home. What about me?"

I flipped the folder open to the last drawing, the only one in color. Green eyes stared back. My eyes.

Herman said nothing. The silence between us grew as he thumbed through the file. I studied my cuticles, hands splayed in my lap. Finally, the silence was too much.

"My mother thought she was being followed. She writes about it. She saw those girls, the ones from the home. She met with some of them. There are interviews in there. They'd been offered a better life. I don't know how, she doesn't say... adoption, I guess? But they aren't happy. Look at the vignettes, Herman."

Herman's face fell as he skimmed a page of handwritten text. A note I'd read over and over the night before, trying to make sense of my birthmother's accusations. I felt a surge of adrenalin as the air in the room shifted, clouding with pulses of emotion. Hot vibrations of anger stabbed at me, spiked with cool fingers of fear. The wave ended with the palpating discomfort of resignation.

"Your mother was...searching for something, Olivia. Something only she understood. When she couldn't find it, she pushed back against the very people who tried to help."

"Searching for what?" I asked.

Herman raised a shoulder, dropping it as he pulled his gaze away from the file and onto me.

"Purpose, perhaps? Your mother had grown attached to those girls at the home. She spent time with them. Some might say, too much time. She saw something in them." He hesitated. "Perhaps they reminded her of you."

He stood, the folds of fabric billowing around him as he headed toward the stairs that led down to Mayhew's Tea Room, the business his wife and daughter ran on the ground floor. "Rose," he called to his wife, not waiting for an answer. "Bring us up some tea and biscuits, would you dear?"

"But she blamed the Garda, Herman...the people she worked with. Blamed them for covering up what really happened at the children's home. Why would she do that if she didn't have proof?"

"After the fire your mother had a hard time. She hadn't been able to save them. It changed her."

"You're saying she was crazy? That she made the whole thing up?"

A slow smile spread across Herman's face as he waited for the beverages. "There are two reasons people abandon everything and everyone they know and love, Olivia. One is guilt. The other is fear. Your mother ran from the guilt, I suspect."

Rose's appearance in the stairwell muted our conversation. She offered a tea service to Herman and nodded slightly in my direction before disappearing back down the stairs.

"Liv, you remind me very much of your mother. She, too, was idealistic to a fault. That, coupled with her innate need to quiet the shadows that haunted her, is what led to this file."

He shuffled toward me, careful not to slosh the liquid from the teacups out onto the silver tray. He sat the service on the coffee table near my feet. Joining me on the sofa, the cushion dipped beneath his weight. My body tipped his direction and I shifted to put more space between us.

"What's wrong with being idealistic?" I asked.

"Not a thing, unless, like Aimee, you live in a world colored by ghosts with agendas of their own. If one spends too much time among the dead, reality starts to get a nip fuzzy."

He met my gaze as I brought the steaming liquid to my lips. Blowing over the surface I said, "She let the images take over."

"That file's sole purpose is to prove the importance of the time we've spent together, Olivia. You need to be able to protect yourself. The energies may seem harmless, but you must never blindly trust what they send you. They are a tool for you to use. Not the other way around. That was one lesson your mother could never grasp."

Herman's gaze met mine, unwavering. Here was the man who had helped my mother through some of her darkest times, had helped me learn to channel energies in the world around me. Had helped me focus enough to manipulate visions I'd never been able to control. Without him, Saoirse would have remained an elusive shadow, rather than the fleshed out girl she became.

"Your mother was a magnificent woman. But what you think you see in that file is the fiction of a brilliant mind under great stress. The Garda investigated her claims. Ask Michael. The fire was an unfortunate accident caused by an electrical short in a building as ancient as this."

I breathed through mounting frustration, careful to keep

my words in check. "So, the fire at the home, my mother's death, the pictures in the folder, they're all just coincidence? Fiction of a mind out of touch with reality?" I tamped down the surge of anger that erupted in my core. "My mother worked on nearly one hundred cases for the Garda, helping to solve almost all of them. But this one...you're telling me this time she was wrong?"

"I'm telling you that we all have limitations. Our passions can interfere with our reality, Olivia. Your mother was no exception to that rule."

Herman placed his teacup on the service tray and reached for mine. I handed it over, skimming my fingers over his before pulling away. For the first time since we'd met, there was not a spark of tenderness or acceptance in our touch, only a pulse of absence I didn't fully understand. He was shutting me out.

"Aimee was human. She needed an explanation for a tragedy. She had a hard time understanding that not everything in life is a puzzle to be solved. You'd be wise to learn from her mistakes. She may have run from the guilt. But you are running, too, Olivia—from fear."

"I'm not afraid."

Herman's gaze found mine. "Remember that. When the truth comes for you, Olivia, remember those words."

5

LIV

The streets hummed as I left Herman's flat, navigating my way across Ha'Penny Bridge toward Temple Bar. Every fiber of my being had been jolted, electrified into action first by my mother's conspiracy theory against the Garda and most recently by Herman's undeniable rejection of Aimee's accuracy. *You have to remember that he's heard this all before, Liv. He's had time to work through it. This isn't news to him.*

The air thickened, pressing in as I walked. I shifted my focus to the people around me, bustling about their own lives even as mine caved in on itself. The hairs along the nape of my neck prickled as I hurried home in the dusky light. Voices filtered in and out of the space. I checked once over my shoulder, half expecting to see someone following, watching. I exhaled and walked faster, my steps keeping time with the rhythmic rise and fall of the city around me.

Dublin City truly is an international hub. Except for a few well-known landmarks, like Ha'Penny Bridge and St. Patrick's Cathedral, it barely resembles the representations in coffee table books and tourism magazines that tout Ireland's lush green countryside and friendly villages. Not that the people in Dublin weren't nice. On the contrary, they were, but if I had to guess, I'd say less than half were actually raised in Ireland.

I resorted to the game I played when the threatening energy of darkening city streets closed in. With each voice around me, I worked to identify the accent, counting how many I found on my way back to my apartment. That night I heard English, French, Dutch, even a hint of Spanish mingling here and there. Focusing in on the tourists brought me a sense of peace. I was one of them, after all. Perhaps now more than ever.

They flocked every evening to this section of Dublin, intent on experiencing the famed pubs and historic bohemian vibe. It wasn't yet eight and there was already a growing pulse of patrons lining the sidewalk outside the red façade of The Temple Bar.

Cohen's Pub and Guest House was just another block down and had been my home for the last six months. Situated on the corner of Eustace Street, it was a short ten-minute walk from the Bridewell Garda Station on the south side of the River Liffey.

The centuries-old boarding house was exactly what I'd imagined when I agreed to take Ashlyn up on her offer to teach me how to use my dreams. Tucked between two brick buildings, the guest house called attention to itself with yellow stucco façade accentuated by bright red trim. It was a far cry from my grandmother's unassuming rural cottage on the banks of Lough Dan.

The en-suite rooms above the pub were comfortable, even had small functional kitchenettes, which had come in handy once my three-week vacation turned into a lengthy sabbatical.

Live music seeped from the front entrance of Cohen's, soothing away some of my tension from half a block away.

Once inside, I could retreat into one of the 150-year-old partitions, cocooning myself from the events scrambling my brain.

I took a seat in a cozy nook in the back by the fire, running my hands over the scuffed, but highly polished wood. Centuries of laughter, celebrations, and frothy pints with friends had been shared at this very table. I let the pulses of leftover energy from those happy times drift over me. Memories like that in a place like this could ease one's worries, for sure. I pulled my hands from the wood before darker energy could seep in.

"Eh, Liv! Will your mates be joining you this evening?" One of Cohen's regular waiters approached the table, already brandishing a dark pint of Guinness on his serving tray. The crooked grin plastered over his boyish face was impossible not to return.

"Not this evening, Ryan." I hoped my smile would hide the churning that remained from the afternoon's encounter with Herman. Evidently, I wasn't successful.

"Rough day, eh?" He sat the pint in front of me, cocking a blonde eyebrow in my direction. "Sorry, then." His grin faded, replaced by a lip tilt of empathy. "Let me know if there's anything I can do to make it better."

"This helps," I raised the Guinness and thanked him, watching him trot off to tend another table. There was something about the Irish, always willing to lend a hand or make an attempt to brighten your day. I would miss that. The thought that maybe it was time to return to Cascade Hills was still playing out in my mind when I noticed Ryan near the bar, pointing toward my booth as a woman nodded at him. I found myself wishing his helpful nature had departed his repertoire of skills.

I rocked my head from side to side, pushing the pads of my

fingers into the flesh at the base of my skull. Coaxing the ball of twisted steel cable in my neck to relax. The little release I found vanished as Ashlyn stepped around Ryan, her eyes focused on my makeshift sanctuary.

I slid my index finger down the curved glass of the pint, addressing Ashlyn before she could initiate conversation. Whatever happened tonight, I had to keep the upper hand. I couldn't let my sister dictate what direction my life would take. She'd spent the last six months doing that.

"How'd you know I'd be here?" It was a stupid question. I lived upstairs, where else would I be on a Friday night?

"Herman called me. I checked with Michael. He said you'd either be at the cottage or here. Since I know how you feel about being in that cottage all alone, I took my chances on the latter. May I join you?"

I nodded toward the empty side of the booth, still not taking my eyes from the pint glass before me.

"So, Michael mentioned you found Saoirse. That must make you happy."

"Happy?" I made eye contact with the woman across from me. The near stranger who shared my DNA, but not my memories. "That's not the word I would choose."

Ashlyn blinked, screwing her mouth into a lopsided frown. How odd to pretend there were no secrets between us. She must have known about our mother's obsession with the girls at the children's home...Aimee's obsession with me.

Ashlyn released an exhausted sigh. Her eyes shifted from me to her fingers as she picked at an imperceptible crumb along the edge of the table. I'd made her uncomfortable. This was a first.

It hadn't taken long once in Ireland to realize that Ashlyn's visions were much different than my own. Her sunny demeanor should have been my first clue. Why shouldn't the glass be half full instead of half empty? If my dreams led me to find people who'd yet to become a statistic rather than unearthing decaying remains, my view of life might be a bit sunnier as well.

Bitterness crept like bile up the back of my throat. Ashlyn's dreams could have saved Saoirse. I shook away the thought. I hated when my mind went there. She couldn't control who she dreamt about any more than I could. Holding it against her did nothing but cause a knot of jealousy to fester inside. I took a hefty swig of Guinness to wash away the taste of failure.

"Michael mentioned you have Mom's file. You shouldn't read too much into it. Those last months after the fire were hard on her."

"How do you know she was wrong, Ashlyn?"

"Because I was there. I'd only been working with the Garda for a few months, but I remember. Michael followed up every lead, every snippet of possibility that Mom could come up with." Ashlyn's shoulder's slumped beneath the cascade of strawberry blonde curls. "Mom wouldn't let it go. She was obsessed. Swore it was some kind of conspiracy that had to do with you. Herman was at his wit's end."

"Is that why he wants me to leave? He thinks I'm going to pick up where Aimee left off?"

"Aren't you?"

The truth of Ashlyn's question hit hard. Is that what I wanted? Everyone involved was telling me to let it go. At some point, maybe I just needed to listen. Maybe Herman was right. I was running from the reality of Cascade Hills. *But if that's the case, what was the point of the last six months?* That query, the one my inner critic couldn't release, was what kept me up at night.

"I just want to do what's right." I let the silence permeate the space between us for a moment. "You know better than anyone, Ashlyn. Saoirse and those girls from St. Mary's chose me. Their faces are sketched in mom's file. There has to be a connection. What if they're trying to tell me that what Mom started isn't over? What if there is something bigger at work here?"

Ashlyn's eyes locked on mine. Her lips pressed in a thin line. "I wish I could answer those questions for you, Liv, I do. But the fact is that the only conspiracy is one you've invented. Just like Mom did. The fire was an accident. It had nothing to do with those girls. I know you've read the reports."

The air shifted before she spoke again. Heaviness. Irritation. "What makes you think you can do what Mom couldn't?"

"I don't think she couldn't, Ashlyn. I think she ran out of time."

Ashlyn didn't need to speak for me to know what she was thinking. Not that I could read her thoughts. Unlike my sister, that wasn't a gift I'd been granted. But the conversation had come up before. And the daggers she shot at me through emerald green eyes were sign enough.

Jealousy was a difficult emotion to hide from someone like me. I'd felt the first prongs of envy in Ashlyn when it became obvious that I could sense energy, just like my mother before me. I could pick it up through objects, flesh, and when it was strong enough, in the atmosphere.

"Look, the fact is, our mother might still be alive if she hadn't been so hell-bent on helping the girls in that file. Whatever she saw, she misinterpreted. You don't know what it's like to lose your mother to a psychic vision."

Emotion caught in Ashlyn's voice and she looked away. She was right. Beth Sullivan, the mother I'd grown up with, had been distant, but for wholly different reasons. And the fact remained, I still had her in my life, still spoke with her every few days or so. Ashlyn had been robbed of that.

"There's a fine line between psychic and crazy, Liv."

"Are you saying you think I'm insane for trying to help these girls? For wanting to finish what our mother began?"

"I'm saying that people like you and I, like Mom, we walk a line between the living and the dead. If we veer to either side too far, the balance is lost. Mom lost that balance and it caught up with her. I don't want to watch you lose it, too."

I felt the weight of Ashlyn's frustration, like pinpricks on my skin, injecting her irritation in a direct line into me. I inhaled and rubbed my hands down my arms, ridding myself of the sensation. Ashlyn slid to the end of the booth, hesitating to lay some euros on the table.

"I'll say to you the words I regret not saying to my mother six years ago. Look around you, Liv. There are people here, in this world, that care about you. Trust that. Let the past, the dead, go."

She rose and gave me a peck on the top of the head before heading out onto Eustace Street. She'd done it again, forced feelings of stubborn inadequacy to bubble to the surface. Before she'd come into my life I'd been a heartsick mess, confused and exhausted by dreams that didn't make sense and a love I'd lost even after risking my life to save it. I owed her a debt of gratitude for pulling me away from all that. She'd allowed me to escape and I was a better person because of her help.

If I hadn't been so wrapped up in Ashlyn's final words, I might have noticed the man sitting across the room from me. His dark hair reflecting the firelight as he watched me pick up my messenger bag, pay for my drinks, and head up the stairs to my second story guest room.

6

RIDGE

The thumping music drowned out any rational thought Ridge might have had as he looked across Cohen's pub toward Liv. It also effectively muted the intense conversation she was having with Ashlyn, a fact that raised his level of irritation with every percussive whack of the bodhrán.

Every time she smiled that perfect smile at the waiter a little piece of his sanity vanished. Lucky for him, the conversation she was having with Ashlyn put an end to the polite smiles. Their past rushed at him. The music of her laughter. The silkiness of her skin. The memory of her lips on his. So much time had passed. He'd been too stupid. Waited too long. Hurt her too deeply.

The last night he'd seen her was eight months ago. A 911 call from Liv's cell at Sullivan Farm lured him there. He could still picture the shock in her eyes when he found her on the stairs in the barn. He'd heard the shot. Knew he'd find Abbott with a bullet in his skull. But the truth of Liv's involvement came out later. Much too late to apologize for trying to protect himself from the pain of her loss. Even now he had trouble rationalizing his own stupidity.

Ridge turned his attention to the pint glass in front of him, twisting it in a circle between his thumb and middle finger. He'd treated her like a criminal that night. Had left her to fend for herself as she fought to clear her name. *You were following orders*, he reminded himself, scrubbing a hand over his face. He might as well have that mantra tattooed to his arm for as often as he needed the reminder.

What are you doing here? He could answer that question, not with any convincing argument, but he could provide an answer. He imagined that's what Liv would ask when he finally summoned the courage to approach her. Part of him preferred lurking in the shadows, providing protection from afar.

Motion from Liv's side of the pub distracted him. She was leaving. Auburn curls hung in ringlets down the back of her green sweater. Her jeans hugged her thighs. The curve of her hips sending a spike of heat through his core. She looked good, even better than he remembered. *Jesus, McCaffrey, pull yourself together.*

He tossed a twenty Euro bill onto the table and tried to act as if he belonged, weaving his way toward the exit that led to the rooms above the pub. He'd scoped them out before she'd arrived. And he knew exactly which one was hers, room 211, on the left-hand side of the narrow hall. He'd even found the sitting area at the end of the hall from where one of the photos found in Garrison's apartment had been taken. It was too close for comfort.

Liv was already at the door when he got to the top of the stairs. It wasn't until then that the reality of the situation crashed in on him. Here he was, a man she hadn't seen in more than half a year, one that should be three thousand miles away, suddenly approaching her from behind in a dark hallway. *Nice. That's one way to get yourself tased—or shot.*

He was almost close enough to touch her when her hand paused on the handle of the door. She froze, her gaze still on the key in the lock in front of her. But her respirations increased, her chest rising and falling with each gulp of air.

"What are you doing here?"

Her voice was almost a whisper. If Ridge hadn't been so intently focused on her, he might have missed it. He swallowed hard, scanning the empty hall around them, wishing he had a better explanation. Jumping on a plane under the guise of protection for a woman he'd purposefully avoided when she needed him most suddenly took on a fresh air of idiocy.

"I was worried about you." Faced with Liv just feet in front of him, it was the best he could do.

She turned to face him. Her complexion was paler than he'd remembered, but those eyes, they were still just as green, and right now they were piercing him to the core. He took a step back.

"You lost the right to worry about me a long time ago, Ridge. Now, if you'll excuse me, it's late and I have work to do."

The messenger bag jutted forward, shield-like as she withdrew the key from the lock and twisted the handle. Her body teetered a bit as she stepped forward. Ridge noticed her brace against the door frame. Either the bag was heavier than it looked, or that third Guinness had been too much. He guessed the latter. Either way, she didn't retreat.

"Can you give me a chance to explain?" He didn't fly three thousand miles against orders from two different commanders to slink away like a frightened dog.

"The last time I saw you, you were checking my arms for track marks," she started. "Trusted a madman over your own girlfriend. Even when the truth came out you never showed your face, Ridge. You've got no right to worry."

Ridge watched the muscle in Liv's jaw contract and release. She pulled her petite frame up to its full height and turned to face him, lower lip tucked firmly in the grip of upper teeth. His reality and hers clashed. The truth was still such a long way away.

He cleared his throat and backed another step, adding to the distance between them.

"I owe you an explanation."

"Why? Are you in some twelve-step program that's forcing you to make amends for all the wrong you've done?" she shot back, venom dripping from every word.

He should have taken Sowards' advice, let Donaghey handle getting Liv back to the States. He focused on the worn carpet under his feet.

Liv sighed, rocking back against the doorframe and Ridge hazarded a look in her direction. Her eyes were closed. Long lashes framed almond-shaped lids. He ached to lean closer, taste the lip she'd reddened between her teeth.

"I just found out the people my mother trusted most thought she was delusional." Liv's eyes fluttered open, scrutinizing him as she continued. "I'm not sure I can take anymore explanations tonight."

She turned toward her room, pushing the door open the rest of the way. Ridge was losing her.

"Liv, wait," he said, still not sure how he'd follow it up if she called his bluff.

"Tomorrow," she said, hand poised on the door. "I'll be at Bewley's on Grafton Street in the morning, nine o'clock. You can meet me if you want."

The door closed behind her before Ridge could respond. What had made him think he could do this? It was clear he was in no condition to provide protection for someone who was, herself, such a complete distraction.

Ridge backed away from Liv's door, a surge of excitement propelling his steps. He took a moment to check the sitting area before trotting down the nearby flight of stairs and out into the night. He crossed Eustace Street to his own room above Connelly's Pub. Cohen's may have been out of rooms, but there was no way he was going to let her get too far from him this time.

He replayed the conversation. Returning again and again to the fact that someone had told Liv that Aimee was delusional. He worked to process that information. Throughout her career, both with the Garda and the Bureau, Aimee Callaghan had been touted as a secret weapon. She'd solved close to 100 cold cases before plunging her car into Lough Dan one dark, rainy night. Something about the sudden tarnishing of her reputation by people who knew better didn't sit right with him.

BEWLEY'S WAS a bustling metropolis at nine o'clock on a Saturday morning. Ridge got there around 8:15, just to scope the place out. After all, this was a protection detail, right? Of course, making sure Liv didn't spot him coming out of the guest house across the street from Cohen's may have been a secondary motive. He shielded himself behind a newspaper at the cafe two doors down as Liv walked by, crossing the elaborate tile work that greeted Bewley's patrons.

Ridge knew Liv's suggestion to meet at the coffee house was a calculated move. She was too smart to invite him into her apartment last night. They'd both been drinking, and she was rattled. Going into her apartment would have ended in one of two ways, and although one situation he would have gladly played out, the alternative would have dug him a hole deeper than the trench he was already in. He was glad she'd suggested the morning meeting.

Ridge took his time folding the newspaper and following Liv inside. He watched as she found a corner booth and situated herself so that much of the room was visible. *Good,* he thought, recognizing her attempt to protect her blind side.

He turned away and studied the pastries in the case at the counter as Liv's eyes flicked around the room. He wondered what she was feeling. His insides hadn't stopped churning since last night.

He'd tried to get a decent night's sleep, but random scenarios tumbling through his brain wouldn't subside long enough for sleep to take hold. They'd made too many memories together, spent too many hours in each other's arms, and no matter how hard he tried to make this the professional detail that he knew it should be, it was impossible to put that history behind him.

He'd called Adam to check in. There'd been no new leads in the Garrison case, and Adam was struggling to hide Ridge's absence from the captain. Ridge apologized for putting his partner in the middle, but Captain Wallace was the least of his worries. He'd smooth things over when he got stateside. Sowards, on the other hand, would present a more serious challenge.

He had to figure out what tie the missing girl had to Liv, and why this apparent stranger had found it necessary to pull him into the middle of it. He kept reminding himself that Garrison had never actually sent the photographs. They'd simply been found in her apartment. There was a chance it was all coincidental. Maybe Liv knew Jessica Garrison somehow. What he wouldn't give for it to be that simple.

He started a path toward Liv's table. "Morning." He slid his Ray Bans off once he was close enough to speak.

"I was hoping maybe I imagined that hallway interlude last night," Liv said, gesturing for Ridge to sit.

She didn't waste any time putting that wall up, Ridge thought. "It's good to see you."

Her face flushed, color washing over pale cheeks.

Ridge pretended not to notice. "You look good."

Liv pulled herself up in the booth, laid her hands in her lap, and cleared her throat before offering a quiet, "Thank you."

Ridge scanned the room once more before settling in, pulling a menu from the holder near the wall and leaning back in his chair, watching his subject as he'd been trained to do. Liv's shoulders slumped a bit and her fingers moved from her lap to the table, playing with the handle of the empty teacup. Nervousness.

"Don't tell me you came all the way over here to deliver a breakfast apology."

Ridge met Liv's gaze. He worked to make it mean something, a combination of apology and unresolved emotion.

"You're right. That's not why I came." Ridge decided to buffer his inner investigator. "I was worried about you. I heard you were here and wanted to make sure you were okay." He hesitated. The truth had never come easy. Part of the reason he made a perfect undercover operative. "I needed to see you again."

A fire lit in Liv's eyes. "I'm fine, Ridge. Did you really think you could just fly all the way over here and walk back into my life?"

"I don't think..." Ridge started. His trench growing deeper as Liv cut him off.

"You can't expect me to forget what happened."

Liv paused to order an Earl Grey from the waitress, giving Ridge a moment to combat the impending explosion.

"Of course I don't expect you to forget," he said as the waitress retreated with their order. "But you're right about one thing. I do owe you an apology." Ridge sucked in a breath, unsure of the effect his next words would have. "I'm sorry...for everything. I never meant to hurt you." He paused, unsure of his next words. "I've missed you, Liv." It was the most honest thing he'd said all morning.

Liv was silent. The expression on her face unreadable. Part fear, part relief. The return of the waitress was a welcome distraction. But once they were alone again, the awkward silence continued, broken when they both spoke at once. Ridge noticed the corner of Liv's lip tip into a tiny smile as he nodded for her to speak.

"That's not the only reason you're here." It wasn't a question, just a statement of fact. She knew. *Idiot.* Of course she could tell he was holding back. He wondered what else she knew. He hadn't taken the time to dig into her records, find out how effective her training had been.

"Your name came up in a missing persons case I've been assigned. Any chance you know a girl named Jessica Garrison?" The words sounded unnatural, accusatory. His insides cringed as he tilted his phone screen toward Liv. He held the edges of the cell so that Liv was forced to make contact. The tip of her index finger grazed his thumb, sending a pulse of electricity between them that had been absent far too long. He swallowed the impulse to take her hand as she pulled the phone free.

"Garrison?" Liv squinted at the picture, once, then twice. "I've never seen her before. Sorry."

Liv slid the phone across the table before taking another sip of her tea. She twirled the edge of her cup as she replaced it on the saucer. The ceramic *swoosh, swoosh* a telltale sign of her lie.

"This woman had a newspaper clipping in her apartment. It was a write up from *The Irish Times* about you finding a missing girl."

"Oh." Liv's voice was quiet, contemplative. "The last time my name came up in one of your investigations, I ended up in handcuffs." She looked at him through long eyelashes. Goading him toward a conversation he wasn't yet ready to have.

Ridge sighed. "It's not like that this time, Liv. Garrison had an envelope addressed to me. There were photographs inside."

He pulled up the pictures Wallace had sent him and slid his phone back across the table. Liv swiped through the images.

"What exactly do you want me to do about this?" Liv's eyes blazed at him. There was nothing he could say to make up for leaving when her life was being torn apart. Honesty was a good first step, but it wasn't one he could take. Not yet.

"I need your help, Liv. I can't do this on my own. Come back to Cascade Hills. She had these pics for a reason. Help me find her before it's too late."

Liv pulled some euros from her purse and stood. Her jaw pulsed, but her eyes told another story. "Sorry you came all this way, Ridge. But you don't need me. Fresh missing persons cases aren't really in my wheelhouse." She squinted, as if that fact pained her. He was losing this battle. "Try Ashlyn. They don't call me in until the hope's all gone."

"Liv," Ridge reached for her, but she jerked away before his fingers could make contact. "I'm sorry, Ridge, really. But I've got a caseload of the dead to worry about."

7

LIV

I vacated Bewley's in record time, pushing through the line of patrons standing in queue for scones and croissants. I'd never let Ridge know that what he'd said spooked me. But the truth was, I'd been feeling it for weeks now. The unsettling notion that someone was watching, even last night, on the way back to Cohen's. But every time I turned there was no one there. Now, Ridge was affirming my fears. There was someone here–watching–taking pictures even. I shivered at the thought and pulled my jacket tighter around my shoulders, walking faster.

I only allowed myself two backward glances as I made my way from Bewley's to the Dooley's rent-a-car station. By the time I arrived I'd relaxed a little, thankful for the mental clarity the walk provided. I knew Ridge was lying when he'd asked me to help with the Garrison case. But I'd told a lie of my own. I may not have known her name, but Jessica Garrison *was* familiar. Her pencil shaded picture tucked in my messenger bag with all the others, sketched in detail by my very own birth mother, long before she'd gone missing. Prickles marched along the nape of my neck, and whether they were caused by her or someone else, I didn't want to find out.

I parked the rental car in front of the St. Mary Home for Children and began the climb to the front door. In the past, Father Kelly had always been there, waiting to escort Michael and I through the dusty catacombs. Today, my visit was unannounced, and with any luck, solitary.

The stone façade of the building was imposing, made more sinister by the smoke darkened patches that encircled each window. I stood on my tiptoes, grasping at the ledge to hoist myself high enough to see inside.

Most of the windows had been boarded after the fire. This was the only one the church had bothered to replace afterward, and it belonged to a room Father Kelly had always avoided.

Concrete stubble bored into the pads of my fingertips as I steeled my grip on the sill. Indecipherable whispers filtered in around the edges of my consciousness and grew louder, competing with the gentle rustle of leaves in the trees around the grounds. I pushed the voices away, focusing instead on the impenetrable sooty blackness beyond the pane of glass. I could see nothing but shadows.

I let go of the ledge and dropped down to the porch, dusting off my hands and sucking in a deep breath to prepare for what was on the other side of the heavy front door. Locked. Trotting down the steps, I made my way around the side of the massive complex.

Above my head, boarded windows studded the stone in perfect symmetry. But near the ground, behind overgrown shrubbery, I found a forgotten access window. I checked my surroundings and turned my back to the frame, kicking in the glass with the heel of my tennis shoe. I flinched at the crystalline sound of the shatter, hoping it was only abrasive to my own hypersensitive ears.

I waited for the sound of an alarm. I'd never seen Father Kelly disarm one, but breaking and entering wasn't an addition I wanted on my arrest record. And the possibility was my sole purpose for renting a car. I needed a quick getaway if necessary, and I refused to drag an unsuspecting cab driver into my personal quest for truth.

When the natural sounds of the woods around me began to overshadow worry, I plunged through the bushes and shimmied, feet first, through the access window, landing with a thump on the cement below.

I flattened my hand against the cold cinderblock wall. As if it would offer some support from whatever waited for me in the shadows. I stood there, blinking repeatedly, urging my eyes to adjust to the darkness.

"Why'd it take you so long?" The woman's voice was clear. And I swiveled my head from side to side, searching for the source of the sound.

"There's no one here, Liv. Just your mind playing tricks on you." I said the words aloud. My own voice pushing creeping fear to the side. They were the words of my father.

I'd been about ten-years-old when the visions started. I'd call for my father from my bedroom and he'd come running, soothing away my fears and ensuring me that there was no one else in the room, that what I'd seen had been mere figments of my imagination. I could still picture him, sitting strong and protective on the edge of my bed stroking my hair and whispering, *"There's no one else here, Liv. It's just the two of us."*

It took the untimely death of my cousin before we'd both realize that just because he couldn't see the visions or hear the voices, didn't mean the spirits were any less real.

I sucked musty air into my lungs and pushed it out in a steady stream, stepping away from the safety of the wall. I flicked on the flashlight I'd borrowed from the Garda office, sweeping it wave-like around the room, hoping to compensate for my maladjusted vision.

The space had been used as a store room. Old cribs, mattresses, and headboards stood in rows like troops, filling the entire east wall of the basement. It explained why the wall had been void of energy. This wasn't an often occupied space. I picked my way through the forgotten furniture to the center of the room and a makeshift pathway that led to the stairs.

From there I could see the opposite side of the basement. Hampers piled with sheets stood next to washing machines, as if frozen in time, waiting for a sister to descend the stairs to put the next load in. Energy was heavier here and a shiver ran down my spine, forcing me to turn from the laundry area and toward the escape of the stairway.

The first four steps disappeared into blackness at a landing, punctuated by a wall that curved to the left. Either a door or more stairs. There was no way to tell without going up. Besides, I was here to hunt for records, tangible proof of the existence of Saoirse and the other girls, not to ghost hunt in a damp, dark basement.

"Get on with it," I whispered, my words scattering the building pockets of energy like fireflies. I headed up the first section of steps and then four more before being stopped by a fire singed door. It took all my strength to force it open. Corroded hinges screaming in protest morphed into wails of trapped children. I jerked my hands away from the wood, forcing the door open with my shoulder instead.

I hadn't considered this when I decided to come here. I knew children had died the night of the fire, eight of them to be exact. I'd seen pictures of each of them in my mother's case file. But I wasn't ready to relive their last moments, frozen in the walls and doors of the burned out children's home.

Once on the main level, I shoved my hands in the pockets of my jacket. From here I knew exactly where to go. I followed the hall that led along the courtyard, peeking in the rooms as I trudged along, careful not to make contact with walls or strewn furniture as I went. I hummed random riffs to keep the atmospheric energy at bay. Dusty orbs caught in the mid-day sunlight seemed to smile at me, urging me on.

Then I saw it. The fifth room on the right. The one I instinctively knew belonged to Saoirse. I withdrew my hands from the shield of my jacket and silenced my vocal cords. Running my fingers down the frame of the door and closing my eyes, I felt for her energy, the reverberations of a young girl who never had the chance to grow up, to love, to have a family of her own.

I shook my head, pressing my fingers more firmly into the wooden frame. But it didn't help. There were too many children. It was impossible to single her out from the cacophony of voices vying for my attention.

"Not now," I whispered to them. "I'm looking for Saoirse," I said, pulling my hands free of the mahogany and venturing inside.

The room was a mirror image of what I'd seen from the courtyard window, twin bed to the left, mirrored dresser to the right. The bed was made, the hymnal still on top of the outer blanket. Dust and mildew had long ago taken over the scent of freshly starched sheets. The fire had never reached this part of the home, but ash and water had permeated every crevice, darkening everything in its path with smoke residue and mildew.

I headed for the dresser, an old waterfall style with a round mirror, secured by leaf-like wooden discs, makeshift fists securing mirrored glass to wooden backing. I drug my fingertips through the soot and grime, exposing parallel trails. I closed my eyes to the pulses seeping from the wood beneath. I'd found her.

A girl's laughter cut through my consciousness–memories of Saoirse's childhood trickling through me. The corners of my lips twisted into a smile. I hadn't expected happiness.

I was too caught up in the images of tea parties and hide-and-go-seek to notice the gust of cool air over my right shoulder, followed by a whispered, "Looking for this?"

8

LIV

I opened my eyes to the voice from behind. My hand stayed planted on the dresser. I pressed the pads of my fingers against the wood, refusing to chance a broken connection.

"We've been waiting for you."

Loose auburn curls hung at shoulder length in the woman's mirror reflection. Grass-green irises shone out from beneath almond shaped eyes. I'd seen pictures of Aimee Callaghan, but we'd never met, and I hadn't noticed just how physically similar we were. I knew now why Michael had done a double take when Ashlyn had first introduced us. There was an uncanny resemblance, down to the way she smiled, the right corner of her mouth curving first.

I followed her gaze to the top dresser drawer. Only when she nodded her approval did I venture removing my palm from the dresser's top and begin tugging at the tarnished brass pulls, wiggling the compartment from side to side to break the glue of grime.

The drawer finally gave to the pressure, sliding open to

reveal a bride's Bible, the white cover now grey with age. As I pulled the book from its hiding spot, energy seeped in, a combination of laughter and loss, fear and gratitude. But another unexpected energy filtered through me, like caramel over an ice cream sundae. An energy I hadn't felt in months. Love.

The apparition in the mirror began to fade, emerald eyes against porcelain skin growing more transparent with each shallow breath I took.

I focused on the Bible in my hands, opening the cover for the first time. I let my fingertips graze the brittle pages. Handwritten in cursive under the stamped bookplate reading, *This Bible belongs to:* were three names. The combination kicked my heart into high gear: Aimee Callaghan, Jessica Mulcahy, and Saoirse Quinn.

"I knew you'd come." The whisper of my mother's voice crawled from the Bible into my consciousness.

I closed the cover and shoved it into the messenger bag hanging at my side, following the urge of my mother's energy. Leaving Saoirse's room, I turned right, deeper into the catacomb of dormitories.

The walls morphed from an aged shade of vanilla to a dingy grey. The air grew thick and stale. Particles of dust and debris floated in the beam of my flashlight. My heart thumped in my chest, a belt of panic squeezed my insides–a warning. But instinct was stronger, directing me down an interior corridor. I closed my eyes as I turned the corner, afraid of what I might see. I exhaled a deep breath and peeked into the darkness in front of me, clear of apparitions. Three doorways gaped at me, mouths into rooms whose contents were charred black.

I breathed a silent, *thank you.* No matter how long I'd dealt with visions or otherworldly energies manifested in worldly goods, the process still petrified me. I knew one day I'd see something I couldn't process, wouldn't be able to unsee. My sister and Michael might be able to think of these abilities as gifts. But for me, the gift had always been a curse.

I panned my flashlight back and forth between each room. There was no light in this section of the home. The windows were boarded and the air hung heavy and stiff, even smoky, as if embers of a fire still smoldered beneath the blackened rubble.

I stood in the middle doorway, hands on what was left of the frame, gazing into the rubble as if there were more to see beyond the petrified remains of scorched wood and twisted iron.

"How long were you here?" I asked the emptiness.

I didn't expect an answer, of course, but I gave it a shot, hoping to direct the energy I was picking up from the burnt remains. My mother had grown up here, of that I was certain. But how she'd gone from Catholic orphanage to a university internship in my father's law firm was a mystery to me.

Whispers of secrets long kept buzzed around me. A young mother with no other choice, a child with nowhere to go growing into a young woman on a mission for the truth. My mother's trajectory hit too close for comfort.

I slid my hand down the charred doorframe, a familiar pressure building in my chest. This is how it started. My legs weakened as dark fingers of energy reached for me. I sunk to the floor, debris crunching beneath the weight of my body. The incessant murmur of ghostly voices replaced the silence of the empty home. I fought against it, pushing a groan from inoperative lungs, jerking my hand away from the doorframe. But it was too late. I'd waited too long.

I squinted against encroaching darkness. Following Herman's advice, I strained to focus on something real as the walls pulsed and throbbed around me. The sensation of being at the mercy of partiers at a nightclub rave strengthened. The constant ebb and flow of energy tugged, pulling in differing directions all at once. Lightheadedness washed over me, and the room spun, a paranormal Tilt-a-Whirl. I reached for the floor in a futile attempt to steady the vertigo.

I struggled to sift through the swirling vibrations, searching for the tenderness I'd felt in Saoirse's room. But it was gone. Replaced by darkness. Heat tickled the tips of my fingers and worked its way through my arms and into my core. I shivered as the temperature of my body rose. The cool mustiness of the hall chilled my skin, raising gooseflesh over my arms and legs.

A bright flash slit through my skull, ending the contact with reality I'd fought so hard to keep. Dark imagery, men in suits leading young women through the halls of the home, fear-laden meetings, locked doors, bound wrists.

Shadows danced along the periphery of my consciousness, cutting through my brain like flashes of electricity. Each jolt pushing me closer to the edge, farther from the safe harbor of reality.

9

RIDGE

R idge had been sitting with Michael Donaghey in Cohen's for nearly two hours. He was doing his best not to show the irritation bubbling beneath the surface as he watched the door over Michael's shoulder. He should have followed Liv out of Bewley's, but Sowards had called, anxious to ream him out after discovering he'd blatantly disobeyed an order.

"I'm sorry we couldn't uncover any information about your missing girl." Michael's voice forced Ridge back to the issue at hand.

"So am I." He twisted the glass of water in front of him. The setting sun shone through the windows, casting prisms of light on the nicked tabletop. He'd never expected the Garda to have any information on Garrison, but considering the connection, it had been worth the shot to ask.

The older man's eyes shifted downward as he spoke. "I must say, I was disappointed to get your call. 'Twill be difficult to watch Liv go."

"The Bureau appreciates what you've done for her." Ridge

glanced around the room before pulling an envelope from his pocket and sliding it across the table.

"So that's it then? She returns to Cascade Hills and...what? I assume your supervisors will make use of her talents."

Ridge ran a hand through his hair before nodding his response. "That's the plan."

"And if the threat continues?" Michael prodded.

"Then we'll protect her."

"Aye." Michael sat back against the padded nook. "The girl has her mother's fire. If she won't let you?"

"She will. We'll figure something out."

Michael took the envelope without opening it, tucking it into the inside pocket of his blazer. "This happened before Aimee died, you know. The threats. Unsolved cases."

Ridge nodded his understanding. He'd read the reports. Aimee Callaghan's last months had been frantic. Official records alluded to delusional tendencies and paranoia. He wouldn't let the same thing happen to Liv.

Michael rose from the booth and secured his hat in place. "Take care, Agent McCaffrey. Got your work cut out, you do." He paused, leaning toward Ridge. "Would you allow me to offer one last piece of advice?"

Ridge nodded.

"If I was a betting man, I lay odds she's at St. Mary's."

Ridge waited for Michael to hail a taxi before flinging the pub door open himself, the tail lights of Michael's taxi still visible, turning North in the direction of Donaghey's home.

When Ridge gave the destination to his own taxi driver, the man eyed him with suspicion, adjusting the brim of his hat before asking for clarification.

"You don't mean the place north of the city. The one that's been closed for years?"

"That's the place. Just drive please." The irritation that had built all afternoon was seeping out around the edges. Liv was alone, vulnerable, and again, he had no one to blame but himself.

"Sorry, then. I'll drop you here, but I can't wait. 'Tis not safe at night." The cabbie kept the car in gear while Ridge pulled euros from his wallet. He waited for the driver to pull away before starting up the drive toward the children's home.

He'd seen photographs, but as he approached the hulking structure he was shocked by the silence of the place. Other than wind and increasingly heavy droplets of rain rustling the trees at the edge of the property, there was no sound—just the charred remains of a tomb.

A compact rental car parked just at the edge of the overgrown driveway was the only sign of life. He shone his flashlight in the driver's side window, illuminating the purse he'd seen Liv carrying that morning at Bewley's.

"Liv!" Ridge hollered as he took the front steps two at a time, trying the knob on the front door before throwing his weight against the slab of solid wood. It didn't budge.

A cool breeze filtered over his shoulder and a rumble of thunder rolled in the distance as he searched the porch for something heavy enough to break the only un-boarded window he could see. Finding nothing, he yelled again, louder this time. He strained to hear a response over the increasing rain. Nothing.

Another breeze washed over the porch, this time strong enough to rattle a loose board on one of the front windows. Ridge grabbed the unsecured corner of plywood and pulled, bracing himself against the building with one leg. The moisture laden wood broke free with the next rush of wind, providing just enough space for Ridge to climb up and over the sill, landing with a thump on the floor inside.

He shone his light around, calling Liv's name repeatedly. He stepped gingerly through the foot-deep debris on the floor. Once an office, charred desks and destroyed filing cabinets littered every corner.

"Liv?" As he turned the knob to exit the room he heard it. A faint whimper, like that of an abandoned puppy. He spoke again, a bit softer this time, his ears tuned for a response.

The hall proved more treacherous than the front office. It was all he could do to stay upright and keep from tripping on burnt remains. Bits of furniture and wall decorations created a carpet of blackened fragments, some of which stuck out at odd angles. If he didn't watch his step, his next destination would end with an ace bandage and a tetanus shot.

The whimper came again, a squeak of breathlessness that drove a spike of panic through Ridge's core. It was closer now, and this time he could tell it was human. He forged through the hall, shoving wreckage out of the way as he clambered on, calling again for Liv before turning the corner.

Her body lay splayed in the debris of the hall. Her arms stretched out to either side. A flashlight, still lit, shone uselessly in the dust just beyond her fingertips. Her messenger bag lay limp at her side. Another oxygen deprived wheeze erupted from her throat.

"Liv, wake up, baby."

Ridge leaned over her face. Her breaths were shallow–light puffs against his cheek–barely enough to keep oxygen flowing through her system. But her eyes were open, pupils dilated. He picked up the light and turned it off, pocketing it before shining the beam of his own flashlight over her body from head to toe. There were no obvious injuries, no reason she shouldn't be moved.

Ridge grabbed the bag and swung the strap over his head. The air in the hall was thick and musty. He needed to get her out and into the fresh air. His heartbeat throbbed in his ears as he slid his arms under her back and knees, lifting her free from the sooty debris.

He made his way down the hall to the front of the building, managing to unlock the massive door before carrying Liv out onto the porch. The rain had turned from a gusty storm into a soft drizzle. He arranged her against the stone façade, making sure she was away from the open sides of the porch, shielded from the elements.

Her head was heavy in his hands as he propped her up, eyes now closed. He was careful to choose a position that would allow air to flow freely through her airway. A rush of some long buried emotion surged through him as the silkiness of her hair slid beneath his fingers. He pulled away and stared at her soot-smudged face.

He tucked a stray curl behind her ear before pulling out his cell to call Sowards. He knew he couldn't risk an ER visit. Not yet. After the obligatory reprimand Ridge was ready for, Sowards was quick to let it go, rattling off an unfamiliar address. And by the time Ridge got his orders, Liv's eyes had fluttered, her breathing deepened, and her whimpers subsided. The bluish hue of her lips replaced with the pink he was used to.

"Hang on, baby," he whispered, folding her against his chest and lifting her from the ground. His breath ricocheted against her temple as he carried her to the rental.

He tucked her limp body onto the back seat, pausing for a moment as regret reared its ugly head. She was truly beautiful. She'd been so sensitive, trusting, when he'd met her. And he'd destroyed her, forced her to divulge her deepest secrets and then left her when the tables turned.

The ache in his chest deepened with each glance in the rearview mirror. She didn't deserve to be caught in the middle like this. And he certainly hadn't earned the right to win her back, no matter how much he wanted that chance. He swallowed the knot of remorse and adjusted the driver's seat before heading away from the empty home and toward Dublin City.

"You want to explain to me what I saw in there?" Ridge's voice was muffled, as if I was listening to it through water. But even so, I could tell he was angry.

I opened my eyes, shifting on the worn settee in Herman's living room, gauging how I might have gotten there. I remembered pulling the Bible out of Saoirse's dresser drawer. Heading down the darkened halls of the children's home. I even remembered sitting in front of the trio of burned out rooms. But after that, all I could access were subtle vignettes. Pulses of memory for which I had no context.

"We've been working on her ability to control the impulses." Herman's voice was a calm contrast to Ridge's anger. "It's not my place to discuss it. As her therapist, it would be against the privilege I share with Olivia to divulge the particulars of her condition."

Condition. The word sliced through me. He was right. That was exactly what this was...an affliction. I squeezed my eyes closed to escape their dry burn. My arms and legs tingled as I stretched, shaking through the remaining fogginess. My fingers still vibrated with remnants of leftover energy and my hands trembled, my body jittery as if I'd had too much caffeine. It always took a while for the effects to wear off.

Herman had warned adamantly against giving myself over to the energy. It made me too vulnerable, he'd said. And the fact that I had no memory of what happened to me physically was grim proof. But this time I hadn't gone willingly. It had drawn me in, targeted me.

I'd been at a crime scene with Michael the first time it happened. The girl's name was Moira Collins, a runaway who'd ended up a tragic statistic in a dumpster near the Dublin docks.

As the coroner dragged her body from the dumpster, Moira's bracelet shimmied loose, falling to the ground at my feet–a delicate silver chain. Appropriate for a thirteen-year-old girl. The letter M stamped onto a circular charm and attached near the clasp. It was as vivid in my memory as it had been when I held it in my hand nearly five months ago.

I should have known better than to touch it, but to pick it up from the ground was instinct. I woke up hours later in the emergency room at St. James Hospital with nothing but disembodied memories and a prescription for Xanax to show for it. That's when Michael persuaded me to see Herman.

"Look, Mr. Mayhew," Ridge's voice quieted. "We both know why she's here. We both want what's best for her."

"Do we?" Herman's voice broke in. "If memory serves, she came to Dublin a broken woman. Now that she's put herself together, you're here to sweep her away again. To use her as your government sees fit. Tell me, Mr. McCaffrey, in your heart, is that what you think is best for her?"

The words cleared the remaining fog, sending a spike of panic into my chest as threats of what else Herman might reveal danced on the periphery. I cleared my throat and pulled myself upright on the settee. Damp clothing sucked at my joints as I moved. But it was enough to get their attention. Both men turned in my direction. Herman eyed me with fatherly disappointment while Ridge's brow furrowed in concern.

I muttered a quick apology to Herman, who waved away my meager defense.

"'Tis a hard lesson learned, but free will is a blessing with which no one should interfere." It was another typical Hermanism. A phrase to be deciphered later. But I couldn't help notice he directed it at Ridge, not me.

Herman excused himself without another word, disappearing down the stairs to the tea room. I held onto the edge of the settee cushion, still working to quiet the buzz filtering through me.

"I'm going to take a stab in the dark here and assume you found me?" I asked.

Ridge nodded. "What were you doing there by yourself, Liv?"

His voice was stern, but his eyes shone something else. Relief, maybe? Concern?

The air between us came to life as he moved closer. I'd forgotten the pull he had on me. Cool fingers of electricity pricked at already heightened receptors as Ridge kneeled in front of the settee. I blew a steady breath through the increasing energy, keeping my head lowered to avoid his gaze. But I couldn't ignore the quickening thumps of my heart, or the sparking vibrations between us.

"I thought—" His voice broke off and his hand went to my hair, pushing a strand of dampened curls behind my ear before twisting its length gently around his index finger.

"Ridge," I warned, pulling my head away.

He leaned back, giving me room to process as he spoke.

"You scared me. With everything going on at home with the Garrison case, it was just a little much."

Of course. The Garrison case. This had nothing to do with me. He just needed to get to the bottom of his latest riddle. Hadn't he always put the badge first?

"Well, I'm fine." I decided indignation was my best chance at masking the attraction I struggled to ignore. Giving in to the energy at the children's home had left me emotionally raw, and he was the last person I needed to be around in that state. "There's nothing to worry about. I just needed a little closure."

For the first time, I met his eyes. Cerulean blue framed by dark lashes. There was no accusation, no disappointment. The only emotions I could decipher were the need to understand against the backdrop of remorse. I swallowed my own knot of regret and looked away.

"Did you find it? Closure?" he asked, rising from the floor and settling onto the settee next to me.

It was a simple enough question. One that made sense, given the circumstances. He studied his clasped fingers. His thumb traced a path over the knuckles of his right hand. The white line of a scar remained, his own tangible reminder of the events that had torn us apart.

The tickle in my stomach grew more frantic, sending a spiral of warmth to combat the damp chill. Attraction was the only energy that always started on the inside. The flush in my cheeks hit as I shook my head.

"Closure's never been my forte," I said, refusing to pull him into my crazy.

11

RIDGE

Kiss her. Ridge fought the impulse as he sat next to Liv on Herman's ancient couch. She was weak. He could see it in her eyes. The wall she'd built since he got to Ireland was crumbling. It had something to do with what she'd seen at St. Mary's, he was sure of it. He'd be taking advantage of her weakness if he gave into the urge, and God knows he'd done enough of that to last a lifetime. But she was close. Too close. He ran his hands over the velvet seat of the settee. *Who owns a settee in this day and age anyway?*

"*Closure.*" Liv's words sliced through him. Twice now he'd held back the closure she needed. The image of her on the floor of the home would haunt him. What would have happened if he hadn't gotten there? Would she have come out of it on her own? Nothing had changed. She was still the truth seeker she'd been when he'd abandoned her in Cascade Hills. And he was still the one keeping secrets.

Ridge practically leapt off the couch when a vibration from his jacket pocket interrupted his thoughts. He glanced at Liv before answering. She looked so small, vulnerable. The muscles in his jaw tightened. If he wasn't careful, a headache would follow.

"McCaffrey! What the hell do you think you're doing?"

Ridge aimed the phone away from his ear, hoping Liv hadn't heard the reprimand. Two in one day. He was batting a thousand since stepping onto Irish soil. Her focus was on the worn carpet, but the tiny smile that curved the edge of her lips was evidence she'd heard.

He took a breath and covered the speaker as Captain Wallace continued screaming obscenities at him. When Wallace grew silent, Ridge did his best to smooth over the situation, telling the captain that Liv was not involved, that she'd never heard of Jessica Garrison. By the time the call was over, Liv's full attention was on Ridge.

He shrugged. "I think I've worn out the Captain's good humor. They need me back in Cascade Hills."

"Has there been a break in the Garrison case?" Liv asked, eyes shining up at him.

"Maybe. We've got a body, not sure if it's her yet." He swallowed. Liv had been working for the Garda long enough to know what that meant. Unrecognizable this early in the game, meant purposely mutilated. *Way to kill a mood, McCaffrey.*

Ridge ran a hand through his hair, scratching at the back of his head. He thought he noticed a hint of worry flicker across Liv's face as he blew out a breath of frustration. He studied her. The way her hair fell over her left eye, the way she twisted the ring on her right hand when she was anxious, just like she was doing now. He followed the curve of her arm toward her face. The way her lips parted. *Jesus.* It was thoughts like this that got him in this mess in the first place.

He scrubbed a hand down his jawline and headed toward the window. A neutral zone where he could ignore the tiny idiosyncrasies of Liv that both drove him crazy and made his world fall into place. He'd forgotten how much there was to miss.

"Do you have my messenger bag?" Liv's voice broke through his self-loathing.

He slipped over to the doorway to retrieve the bag, resting it at her feet as she thanked him.

She reached in, pulling out a small Bible, greyed with age.

"I found something in one of the rooms that might interest you."

Ridge's eyes narrowed before he could check his expression. The one thing he could count on from Liv were surprises. He hoped she hadn't noticed the hint of disbelief.

She turned the book over in her hands. And he couldn't help but wonder what she was feeling. What to him was nothing but a cold, hard book, to her was something alive with energy. It was hard to imagine remnants of life trapped between the covers of an inanimate object.

She flipped through the tissue-thin pages, hesitating every so often to study handwritten notes in the margins.

"I found this in the bedroom that belonged to Saoirse, the girl we just found. There's something inside you should see."

Liv flipped to the names listed inside the front cover. She held the book out to him, and his fingers grazed hers as he grasped it. *Aimee Callaghan. Jessica Mulcahy. Saoirse Quinn.* He read the names several times in silence before snapping a picture of the page with his phone.

"The surname is different. It could be anyone." Ridge tried to make his voice as gentle as possible. Sometimes talking to her was like trying to approach a deer. You had to be careful not to scare her off.

Liv shook her head from side to side. "It's her, Ridge. I can't explain how I know, or why, I just do."

Ridge narrowed his eyes at Liv, not bothering to conceal his disbelief. Liv shifted to the far corner of the settee. *Shit.*

"Have you ever had déjà vu?" Liv asked.

Ridge checked her expression. She was serious. He nodded. "Sure."

"The blackouts are kind of like that. Like waking up with someone else's memories."

"Can you only read certain people? Or can it be anyone?"

Liv shrugged, but Ridge had already seen the contraction in her jaw, the flush of color in her cheeks that gave him his answer.

"If I had something that belonged to them, it could be anyone."

Anyone. That meant she could read Garrison. Now that she'd admitted it, all he had to do was get her home and get something of Garrison's into her hands. It could work. It could be the break he needed. Liv tucked her lower lip under her top teeth, a sign Ridge had learned long ago to read as nervousness, and that still sent a pang of attraction through his core.

"I'm going to need to keep this." He held up the Bible before grabbing his jacket from the back of the settee and shrugging into the leather sleeves.

"I need to make some calls, pass this information along. If you're feeling up to it, why don't you let me walk you back to Cohen's?"

Ridge expected a protest, but Liv didn't speak, just nodded. She started to sling the messenger bag over her shoulder, but Ridge caught the strap, hooking it over his own. He offered her his hand as she stood, but she declined, the corners of her mouth turned down in the hint of a frown. Her steps, wobbly at first, evened out by the time they got to the doorway.

They walked in silence most of the way back to the guest house. Even in the darkness of the evening, Liv's grimy clothes earned a few suspicious looks from passersby along the route. Ridge struggled with what to say to her. Dumping several options before running out of time. They were standing in the hallway outside of Liv's room before he spoke.

"Is there anything else you want to tell me about what happened at the home? Anything else I should know?"

Words he meant to deliver soothingly, as a sign of how much he cared, sounded brash and critical to even his own ears. He shook his head.

"Those pictures you showed me. I've seen her before. Jessica, I mean. Michael gave me a folder of Aimee's sketches. Jessica's face was one of them."

Ridge didn't know how to respond. He watched as she shuffled her feet over the worn carpet.

"And I know someone's been following me. I've felt it for the past few weeks. After this morning, I thought maybe it was Garrison. But now...I guess I wish it was."

Protective instinct built with every word Liv spoke.

"Come back to Cascade Hills with me, Liv." He'd been practicing that phrase since they'd crashed and burned at Bewley's that morning. The words slid through his lips, and he bent to plant a kiss on her forehead. Coconut and jasmine shampoo mingled with the trace of damp mustiness from the children's home. Temptation overpowered him, forcing him a step closer. "You're not safe here anymore."

His hand grazed her arm, from shoulder to elbow, and he knew he'd pushed the moment too far. But she hadn't retreated, hadn't moved to stop what was about to happen. Inching closer, he leaned in, the sweetness of her breath warm against his skin.

His heart hammered as he tilted her chin upward, brushing his lips over hers. He lingered a moment, giving Liv a chance to respond. He leaned into the warmth of her hands on his chest, closing his eyes as she pushed up onto her tiptoes. The heat of her mouth covering his. She slid her hands to the back of his neck, fingers tangling in his hair.

A spike of heat drove through his core, his need for pleasure clouding all rational thought. But almost as quickly as it started, it was over. She pulled away, running her hand down his chest before pushing him away.

"I can't do this," she whispered. He thought more for her benefit than his. "I'm sorry. Thanks for walking me home."

Liv slid the messenger bag off Ridge's shoulder and slipped through the door, leaving him alone in the dimly lit hallway with a barrage of regret and a tangible reminder of his own weakness.

I stood in the cramped shower stall, rivulets of steaming water cascading over my body, warming chilled skin. My mind twisted back and forth between the pleasure of my lips locked with Ridge's, and the sheer stupidity of it all. Wasn't there a saying? Fool me once, shame on you, fool me twice... There was no question. I was the fool.

The logical part of me knew turning away had been the right thing to do. But the scent of him remained, filling my senses and stabbing me with a plunging sense of regret. And no matter how much my inner critic chided me, I knew Ridge felt it, too. I stepped out of the shower and wrapped a towel around my midsection. My eyes lingered a moment over the red line of scar tissue running across my abdomen.

Thoughts of that night washed away the lingering hint of pleasure, like a wave scrubbing away sand-written words. *You can't put yourself in that position again*, I told myself. But no matter what line of reasoning I used with my psyche, it didn't change the fact that I wanted more.

For the past six months I hadn't allowed myself to miss

Ridge. I'd thrown myself into my role with the Garda, desperately searching for purpose. But with Ridge's return, something inside loosened. Maybe it was the darkness I'd felt at the home, the knowledge that whatever was going on was bigger than one lost little girl. Perhaps it was sheer loneliness that made me need him in a way I'd been forcing myself to ignore. Regardless, I wasn't sure if I was ready for the repercussions that accompanied a relationship with Ridge McCaffrey.

I'd put myself out there once. Fallen hard for the handsome detective with a dimpled grin. But all I had to show for it now was an arrest record and an angry scar. *That wasn't his fault.* The words pelted me. "But I can blame him for not coming back," I said to the mirror, swiping my hand across foggy glass.

I'd just finished towel drying my hair when the lights in the room flickered twice and died. I slid into a pair of jeans and a sweatshirt just as a blast rocked the floor of my suite. The building shuddered, swaying as if a shift of tectonic plates had knocked it off its foundation.

The smoke came first, heavy and metallic in my nostrils. Screams and furious beating on the walls and doors up and down the hallway split the calm of the night. I turned away from the door, toward the far corner where I'd dropped my messenger bag. I reached for the strap, my fingers grazing the woven canvas, as a second blast hit. The force sliced a zigzag lightning bolt onto the plaster wall and knocked me off my feet. The dresser next to me teetered in the aftershock. And the television slid onto the floor with a crash, narrowly missing my feet.

I pulled on the bag with every ounce of strength I had. My heart pounded like a freight train in my chest, pulsing thunder in my ears. The dresser shifted again. I gave up on the bag and scrambled away, just before the wooden beast toppled to the floor where I'd been.

I climbed onto my feet and threw open the door, joining the mob of guests stampeding toward the front stairway. I glanced over my shoulder at the closest exit, a rear kitchen entrance that led to an alley out back. Flames flickered up, licking the doorway. The front was the only way out.

The throng of people ebbed and flowed, sucking me down the hall like a tide. Guests rushing in droves from the third floor complicated escape for those on the floors below.

It took only seconds to reach the landing, but the stairwell had already filled with smoke, choking and burning the back of my throat. I tugged the neck of my sweatshirt up over my nose and sunk lower, crouching, as grey-black wisps chased me from behind. Smoke belched forward, propelled by a third explosion from the back of the building.

A surge of screams erupted as chunks of wood and plaster rained down on us. I dropped to my hands and knees. My eyes stung as I crawled toward the doorway, following the crowd toward blind exits.

A hand grabbed me from behind, jerking me out of the way and flattening me against the floor as a billow of black smoke erupted from a first floor doorway. I struggled against the pressure on my back, straining to find a face to go with whoever was holding me down. Even once I was released, the flow of panicking guests kept me pinned. When the stream ended, I found myself tucked between an open hall door and the wall. Alone.

I pushed my arms out into the surrounding blackness, searching for someone or something to show me the way out of the smoky inferno. My vision was cloudy, a dark veil over my face. The sting of smoke made it hard to focus, and I rubbed at my eyes, trying to end the incessant watering.

I swiveled my head back and forth, searching for the glow of a red exit sign. But there was no visible difference between the way I'd come and the way I needed to go. Each end of the hall morphed into walls of orange-black flames. I closed my eyes against the scorching smoke, held my breath until my lungs screamed in protest.

Emergency sirens wailed from outside. Over the thunder of fire, they seemed to be everywhere and nowhere all at once. Heat crept closer. The roar of flames threatening from every direction.

I sucked in gulps of air but couldn't catch my breath. Logic kicked in, coaching me to take small regulated mouthfuls of air, but it was impossible. Thoughts of the St. Mary's fire filtered in around the edges of my consciousness. Blurring the line between my world and theirs. This was how they would have felt, victims trapped within the walls of a home they only ever wanted to escape.

I coughed. Sinking back onto my heels against the wall.

"*Not yet,*" I heard. The voice a whisper in my ear. My birthmother's voice. "*It's not time.*"

I yelled, an incomprehensible guttural sound. My lungs burned like lava as I scuttled away from the wall in a last ditch effort to save myself.

"Got one!" I heard a man shout as strong arms grasped my shoulders, slinging me forward along a chain of masked men until a blast of cool night air hit my face.

I watched from the curb alongside an emergency van. A medic-issued blanket tucked tightly around my shoulders as Cohen's Pub and Guesthouse went up in flames. When the fourth blast rocked the pavement, collapsing a portion of the roof, a group of hotel guests and I cringed in unison, mumbling soft exclamations of disbelief. Each of us was being treated on scene for smoke inhalation, freeing up paramedics to transport the more serious cases.

A woman on a gurney screamed as two medics shuttled her into one of the nearby vans. The skin along her left side was blackened, sloughing off in sections, leaving raw red swaths of flesh exposed. Within moments, a shot to her arm calmed her cries, ushering her into what I hoped was blissful unconsciousness.

I'd been sitting with the others for almost an hour when the man next to me nudged my shoulder, withdrawing his oxygen mask and asking, "Isn't that you?"

I looked up at the nearby tech who was trying to make announcements over the roar of flames and drone of emergency equipment.

"Olivia Sullivan," the tech called again in a thick Irish brogue, glancing at his clipboard, then back at our group.

"Here," I answered, swiping the oxygen mask off my face and raising my hand. He nodded at me, signaling me to stay put while he turned to a small group of onlookers.

Ridge pushed his way around the tech, knocking the clipboard from the medic's hands as he rushed toward me.

His arms were strong and warm as he lifted me from the ground in one smooth swoop. The ferocity of his embrace prompted an eruption of coughs from my oxygen deprived lungs. Another tech hurried over to admonish Ridge and reattach the mask to my face, settling me back on the curb with the blanket around my shoulders.

"I'm sorry," Ridge whispered over the rumble of the fire, lacing his fingers through mine.

I fought the urge to pull away. But gentle pulses of energy

overcame my personal crusade to keep him at bay. He brought the back of my hand to his lips, kissing gently.

"I'm sorry for leaving you then. I'm sorry I left you tonight." The look of terror in his eyes meshed with the tingle of fear that vibrated from his fingers into mine. My instinct to end the connection evaporated as the heat of his panic was replaced by the gentle warmth of relief. The raw emotion I'd kept contained until now broke free, forcing the first tears of the night down my smoke-stained face.

"I'll go back to Cascade Hills," I said, sliding the mask off. My eyes remained glued to the flames–a fire I knew was meant for me. One that had destroyed every reminder I had of my mother. Someone had been watching. Was watching still. But why they'd go this far, injuring innocent people when they only wanted me, was beyond comprehension.

Ridge pulled his hand away from mine, breaking the connection as he tilted my face toward his, pushing my mask out of the way. His lips caressed mine, tentatively, as if asking permission. I relaxed into his kiss–warm, safe, hungry.

I needed this. I needed him. Someone to make me feel normal. Like the images and energies I faced every day weren't dictating the path of my life. Like I could be something more to someone than a conduit for unsettled souls. Ridge pulled me closer, trailing soft kisses down my neck before returning to my lips. Only the inability of my singed lungs to keep up forced us apart.

13
———

LIV

"Are you sure you want to do this?" Ashlyn asked, her voice low, conspiratorial.

I stood with my sister in the bedroom of her downtown apartment. It was two o'clock in the morning, but with the commotion since the fire, it felt closer to noon. Every light in the apartment was on, and coffee and high-octane tea flowed like water, urging everyone involved to stay awake just a few more hours.

"It's time, Ashlyn. I never should have stayed this long. I can't be the reason innocent people die."

"You don't know that blast was meant for you." I heard the confidence in her voice, but vibrations of uncertainty wavered in the air between us.

I didn't answer, just pulled the borrowed robe tighter around my midsection and lowered onto the edge of the bed.

Ashlyn jerked shirts off hangers and piled them next to me. She glanced over her shoulder toward the open bedroom door. Ridge and Michael's voices echoed down the hall from the sitting area nearby. "This is his idea, isn't it?" Her eyes were on mine, searching.

My sister shoved the small pile of clothes to the side and tucked in next to me. She slid her arm around my shoulder, pulling me close. For a long moment she stayed silent. Her focused breath the only sound between us as she clutched me tighter.

Vibrating pulses of regret sloughed off her in waves. I could hear the catch of her breath in her throat as she struggled to speak. A clot of emotion that had nothing to do with Ridge. The heat of her energy bound around me, trapping me in a bubble of remorse that wasn't my own. I pulled away.

"Ashlyn, it's okay. We both did the best we could under the circumstances."

"I was never the sister you needed me to be," she said.

"Without you, I never would have called Michael. You listened when those first few cases nearly sucked the life out of me." I studied my sister. Pain and loss radiated from her body into the air between us. "Most importantly, you're here now."

Ashlyn grabbed a shirt and began to fold. "Ridge hurt you once, Liv. What makes you think he won't hurt you again?"

"He found you. That should be worth something," I said.

Ashlyn's eyes locked on mine, and a flicker of fear sparked between us. I brushed it away, tucking a pre-folded shirt into the bag.

"I'm not going back for him, Ash. For once, I'm doing this for me."

She stopped folding, cocking a skeptical eyebrow over an already doubtful stare. And for the first time I suspected she could read me as easily as I read her.

"Mom's name turned up in a Bible I found at the children's home."

Ashlyn went back to folding.

"She lived there, Liv. After she came back from the States. You know that."

"Saoirse's name, too. And Jessica, the missing girl from Cascade Hills." I hesitated, hoping for a reaction. Nothing. "There's a connection, Ash. I already know how things turned out for Saoirse. Maybe there's something I can do to keep the same thing from happening to Jessica Garrison." I lowered my voice. "If it hasn't already."

"You've never worked an active case. It's a different beast." Ashlyn smoothed her hand over the green knit blouse that topped the stack of borrowed clothes.

"Doesn't mean I can't." I struggled to keep indignance from my voice.

"Doesn't mean you should." Her eyes blazed back defiance.

"How's the packing coming along?" Ridge's six-foot-two frame filled the doorway, scattering shards of charged emotion.

A perfect smile lit up my sister's face as she turned to face Ridge. She'd always been the better pretender, an inherent master of façade.

"We're just about done." Ashlyn stood, pulled a couple pair of jeans from a dresser drawer and tucked them neatly in the open suitcase at the foot of the bed. She tossed another pair and a comfortable-looking sweatshirt my way before excusing herself, slipping by Ridge with a painted on smile.

"You okay?" Ridge asked as he entered.

I nodded, surprised by the sudden surge of emotion coiling itself around my vocal cords. I picked up the pile of shirts and snugged them into the suitcase.

"My flight leaves this afternoon. Michael and Ashlyn have promised not to let you out of their sight until they can get you on a plane to the States. The Garda has patrol stationed outside." Ridge moved toward the windows facing the street below. He pulled back a curtain and peeked out. "You're safe."

"Do you still have the Bible?" I pushed the words through the steel lump lodged at the base of my throat.

"Yes." Ridge's voice was quiet, reassuring.

"Everything else is gone. Aimee's drawings, her notes, everything." I sucked in a ragged breath and forced myself to face those soul-scorching eyes. From the first time I'd seen them under the mercury light at my grandmother's farm, they'd done something to me. Melted me from the inside out. He'd been the first person in a long time to make me feel safe–wanted. Every part of me ached to feel that again, even if he hadn't earned it.

Ridge nodded, thumbing toward the open doorway. "Michael thinks maybe that's what they were after."

A spark in the air ignited as I studied Ridge, lifting the hair on my arms and across the back of my neck. A gentle buzz skimmed along exposed skin. Ridge was holding back.

"You know, don't you?" My heart kicked up a notch as Ridge stepped away from the window, toward me. The sensation along my extremities intensified into a harsh prickle. I worked to stifle mounting panic in my voice. "Who did this, Ridge? Who's been watching me?"

Ridge's hands went up, eyes wide, palms facing me in a gesture of surrender. "Liv, please–if I knew..." He let the statement drift in the air between us.

The buzz against my skin vanished as quickly as it had come. I rubbed my arms, disintegrating the leftover tingle of energy. Maybe I'd imagined it. Maybe I wanted an excuse not to go home. Maybe. But for once, I wanted to be wrong.

14

LIV

Going back to Cascade Hills was like traveling through a time warp. The ten-hour flight gave me plenty of time to make a mental list of all the reasons why heading back to the place where everything fell apart was a terrible idea. The decision looked different in the light of day. There were consequences of going home I hadn't considered.

As far as I knew, Ridge was the only one outside my immediate family who knew the full extent of my abilities. I'd have to deal with all the piercing questions from everyone else. But that I could manage. Besides, what I'd been doing in Dublin was a matter of public record. The newspaper clipping in Jessica Garrison's apartment proved as much. It was too late to lie.

I glanced around the darkened cabin of the Boeing 767. Families returning from vacation, full of memories that would sustain them until finances would allow the luxury of international travel once more. Everyone I'd met on the plane was in the midst of experiencing life. A concept I'd been so far removed from in the last six months that it felt foreign to me. Instead, I'd been living in the past, shaped by memories that were not my own.

There was an elderly couple in row 15 hoping to shape a relationship with the grandchildren they'd yet to meet living three thousand miles away. I'd helped them stow their bags as we boarded the flight. They oozed excitement, and I only hoped their grandchildren would appreciate the effort. What I wouldn't give for a few more moments with mine.

I'd glimpsed what it was like to live in the now, before my relationship with Ridge had been torn apart by the lies of a man bent on destroying my family. But Ridge had been there to catch me when Grandma died. When the world as I knew it ceased to exist.

The last couple days with him had unearthed all those old feelings. He'd provided the apology I thought would never come, even if it was six months late. I'd tried to stay angry, but being with him was like slipping into a favorite pair of jeans. It was comfortable. Too comfortable, maybe.

I was glad he'd gone home ahead of me. Captain Wallace was on his case about the Jane Doe that had been found, and the doctors I'd followed up with after the fire weren't quite comfortable releasing me for a ten-hour flight on recirculated air. Everything had fallen into place, giving me some much-needed space to think, and time to say my good-byes.

The months in Ireland had shaped me, molded me into a person I hardly recognized. The people, the cases, all of them colored the woman who stared back at me from the mirror. Only since Ridge had shown his face had the tendrils of who I used to be filtered through.

I liked the old me. The me that existed before the jagged blade of a knife transformed my world. I missed the ability to trust that the people in my life were who they presented themselves to be. All of that seemed intrinsically better than the cynical, distrustful being I'd become. Always on the lookout for a wolf dressed in sheep's clothing.

Six months had felt like a lifetime. And no matter what repressed feelings Ridge was stirring up in me, I couldn't shake the nagging thought that he could turn out to be the biggest wolf of all. There were reasons he wouldn't tell me why he'd left, and no matter what his energy said, a big part of me was terrified of his explanation.

The animated plane on the seat back in front of me crawled closer to the heart of the United States. Waves of anxiety lapped at me like an incoming tide, gently wearing away the stony façade of the woman I'd spent the last half year pretending to be.

I exhaled through the confines of the emotion, telling myself for the umpteenth time that going home was the right thing to do—the only thing—under the circumstances.

Right now, Jessica Garrison needed me. Her name scrawled in a dead girl's forgotten Bible. Her face sketched by my mother's hand. This was my chance to put the pieces together that my mother never could. My chance to make things right for the faces in that folder. I couldn't change the past, but if Jessica Garrison was still alive, I'd do everything in my power to change her future.

A fit of giggles erupted from a seat a few rows ahead of me. A man whispered in a woman's ear. Her eyes shone pure happiness as she looked at him and snuggled onto his shoulder. I felt a smile creep onto my face as I watched them. The possibility of Ridge waiting for me, memories yet to be made, followed close behind.

The days since the fire helped me realize just how important it was to have someone to share life with. I'd been pushing people away for too long, cocooning myself in a world only I understood. Whether it was loneliness, or sheer stupidity, the fact that Ridge McCaffrey had been able to penetrate that shell was nothing more than a form of unbelievable magic I'd never fully understand.

I glanced again at the monitor. The lurch of our initial descent already registering in my gut. The cartoon plane now hovered directly over the state of Ohio, covering most of the state with its oversize proportions.

Mom would be waiting for me outside the terminal. Although my birthmother's words nagged at me in whispers, it was my adoptive mother who'd made this life possible. I may have spent a good majority of my life at odds with Beth Sullivan, but if the last year had taught me anything, it was that strength comes in all shapes and sizes.

The fact that she'd been able to unearth hers from a fortress of deception and embrace the daughter who was a daily reminder of her husband's infidelity awed me.

I SCANNED the line of cars outside arrivals at John Glenn International Airport twice, but my mom's black Mercedes was nowhere to be found. I hung back as a group of travelers forged ahead, finding their rides within moments. I listened idly to their chatter as I slid my phone from my pocket and waited for it to reboot. Maybe she was running late. The woman next to me leaned in as she passed.

"I wonder who he belongs to?" She jabbed me lightly as she spoke, as if we'd been friends forever, instead of seat mates on an international flight. I followed her gaze.

I sucked in a nervous breath, the tightness in my chest finding a partner in the flurry of butterflies that let loose in my stomach. I cleared my throat before responding, "Actually, I think he's mine."

The woman gave an approving grunt before walking off in the opposite direction, muttering, "Lucky girl," as she left. If she only knew.

Ridge did make quite a spectacular sight. He was leaning against his black Shelby, the lines of the car the perfect backdrop for his powerful form. Dark wash jeans and a light grey t-shirt stretched perfectly over a solid chest, camouflaged under a black leather jacket. I didn't remember him looking so good when he was in Ireland. *You didn't give yourself the chance.* There she was, my inner critic, right on cue and wholly accurate.

Even the air was different here. Cooler and less humid, but charged with something else...possibility? For a moment, I wondered if there was a way to forget the better part of the past year, to overlook explanations and start over. Jumping in when things were good between us, no secrets, no mistakes, just each other. I'd been gone so long that it almost seemed possible.

Ridge's focus was on the airport security guard who was admonishing him for being parked in the pick-up zone. I watched as he uncrossed his arms and flashed his badge at the guard, who put his hands up in defeat and walked away. Steps later I was within earshot.

"That's a gross abuse of power, Detective McCaffrey." I bit my lower lip to keep a goofy smile from taking over my face. I hadn't meant for that reaction to come through, but surprise at seeing him instead of my mom and a creeping desire to leap with both feet, got the better of me.

His head snapped my direction, his hand flying up to his face to remove a pair of dark Ray-Bans. Jesus, those electric blue eyes were a killer. I wracked my brain trying to temper the physical reaction I was having with logic. *Take it slow,* I coached myself. Funny how a shift in location is all it takes to dredge up old emotions you thought you had under control.

Even after the fire, I'd forced myself to keep my emotional distance. I never let it move past the gentle kisses we shared that night. I'd have to learn to do the same here. If we were going to be together, as colleagues or otherwise, I wanted to do it the right way. Truth first. Rushing headlong into a relationship after all this time with unresolved secrets at our heels was definitely not best practice.

"Liv." It was more breath than word, and before I knew it, strong arms were around me and my feet were no longer connected to the concrete below. Good to know I wasn't the only one suffering from location based insanity.

My luggage slipped through my fingers, falling with a thud. I hoped the sound of it would break whatever spell was taking over. We'd agreed to take things slow. Focus on the case. See what happened. No expectations. I pushed myself away as Ridge released me, grabbing my bag and studying me again.

I tucked a stray wisp of hair behind my ear. *Don't do that,* critical me chimed in. *Playing with your hair is a signal you're interested. Watch your body language, Olivia.* I chomped the inside of my cheek against the threat of nervous giggles. Casting my eyes toward the cement, I waited for him to open the trunk.

"These last couple days have been worse than the past six months." Ridge said, popping the trunk. "You look good."

I glanced down at the oversized sweatshirt and too big jeans, feeling completely inadequate in the borrowed wardrobe. His eyes smoldered though as they combed over my body, sloppy attire and all, coming to rest on my face. A smile broke out across his lips.

"I was worried you might have second thoughts." Ridge swallowed. "I'm glad you're here."

"Thanks," I said like a love-struck teenager. "I'm glad to be back. I think."

Ridge tossed my bag into the trunk of the Shelby before opening the passenger door for me. His hand on the small of my back sent a rush of blood flow to recently neglected regions, reminding me once more what a challenge going slow was going to be.

We drove in awkward silence, the interior of the car saturated with the tension of words left unsaid, secrets kept, past betrayals, and recent apologies. All of that mixed with the sexual energy of two teenagers on their way to prom. I wondered if he felt it too, or if it was just my own hypersensitivity.

I got my answer as we exited the garage. The muscle in his jaw ticked, a sure sign the tension was affecting him, too. The light at the intersection just past the airport stopped us and his eyes fixed on the red glow above, his hand planted firmly on the leather-wrapped gear shift between us.

As red gave way to green, Ridge floored it. The growl of the V8 sent a tremor through me, slamming my body against the seat back. He blew through three gears in the span of mere seconds before yanking the car over into the turn lane and into a hotel parking lot.

My heart pounded as he silenced the engine and lunged over the console toward me. He wrapped his hand in my curls, tugging firmly. That simple act sent a spike of desire through my midsection as I met his lips, ignoring screams of protest from the logical side of my brain.

An airy groan escaped Ridge's mouth as our kiss deepened, the vibration causing a series of spasms in my core. I worked my hand from his jaw down his neck and onto his chest, tangling my fist in his t-shirt. His heart thumped as mercilessly as mine, muting the little voice in my head for the few seconds it took to gain the mental clarity necessary to convince my muscles to push him away.

"I can't do this." My voice quivered, hinting at the conflict playing out in my mind.

He held my gaze.

I found myself shaking my head, retreating from him as far as possible within the confines of the car. My lips throbbed. My body buzzed with the afterglow of his kiss. I wanted to lean over the console and initiate another, taste the saltiness of his skin, feel his hands on my body. To hell with taking it slow.

But fear has a way of creeping up on a person. I was scared of losing what little bit of independence I'd gained over the course of the last half a year. *Independence? That's what we're calling it now?* I silenced the voice. Scared to put myself in the same position I'd been when he'd driven away from the farm and never returned. No man was worth that.

"Just not yet," I finally choked out.

We sat in that Marriott parking lot in silence for several moments. Just as I was starting to consider apologizing, Ridge leaned over and planted a soft kiss on my temple. He squeezed my hand, a tickle of warmth sliding from his skin into mine. The same warmth I'd cherished at the children's home. A lump rooted itself in my throat as the realization hit. Love.

15

RIDGE

R idge fiddled with the radio as he drove Liv from Columbus to Cascade Hills, turning it from one station to the next just to fill the space between them.

"You can't even tell what's playing," Liv said. Her hand brushed his as it hovered over the steering wheel control. "Just pick one, okay?"

Ridge stopped pressing buttons just as a techno beat with hip-hop vocals screamed through the speakers.

"Okay, maybe not *that* one." He heard the smile in her voice as he switched to a pre-programmed standby, exchanging rap for guitar laden riffs. He checked her reaction.

Liv swiveled her head toward the passenger side window, her fingers dancing along the hem of her oversized shirt. He blew through his own frustration, wondering if he'd already made her regret returning to Cascade Hills.

He'd gone too far in the hotel parking lot. She needed time to readjust. And he'd agreed to take it slow. What choice did he have, really? But damn it, it would take every last ounce of his self-control to navigate this arrangement.

The past seventy-two hours had been a whirlwind. From the moment he'd found her outside Cohen's the night of the fire something snapped. The Garrison case, the secrets he was keeping, all of them sucked into the background. She was what he wanted, he knew it now more than ever. And he'd be damned if he'd let the job get in the way this time.

Of course, it wouldn't be that easy. He had responsibilities, duties to fulfill before he could even think of a future with Liv. He shook away thoughts of Marcus Sowards and the impending doom of his assignment.

"Your mom put a little something together. A welcome home party." He struggled to keep the frustration out of his voice. "It's why she sent me to pick you up."

"That wasn't necessary."

She sounded sad, far away. He glanced her direction to get a better read, not that his skills of perception had done him any favors at the airport. But her head was still turned, taking in the scenery.

"The party starts at eight, at Murphy's. I could swing by and pick you up on my way." He cringed at his offer. She knew better than anyone that Sullivan Farm was nowhere near "on the way" to Murphy's Pub. *Ridiculous*, he thought.

"Okay," she answered.

The Shelby swerved just a bit toward the edge of the road as Ridge bit back his surprise.

"Okay," he repeated under his breath, trying to remember the last time he'd felt so nervous around a woman. High school prom, maybe? He came up empty.

The cityscape dissolved into corn and soybean fields, a mix of withered stalks ripe for harvest and empty fields already stripped bare. The typical October landscape of rural Ohio flashed by both windows as he pushed the speed limit toward Cascade Hills.

"Tell me more about Jessica," Liv said, turning to face Ridge. "If I'm going to help, I need to know more about her."

Ridge focused on the road ahead. "You were right. Her parents confirmed that her surname was Mulcahy before she was adopted. We're in the process of digging up records, but we're not having much luck. Everything official says Garrison."

"The original paperwork would have been lost when the children's home burned." Liv said. "That's why the case with Saoirse went cold, too."

Ridge bit back the urge to tell her who Jessica Garrison really was. To drop the charade he'd been living and come clean.

"Garrison's the sister-in-law to the district attorney," Ridge started, filling Liv in on the most basic details of Garrison's life, hoping it would satisfy her curiosity while keeping her on the periphery.

"Important family members. That explains a lot. I guess you must be getting a lot of heat about finding her?"

Ridge felt Liv's eyes boring into the side of his head as he drove. He didn't have a comeback. But the bitterness he detected in Liv's voice worried him. To her this was about equity. Equity for an orphan girl dumped in the foothills of Dublin and a successful woman with a family that would do anything to see her returned safely.

"What about Jane Doe?" Liv asked.

Icy dread crept from the back of Ridge's neck, over his shoulders and into his chest. Sowards had been right. Bringing Liv home could end up being his biggest mistake yet.

"We'll talk more about the case tomorrow," Ridge said. He had to keep Liv from forcing more than he could give. Had to keep her from realizing just how much he was holding back.

Staying in Liv's good graces without sacrificing his future with the Bureau was going to be a delicate balance.

Liv turned toward the window without a word, twisting her grandmother's gold Claddagh ring on her right hand. Leaving Ridge to wonder if he'd done more harm than good by trying to pacify her. He needed time, and with Liv back in Cascade Hills, time was likely in short supply.

He downshifted to turn onto Sullivan Road. Headlights flooded the interior of the car in the dusky light. A combine in the corner field, heading down the rows of corn closest to the road blinded him momentarily before he could gain his bearings and drive past.

Less than a mile and the farmhouse drive would appear on their left. He'd been checking on the place regularly. She'd hired gardeners and a cleaning service, even had the lights set on a timer to make it appear as if someone was home. But this was a small town, and most people knew the house was empty.

Liv shifted in her seat as Ridge pulled into the driveway. Her whole body seemed to tense as the sound of gravel crunching under his Michelin's filled the space between them.

He drove slowly, scanning the barn lot as he went. The mercury light shone down, encircling the parking area between barn and house with a flood of bluish light.

Ridge pulled to a stop as close to the sidewalk as he could, searching each window of the three-story farmhouse as the car grumbled idly.

"Thanks for the ride, Ridge." Liv pulled on the door handle, bathing the interior in the warm glow of the overhead light.

Ridge scrambled to quiet the engine and pop the trunk before Liv could do it herself. He may be a liar, but he could still be a gentleman. He heaved her bag from the trunk of the car and followed Liv up the walk to the front door.

He'd never seen her so hesitant. She glanced back at him twice before grabbing the handle of the storm door and flinging it open with more force than necessary. Catching it with the toe of her tennis shoe, she kept it propped open as she fiddled with the key, pushing it into the lock and turning just enough to release the locking mechanism.

That's when it hit him. The psychometry. She hadn't been able to sense emotions through touch before she'd left. At least, not to the degree she could now, according to Donaghey's reports.

Now, she was faced with a century worth of history encased within the walls of her own home. At least, she would be, if the research he'd done on the phenomenon had been accurate.

"Here, let me—" Ridge tucked the bag under one arm and stepped forward, ready to open the door.

"No!" She practically shouted the word. "I can do this."

She'd told him she could control it, but it sure didn't look like it from where he stood. Ridge held his breath as Liv finally gripped the bronze handle and turned, forcing the door inward with her shoulder.

She stepped inside and fumbled with the beeping alarm system, apparently unscathed by lingering psychometric energy. Although, he did pick up on the tremble in her hand before she slid it down the front of her jeans, as if rubbing off a layer of grime.

"You can leave the bag just inside the door there. I'll get it from here."

He nodded at her, his stomach turning a little flip as she tucked the corner of her lower lip under her front teeth, biting gently. He had to get out of there before he committed another classic act of stupidity. *Slow, MCaffrey,* he coached. *Take it slow.*

He had no choice but to hold up his end of the bargain. In spite of the moments they'd shared the night of the fire, that wasn't why she was here, and he knew it. She'd come home, provide what help she could on the Garrison case, as long as he promised to take it slow–see where things went.

He already regretted using the case to get her back to Cascade Hills, but it was too late to change that. Now, he'd volunteered to pick her up for a party that was sure to involve alcohol. *Nice.* He was bound to execute some other social sin in the hours to come.

"I'll see you around 8:00, then?" he managed.

She smiled as he pulled the door closed, looking up at him with those emerald eyes. How did he ever think he'd be able to focus on the Garrison case with her so close? He hadn't been able to separate his feelings for Liv when the job brought them together nine months ago. How was he supposed to do it now?

He trotted down the porch steps and back to the Shelby, his insides churning. Time had obviously done nothing to calm his feelings toward Liv. And with her home, the responsibility of protecting her from enemies she didn't know existed was now more important than ever.

He sucked in a breath and growled through the exhale. He had no idea how to balance it all. Liv had proven her worth to the Bureau when she'd confronted Lyle Hunt. This test would be his. The Garrison case had chosen him, and Liv would either end up his secret weapon or his Achilles heel.

16

LIV

I was sitting in the passenger seat, halfway up the drive to Sullivan Farm before I realized the fallout this new "gift" would bring me. A century-old farmhouse occupied by my grandparents and theirs before them was sure to have some lurking energy.

I spent what was left of the uncomfortable ride talking myself through what was about to happen, internally chanting a mantra. *You can control this. This does not control you.* Herman taught me that trick in the very beginning, when I first started to understand that the pulses of energy I felt were the result of others' emotion. But now that I was faced with vibrations of a past to which I was so closely linked, I was petrified.

I slid down the inside of the leaded glass door as Ridge closed it behind him. The air in the farmhouse hung thick, permeated with the stale heaviness of an empty home. A twinge of pine scent wafted toward me. Barely noticeable proof that the cleaning service I'd paid for months had held up their end of our agreement.

I inhaled deeply. Still missing the sweet cinnamon and lavender aroma that used to greet me when I entered my grandparents' home as a child. And for a moment, I almost thought I detected a whiff. That life seemed so far away, as if it had been lived by another person entirely.

I scanned the familiar space in front of me. The foyer opened into the living room. To my left was the office and stairs that led to the second floor. To the right of the living room, the hall disappeared into the kitchen and dining area. Everything was just as I'd left it. I took a deep breath and stood, Herman's voice echoing in my head, *"You are in control of your own gifts."*

The visions were one thing. I'd grown used to them, almost took comfort in them, like a visit from an old friend. But psychometry was a different monster. It took incredible focus to block the vibrations from seeping through my fingertips. I slid my hand along the hardwood floor. Bracing myself against the pulse of energy. I might have to start wearing gloves again.

WHEN THE DOORBELL rang at exactly 8:00, it was hard to remember that the man on the other side played a bigger role in my history than in my present. I may not be ready to admit it, but I was open to the possibilities. More than that—I wanted a relationship with him. But it would take time to silence the voice in my head that kept reminding me of Ridge's betrayal. A pang of regret stabbed my chest. Chances were he'd always meant more to me than I did to him.

I added that thought to the list of the many conversations I knew we'd need to have in order to move forward. I'd learned during my time with Michael that trust is the most important aspect of a partnership. And right now, no matter how much I wanted to start over, complete trust in Ridge was out of reach.

"I brought you a few things." He picked up grocery sacks from the porch as I swung open the door. "Just milk, bread, Froot Loops...the basics."

Damn it. Just when I'd talked myself into believing he was an enemy, he had to go and do something like this. Something so sweet and thoughtful that I couldn't ignore the tickle in the pit of my stomach.

I thanked him and followed him into the kitchen as he started unloading the packages. Lit only by the interior light of the refrigerator, he slid the gallon of milk into the empty fridge. Turning to face me, a smile crinkled the skin at the corners of his eyes.

"Ready to head out?"

Stubble from the day roughened his cheeks and chin. I forced my hand into a fist at my side to keep from stroking his jaw line. And those lips. I chomped on the inside of my cheek, a reminder to keep myself in check.

Thankfully, the ride into Cascade Hills was less wrought with tension than the ride from the airport. Ridge kept initiating conversation, nothing more than small talk, but enough to keep the mood light. I wondered if he'd spent that last couple hours coming up with a list of safe topics for discussion. I pictured him trudging through the supermarket for milk and bread, all while compiling a mental list. I bit back a smile. Probably.

Ridge found a space in Murphy's already packed lot. As the site of our first date, Murphy's Pub held a special meaning for us, but more than that, it was Brian Murphy's pride and joy.

Brian and Ridge had been friends since high school, as far as I could tell. And that friendship had rubbed off on me. Without Brian, I wouldn't have survived the confrontation with

Lyle. I was eternally grateful to both him and Ridge's partner, Adam, for the part they'd played that afternoon.

I'd never worn a wire before that day, and near death experience or not, I'd gotten the information from Lyle I'd been looking for. Proof that I hadn't betrayed Ridge, and more importantly, that Lyle had been targeting my family for decades.

There was a playful glint in Ridge's eyes as he opened the passenger door for me. One I couldn't help but return. I smiled as he drew me into him.

"There it is," he whispered, his breath teasing the top of my ear. "I've been waiting for that smile." He pressed his lips onto mine before I could object. A quick kiss, leaving me wanting more. He clasped my hand in his and directed me toward the entrance of the pub.

A tingle of energy slid through my fingers before I could shield myself. My first instinct was to pull away, but the heat of his hand in mine was too tempting. The idea that I could use my abilities not only to help a missing girl, but to gauge Ridge's true intentions intrigued me more than I cared to admit.

A wave of heat, propelled by the unexpected force of Ridge's energy, crashed over me. Greater than the gentle pulses I'd felt the night of the fire, and more focused, it spiked against my skin, sending a chill down my spine.

There was no maliciousness, no malintent. Regret was the first clear emotion, followed by a veiled pulse of want. And something else, a void, hidden behind a wall I couldn't penetrate.

Ridge stopped short of Murphy's heavy wooden door, giving my hand a squeeze.

"Just enjoy your night, Liv," he whispered as he pushed open the mammoth slab of wood.

A cacophony of music and voices filled my ears as we

entered the pub. The immaculate mahogany bar reminded me of Cohen's. Everything about Murphy's was authentic, from the dark wood of the cozy partitions, down to the way Brian drew his pints, never shorting the Guinness its recommended two-minute draw.

A band was set up in the corner by the bar, playing classic rock covers as familiar faces milled about. As soon as we entered the room, each face turned in my direction, glasses raised, as an ill-timed, "Welcome home, Liv!" filled the air.

A surge of appreciation washed over me, mingling with memories of the last half a year. I pushed back the threat of tears. Uncertainty siphoned away some of the joy of my homecoming.

Balloons and streamers marked every inch of the pub, and a large green banner with shamrocks on either end announced the sentiment I'd just heard erupt around me. I had to admit, Beth Sullivan was incredible. How she'd pulled this all together in the span of twenty-four hours since I'd told her I was coming home was nothing short of amazing.

I managed to squeak out a thank you before emotion rocked my voice. Mom was the first to embrace me as the group gathered around. I fought to keep tears at bay as my mother's arms tightened around me. Her smile a reminder of the month we'd spent together as I healed from Lyle's attack. The tragedy had led to the chance to get to know the woman my father had fallen in love with, the one that existed before a veil of secrets and rejection clouded her world.

I learned more about her in that short period of time than I had in the 27 years I'd been her daughter. How could I have stayed away so long? A glint of Aimee's energy tugged at me, her voice nagging from the recesses of my brain. *"It's been here the whole time. You just pushed it away."*

"I'm so glad you're home, Olivia."

"Thank you for this, Mom. It's wonderful."

"Well, you certainly didn't give me much time," she teased.

Mom withdrew her hug and passed me off to Brian. He came forward and wrapped his arms around me, deep blue eyes locked on mine. They were full of mischief as always, but I detected a flash of sincerity there, too, as he welcomed me home. Like a big brother, he gave me a squeeze before releasing me back into Ridge's arms. The heat of them around me prompted my inner critic to jump in, reminding me that we had work to do. I stepped away from his embrace.

Everyone was there, Brian and Mom of course, but others as well. Ridge's precinct Captain, Frank Wallace, and his wife made it. Other officers with the Cascade Hills PD, including Ridge's partner, Adam Miller, were gathered around the extended table Brian had arranged for the occasion.

Another scan of the room revealed two new faces. I glanced up at Ridge as a flicker of nervousness clenched my chest.

Ridge nodded reassuringly, tilting his lips up in a playful smile before sliding his hands over my shoulders and guiding me toward the waiting strangers.

"Dad, Skylar, this is Olivia Sullivan. Liv, my dad George, and my sister, Skylar. They're in town from Virginia."

"It's so good to finally meet both of you," I said, holding my hand out to George first, bracing myself against the energy to come. "Ridge has talked a lot about you."

He ignored my hand and opened his arms wide, grasping my shoulders and folding me into a hug. I turned my head just in time to avoid face planting the man's shoulder, returning his hug the best I could with my arms pinned awkwardly to my sides.

Skylar giggled and whispered toward me, "Dad's a bit of a hugger."

When he released me, I took him in. He was a touch

shorter than Ridge, but with the same vibrant blue eyes. His thick brown hair was cut short and graying at the temples. His skin was a deep tan, undoubtedly the product of years spent on outdoor construction sites. Crow's feet buckled the delicate skin around his eyes and smile lines framed his lips like parentheses. He was heavier set than Ridge, and the buttons on his shirt strained just a bit over his midsection.

Skylar caught my attention and opened her arms. "Hope you don't mind, but I'm kind of a hugger, too."

I leaned into her embrace. It was soft and easy, quite different from George's aggressive grip. When she pulled away she took hold of my hand and smiled at me. I bit back the urge to pull away, fighting the sparks of energy that filtered through my fingers, punctuated by an eerie darkness I couldn't quite interpret.

"Thanks for putting up with my brother. I know he can be a handful at times."

I glanced at Ridge, taking the opportunity to reclaim my hand, and wondering what exactly Ridge had told his family about us. They seemed to be under the impression we were still a couple. Ridge shrugged at me, mouthing the words, "Just go with it."

"Let's save the embarrassing stories for another day, okay Sky?" He gave her shoulders a tweak before pushing her toward Brian who folded her into an embrace before heading to the table.

I should have reneged then, pulled out of whatever charade Ridge had decided to unload on the people in our lives. Something in me couldn't, though. Maybe it was the remnant of his energy I was holding onto like a security blanket. Or the need to find out what he was hiding behind the veil. Regardless, it felt good to pretend that what I once wanted was possible.

I watched Skylar and Brian as they found seats at the table. There was only one way to describe Ridge's sister–beautiful. Long russet hair complemented light blue eyes rimmed with a darker shade, making them appear larger than they were. There was a familiarity about her, though, one I couldn't quite work out.

Her complexion was perfect, dark eyebrows and hair framed her light skin, a twenty-first century version of Snow White. She was taller than me by about three inches or so and had a thin athletic build with curves in all the right places. I couldn't help being a bit envious as I compared her to my own petite frame. The McCaffrey family definitely had good genes.

The warmth of Ridge's hand found the small of my back as we rejoined the group. Brian had brought some of the wait staff in to serve for the party, which I knew took a load of responsibility off him.

By the time we were a couple hours in, the smile Ridge had been waiting to see couldn't be erased from my face. The band started in on Ed Sheeran's *Perfect* and all the couples in the room headed toward the bar and the makeshift dance floor. I'd heard the song performed live in Dublin and it had become a favorite.

Maybe it was the Guinness, or just the overwhelming sense of belonging, but when Ridge offered his hand, I accepted. Following him out to the dance floor, I draped my arms around his neck. Tucking my cheek against his chest, we swayed back and forth to the licks of the guitar. Never once did I wonder how he'd known.

I gave in as he stepped closer, his hands wrapping tighter around me. The rhythm of his heartbeat, the rise and fall of his breath, each was hypnotic. He moved his hand from my waist to push curls from the side of my face, exposing my neck to deliver a line of kisses. His lips soft against sensitive skin.

With my eyes closed in the dark of the pub, alcohol subduing my inner critic, it felt right. For the first time in a long time, I knew–I was exactly where I was supposed to be.

17

RIDGE

"Can I ask what you were thinking?" Ridge asked as he drove away from Murphy's followed by his father's grey Mercury.

"They just got in town. Would you rather they stay at your place in one tiny little bedroom?"

"That was the plan."

Liv shrugged in the darkness of the car. "I have plenty of room. It seemed like the polite thing to do. Besides, you're the one who told them we're still—"

"Just—" Ridge cut her off. Ignoring the hint of amusement in her voice. She'd had too much to drink. He was regretting his decision to be the designated driver. He sighed and gunned the engine as they headed down rural Route 3 toward Sullivan Road.

"Why'd you do that? Why'd you tell everyone that we're together?" Liv asked quietly, as if afraid to upset him. Part of him died a little with that thought. Maybe she wasn't as drunk as he thought.

Because my life isn't the same without you in it. Because I

*can't forgive myself for leaving, for choosing the job over you.
Because I'll do anything to make it up to you.* All those thoughts
screamed through his skull. The moments they'd shared on the
dance floor solidified them, but he had to stay in control. At
least until the Garrison case was behind him. *Then what?*

"It wasn't intentional, Liv. Your mom assumed that we'd
smoothed things over in Dublin. I just let her believe it. I guess
I figured you would set her straight."

"That explains the Cascade Hills crowd, but what about
your family?"

"They went straight to Murphy's. Got there before I got
back from taking you home. Your mom had already done the
damage."

"She invited them?"

"No, I did. They're here to see–" *Shit.* "Sky doesn't miss
many opportunities to visit Brian," Ridge redirected. "But
they're here to see me."

Liv went quiet. And Ridge spent the rest of the drive
wondering if she believed him.

A COOL BREEZE washed over the front porch where Ridge sat.
Liv was inside with Skylar and George, getting them situated
into rooms on the third floor. It was a clear October night. A
half-moon shone down onto the barn across the lot, casting
ghostly shadows across the cars.

Sowards' words haunted him. He'd warned against
bringing Liv home. The operation was fragile right now. No
one, not even Sowards, seemed to know what direction it was
going to take. He scrubbed his hands down his face. *What had
he done?*

The squeak of the screen door saved him from his thoughts

as Liv padded out onto the porch. He glanced over as she sat in the rocker next to his. Bare feet with green sparkly nail polish poked out from under a fluffy white robe.

He sucked in a breath.

"I think it's only fair that you know something," she said.

Ridge watched Liv as she rocked gently back and forth, pushing up off her toes with each forward pitch. He stayed quiet, waiting.

"It's about the psychometry. I don't need an object necessarily." She never looked at him, just continued the gentle sway of the rocker. She thought he didn't know.

"I didn't mean for it to happen. But when you took my hand outside of Murphy's it just came too fast. I didn't have time to block it."

She stopped rocking, focusing her attention fully on him.

"I didn't want to."

Ridge looked at her. This was a dangerous game. His life was a closed book and she was the only one with the ability to break it open. In some ways, he wished she could.

"Do I want to know?" he asked.

"Just tell me one thing. If you cared this much last spring, why'd you run?"

Ridge didn't know what to say. A trickle of disappointment filtered through him. His secrets were safe. As it stood though, he was damned if he told the truth and damned if he didn't.

"It wasn't my choice, Liv."

The glitter in Liv's toenail polish caught the moon's light as she rose from the rocker.

"It wasn't mine, either." Her words were a punch to his gut. "Maybe we should make sure we're making our own decisions from here on out."

As Ridge watched the woman next to him, moonlight

illuminating her face, he knew exactly what decision he wanted to make.

"Tonight, at Murphy's...I know us, together, was all a misunderstanding." Her voice rolled over him like a warm tide. "I know we agreed to take it slow." Her breath hitched, hardly more than a whisper. "But I forgot how good it is to feel wanted." A clench of guilt snagged in Ridge's chest. She still hadn't looked at him. "I'm not ready for that to end."

She couldn't be asking what he thought she was. After days of pushing him away? She shivered, cinching the robe tighter around her waist. Heat melted through Ridge's core.

"Tonight?" he asked.

Liv shrugged. "You've got to sleep somewhere." She smiled, a true, unfiltered smile. The first he'd seen since before Lyle's attack. He could almost feel it liquifying his heart.

"You've been drinking," Ridge said.

Liv's smile faltered. "I know what I'm asking." She lifted her gaze to meet his. "No expectations, Ridge. Just consider it. I'll be upstairs."

She left him on the porch, weighing the options. For most red-blooded men this proposition was a no-brainer. But this wasn't just some girl he'd picked up at a bar. This was Liv.

Professionally, he should walk away, get back in his Shelby and drive home. Life had changed in the months they'd been apart. And he wasn't the man she thought he was. That, in itself, should have been enough to stop him. But, sitting there in the moonlight, he knew he'd never be able to let her go. Not tonight. Not when this operation was over. Not ever.

18

LIV

I'd spent the last minutes obsessing over how I'd face Ridge if he chose not to follow me upstairs. I decided that if he didn't, I'd put it all behind me. Move forward with my life. Figure out the connection between Jessica and Saoirse and then I'd be done. We'd part ways. Maybe I'd open that photography studio I'd always wanted.

I'd almost resigned myself to those options when two soft knocks gave way to Ridge's form silhouetted in the bedroom doorway.

"I'm glad you came," I said as he made his way toward the bed.

I breathed into his neck as he pulled me up from the side of the mattress, savoring the spicy hint of his aftershave. As much as I'd enjoyed the party and getting to see everyone I'd missed over the last several months, the moments I'd spent in Ridge's arms had left me wanting more. More contentment, more desire, and as a bonus, more time to penetrate the wall that blocked me before.

I stood on my tiptoes in front of him. My body pressed against his as I slid his jacket off over his shoulders. My fingers tugged at his t-shirt, probing for bare flesh.

The hardness of him, coupled with the energy I'd felt in Murphy's parking lot, sparked a current of electricity through my core, blinding me to the inevitable consequences of my actions.

Ridge's eyes shone their clear cerulean blue as he looked down at me, peeling his t-shirt off his torso and over his head. The sight of him sucked the air out of my lungs. My eyes devoured the muscular cuts my hand had been exploring.

"Are you sure this is what you want?" The vibration of his voice curled through me. His eyes searching mine.

I nodded, forcing a vocal affirmation through impatient lips.

He stepped away and slowly untied my robe, sliding it over my bare shoulders until it fell in a puddle around my feet.

His lips parted as his eyes gravitated downward over my bare chest. He clasped his fingers through mine, holding them on either side of my head as he pushed his body against mine.

My hands tingled with his desire as it meshed with my own. I tilted my head and closed my eyes, absorbing his energy, allowing the heat of him to flow through me. The air around us hummed as he bent to trail kisses down my neck.

"I missed you, Liv."

His words melted into me. The soft hunger of his kiss liquified rocks of remaining uncertainty. I fought to find the veil I'd felt earlier, but desire dulled my focus, keeping that energy hidden in the shadows. Our kiss deepened and my pulse pounded in my ears.

His energy siphoned away as he unclasped his hands from mine, returning in short sparks whenever he skimmed his fingers lightly along bare flesh. He reached to turn down the bedclothes behind me. The cool air of the bedroom lifted gooseflesh as he jerked the sheets down to the foot of the bed in one lithe movement.

Ridge's searing eyes grazed over me before a low growl echoed from deep in his chest, igniting another spike of desire as he laid me down on the mattress.

My body quivered as his hands roamed over sun-starved flesh. He slowed, his eyes lingering on my abdomen. The warm energy of desire shifted. Anger pelted my skin like shards of glass, growing sharper the longer he hesitated. A tremor of irrational embarrassment washed over me, driving my arms to hover protectively around my midsection.

I fought for control. Forcing rational thought to riot alongside the raw emotion sliding off Ridge. This was the first time he'd seen the scar. And for some reason allowing him to inspect it terrified me. I lay motionless in front of him, breathing through the senseless panic brewing inside.

His eyes blazed into mine as he pried my arms away from my belly, fully exposing the jagged red line that ran from my ribs toward my navel. He bent to kiss the center of the mark before meeting my gaze.

"Does it hurt?" he whispered.

"Not anymore," I answered. *But your anger does*, I wanted to say.

His eyes seared across my skin, following the scar. The muscle in his jaw contracted as if in rhythm with a silent band.

I tilted his chin upward so that he was looking at my face, the reminder of Lyle's attack tucked away in the shadows. I studied his expression and sat up. Desperate for relief from the shrapnel of his emotion, I reached for the button on his jeans. The fire of anger in his eyes slowly receded, replaced by a growing glimmer of want.

I worked the denim down over his thighs. Relief flooded me when he kicked out of the jeans, ending the pinpricks against my flesh. He hovered over me, and I traced the defined muscles in his shoulders with my fingertips as he lowered himself over me, his lips covering mine. His touch stoked embers of desire left cold for too many long months.

A moan escaped my lips as our bodies melded together. The beginnings of what I now realized I'd been so desperately missing stirred inside my chest. Connection. An undeniable link with someone in this world who needed me as much as I needed them.

A GLANCE toward the window told me it was still the middle of the night. The expanse of mattress next to me lay empty and cold. A pleasant ache and unjustifiable feeling of peace were the only lingering reminders of Ridge's bedroom visit. I listened carefully for the sound of the downstairs television, but there was only silence.

Faintly, a thump, like a car door closing, resonated in my ears. I lifted myself from the bed and tiptoed to the window, looking out onto the barn lot. A trickle of uncertainty shimmied down my spine as faint lights reflected off one of the outbuildings. The glow hadn't come from the direction of the driveway, but from the woods near the lake. They disappeared as soon as they'd come, my overactive mind playing tricks on me.

The floorboards above my head remained quiet as I stole down the hallway. It wasn't until I approached the landing that I heard voices, hushed whispers that became clearer as I descended the stairs and crept across the living room toward the kitchen. I recognized Ridge's rich baritone immediately.

The second voice had a matching timbre. The only major distinction between the two was a hint of gravel and age. George. I stopped short in the hallway when I heard the discussion.

"When are you going to tell her?"

"I don't know. Not until I have to, Dad."

George sighed, "Ridge, I realized a long time ago that trying to tell you what to do was like pissing into the wind, but this is different, son. She needs to know, especially now."

The screech of one of the kitchen chairs scooting away from the table grated against my eardrums. I briefly considered racing back upstairs rather than get caught in the hallway, but the sound of the refrigerator door opening calmed my nerves.

"No, thanks," George said before the fridge door closed and the slosh of liquid being poured into one glass confirmed that he'd declined a beverage. Chair legs on wooden planks sounded again as Ridge returned to the table.

"She just got home. How am I supposed to tell her something like this?" A sigh. "I'm trying to rekindle this relationship, Dad, not destroy it."

"The longer you wait the harder it's going to be. I'm not telling you it's going to be easy, but she's stronger than you're giving her credit for, Ridge."

There was a lengthy pause. Ridge spoke with resignation in his voice. "Look, I don't want to give her a reason to leave again. If she thinks I've been..." Ridge paused, not finishing the sentence. "After everything that happened last spring, I can't risk the outcome. Not yet."

"Are you listening to yourself?" George's voice was getting louder, more impatient. "You *have* made some questionable decisions, Ridge. You think she'd hit the door if she knew about this one? Is that what you're afraid of?"

"It's more complicated than that, Dad." Frustration grew in

Ridge's voice. He paused, allowing it to evaporate. "What if she does leave?" His voice was quiet, reflective. "I don't want to talk about this anymore."

"Okay, fine. But let's be clear about one thing. If you don't tell her, and she finds out some other way, which we both know she will in a town this size, any hope you have of smoothing things over would go out the window. Tell her now, Son. Before it's too late." There was a loud screech of a chair being pushed away from the table.

Ridge was silent. I stood draped in the hall shadows with nowhere to go as George strode out of the kitchen. My heart leapt into my throat as we locked eyes.

His gaze softened and he reached out and patted me on the shoulder, nodding in the direction of the kitchen and mouthing, "Go talk to him," before striding out of the hallway and toward the stairs. I waited until I heard his footsteps on the wooden risers before creeping into the kitchen.

Ridge sat at the table, his back to me and his head bowed toward the walnut top as he rubbed his temple with his left hand. The only light illuminating the kitchen was the 40-watt bulb above the stove.

"Want some company?"

Ridge turned to face me. He didn't seem at all surprised. His eyes were dark and distant, but he motioned me toward him anyway. When I was within arm's reach he took my hands and pulled me into him. This time I made sure I was ready. I blocked what I could, but tendrils of negative energy, the hardest to keep out, filtered like smoke through my veins, heating my skin. I was relieved when he dropped my hands and gripped my waist instead.

"How much did you hear?"

Memories of the night I met Ridge flashed through my

brain. I'd been hiding in the shadows in the same hallway that night. My choices then had been to step out of the darkness and reveal myself or continue to hide. I'd made the right decision that cold March night. Now it was Ridge's turn.

"Enough to know that you're keeping something from me."

"But you already knew that." He brought his left hand up and watched his fingers as they twirled through my hair.

"Whatever it is, Ridge, I can take it."

Ridge sighed heavily, moving his hand back to my waist and pulling me close. "I should have said something before last night."

I swallowed the knot of emotion that surged into my throat. Forcing the, "But you can tell me now."

"This is going to sound crazy."

I released a worried breath and smiled down at him. "Come on, Ridge, I see dead people in my dreams and read energy through objects. You're talking to the queen of crazy, remember?"

The corner of his lips turned up just a bit as a single chuckle rose with his words. "God, I love you."

My lungs seized mid-breath. I hadn't expected that.

"Is that the crazy part?" I whispered.

His hands tightened on my waist, fingers splayed on the small of my back as his thumbs slid in arcs down to my hipbone and then up again, as if he was trying to massage away my expected reaction. His head bent to watch the motion. "I don't know where to start."

"The beginning is good."

Ridge looked into my eyes. I didn't try to hide the fear that I knew was there. Telltale evidence of the battle between the me that wanted him to feel even a portion of the fear that I'd experienced alone in Lyle's office last spring, and the me that wanted to start over, forget all the hurt and betrayal that swirled between us.

I shrugged like whatever he was going to say was no big deal. But with each silent second that ticked by, the instinctive clench in my chest proved otherwise.

"Ridge? You're scaring me. What is it?"

19

LIV

"I sold my house," Ridge said.

"Okay. That's not at all what I expected you to say."

Relief lapped at me. This was the news he was afraid to tell me? I threaded my fingers through his sleep-mussed hair. There was more.

"That is kind of a crazy thing to keep secret. Where are you living?"

He studied me.

"I want you to know I didn't expect this to happen. It just seemed like the best option under the circumstances. I didn't even have it listed. I guess you could say I got an offer I couldn't refuse."

He was babbling, trying to ease whatever tension he predicted I'd have. I couldn't help but giggle, partly at his insecurity, but mostly to mask my own. I wasn't used to seeing him like this.

"You know, I had a teacher once who sold her house that way. Someone just walked up to her doorstep and made her an offer. Of course, she lived in a historic Victorian, not a fifties era

Cape Cod." *Nice, Liv. Now you're making fun of his house.* I cringed at my own comment. Now I was the one babbling.

Ridge took a deep breath. The Adam's apple in his neck bobbed as he swallowed hard. He straightened, muscles tightening as he looked away. Something was up. I didn't need to be psychic to realize it. Although, in that instant, I wanted more than anything just to take his hands, force truth in the only way I knew how.

"It was someone who knew the house. Had lived there before," he finally said.

"Oh, well, that's good. They didn't mind the girly décor?"

I smiled at my attempt at humor. Walking into Ridge's house for the first time had been like walking into a rose garden. Loud flowers and hues of pink had assaulted me from every angle. The memory was wiped away by Ridge's silence. He removed his hands from my waist and slid one through his hair, avoiding eye contact.

"She didn't mind it. She decorated it, so..." He let the statement drift off, waiting for me to make the connection.

My heart stopped in that moment. A knot cementing itself in the center of my chest. Insecurity crept over me, sending prickles like pins and needles across my skin. Ridge continued to avoid my stare.

"Bridget? Bridget bought your house? Your ex-wife? In Cascade Hills? When?"

I couldn't form complete sentences, only bursts of incoherent thought. Ridge finally brought his eyes up to meet mine, the angle of his jaw pronounced in the waning moonlight that streamed into the kitchen. He didn't say anything, just gave me time to process.

I turned away and walked toward the window, staring out over Cascade Lake as I worked to tamp down the threatening tears that had started a slow march upward from inside my chest. Here it was, one of the consequences of allowing myself to give in to my desire. How could I have been so stupid? Last night was supposed to have given me the upper hand. Instead, all it did was turn me into a needy, weepy basketcase.

"You're still living there." The realization punched me in the gut.

Ridge hung his head. That was confirmation enough. He might not care to admit it, but it was clear to everyone that knew him that Bridget was the one who got away. She'd done horrible things to him over the course of their short marriage, not the least of which included cheating and the drug induced miscarriage of their baby. But in spite of all that, Ridge had loved her. Maybe he still did.

Brian had been the first to tell me that Bridget had a knack for showing up just when Ridge was finally getting on with his life. She'd toy with his emotions just long enough to mess him up again. How long had she been toying with him this time? I turned back to face Ridge.

"When?"

I noted his anxious swallow again, his eyes returning to his lap.

"Ridge?" I prompted, not bothering to hide the irritation in my voice.

"Not long after I came back to Cascade Hills. A couple weeks or so."

I did the math in my head. He'd come back two weeks after I left. That much he'd admitted. "You've been living with your ex-wife for the last five months?"

Putting the words out there felt like ramming my head against a brick wall. I didn't understand why, or even how, but everything I'd read in Ridge the night before, I'd misinterpreted. Bridget had been in Cascade Hills, living in the same house as Ridge, almost the entire time I'd been gone. That was a long time to screw with someone's head. I sucked in a breath.

"Then, what is this?" I motioned between us. "For old time's sake?" I knew better than to hope his head was all she'd screwed with.

"Jesus, Liv. It's not like that." He tried to backpedal. "Come on, you know it's not. You said it yourself. You felt it." He gripped my waist again, pulling me closer.

"Why didn't you tell me?"

Ridge squared his shoulders and fixed his eyes on a point beyond me.

"Would you have come back to Cascade Hills if you had known?"

He had a point there. Not in a million years, no matter how many missing girls were vying for my attention.

"Why not just move her into your house? You two could cozy up together without all the legal paperwork. Why sell?"

"Because it wasn't about her, Liv." The fire of indignation began to blaze in his eyes.

"Right," I scoffed.

"I stayed so I could be there for my son."

I don't know how to explain the hurt that crashed over me in that moment. It was as if Lyle's knife had twisted through the scar in my side. I stared at Ridge, dumbfounded.

"That's why Dad and Skylar are here. I'd been putting Dad off about coming to meet Colton. Skylar already knew. She was here on internship all summer, but bringing Dad into it made it real. You know? I told them they could come up when I got back from Ireland."

"I don't understand," I finally choked out between alternating waves of hurt and confusion. "She's pregnant?" Numbness overpowered me, my thoughts jumbled and non-cohesive. "Is this why you left last spring?"

Ridge shook his head. "No. She's not. I didn't know then. Please, Liv." He reached for me as I backed away. "His name is Colton. He's three-years-old."

Three. The number echoed in my skull. *Three.* That meant he was born well before Ridge and I were together. *Three.* Ridge hadn't cheated on me. *Three.* Jesus, Ridge was a *dad.*

My heart rate slowed a touch, the pounding of blood no longer muting sound. Ridge pulled a chair up behind me and guided me into a seated position.

"I didn't know anything about him until I came back to Cascade Hills and Bridget showed up."

"Bridget." I repeated stupidly.

I drew in a breath and leaned back against the spindles in the walnut chair. The design pressed a blessed distraction against my spine as I processed the information.

It was one thing for Bridget to be back in Cascade Hills but quite another for her to be the mother of Ridge's child. She would never be out of his life. For at least the next fifteen years, Bridget would remain a constant temptation. One more reason to forget last night ever happened. I blew a shaky breath through tight lips.

"Liv?" I focused my attention back on Ridge. "Please say something. Tell me what you're thinking."

Honesty, I told myself. If he wanted to know what I was thinking, I should tell him. A thousand questions flooded my brain. I took another focusing breath.

"Are you sure he's yours?"

As soon as the question hit the air I wished I could take it back. It sounded heartless, cold. But Ridge didn't flinch. He nodded.

"We had a test. He's definitely mine."

My thoughts drifted back to the conversation I'd overheard as I lurked in the hallway.

"You didn't want to tell me." That hurt almost as much as the fact he'd chosen to live with her.

"I didn't know what to say," Ridge admitted.

"A person can't have a relationship with someone who has a child and not know about it." Anger began a slow march from somewhere deep inside. "You're *living* with her." The unspoken accusation hung heavy. Words bit at the air between us.

Ridge pulled back and sucked in a breath. "I didn't know how much longer I'd be here. We might have shared a house, Liv, but I never slept with her." He paused, his voice dropping. "I didn't know what else to do."

Frustration spiked through the air. And watching him struggle against it cut into me. Somehow I knew what he was saying was true. But the hurt churning through my gut wouldn't let me let it go.

"So, last night was–what? For old time's sake?"

I shook my head. Having a son wasn't an unforgivable sin. Besides, I had initiated last night's mistake. He may have started the ruse, but I was the one who took it to the next level. There was no one to blame but myself.

I gave into the temptation to apologize. "Don't answer that. Last night was my fault. I should never have pushed it that far."

"No, Liv." Ridge's voice was sharp, slicing through my sentence like a knife. His eyes blazed as he stared me down. "Don't do that. Don't say you're sorry. This is not you. This is *me*. Do you understand that? *I* made the decision to stay in that house. *I* fucked up."

Ridge stood, the chair falling with a clatter against the floor. He brushed past me, his turn to stare out the kitchen window.

"I always saw myself as a dad someday. Back when Bridget and I were married, when she got pregnant, that was a good time. I was young, but I was ready, you know?"

I watched silently as Ridge righted the chair before turning toward me.

"But now–" His eyes bored into mine. "I know we have a lot we need to work through, Liv, but what you felt last night, the way I feel about you, that's not fake." Ridge's voice softened. "Bridget and Colton showing up provided the distraction I needed to try to get over what I did to you. But, the fact is, being a father is something I thought I'd be sharing with you, not her."

"Whatever happened with Bridget four years ago may have changed some dynamics, but it's not what changed things between us. You have to know that. As far as getting over what you did to me...where were you, Ridge? Where were you when I confronted Lyle? And after?"

"Liv, it's not that simple."

"It is. It really is that simple, Ridge. You have an obvious sense of responsibility, or you wouldn't be staying with Bridget right now. You'd find another place. You can be a father to your son without living with your ex-wife. People do it every day. But she needed you, so you did the right thing. You stayed. Where were you when *I* needed you?"

I felt the tear start down my cheek. I wiped it away angrily, before Ridge could do it for me.

His eyes darkened, a crease appearing between his brows. He opened his mouth twice as if to speak, but nothing came out.

Finally, words came. "I can't tell you."

I turned toward the door that went out onto the sun porch. Every fiber of my being ached with the pain of loss.

"Wait." He grabbed my arm before I could escape the situation, pulling me to face him. "But I can tell you this, I will never forgive myself for not being there that night. And the three nights after as you laid in that hospital bed, or the month you stayed here with your mom before leaving for Ireland." He paused, reading my expression. "I will forever regret the mistakes I made."

We stared at each other. I'd never seen him like that. Jaw clenched, close to tears. Desperation permeated him, revealing a side of Ridge that was new to me.

"Please, Liv. Please give me a chance to prove how much I care about you."

I averted my eyes from the intensity of his gaze.

"I want to hate you," I admitted. "But I can't imagine my future without you." Even as I spoke the words they sounded as if they were coming from someone else. A wave of panic crashed over me, as if I'd been stripped bare, vulnerability the only blanket I had left. *Stupid.*

A gentle hand lifted my chin. Strong arms wrapped me in warmth, cradling me against a muscular chest. I closed my eyes and listened to the steady heartbeat beneath my cheek. My breath caught as he leaned down and kissed the top of my head. There was no question who the weaker party was now.

"Give me a chance to make it up to you."

Skylar bounded into the kitchen before I could answer. "Morning booger," she shot at Ridge. "Oh, geez, sorry."

"Morning, brat," Ridge returned after pulling away, never taking his eyes off mine.

"I didn't mean to interrupt."

"It's okay, Skylar. You didn't," I said, sliding out of Ridge's embrace and forcing a smile in her direction. Walking around to the other side of the breakfast bar, I busied myself with the coffeemaker, trying desperately to force down the hurt and anxiety bubbling just beneath the surface.

"Liv, I just wanted to say thanks for letting us stay—"

She stopped abruptly as she came around the bar into the kitchen. I noticed her glance at Ridge before turning her attention back to me. I'd never been very good at hiding my emotions.

In hindsight, that was probably what had tipped Lyle off that afternoon in his office. It's a good thing I never aspired to be an actress. Her voice was softer when she continued.

"Are you okay?"

"I'm good. Fine." My voice was forced, too loud for the situation. "I just need a minute, I'm sorry, Skylar." I let my fingers graze her arm before I retreated out onto the back porch. Concern vibrated through my fingertips. I escaped just as Skylar began laying into Ridge in the kitchen.

"Did she just now find out?"

"Take it down a notch, Skylar, it's complicated."

"No, Ridge, it's really not. You have a *son* for Christ's sake." My jaw clenched as she said the word, son. "You've known for months and you never bothered to tell the woman you claim to love?"

"Watch it, Sky. I do love her." I could tell by Ridge's voice that he was short on patience.

"Funny way of showing it."

I heard Skylar stalk back down the hallway away from the kitchen. I inhaled a deep breath of the cool morning air. The sun had just begun its ascent over the lake.

I was stronger than this. Ridge and I had been through a lot in the short time we'd known each other, and we could get through this. Who knows? Maybe I could even learn to like Bridget. Although the mere thought of that sent a spiral of skepticism down my spine.

I finished pulling myself together and turned to head back into the kitchen. Ridge was leaning against the doorframe, watching. He offered me one of the cups of coffee he was carrying, and waited.

"Can I ask another question?" I said as I reached for the cup of steaming black liquid.

"Anything."

"Does Bridget know about me?"

"Yes."

A weight lifted off my chest. I ventured one more question.

"Do you think she'd mind if I met Colton?"

20

RIDGE

"You're late." Captain Wallace was waiting in the station as soon as Ridge walked through the door.

"Sorry, Captain. Bit of a tricky morning." Ridge said, putting a tumbler of coffee on his desk and shrugging out of his jacket. He pocketed the vibrating cell with Sowards' number illuminated across the screen.

"I bet it was," Adam teased from the chair opposite Ridge's desk. A sly smile parted his lips as he raised his eyebrows to his partner.

"Shut up, Miller."

Adam raised his hands in defeat.

"When you two are done revisiting middle school, the medical examiner wants to see you in her office. The tox results are back on our Jane Doe."

"Still waiting on positive ID?" Ridge asked.

Captain Wallace nodded.

"What's taking so long?"

"You know, I had a detective once that would've been able

to answer that question by now. Why don't you ask the doc when you get down there?"

Ridge took the jab and offered a little salute to Captain Wallace before grabbing his jacket and following Adam out the door of the precinct.

"Did you tell her?" Adam asked as soon as they'd climbed into his pickup truck.

"About Colton, yeah." Ridge focused on the buildings outside the passenger side window.

"How'd she take it?"

"About as well as you might expect. She wanted to know where I was the night of the attack."

Adam's face fell. "You didn't tell her."

"Of course not." Ridge fixed his gaze out the passenger window.

"Ridge, come on. I know how difficult this must be for you. And I'm not gonna be the one to say, 'I told you so,' but the fact is, getting involved with Liv was a mistake from the beginning. You know as well as I do that you can't risk telling her. It's too dangerous for everyone involved. Including Liv."

"Yeah, thanks for that helpful piece of advice, brother." Ridge let the sarcastic comment hang in the air between them. He could feel Adam watching, gauging his reaction. Judging him.

"Telling her why you weren't there would jeopardize everything we've worked for. The job comes first. You should know that better than anyone."

Ridge ran a hand through his hair and allowed the silence of the truck to replace conversation. He'd wanted Liv to come home, but now that she was here, life was growing increasingly complicated. It wasn't just because of Colton and Bridget. Liv wanted the one thing he was incapable of giving. Honesty.

"Oh, I almost forgot. You're gonna love this. Lyle Hunt's plea deal was finalized yesterday."

"And," Ridge prompted after waiting for Adam to continue.

"Five years."

He couldn't have heard that right. He'd seen the scar, read the medical reports. Liv was lucky to be alive.

"He'll be out in three," Ridge speculated. Fury heated nerves already frayed by the morning's events.

Adam shrugged before going into the details. "He pleaded guilty to aggravated assault. They granted him the minimum sentence because of his full cooperation." Adam used air quotes around those words. "He gave up some intel. Nothing earth-shattering from what I hear. I hate to say this, but I think the biggest factor was that Liv didn't hang around to assert her own rights. You can't claim a victim has been irreparably harmed when they're off gallivanting around another country."

"She wasn't–" He breathed through the anger. Was there any way he hadn't failed Liv? He was beginning to doubt it.

"I know," Adam soothed. "I'm just saying that I think that had a lot to do with the short sentence."

"Jesus, this day just keeps getting better and better."

"It only just began, brother." Adam chuckled as they pulled into a spot in front of Foster's Mortuary.

FOSTER'S WOOD paneled office hadn't been renovated since her father was the town's M.E. over fifteen years ago. Every time Ridge opened the door, the stench of stale cigars intermingling with formaldehyde and rubbing alcohol assaulted his senses.

Megan had installed plug-ins, but it was going to take more than electrified tiles of scented paper to overcome the decades of death that permeated the room.

Ridge couldn't help wondering what it must have been like to grow up the daughter of a medical examiner. Especially one whose office was attached to their own home by a skinny enclosed breezeway. He imagined her sweet sixteen party took place elsewhere.

He was studying an old photograph of Megan with her dad when the leggy brunette came through the door.

"Good morning, gentlemen."

She smiled at Ridge, flashing him the perfect white smile he'd come to expect when he visited. She smoothed her long hair away from her face and tucked it over one shoulder, exposing the curve of her neck above the lab coat she wore. He was used to playing this game with her. He'd been doing it since she took office three years ago. Today, though, the game didn't hold his interest as much as it had in the past.

He returned a quick smile before cutting to the chase. "Any news on the ID of our Jane Doe?"

"Sorry to disappoint you boys, but no. I think we're getting close though." She tossed them both a mask and a pair of gloves before inviting them back the hall to see the body.

Megan pulled back the sheet that covered the woman's face, what was left of it anyway. Adam cringed and took a step back. This part of the job had never been his forte. Surveillance? He was a pro. Dead bodies? Not so much.

To Ridge it looked like she'd been peeled. There was no flesh left on her face or hands. A layer of gelatinous membrane spread over bloody tissue and bone.

"These are chemical burns," Megan explained. "Basically, they put something on her to obliterate her face and her hands. As you know, that makes it difficult to get a positive ID."

No face. No fingerprints.

"What about dental records?" Ridge asked.

"We're working on it. Her teeth were rasped–ground down

to the point we can't get a positive ID. Someone didn't want us to know who she is. But I do have one thing I think you'll be interested in."

She pulled a manila folder from the counter and unsheathed the papers inside, handing them to Ridge.

"What am I looking at?" Ridge asked as he scanned through the lines of numbers, the results of extensive lab tests. He could feel Adam looking over his arm, eager to be able to focus on something other than a mutilated corpse.

"Most of her labs came back within normal range. Except for these." She pointed out a column on the second page. "I'm assigning cause of death as a drug overdose."

"Heroin?" Adam guessed. It had become an increasing source of concern for the Cascade Hills PD.

Megan shook her head. "No way. There are three different drugs, but I don't think they were administered separately. There's something in the way they interacted with each other. This is something new, a cocktail of some kind."

Adam continued to probe. "What exactly are we talking about here?"

"There's evidence of a neuromuscular-blocker. Like Pancuronium, maybe. It would have paralyzed her, at least temporarily. Then there's a central nervous system stimulant, something similar to meth, or cocaine, maybe. I can't imagine anyone using the two of those together. It doesn't make sense."

Megan paused, taking a good look at Jane Doe.

"And the third?" Ridge prompted, pulling the medical examiner back to the conversation.

"It's a neurologic. Unknown origin. I've sent a sample to the federal lab to see if they've seen anything like it before. This wasn't some run of the mill OD. Somebody did this to her."

"Are you telling us we've got someone out there killing girls with a new street drug?" Adam asked, his attention piqued.

"This is no street drug, Detective Miller. It's a neurologic. It did a number on her brain, increased her levels of glutamate. Lit her neural receptors up to the point of serious damage. Someone out there knows what they're doing. There's chemistry involved, way more than is required with heroin or even meth. Whatever this is. It's potent. There's a chance that whoever administered the drug didn't intend to kill her."

Ridge absorbed what Megan was saying. He'd been sitting in this sleepy town for almost six years, working leads handed down to him and getting nowhere. If the M.E. was right, and this drug was a neurologic, and if the girl on Megan's table was Jessica Garrison, then this could be the break he'd been looking for. The break that would make it possible to end the lies. Start over.

"Is there anything else?" He handed the folder back to Megan. "Any other identifying marks or anything on the body?"

"Just this."

Megan pulled the sheet back to expose the girl's right hip. A small divot, oblong and less than a centimeter deep, gouged a hole in the flesh just to the left of her hipbone.

"Ideas?" Megan asked.

Ridge and Adam exchanged an uncomfortable glance.

"I chalked it up to an unrelated injury. Maybe catching her hip on something when she was dumped. It's post mortem."

Ridge nodded. It was exactly what he didn't want to see. There was no need to wait for dental records. She'd had a microchip, in the exact location as the other assets. There was no doubt in his mind now. This was Jessica Garrison.

21

LIV

The quiet of the farmhouse settled in after Ridge left for work. After breakfast, George took the boat out on the lake to go fishing. I watched from the kitchen window as he motored out into the middle of Cascade Lake and readied to cast his line. I liked George. He was honest and straightforward. Qualities I hoped I'd be able to find in Ridge someday. Getting to know Ridge's dad gave me hope.

Skylar conned Ridge into dropping her off at Murphy's on his way to the station so she could spend the day with Brian. They made an adorable couple. Brian with that boy-next-door grin, Skylar with her Snow White complexion and blue eyes. Both with selfless personalities to match their exteriors. They were perfect for each other.

I scrubbed the bottom of the sink as the last of the dish water disappeared down the drain. The conversation of the morning rung in my ears. It was hard to believe Ridge was a dad. It wasn't that I didn't believe he'd be a good one. The opposite, really. Colton was a lucky little boy. He had two parents who loved him. Which was more than I could say for

Saoirse. Darker thoughts filtered in alongside sunnier ones. Memories of the children's home danced in my mind.

Now that the initial shock of Ridge's news had worn off, it was time to tackle number one on my to-do list. And her name was Jessica Garrison. Who was she? How did she know Saoirse? And why did she have photographs of me?

JESSICA'S APARTMENT was on the other side of town in an upscale development that had gone up on the outskirts of Cascade Hills within the last five years. The town barely resembled the one I'd grown up in. The four-stoplight town of my childhood had expanded around the edges, spreading through fields farmers no longer deemed lucrative. One day it would merge with the surrounding villages, I was sure.

I'd done a Google search to find Jessica's address, but it hadn't given me her unit number, only the general mailing address for the apartment complex office. But as I pulled in the drive, winding toward triplex townhomes arranged around a central courtyard, it wasn't hard to tell which rental was hers.

Fluorescent yellow police tape flapped in the breeze from the front porch railing of an end unit. I parked a few rows away from the curb, hoping not to draw attention to myself, and sucked in a breath before popping open my car door. I'd picked a good time to come. It was the middle of a weekday, and the parking lot was nearly empty. Most of the residents away at work, I assumed, their homes empty and waiting until the five o'clock hour brought them back to life.

Standing in that parking lot with the cool October breeze washing over my face, the weight of the situation crashed down on me. Ashlyn was right. This wasn't what I was used to. The faces that troubled me in my dreams were those of girls long dead, looking for some sense of closure before they could move on to whatever was beyond this life. But now, here I was, hoping to help find a girl who'd been missing for days. One I hadn't seen in a vision. One who, with any luck, would still be alive. For the first time, there was hope.

"Liv? What are you doing here?"

My head snapped toward the familiar voice.

"Adam." I gave in to the ripple of a nervous giggle. "You startled me."

Ridge's partner apologized with a cock-eyed grin before joining me in inspecting the apartment from afar.

"I take it Ridge told you about the Garrison case." He slung an arm over my shoulder and gave it a squeeze. "But you really shouldn't be here."

I ignored Adam's last comment. "Where is Ridge?"

"Back at the station. I've got an appointment this afternoon and he wanted to catch up on some paperwork."

I could feel Adam watching me as I kept my gaze fixed on Jessica's apartment. "They still don't know what happened to her?" I asked. Anything to distract him from the oppressive stare that burned into the side of my head.

"Nah. Nothing yet."

I released a pent-up breath as he looked away, starting the walk toward the townhome.

"Listen, I've got to go inside for one last look before they unseal the place. BCI's crime scene unit has already combed it. Didn't find much. But I guess Ridge probably already told you that."

"No," I admitted. "Since I got back he hasn't talked about it."

"It'll just take me a minute," Adam said as he ducked under the waving police tape. "Wait out here, will you?"

I nodded as Adam disappeared into the apartment,

obediently staying behind the fluorescent barrier. I craned my neck to see through the open door. The cream-colored walls of a hallway and a flight of stairs were all I could make out.

I could hear Adam shuffling through the rooms, opening and closing drawers and cupboards. A few minutes later he was back, securing the door behind him.

"We should probably go. I've got to get to my appointment."

I nodded and followed Adam from the front stoop. Static in the air between us sparked at me as we walked.

"Were you looking for something in particular?" I asked, already sensing the answer.

He shook his head. "Anything, really. Just wanted to give it one last look." Adam hesitated, turning toward me, "Why are you here?"

It wasn't an accusation, just a simple question. But I was ill-prepared just the same. The *"um"* came out before I could censor my hesitation.

"What all did Ridge tell you about the Garrison case?" Adam's friendliness deteriorated into words tinged with a hint of accusation. His chocolate eyes held firm on mine, forcing an answer.

"Not a lot. He just thought since I'd been working with the Garda, that I might be able to help with this case."

"So the story's true, then." He crossed his arms in front of his chest. "You're a freakin' psychic."

Adam's lips turned into a smile, but the word hit me with the force of a blast. I hated it. After a lifetime of visions, you'd think I'd be used to it, but I wasn't. It grated on my eardrums like nails on a chalkboard.

"I'd prefer the word empath," I said softly.

"Empath." Adam returned, stretching out the syllables. "I'll be damned."

A ball of nervousness grew in my stomach, vibrating as I stepped away from Ridge's partner and toward my car. My expression must have given me away. Adam's body relaxed as he stepped closer, reaching toward me with palms raised.

"I'm sorry, Liv. It's just that Ridge never came clean about that. I asked. Not long after you left there were rumors flying around, but he never gave me a straight answer."

Adam watched me for a beat as I unlocked my car, stepping out of the path of the driver's side door as I swung it open and slid inside.

"It's a small town, Adam. Word gets around."

Adam's grin returned as I brought the engine to life and pulled away from Jessica Garrison's apartment. Only when I was out of the parking lot, back on the main drag, did I question why he'd been searching the apartment one last time–alone.

22

LIV

Skylar phoned as I headed back to the farm, inviting me to Murphy's for a late lunch. I accepted without thinking–a much needed reprieve. My brain was spinning, working over the conversation I'd had with Adam, and the fact he now knew for certain that I was a freak. I'd seen it in his face, heard it in his voice as he repeated the word, *"empath."* The entire exchange was eating me up from the inside out. If Ridge hadn't told him when he asked point blank, then what did that say about Ridge? He was too ashamed to admit it?

Ridge's sister was leaning against the stone façade of the pub, between Murphy's main entrance and the empty storefront that was once slated to become my photography studio. I hadn't noticed it in the dark the night before. But seeing it now caused a rock to solidify in my chest. That world was a remote dream for my future that I'd shoved aside for too long, now nearly hidden in the cobwebby recesses of my mind.

"Why didn't you ever open it?" Skylar asked as I

approached, my eyes drifting toward the paper covered glass door.

"It just didn't work out," I said. Shrugging it off as if it was no big deal. It had been, though. Once. In another life.

"Brian said he hopes you'll finish it now that you're home."

"He's been too nice to me. We'll see." I smiled at Skylar. I wasn't sure how much she knew.

"Just a sec," she said, heading toward the back stairway, the one that led to Brian's apartment on the second floor. I waited at the bottom as she climbed the stairs to retrieve whatever she'd forgotten. She returned a moment later with a sweater draped over one arm.

"What happened to make you leave? In the spring, I mean. Ridge did something, didn't he?"

My breath caught in my throat at the abruptness of the question. She met my gaze as I glanced at her. I wanted her to relent, realize I wasn't ready to answer such a personal question yet, but she didn't. She just stared at me with wide, probing eyes. I could lie, but then I wouldn't be any better than Ridge.

"Come on, Liv. He's my brother, and I love him, but he's far from perfect. And now that I've spent a little time with you–" She shrugged, shifting her attention to the pebble she was rolling with the toe of her tennis shoe. "Cascade Hills is your home. There has to be a reason you stayed away so long."

I hadn't spoken to anyone about what drove me away. Michael and Herman only knew parts of the story. Ashlyn knew a bit more, but because she could sense it, not because I'd volunteered the information. I'd even avoided the subject with my own mother before leaving for the fair isle, although she'd been around to witness most of it.

"It's kind of a long story, I guess."

Skylar shrugged, heading away from the storefronts and

toward a bike path that paralleled a nearby fencerow. "I've got time."

"I don't know how much you know, but I met your brother when I came back to Cascade Hills for my grandmother's funeral. He stopped me for trespassing at the farm, actually."

I glanced at Skylar as we walked. She was taking it in, urging me on with her silence.

"I guess I fell too hard too fast. It had been a while since I'd had that, you know? But our relationship was going really well," I reasoned, more for my own understanding than hers. "I decided to move back to Cascade Hills from L.A. for good, to live at the farm like my grandmother wanted. Then, everything started to unravel."

I stopped talking. Reconsidering the decision to dump all of this on Ridge's younger sister.

"Go on," Skylar said, taking my hand in hers. Her eyes pleaded as pulses of compassion filtered from her skin to mine.

"I had an ex-boyfriend. From school in California–Jason. He showed up, making threats. Adam got shot. It was a mess. When they finally caught up with Jason he spun this story about how he and I were still together, that I'd helped him drug my own grandmother to get the inheritance."

Skylar stopped, dropping my hand and turning toward me. Leaning against the wooden fence, her eyes opened wide. Judgment. I clenched my jaw against it and kept walking. Human nature at its finest.

"I didn't, of course." It seemed like an important point to make. Skylar trotted back up to my side. "Anyway, our relationship fell apart after that. All the evidence pointed to my involvement. I was arrested and charged with felony counts of drug possession."

My chest tightened. It had been so long since I'd forced

myself to remember the details. I propped myself into a sitting position along the top rail of the roughhewn fence.

"That's when you left?" Skylar asked as she joined me.

I shook my head. "No, but Ridge wouldn't talk to me. Wouldn't let me explain. Even after Jason admitted everything and committed suicide in the barn at the farm—" The memory sucked the breath out of my lungs. "Ridge didn't want my side of the story. Brian was the one who pushed me, helped me come up with the plan."

"What plan?" Skylar prodded. I'd hesitated too long, lost in memories I'd just as soon forget.

"A plan to prove to Ridge I wasn't the person Jason made me out to be. The whole thing, Jason's attacks, the charges, it was all a set-up. Jason was a pawn in a bigger game. He told me as much, but after his death, I had no proof."

Skylar was taking it all in. There was a look of concern in her blue eyes that urged me on.

"Brian got Adam involved and they set me up with a wire. They stayed outside and monitored while I went in to meet with Lyle. He owned The Hunter, one of the nicer restaurants in Cascade Hills. It's closed now, of course." A bubble of nervous laughter surged in my chest. "In a crazy twist of events, Lyle was dating my mom at the time. But he was the one who put Jason up to it, conned him into framing me."

"So you cleared your name?"

I nodded. "Lyle admitted he was after the Sullivan money before he stabbed me."

Skylar stifled a gasp, her hand flying up to cover her mouth as her eyes grew unnaturally wide.

"The last thing I remember is Brian standing over me, yelling for Adam to call for help."

Silence stretched between us as she processed. I might have

regretted my decision to tell if it didn't feel so freeing. The knot that I thought was permanently lodged in my gut loosened.

Spilling the details to Skylar didn't make sense on any level. Maybe I'd just shut everything up inside for so long I couldn't take it anymore. Needed to let it out, admit that what happened had changed me.

A gust of wind slipped around the corner of the building, sending Skylar's hair away from her face in raven wisps. She smoothed it with her hand before twisting to look at me.

"And when it was all over, Ridge was–?"

I shrugged. "Gone. Dropped off the face of the earth."

"Well," she said. Hopping off the fence and dusting off the back of her jeans. "He's had some experience running away."

Skylar held out a hand to help me down.

"We should probably have that lunch before we hit the road," she suggested.

We walked in silence toward Murphy's kitchen door, slipping in the back and weaving our way through the sparkling white tile walls and gleaming stainless steel appliances. The contrast of high tech kitchen and old world pub provided a grim reminder of my own lack of assimilation. I had a long way to go to catch up.

I tried to look the other way when Brian pulled Skylar to the side as we made it to the bar, folding her into a kiss that lasted a touch longer than it should have given the public space. *Who are you to judge?* My inner critic quipped in irritation.

Brian came and went as Skylar and I sat on bar stools, eating club sandwiches and twisting back and forth like kids at a soda fountain. Skylar took a long sip of her cherry Coke. Her eyes fell, a glimmer replaced by harsh reality.

The corner of Skylar's mouth tipped into a smile as she started to speak. "When we were kids, Ridge used to take me to the 7 Eleven a couple blocks from our house. He'd set me up on the seat of his bike and then he'd stand and pedal the whole way. Buy me candy with the money he made mowing lawns."

Skylar hesitated, picking apart her cocktail napkin as if lost in the memory.

"Ridge must have been about thirteen or fourteen then, I guess. I remember once, when we got to the store some older kids were there. They poked fun at him for dragging his little sister everywhere. Called him names. It made him furious, I could tell. But he never let on. Never let me see him get upset about it. In fact, I think he dragged me up to that silly 7 Eleven more often after that just to prove a point."

Skylar smiled, glancing at me. "Those are some of my favorite memories. Those rides up to the convenience store with my big brother. Of course, the fire changed all that. It changed him–all of us. We never went back to the 7 Eleven after our sister died."

"I'm sorry." It felt like the only thing to say to break the silence that strung between us.

Skylar smiled at me, "Oh, Liv. It's okay. We all have sad stories. That's what makes us who we are, right?"

"I guess." I twisted my own Coke glass in circles on the bar.

"The point is, I see some of that old Ridge when he's with you, Liv. Last night at the party? For the first time in a long time he was genuinely happy."

My breath clenched, constricted in my chest as Brian slid up on the other side of the bar. Once again, I'd been saved by Brian's impeccable timing.

"Don't look now," he whispered toward Skylar, "but we have a visitor." His usual jovial grin had been erased by a scowl. His eyes flared angrily as Skylar followed his gaze.

"Oh my God. She's here," Skylar whispered as I swiveled my head to see what they were looking at. "It's Bridget."

I scanned the woman who stood at the hostess stand. Long

legs, accentuated by skinny jeans and knee-high boots, were hard to miss. She wore a tunic length blue sweater that clung to her hips and breasts.

If Barbie had a raven-haired human equivalent, Bridget would certainly be it.

Skylar's blue eyes settled on mine as I turned back around. Brian watched me, as if waiting for a reaction. Neither of them spoke, just eyed me like frightened deer in a clearing.

I fiddled with the hem of my shirt and broke through the heaviness of our awkward silence. "Do you think she wants Ridge back?"

"Definitely." Brian and Skylar spoke at once.

"She was never good for him, Liv." Brian started to explain. "I thought for sure she was making up the whole Colton story to trap him. Then, of course, the paternity results came back. Once you meet him, though, it's pretty obvious. Big blue eyes, just like Ridge. He's a cute kid."

A dagger of hurt stabbed my chest, the first one since I'd opened up to Skylar in the parking lot. I wasn't sure why the idea of Colton looking just like Ridge bothered me so much. It's not like I wanted the kid to be ugly or anything. Maybe I wanted to save Ridge's genes for our future offspring, assuming there would be any.

The insatiable desire to meet the woman who could get under the skin of Ridge McCaffrey more than any other surged through me.

"I should go introduce myself."

Brian gave me a disapproving look and flung the towel off his shoulder, rubbing hard circles across the bar. "She's not worth your time."

Since I'd met him, Brian had always been the one I could count on for support and a witty joke. I'd never seen him so agitated.

"It's bound to happen sooner or later, Bri. I promise not to start a cat fight."

Brian studied me a moment. "It's not like I can stop you."

"Thanks, Brian. I'll be back in a minute, Skylar."

"You don't want me to come with you?"

My chest filled with a balloon of anxiety as I declined her offer and strode around the bar, following the path of the hostess. I pulled my shoulders up and straightened my blouse, feigning as much confidence as I could muster.

As I turned the corner, Adam Miller saw me first, the look of surprise on his face comical. And likely in keeping with my own. He jerked up from the booth, knocking the table with his legs and tipping an almost empty glass of water.

His eyes flicked between Bridget and me, and he stumbled over his words. Righting the glass he asked me what I was doing there. Interrogated twice in one day. I was on a roll.

"I'm here with Skylar. We stopped in to visit Brian and he mentioned he'd seen you," I lied. "I just thought I'd say hello."

I let my eyes shift to the woman sitting across from Adam. From a distance, she'd been pretty. Close up, she was model gorgeous. Shiny black hair fell in curls down her back. Some of them looked tinged with purple and blue hues, the only indication I had that black wasn't her natural color. Perfectly groomed eyebrows arched above large long-lashed eyes set in a perfect ivory complexion. Her eyes were a flinty grey, the color of the sky before a thunderstorm.

"Sorry. I didn't realize you had company."

I waited for Adam to recover from the shock of seeing me, hoping for an introduction. A few seconds later, I gave up, extending my hand toward Bridget.

"I'm sorry, I don't think we've met. I'm Liv Sullivan, a friend of Adam's."

I smiled my best smile, doing everything within my power to hide the intense dislike I already had for this woman.

"Liv." A streak of recognition flickered briefly across her face and she glanced at Adam before getting it under control. "It's nice to meet you. I'm Bridget McCaffrey."

McCaffrey, the name was like a punch to the chest. I'd been naïve to think she wouldn't have kept Ridge's name.

I bit the inside of my cheek to keep from showing emotion, and she finally accepted my handshake, planting her thin, cool fingers briefly in mine. A grip that makes you feel as though you've taken the hand of a princess, or maybe a wet eel. I breathed through satisfaction when the wall I'd erected against her energy held.

Adam finally chimed in, "Liv is–"

"Ridge's girlfriend," Bridget interjected. A small smile turned the corners of perfectly glossed lips.

I glanced at Adam, who had finally reseated himself in the booth. His eyes were wide as he glanced from Bridget, to me, and then back again.

"Well, I've heard a lot about you, Bridget. It's nice to finally put a name with a face. I'd better get back. Nice to see you again, too, Adam."

I silently complimented myself on the ability to sound like an adult. I even walked away slowly, without ever turning back to catch a reaction.

When I got back to the bar I let loose, though. Sinking onto the stool with my head in my hands, exhaling a curse. I felt Brian's hand on one side and Skylar's on the other as they rubbed circles over my shoulders.

"So?" Skylar finally asked.

"She kept his name. They've been divorced for–what? Eight years? Who does that?"

"Shit, Liv. I should have told you. I'm sorry." The sincerity in Skylar's voice was palpable. "Come on, we should get back to the farm."

23

RIDGE

Ridge spent the afternoon poring over every scrap of evidence in the Jessica Garrison file, including the information he hadn't bothered to share with his partner. Adam had left just after they'd returned from the M.E.'s office and hadn't been back. Working a lead for another case Wallace had him assisting with. Or so he'd said. It didn't matter. Ridge was glad to have the time alone.

Adam and Ridge had been transferred by the Bureau to Cascade Hills as a team six years ago. But Adam's training was as a support specialist. He'd never seen distinguishing marks peeled from a body. Ridge had seen photographs of similar injuries in his training at Quantico. It was one of many factors Sowards assigned him to notice in his current detail, but it was the first time he'd seen anything like it in Cascade Hills.

The GenLink Counterintelligence Research Program had spawned as a result of Reagan's Cold War era. The program had gone through several reincarnations over the years, but the goal of the research had remained steady–discover ways to utilize psychic abilities to enhance National Security.

Since the 1980s, when GenLink was in its infancy, each asset who came through was marked. In the 80s the Bureau used tattoos. In the 90s, they made the shift to microchips. To Ridge's knowledge, all but one of the GenLink assets had been marked this way. And although the Bureau had instituted strict protection orders for each of them, the women involved were slowly starting to disappear. Aimee Callaghan had been the first active asset to go, but more followed. The Bureau refused to provide an official theory, but that hadn't stopped Ridge from doing some research and developing one of his own.

The feds had been careful. Each agent assigned to the operation only knew about his or her own asset. Other than basic historical briefings, no other information was provided. Which accounted for Sowards' tight lips once Liv came back to Cascade Hills. Ridge had put a few things together with the help of contacts like Michael Donaghey, though. And once he figured out that Ashlyn Callaghan was Liv's biological sister, his suspicion of the Bureau's motives morphed into full-fledged conspiracy theory.

The brass knew more than they were telling about the disappearance of assets. In fact, it was Sowards' mandate that he not bring Liv back to Cascade Hills that made him want to get her out of there as soon as possible. He wasn't the only one keeping secrets.

It was obvious to Ridge that Garrison was an asset, although no one would admit as much. He'd asked his supervisor point blank when the photos of Liv surfaced in the girl's apartment. But Special Agent in Charge Marcus Sowards either didn't know or couldn't tell him. Ridge was banking on the former. It was the only explanation for the dissected divot on her hip and her distinct lack of footprint when it came to official records.

Every document he'd found so far had been doctored in

some way. From her birth certificate to her cell phone records, all of them had been professionally cleaned. He just didn't know by whom.

Ridge propped his elbow on his desk and sighed as he turned his attention to her bank statements. Again, too perfect to belong to a 24-year-old single woman. Every line item, every transaction had been carefully selected to throw suspicion away from Garrison. But Ridge had been in the Bureau long enough to notice the telltale signs. Deposits made at exact intervals, down to the minute. No direct deposits or ACH withdrawals. Cash withdrawals were always under $60, and other than rent, no single transaction was above $120.

The image of Garrison on the table in Megan Foster's office haunted him. Who had been protecting her? Everything spread out in front of him left him with more questions than answers.

How did Garrison know about Liv? None of the assets were ever supposed to know about one another. Did the photographs prove Garrison knew Liv was an asset? Or was it the connection Liv had with the girls at the home that led Garrison to Liv? Either way, Ridge worried, information about Liv could have been leaked to the wrong people.

Why eliminate Garrison? Had she been trying to warn him with the photos or were they blackmail material? It wasn't out of the realm of possibility that she'd been coerced to the other side. But none of that mattered much right now since he had a very limited idea what, or who, the "other side" was.

Someone in Dublin had tracked Liv, watched her. He could only hope that whoever had taken the photographs was affiliated with the Bureau, or at the very least, that the person responsible for the fire at Cohen's hadn't realized Liv was back on US soil.

As far as Ridge knew, Liv was the only remaining asset that had yet to be microchipped. It had taken a lot of convincing on his part, but it was a feat of which Ridge was particularly proud. He'd hoped it would help keep her safe from whatever group was hunting the assets. At least this way, they couldn't know for sure that she was part of the program.

Guilt crept in as he wondered how much longer he'd be able to keep Liv in the dark. She hadn't known Garrison personally. That was a blessing. And despite what he'd told her in Ireland, he wanted to keep her out of it. She deserved a chance to breathe, get settled back in. Who was he kidding? He wanted a chance to make amends.

It was nearly seven when his phone broke the silence of the station house. He glanced around the open room. Cascade Hills was a small town, and everyone but the night dispatcher and the on duty patrol had gone for the day.

Skylar's number shone on the screen.

"What's up, Sky?" He worked to keep his voice light, unaffected. The last thing he needed were probing questions from his little sister. He'd gotten enough of her know-it-all attitude that morning.

"Dad caught some fish today. We wondered if you'd be here for dinner."

Ridge folded the phone between his shoulder and cheekbone and began loading everything back into the file box. He slid it under his desk and grabbed his jacket from the back of his chair, heading for the door.

"I lost track of time, Sky. I'm on my way."

"Okay." Skylar lowered her voice, forcing Ridge to tuck the mobile more tightly against his ear. "Ridge, before you get here, you should probably know that Liv met Bridget today."

The statement stopped Ridge in his tracks. A plummeting sensation in his chest shot a pulse of adrenalin through his veins.

"I'll be right there."

He didn't wait for a response, just thrust the phone in his pocket and pushed his way out the door. As he fired up the Shelby, his mind roared through the possibilities of Liv's reaction to meeting the mother of his son. He tried to put himself in Liv's position. Doing so only made him feel worse. He wasn't sure it was possible to betray someone quite as much as he'd betrayed Liv.

You have no one to blame but yourself, he thought. *You should let her go. Resign this assignment and let her get on with her life without you.* He knew that was true, but he couldn't ignore the feelings he had for her either. Besides, if he didn't protect her, who would? She'd end up on Megan Foster's exam table, just like Jessica Garrison.

Liv was standing near the lake when he pulled to a stop in the driveway of Sullivan Farm. He wouldn't have noticed her in the late evening dusk, but the light on the dock cast an eerie glow along the shoreline, stretching her shadow along the ground. She didn't turn, just kept chucking rocks at the mirrored surface of Cascade Lake. She'd never been able to skip stones, but the hours he'd spent trying to teach her last spring were embedded in his cache of favorite memories.

"Everything okay?" Ridge asked as he approached.

She choked out the word, "Fine," before Ridge got close enough to touch her. When she turned toward him he could tell she'd been crying. Even in the low light, thin makeup free trails lined both cheeks. He pulled her close and wrapped his arms around her, holding her until he felt her resolve weaken, her body melting into him.

"Come on, let's go for a walk."

Ridge hollered back toward the house, letting Skylar and George know they'd be back in a few minutes. His sister waved from the kitchen window, worry etched across her brow.

Ridge stayed silent as they walked along the stone path that led from the lake to the woods. What could he say, anyway? He focused on the crunch of their shoes on the pea gravel. Four steps whittled into two as their strides synced.

"She's beautiful." Liv's voice was small, scared.

"So are you," he responded without hesitation.

"It's stupid, I know, but it never occurred to me that she'd still have your name. That was hard to hear."

Ridge sucked in a deep breath. Another failure.

"I should have told you."

Liv stopped walking, turning to face Ridge. "Are you sure this is what you want?"

He studied her. Heart shaped face, green eyes, those full, soft lips. He cupped her jaw and ran a thumb across her bottom lip. Her eyes fluttered closed, but she pulled away.

"The three of you–you'd make a beautiful family."

The words hung like fog in the air between them.

"What?" Ridge shook his head. "Absolutely not."

He tilted her head, forcing her to look him in the eye. Everything he'd been wanting to say for the past nine months rushed at him. He exhaled a curse. Deciding on the only words that wouldn't get him fired.

"I never knew I could be as happy as I am when I'm with you, Liv. Regardless of our issues, what I had with Bridget is over. It's on me to find a way to be in Colton's life without hurting you in the process. And I'll be the first to admit that I have no idea how to make that happen. But I need this. I need you to tell me when you're hurt so I can make it right."

"Today was fine," Liv started. "Bridget was fine. Meeting her just reminded me of everything that's wrong between us. I'm pretty sure that nothing short of time travel would fix our problems, Ridge. Colton isn't even one of them."

There was an edge in her voice. Her head seemed to be telling her one thing but her body was out of sync. She stepped forward, running her hands slowly down his chest, tugging at the buttons on his shirt as she went.

"You'll be a great dad."

Ridge tangled a hand in her hair, tipping her head back just far enough to kiss her. He felt her lean in, her lips softening under his.

"We can't keep doing this." She pulled back, tucking the corner of her bottom lip under her teeth. "We need to make a decision about what we're doing, where this is going."

The gentle lap of the water as it washed onto the rocks at the lakeshore drowned out rational thought as Ridge twisted one of Liv's curls around his index finger. She leaned into his touch, closing her eyes. He should have stopped then, walked back up to the house for dinner followed by an honest conversation. That's what any normal human being would have done. But he knew what he wanted.

"I know what I want," he said. "Marry me." The words slipped out before he could censor them.

Liv's eyes flew open as she jerked back, pushing away from Ridge's embrace.

"No." Her eyes were wide, hurt. "Not like this, Ridge. Not because of her. Not because you're trying to fix a mistake."

A single tear began a slow march down Liv's cheek. She brushed it away.

"Liv, that's not what this is. Please."

Ridge reached for her shoulder but she turned too quickly, her shoes crunching an upbeat rhythm against the gravel as she ran toward the house. He called after her, but she didn't look back. He stood on the path wondering what the hell he'd been thinking and cursing himself for being an ass. No matter what his job was or who he was trying to protect her from, right now he was the only enemy she knew.

HE'D TRUDGED to the house, watched her run up the stairs, and flinched when the door slammed behind her. He'd followed her up. Pecked on the door until she yelled for him to go away. Short of breaking the door down to get his point across, he'd have to wait this one out.

Now, as he sat with his Dad and Skylar at a dining room table that didn't belong to him, in a house he was no longer welcome in, pushing freshly grilled trout around on his plate, he considered his options. *Leave,* his inner voice asserted.

"Why would you ask her that?" Skylar asked after dinner as they sat in the living room. Ridge kept one ear tuned to the stairway as they talked. Hoping for a break. George headed to the kitchen to clean up, leaving them alone. "You need to take a step back. Look at this from her perspective."

"Now you're an expert on a woman you met less than twenty-four hours ago?"

"We had a nice talk." Ridge watched his sister as she shrugged. "I like her."

"Yeah, well. So do I," Ridge admitted.

"I know. That's why you need to tell her the truth. That's all she wants, Ridge. Tell all of us the truth. Liv told me what happened before she went to Ireland."

"She what?" Ridge worked to keep irritation out of his voice. What happened to Liv was none of Skylar's business.

"You expect her to forgive your mistakes, even one that almost killed her. You want a chance to start over. That's fine. But you can't expect her to forget what you did. Where were you?"

"She had no business telling you."

"Why?" It was Skylar's turn to be angry. "It's her life, too. You aren't the only one whose feelings matter."

"She has no idea what happened, Skylar. None. This is–"

"Then tell her. You can't just fall off the face of the earth when someone you care about needs you and not bother to explain why."

Ridge went silent. Frustration twisted in his gut. He'd be damned, but Skylar was right. His little sister was all grown up, and giving him relationship advice. Boy, how the tables had turned.

"What's done is done, Ridge. You can't go back. And no matter how much you want to, you can't just start with a clean slate. Her reaction tonight had nothing to do with you posing the question, and everything to do with what happened last spring. You've got to give her a reason to trust you again."

24

LIV

The longer I stayed holed up in my room, the more frustrated I became. Not at Ridge or Bridget, but at myself. The fallout of the past few days had me acting like a toddler who'd lost her favorite toy. Part of it was fear. That was clear. I yearned for safety, a new life. But the past wouldn't loosen its grip.

I turned the handle on the bedroom door and slipped out into the darkened hall. Tucking myself into the shadows at the top of the stairs, I listened to the rise and fall of gentle conversation in the living room below. Easy banter between family members who had, too quickly, begun to feel like my own. I hugged my knees to my chest and rocked back and forth, quieting the urge to join them.

I snuck back up to my room when Skylar's conversation with Ridge turned to me. I stayed long enough to understand that even his sister wasn't going to change his mind. Knowing Ridge kept secrets from his entire family should have been a warning sign. But instead, sorrow tugged at my heart.

I knew the pain of keeping secrets, of hiding in plain sight from the people you cared about most. Guilt bubbled in my chest. I closed the bedroom door as quietly as I'd exited, waiting for the silence of night to engulf the farmhouse. Waiting for my moment of purpose, the chance to live up to the promise I'd made to Jessica and the others.

A hush had descended over the house by the time I ventured out again. I crept downstairs and out the front door, wondering, only briefly, which room Ridge had chosen to sleep in. I forced thoughts of him away. Tonight was Jessica's night. She needed me, and I refused to let her down.

I tugged the front door closed behind me, skipped the squeaky second to last step, and trotted on tiptoe to my Mustang. I flinched against the sound as the motor roared to life, checking the windows for a sign that someone had heard. My eyes darted from pane to pane, but the house stayed dark.

A FEW LIGHTS glowed in windows and porches in the development around Jessica's townhome, making it easy to spot the darkened rectangle that now stood empty, shrouded in the mystery of a young woman's disappearance.

I bypassed the front door. Adam had checked the lock as we'd left that afternoon. Instead, I headed around back. If there was any way in, it would be through a window. I checked each one, pushing the screens upward, out of the way, before using the palms of my gloved hands to coerce the sash northward.

My fingers ached with the challenge of pushing and pulling against each pane of glass. I was down to the last window when I felt the frame shift beneath my fingertips. With renewed persistence, I pried the window open, forcing my fingers into the tiny space between window and sill, gaining what leverage I could to slide the double paned glass upward.

I must have been out there, poised at the window, for fifteen minutes. I kept looking over my shoulder, wary of insomniac neighbors. All I needed was someone to report a stranger breaking into a vacant crime scene. Just as I was about to give up, the window gave way, sliding into a fully open position with a *thunk*.

The cool October breeze washed over me, sending stray strands of hair across my face. I wrapped my arms over the sill and walked my feet up the vinyl siding until I was level with the bottom of the casing, close enough to thrust my torso inside. My triceps burned in protest as I lurched forward. Halfway through, I lost my grip, landing cheekbone first on the hardwood floor of Jessica's dining room. Wooden chairs scraped against the floorboards, creating space for my body to fall forward in an accidental somersault.

The darkness of the room closed in around me. I sat crumpled on the floor, allowing my eyes time to adjust. I pulled off one glove, pushing the pads of my fingertips along my cheek, checking for signs of blood. None, thank God. But I was sure to have a winner of a bruise tomorrow.

I replaced the glove and struggled to my feet, exploring the walls around me to orient myself. The dining room emptied into a galley style kitchen, which ended in the cream-colored hallway I'd seen through the front door earlier this afternoon.

By the time I climbed the stairs to Jessica's room, the moonlight through the windows was providing just enough light for my adjusted vision. There were three rooms upstairs. I bypassed the first two, leaving the open doors of a bathroom and a guest room turned office behind. A four-panel slab of hardwood at the end of the hall was all that separated me from Jessica's most intimate space. I sucked in a jagged breath, tamping down the nervousness that tingled up through my core.

I tugged the gloves off my hands and shoved them in my pocket. The hum of energy formed a bubble around me, vibrating in my chest like a response to a percussive band. I reached for the door, my palm flat against the smooth white paint. The shock was immediate. Pulses of confusion and fear stabbed into my skin, giving way to hot spikes of anger and betrayal. I jerked away. My heart banged a racehorse rhythm in my chest as heat penetrated from all sides.

You can do this, I coached, closing my eyes and pulling my hand up into the sleeve of my fleece pullover. I took hold of the knob and twisted. *There's nothing here that can hurt you,* Herman's words, my safety net.

The first vision plowed through me with the force of a tractor trailer, sucking the air from my lungs and plunging me into another world. My hold on the knob tightened, securing the only connection I could to the real world. The door creaked open with the force of my grip, dragging me to my knees.

The knife glistened at her throat. Dark curls fell around the sinewy hand controlling the blade. A tattoo, black Celtic cross, marked the flesh between her attacker's thumb and forefinger.

"Shh...it will all be over soon, love."

"Why are you doing this? I've given you what you want." The words morphed into a whimper, transforming her delicate throat. A thin line of blood appeared against china doll skin.

"Did you really think we could just let you go?" His voice seethed in her ear. Stale breath sending wisps of hair across her face. She squinted against the onslaught. "One more time Jessica. Help us find her, then you'll be free."

"Please, no," she pleaded. But he ignored her. His knee on her back. His fists secure around her wrists.

The rush of breath from my own lungs meshed with Jessica's. A faint squeak from downstairs dimmed the image.

"Don't go." My own voice this time, begging to stay

connected.

Deep brown eyes pleaded, imploring me through long lashes matted with tears. "Help me."

Another sound from the real world jutted through the connection. Footsteps. But Jessica refused to let go. Her scream echoed in my ears. His hands pushed against her back, holding her down against rough floorboards. The needle plunged into her arm. Heat liquified her. Filled her lungs. And he watched.

The space around me dulled, the high of the vision dropping me onto the coals of real life. Quiet footsteps closed in. The creak of floorboards. I bit back the urge to give voice to my own fear.

Pushing into Jessica's room, I sealed myself inside before leaning back against the door, opening myself to the pulses of energy that still buzzed across my skin. I glanced at the doorknob. Simple metal that yielded so much. Another creak from the hall. I shot my hand up, engaging the lock, and scuttled away from the door. Crab-crawling as fast as I could, I flattened my back against the sideboard of Jessica's bed.

The brass knob gleamed in the moonlight filtering through the window. It turned. Once. Twice. My breath caught. A belt squeezed my lungs, constricted my throat. The prod of the needle against sensitive flesh. *Why?* I closed my eyes, coaxing Jessica back in. She came willingly. Fear filling my chest as it did hers.

My muscles screamed against the firm grip of her attacker. She squirmed against his hold. Her eyes locked on mine. But only for a moment before a bee sting of heat ushered in complete intoxication.

Life drained from her eyes as he lowered her to the ground at his feet. He cursed as roughhewn boards scraped against the soft flesh of her cheek. The last glimmer of her energy stabbed through me, her voice an echo in my skull. "It's you they want."

25

RIDGE

"Liv?" Ridge tapped on Jessica Garrison's bedroom door. "Come on, I know you're in there. Open up." He twisted the doorknob. Once. Twice. A thread of panic seized in his chest. Michael had warned him about this.

"Don't let her get tangled up with another asset," Michael had said when Ridge told him she'd agreed to go home. *"This girl, Jessica. You don't know who she is. Until you do, don't get Liv involved."* Ridge had blown him off. But now, the risk was real. *"You saw her at the children's home. That connection could be doubled, tripled even, by an asset, especially one who's been trained. This isn't some parlor trick, Agent McCaffrey. The physiological symptoms of this gift can be deadly."*

Deadly. The word reached into Ridge's chest and wrapped its fingers around his heart. He called her name again, pounded his fist against the smooth solid of the bedroom door. Neighbors be damned.

There was no response. He checked the knob, a basic interior room door, the kind with the hole on one side to pop the lock if necessary. But that wasn't the problem. Below that, Jessica had installed a deadbolt. He'd made a note of it when they'd done their preliminary search. But only now that Liv was locked inside did he care why she'd put it there in the first place.

"Liv, listen to me. I know you're mad, but I need you to unlock the door." He hesitated. Still no sound from the other side, no scrambling of feet, no whimpers like he'd heard that night at the children's home. He lowered himself to the floor, peering through the space where the hardwood of the hall met the carpet of Jessica's bedroom.

Legs. Outstretched toward the door. The soles of Liv's tennis shoes. A hand, open and limp on the ground. From what he remembered of the room, Liv was sitting, semi-propped against Jessica's bed.

Ridge stood. The coils of tension at the base of his skull tightened. There was only one option. And he'd pay for this later.

Ridge rammed the door with his shoulder. Once, twice... nothing. He kicked with the heel of his boot. A shimmy of hope rattled through the lock and surrounding trim. One more kick. The trim splintered, sending the slab inward, bits of loosened pine sprinkled the carpet near Liv's outstretched palm.

Ridge flipped the light switch on the wall. An instinct, as if the light would scare away the monsters dragging Liv into unconsciousness. She lay on the floor, open-eyed, pupils dilated. The green of her irises thinned into to slivers around a blackened orb. *Jesus.* Panic surged up from his gut as he lunged toward her, his knees sinking into the bedroom carpet.

Liv's head lolled to the side as Ridge pulled her limp form to him and nestled her head in the crook of his arm. He whispered her name, pushed tendrils of curl off soft skin. He struggled to ease her body from the floor. His heart pounding in his chest. Michael's words echoed in his skull. He should have listened, should have paid more attention.

He watched her chest for the rise and fall of life as he carried her from Jessica's bedroom down the stairs and out the front door of the townhome. He was beyond giving a rat's ass if anyone saw him. At this point, the only thing that mattered was the woman in his arms.

"Liv, stay with me." Ridge said the words loud enough that he hoped they'd break through the otherworldly wall between them. He skimmed his hand down the side of her face as he lowered her into the passenger seat of his car. Her skin was cool, clammy. The touch sent a spiral of shock through him. The image of Jessica Garrison on the medical examiner's table crept up on him. He wouldn't let Liv be next.

The engine roared to life, tires squealing as he launched the Shelby toward Sullivan Farm. There was no movement from Liv's side of the car, no noise to prove she was still with him. He pulled her arm onto the console between them, checking between shifts for the faint, but steady, pulse. Only that throb of hope kept him from veering straight to the emergency room at County Memorial rather than heading for the protection of Sullivan Farm.

They were halfway to the farm before Ridge heard the first whimper, the first indication that Liv wasn't lost to him forever.

"Liv," Ridge said her name, pulling her hand toward his lips. He made every effort to pour his energy in, combat whatever darkness had taken over.

In a gasp of breath she lurched forward, her forehead nearly smacking the dash before the sudden forward momentum engaged the seatbelt, tugging her back against the seat. Ridge stuck out a hand, soccer-mom style, reaching to soothe her as her panic erupted in a wave of coughs.

"Liv, look at me." Ridge ground the car to a halt in the gravel at the side of the road. She clawed at her neck. Red swaths carved onto perfect porcelain skin. He jerked the emergency brake and grabbed her hands. For the first time, she looked at him. Her eyes were wild, scared. Her chest heaved as she sucked in one lungful of air after another.

"Just breathe. Take it easy." He tried again. "You're okay. It's just us." Her fit of panic morphed into a wave of fear. He watched as the emotion gathered behind her eyes. He was ready when the first tears slid free, skimming down her cheeks in rivers.

"She's dead." The words sent a knife to Ridge's heart. He should have warned her before now. "Jessica Garrison is dead."

RIDGE BREATHED a sigh of relief when they pulled down the drive to the farm. The lights in the windows still blessedly dark. Liv hadn't spoken since the announcement at the side of the road, but she'd allowed him to hold her hand as they made their way back toward her home.

"I'm going to go get cleaned up," Liv said, dropping his hand and making her way through the foyer, toward the staircase.

"Do you need help?" The words felt foreign, yet necessary.

She shook her head, wobbling a bit before righting herself against the living room sofa.

Ridge watched her disappear into the shadows of the second story, her gait unsteady. The grip she took on the bannister proof of her instability. He stood at the bottom of the stairs until he heard the water of the shower.

He pulled his phone from his jacket pocket and dialed the

number that had been vibrating through the leather for most of the ride to the farm.

"Christ, McCaffrey. Correct me if I'm wrong, but you are still on Bureau payroll, correct?" Special Agent in Charge Marcus Sowards' voice was rough, loud against the quiet of the sleeping house. He let the rhetorical question go. "We have some intel you should be aware of."

"Garrison was an asset, wasn't she?" Ridge ignored his supervisor's comment. Anger roiled like lava through his core, driving a hot spike of helplessness through him. Liv, lost in a world he didn't understand, fresh in his memory. Ridge waited out the silence on the other end.

"You know I can't confirm that."

"You don't need to. I saw confirmation tonight."

"I told you not to bring her back, McCaffrey." Sowards' voice had lost its edge. "What happened?"

Ridge turned toward the kitchen, and the possibility of caffeine induced clarity. "I don't know yet. I found her in Garrison's apartment–alone. I haven't pushed her."

"Find out. I hate to be the bearer of more bad news, but we have a sighting of O'Malley." The name hit Ridge like a punch to the gut, lacing the coils of tension at the base of his skull tighter. He rubbed at them with his free hand.

"Where?"

"Street cam outside Cohen's the night of the fire."

Ridge exhaled a curse into the receiver. "Does he know Liv survived? Where is he now?"

"Slow down. We're working on it. He's been so far off grid, it's been impossible to track him. The fact we caught him on camera means he wanted us to see him."

Ridge nodded a response, bracing himself on the counter. "I want to know who killed Garrison. And I want to know if they're after Liv."

"We're doing what we can. You worry about Olivia. Right now, she's all we've got. The future of GenLink depends on her."

Ridge ended the call without saying goodbye. His jaw ached, set in an angry clench. As if he needed Sowards to tell him what the stakes were. But GenLink be damned, for once he was clear. Liv's life, her happiness, meant far more to him than any government program. He pushed his flattened palms against the cool of the countertop.

"Coffee's in the cabinet to the right."

Ridge spun to face Liv. Wet ringlets framed her face. Even with dark circles shadowing her eyes and the ghost of her limp body hanging in his memory, the sight of her loosened a knot inside of him.

"How long have you been standing there?" He acted nonchalant, pulling the coffee from the cabinet and rinsing the basket to ready a new pot.

"Not long. Your secrets are safe."

He might have laughed if her words hadn't stabbed directly into his heart.

They stood in silence as the coffee pot gurgled and bubbled, spewing forth its black gold. Ridge wasn't sure how much longer he could operate under his current level of sleep deprivation.

Liv reached into the cupboard behind him. He inhaled her beachy sweetness, forced himself not to touch her. Had it really only been two nights ago that she lay in his arms? God, it seemed like a lifetime. She stepped back, offering him a mug. She filled hers first. He could feel her watching as he poured his, sprinkling in a teaspoon of sugar and swirling until the crystals dissolved.

"You can ask me anything," she said between sips. "That's why I'm here, right?" A fresh wave of panic clenched his gut.

"To help with the Garrison case?"

Jesus. He had to get it together. He blew relief over the top of his cup, glad to have some way to mask his reactions.

"Did you see who killed her?"

26

LIV

Of course, Ridge had to ask the question I had no way of answering. I swallowed against the kernel of failure that curled its way into a knot in my chest. I sipped the coffee, grateful for the burn as it slid down the back of my throat.

"You don't know." Ridge guessed before I could form the words.

"It was a man. I couldn't see his face. He had a tattoo, a black cross, like the Celtic ones in Irish cemeteries." The image appeared in my mind. "With the circle woven around the top."

Ridge nodded. "Think you could draw it?" He passed a pad of paper across the counter toward me. He followed as I moved from my perch against the counter toward the table. I tugged on a chair, the feet scraping against the hardwood beneath. We sat in silence as I sketched a passable rendition of the cross I'd seen on the hand of Jessica's attacker. I wasn't terrible, but it was clear I hadn't inherited my mother's drawing skills.

Ridge twisted his cup in circles, watching. "Is it always like that, Liv? Do the visions always—"

"Turn me into a freak?" I cut in.

"That's not what I was going to say." Ridge's voice was quiet, tentative. "You scared the shit out of me tonight. I don't know what to do when the visions take over. How am I supposed to get you back?"

Hurt constricted his voice. Anxiety pricked at the air, raising gooseflesh along my arms and legs.

"Sometimes the end isn't up to me. Sometimes they have something to say and they don't let go until it's been said. That's why Herman was so adamant. Never invite them in. Never ask for more. But giving in to their energy is the only way to get answers."

I slid the pad of paper toward Ridge, being careful not to get too close.

"This is it?" Ridge studied the cross. "Are you sure?"

"I'm not the artist my mom was, but yes. That's what it looked like. It was on his right hand." I rubbed the spot with the pad of my thumb. "Between his thumb and index finger."

Ridge leaned forward in his chair. The pad gripped in his fist. Negative energy sucked the oxygen from the room, sending a film of heat over my skin. I scooted away from the table, standing to put my half-full coffee cup in the sink, anything to get away from the ions that poured off Ridge.

"Your dad and Skylar should be up soon." It seemed like safe territory and I needed the relief. "Sky said they're taking Colton to the zoo today." The grip of fury eased. "Are you going with them?"

"No. This is their last day here. They wanted a day to spoil him without any parental interference." Ridge's eyes met mine. "I need to know what you saw. Where was she?"

"Not her apartment. It was damp, cold. I only saw the boards of the floor. They were rough sawn planks. A cabin, maybe?"

"Was anyone else there?" Ridge's voice was dark. Serious. Official.

"I only saw Jessica, and parts of her attacker."

Ridge leaned back and ran a hand through his hair. Frustration. I clenched my jaw to keep emotion at bay. "The injection is what killed her." I lowered my voice. He'd never asked how she died. "But you already knew that."

"Liv–" Ridge started.

"You should have told me. What else do you know, Ridge? What else are you keeping from me?"

"I didn't have a chance to tell you. The M.E. found traces of a drug in our Jane Doe. She couldn't identify what it was, and we still have no positive ID on the body. Until we got that, I didn't want to worry you."

"Well, I'd say you've got your positive ID."

Ridge nodded. "I'm not used to working with..." He stumbled with the words.

"You can say it–someone like me." I forced a chuckle. "Maybe Michael can give you notes."

A surge of emotion ran through my chest. I missed Michael. Missed the way he'd listen when I told him what I'd seen. I'd never felt interrogated when we'd worked a case together. Maybe it was the time he'd spent with my mother, maybe just his personality, but he understood in a way I knew Ridge never could. Ridge wanted facts and details. Michael knew better. Michael relied on my interpretations. Trusted them. I sighed through the clench of loneliness.

Give it to him anyway, whether he wants it or not. My inner critic had a point. Might as well dump the rest of my freak show in Ridge's lap. "Whoever killed Jessica, they aren't done. It's me they want."

A bubble of hesitation hung in the air. I could imagine him thinking, *"Oh, not this shit again."* But instead he crossed to my post at the sink, pulled gently at the tie of my robe, urging me toward him. The python of anxiety wrapping around my chest began to loosen.

"I'll never let anything happen to you. I promise." Honesty glowed from his eyes. And I wanted to believe he had that power. But the experience I'd had in Jessica's bedroom left plenty of room for doubt.

"You shouldn't make promises you can't keep," I whispered.

Ridge's phone buzzed from the nearby countertop. His shoulders slumped, and his jaw ticked. Irritation. He reached for the cell.

"McCaffrey," he answered. I took my cup from the sink and refilled it while Ridge took the call. "When?" The panic in his voice was palpable. "I'm on my way."

Ridge pocketed the cell and shrugged into his jacket.

"I'm sorry. I know everything seems upside down right now. But we'll figure it out. I've got to go in. You stay at the farm today, okay?"

I nodded in response.

"You won't be next, Liv."

He leaned in to kiss me. The heat of his lips softening the nugget of nagging anxiety. I didn't have the energy to stay angry with him. Blame only clouded my abilities. The last thing I needed were more barriers to the truth.

"I'll call as soon as I can," he promised before heading through the dining room to the front door.

27

RIDGE

Ridge pulled up as close as possible to the Cape Cod, which was still two houses away. His heart thundered in his chest, ramped up by the police and emergency presence that had consumed the typically quiet neighborhood following Bridget's frantic 911 call. Ridge kept his head down, ignoring the neighbors lining the sidewalk to see what was going on at the McCaffrey house.

Adam jogged from the back corner of the structure when he saw Ridge. Intercepting him before he could get to the driveway.

"Where are they?" Ridge asked when his partner got within earshot.

"At the precinct. They're fine. Said she was giving Colton a bath when the explosion hit. She's pretty shaken up, but Colton seems oblivious."

For the first time since the call had come in, the knots twisting in his side relaxed a bit. He scoured the front of the house. The façade of the white Cape Cod looked just as it always did, neat and tidy, fitting in perfectly with all the other well-kept houses on postage stamp lots in this neighborhood.

Ridge could smell the damage, though. A telltale tendril of smoke rose like a ribbon from the rear of the home, proof that what he was doing had painted a target on his family's back.

Adam fell in step with Ridge as they hiked across the front lawn, past the federal bomb unit van parked in front of the garage. Ridge made a point not to look inside. The last thing he needed was to be outed by another agent. Not here.

He ducked under the crime scene tape and entered the front door, passing through the formal living room and into the kitchen. There was no doubt about the damage now. The entire rear wall, once home to custom maple cabinetry and the kitchen sink, was gone. A gaping hole, framed in black, exposed the backyard lawn on the other side, complete with primary-colored plastic playset.

"Jesus," Ridge exhaled, running a hand through his hair as he surveyed the damage. The relief that had come with the knowledge that Colton was safe suddenly replaced by the heat of fury.

He glanced down at what was left of the area rug. A half circle of the woven oval was missing. Outlining the newly formed hole in the hardwood floor with blackened wool threads.

Colton often played on that rug after meals, while he and Bridget cleaned up the kitchen. Ridge could almost see his son sitting on the carpet, running Matchbox cars up and down the linear design, sometimes catching the wheels up in the loose loop texture.

He shook away the weight of what could have happened, trying to focus on what Adam was saying to him. Something about an IED under the kitchen sink.

"There's no sign of forced entry." Captain Wallace's voice.

Ridge clenched his jaw, pulling himself together as Wallace's hand gave his shoulder a squeeze. "No way to know yet who planted the device."

Ridge could only nod. His training had prepared him for a lot of things, homicides, catastrophic wounds, even bomb blasts. But seeing his own home blown down to the studs was one experience no level of training could have prepared him for. The foul odor of burnt insulation and molten siding was a combination he wouldn't soon forget.

"You KNOW I can't let you work this case," Captain Wallace said.

Ridge stood in Wallace's office, staring out the window into the parking lot beyond. The past few hours had been a blur as Ridge tried to pry information from the assigned officers. Wallace hadn't even let him see Colton yet. That part was about to send him over the edge.

"Let me see them, Captain."

"I sent Miller with them to get some lunch. They're meeting up with your dad and sister. As soon as they get back, they're all yours. But in the meantime..."

Ridge turned to face his superior. He knew there would be questions. Questions about his relationship with Bridget, his relationship with Liv. Why he wasn't there when the blast hit. On the surface, he knew how bad it looked. If the tables were turned, he'd be taking a good hard look at the ex as well. Even harder if he knew there was a recently returned romantic partner in the mix. He pulled a chair out on the other side of Wallace's desk and sunk into it, folding his hands into his lap.

"Any idea why someone would want to hurt Bridget?" Wallace began.

"Of course not." Great. First question and he'd already lied. She didn't exactly make friends everywhere she went.

Wallace nodded. "Tell me a little bit about the relationship you have with your ex-wife."

"She's the mother of my son."

"But you've been living with her. Come on, Ridge. You're telling me it never once got physical in the last six months?"

Ridge's heart thrummed inside his chest, anger boiling his blood pressure to the breaking point. Heat flushed his cheeks. "I don't see what that has to do with what happened this morning."

"You know how this works, Ridge. I'm just trying to get a handle on your relationship. You've been staying at the farm since Liv came home, right? You might save yourself a hiccup with Liv if you could get Bridget out of the picture."

Ridge stood, the chair he'd been sitting in wobbled before toppling to the floor. He leaned over Wallace's desk, fury-forced words escaping through clenched teeth.

"You know I would never do anything to jeopardize Colton. I stayed with Bridget because Colton is my son. That's all there is to it."

"And Liv? She's got to be upset. She's been in Ireland with the Garda. Is it possible that she could have done this?" Wallace was pushing him, urging an explosion.

Blood pounded against Ridge's eardrums. He reached for calm that was just beyond his grasp. "No. Liv would never do this."

"How can you be so sure?"

"Because Liv is..." What could he say? Adept at breaking and entering? Hurt by the fact that Bridget was a part of his life? The target of an undercover operation? The woman he loved? There was no good answer. He retreated, distancing himself from Wallace. The captain gently closed the door to his office, lowering the blinds before turning back to Ridge.

"How long has Liv been your target?"

Ridge's fury morphed into some version of panic, hidden behind the stony façade of a well-trained special agent. A shiver climbed down his spine. How could Wallace know?

"Have a seat Detective...or should I say Special Agent, McCaffrey. It is McCaffrey, right?"

Ridge righted the overturned chair and lowered into it. There was no easy way out of this one. Someone at the crime scene must have recognized him.

"Why don't you start by telling me what you're doing in my department."

Ridge hesitated. He should continue the cover-up, that's what he was trained to do. But Wallace had a right to know the basics of why he was there. Besides, if this morning's explosion was any indication, someone in Cascade Hills already knew who he was.

"You get this from the crime scene this morning?" Ridge asked.

Wallace nodded. "Prompted me to do some checking. You can imagine my surprise when they told me my best detective wasn't a detective at all."

"Well, you can rest easy, Captain. It's not personal. I was assigned to your department because it offered a base for me to keep tabs on certain targets. The proximity of your unit gave me the means to carry out my assignment without raising unnecessary questions."

"What exactly is your assignment?"

Ridge fidgeted, flipping at the edges of papers that littered the Captain's desk.

"I'm here to protect a Bureau asset. That's all."

"And you had to infiltrate my department to do that?" Wallace's round face reddened.

"I'm sorry, Captain." Ridge meant it. He'd always liked Frank Wallace.

"I can't have you working cases that don't involve your target. Do you know how many prosecutions could be jeopardized if the public found out that you weren't a trained detective?"

"I'm a Special Agent for the FBI, Captain. A trained law enforcement officer. Nothing I've done here can come back on the department."

Wallace's jaw ticked as he stared at Ridge. "I need you to take a couple of days. We'll work to see who planted the IED, but you're off the Garrison case. It's too high-profile."

"Captain," Ridge started to refute.

"It's not up for discussion. Now get out of my precinct."

Ridge hesitated a beat before Wallace jerked his chin in the direction of the door. Ridge exited just as the front door of the station house swung open. Adam and Bridget came through first, followed by George and Skylar. His sister had Colton perched on her hip.

"You're okay?" Ridge asked Bridget. She nodded, a tight smile curling her glossed lips. She'd never enjoyed time with his family. Ridge was sure today was no exception. Adam gave Ridge a pat on the shoulder before disappearing toward the maze of desks.

Ridge swung Colton into his arms, holding him to his chest and inhaling the comforting scent of lavender baby shampoo. He felt the warmth of his father's hand on his shoulder. Assurance that everything would be okay. Ridge palmed the back of his son's head, holding him close, the desire to let go nonexistent. His heart skipped in his chest. Today could have ended so differently.

28

LIV

W hen the pressure of dreams and visions became too much, there was only one way I knew to cope. With a camera. Since I was a kid I'd been venturing off alone to find lost nooks and crannies to photograph. With every shutter click the world would fall away, and right now that was exactly what I needed.

Fall was my favorite time of year. The orange and red and gold of the landscape drew the artist in me out a little more than usual. The crisp air cooled my skin as I walked from one end of Sullivan Farm to the other, pausing to remind myself through the lens of my camera why I loved this piece of the world so much. Forgetting why my life was in shambles was a pleasant side effect.

The click of the shutter was cathartic. With each snap, reality receded, long enough to provide a momentary reprieve from the guilt of the Garrison case and the threat of the visions.

When Ridge found me late that afternoon, I was stretched out on my stomach along the rocks near the lake with my Nikon aimed at what must have looked like a ridiculous angle.

My subject was a maple that stood at the edge of the woods, twenty feet or so from the shoreline. The sunlight glittering through the branches made a perfect autumn study. I waited for a gentle breeze to rustle through the leaves, snapping in rapid succession until the foliage grew still again.

"You want to go for a walk?"

I'd been too lost in my own world to hear Ridge pull in the drive. I tucked my legs under me and indulged myself in a smile as I rose, letting my eyes wander over the man leaning against a willow just a few feet away. Ridge's jeans hung perfectly on his hips, hugging the muscles of his thighs in just the right places. His shirtsleeves, rolled up to the elbow, revealed a sprinkle of dark hair over muscular forearms.

His hands were shoved into his pockets, pushing his strong shoulders a little higher than normal. He almost looked shy standing there. A *Rebel Without a Cause* pose by an invincible man secretly afraid of rejection. As if I'd refuse his offer. As if *anyone* would refuse that offer.

He held out his hand to help me up, the warmth shocking against the coolness of my own. Energy nagged at me from his flesh. Dark pulses that I couldn't quite understand. Frustration? Fear?

"Your hands are freezing." He drew all ten of my digits together and sandwiched them between his own, the pulses doubling in strength. "Is this okay?"

I nodded, fighting the urge to pull away. Grasping at normalcy for once as he looked at me.

"Can you always sense it? Like right now, can you feel what I'm feeling?"

I shook my head, fighting against unwelcome tears that rushed to burn the backs of my eyes. "Not always. I'm usually pretty good at shielding myself." *Right now, I feel hurt, anger,* I wanted to say. *What happened today?*

"What's it like?" he asked.

I shrugged. I'd been asked this before, but it was difficult to explain. He let me off the hook. "Does it hurt?"

I swallowed, not wanting to answer. "Sometimes."

He just nodded and dropped my hands as we continued in silence, walking through the trees along the edge of Cascade Lake. I hooked my pinkie finger around his when the distance between us started to be too much. Normal couples held hands. Normal couples took walks in the woods. He glanced at our entwined fingers as I latched on, skimming his thumb across the back of my hand, a pulse of contentment.

We walked the same path I used to follow with my grandfather. There was a clearing on the other side of the woods and Grandpa would take me there, his cheery voice pointing out the different wildlife and vegetation along the way. A few times he'd even packed a picnic for us to enjoy when we reached our destination.

On more than one occasion we'd stayed until well after sunset, not venturing back to the house until Grandma's voice broke through the crickets' call. It was impossible to think that he'd been gone sixteen years. That seemed like a lifetime ago.

"I need to tell you something," Ridge broke through my memory.

"What is it?" The pulses from him deepened, growing more painful as the energy sparked into my skin.

"There was an explosion today. At Bridget's. She and Colton are okay, but they're homeless." Ridge hesitated. "I'm working on getting them set up in a hotel, but Colton asked if he could spend the night. Dad and Sky already headed home."

"I thought I saw them pull in an hour or so ago. I didn't realize they'd left already." It was easier to focus on George and Skylar than Bridget and Colton.

Ridge nodded. "I thought the four of us could have dinner.

See how it goes. Maybe it would be okay for them to stay the night, just until I can get them settled somewhere tomorrow."

My breath caught in my throat and I swallowed hard. "Of course."

I wanted to say, "No." I wanted to ask why it was up to him to get them settled. *These aren't random people,* my inner critic promptly chimed in. *This is his family.*

Ridge stopped walking and sighed, shoving his hands back into his pockets. Aggravation or frustration heated the air around him.

"It will be just one night, Liv. I promise. I thought maybe if you spent some time with them it would get easier."

For some reason, he still thought having a son was our biggest obstacle. We needed time alone–time to talk.

"I would like to meet Colton," I admitted.

Ridge smiled down at me as I lifted onto my tiptoes to cover his lips with mine. I pulled him toward me, a last-ditch effort to mask the fear churning in my chest. He finally reciprocated, removing his hands from his pockets and wrapping them around my midsection, intensifying the flurry of butterflies that took flight inside.

The crunch of tires on gravel cut into the moment. "Sounds like our company has arrived," I said, pulling away.

Ridge nodded and we started toward the house. Bridget was heaving a little blonde-haired boy from the back seat of her BMW as we rounded the tree line. She gave a short wave and set the boy on the grass. Within seconds he'd spotted Ridge and emitted a high-pitched squeal.

His tiny legs carried him far faster than I ever expected, and Ridge started toward him as Colton hollered, "Daddy!"

The simple word stopped me in my tracks. I watched as Ridge scooped Colton up and swung him around. The smile on his face reflected the pure joy Colton wore across his.

Ridge's face fell as he noticed me watching, driving a spike of guilt through me. I had no right to limit the happiness that little boy gave him. I only wished that I could make him as happy. So far, I was failing miserably.

I'd brought nothing but guilt and frustration to him since I'd been home. I wanted what we had last spring, and if I could bring myself to forget the scars I'd happily do so. So far, I hadn't figured out how to let it go, though. The emotional roller coaster I'd been on was too much for even me to understand.

My insides churned as I trudged toward the house, hanging back as the three of them gathered on the front porch, looking exactly like what they were—a family.

29

LIV

One look at Colton up close and I knew the paternity test had been unnecessary. The little boy had his father's electric blue eyes and the same angular jaw line, buffered only slightly by baby pudge. Wisps of honey blonde hair framed his face, certain to darken with time. I'd never seen a childhood picture of Ridge, but I had no doubt Colton was the spitting image.

We'd just finished pizza and I was sitting with Colton on the back porch glider, studying him while he showed me some of his new Hot Wheels. I grinned as he pulled his most recent addition out of the canvas bag of toys at our feet. He pointed out the spoiler on the black Shelby he held in his hand. I giggled. Like father, like son.

The evening crept by. Bridget flirted shamelessly with Ridge, and showed no concern over whether or not I was within earshot. Ridge didn't act on any of her flirtations, but he certainly didn't put an end to them either.

He'd been in the kitchen with her since dinner, engrossed in what looked to be a private conversation. My inner critic was in the midst of spouting some nonsense about being used as a glorified babysitter when Ridge started around the corner.

Just as he was about to join us on the porch, Bridget's thin ivory hand skimmed down his bicep, drawing his attention back to her in the kitchen. I shook the twinge of jealousy away, reminding myself that technically, Ridge and I were not a couple. Forcing my focus back to the little man next to me, oblivious to the tension rolling off me in waves, was my only saving grace.

"Here," Colton said. "You have this one." He slid off the edge of the glider, tucking a blue Corvette into my hand before rolling his black Shelby over the armrest of the patio glider, making *vroom* sounds as he played.

Moments later, Bridget stuck her head around the corner. "Come on Colton. Daddy says we can stay the night, but it's time to get ready for bed. Say good-night to Livvie." I hated the nickname when she said it, but when it came out of Colton's cherubic lips it sounded nothing short of precious.

"Okay, Mommy. 'Night Livvie. See you in the morning!" He reached up on his tiptoes and planted a wet kiss on my cheek. If this one turned out anything like his father, he was sure to be a lady-killer. Let's face it, in the span of just a few hours, he'd already managed to wrap me around his pudgy little pinkie finger.

Ridge sat on the glider next to me with an exhale. "So?"

"He's adorable. Just like his daddy."

Ridge's eyes glowed. "He is pretty great, huh?" He slid a hand across the top of my thigh as we sat side by side, exhaling deeply. "I could have lost him today, Liv."

I wrapped my fingers around his hand and waited for the flood of energy. Unadulterated fear mixed with ribbons of relief pulsed through him with every heartbeat. I pulled his hand to my lips and kissed.

"He's still here," I reassured. Sucking gently on the tip of his index finger before pulling away with a kiss. "And so am I, if you still want me. I'm sorry for the way I've acted, Ridge."

He put a hand up to stop me, but I went on. I needed to get this off my chest.

"I'm just not sure what this is, who I am anymore. So much has happened in the past six months to change me, but it's so easy to fall back into old patterns."

"You're still the same Liv Sullivan I fell in love with." Ridge pushed a few curls off my shoulder, exposing my neck to his lips. The tension that wound my insides into tight coils began melting away. I closed my eyes as his kisses lingered, venturing my own hand onto the bare skin of his arm. Quick footsteps from the kitchen forced the anxiety to return.

"Ridge?" Bridget's porcelain face appeared in the doorway. "I don't mean to interrupt, but Colton wants nothing to do with the bedroom upstairs. He wants to sleep downstairs, with Daddy."

Bridget's eyes met mine, and I could have sworn there was a smirk on those perfectly glossed lips of hers. Way to kill a mood. Ridge sighed lightly and patted me on the leg. I watched as the two of them retreated through the kitchen door.

I could hear Ridge talking to Colton in the living room, trying to persuade him to sleep upstairs rather than on the living room couch. Eventually Colton's will, and odd fascination with the fireplace, won out and the room became quiet.

I finished tidying up the kitchen, giving it a more thorough cleaning than I could remember since returning to the farm. It was an unnecessary but effective method of distraction. And by the time I headed through the living room to go to bed, Ridge and Colton were snuggled together on the couch, asleep.

The moon's glow through the big bay window shed a silvery light across their faces and I stopped to pick up my camera off the end table and snap a picture, without the flash of course. Replacing the Nikon, I grabbed my grandmother's quilt from the nearby chair and covered the two of them, letting my hand drift over Ridge's jawline and into his hair before pulling away.

"This must be hard for you." I nearly jumped at the voice. Bridget was sitting on the stairs just above the landing. Hidden in the shadows, I never would have seen her if she hadn't spoken. "How long have you known?"

I walked up the first few stairs, unsure whether or not I was ready to admit that the bombshell had only been dropped a few days ago.

"About Colton? Less than a week," I admitted, settling on the step next to her. We sat in silence for a while before I got up the nerve to ask more. "Why did you wait so long? To tell Ridge, I mean."

Bridget let out an airy laugh. "I guess I just wasn't ready yet. It never occurred to me that there might be a statute of limitations."

I gave Bridget a quizzical look, unsure what she meant. She caught my gaze and looked away.

"I came back to Cascade Hills hoping for a fresh start. I never really thought he'd say no."

I could have sworn a look of true regret passed over Bridget's complexion as she made that admission, but in the shadows it was hard to tell.

"Why didn't you just hang around four years ago? Ridge obviously said yes back then."

That breathy laugh came again. "I've never been very good at relationships, Liv. At the time, I wanted a child, not a husband."

"So, this wasn't–" *an accident?* I wanted to say, but I didn't. Instead I let the question remain unspoken.

"Come on, Liv. Look at him. Who wouldn't want those genes in their offspring?"

"Did Ridge know you were trying to get pregnant?"

I felt Bridget's eyes on me.

"Of course not. I told him I was on the pill. He still thinks it was an accident." She made little finger quotes in the air between us when she said the word, accident. "Guess that makes me a horrible person, right?"

"Not horrible, just dishonest." The words slipped out before I could censor them and I immediately regretted the retort. "I'm going to head to bed. Is there anything you need before I go?"

Bridget gave her head a little shake and I continued up the steps, wondering if she was going to watch Ridge and Colton all night long.

"Liv?"

I turned to face her.

"Do you really dream about dead people?"

I stared through the darkness at her, shock halting my ability to speak.

Bridget shrugged. "What kind of things do you see?"

She never turned to look at me, her thunderstorm eyes planted on Ridge and Colton. When I gained enough wherewithal to speak, the thoughts that came to me were grossly inappropriate.

I owed this woman nothing. The fact that Ridge had divulged my darkest secret to a woman I loathed slashed me as deeply as Lyle's knife so many months ago. In fact, I realized, if I had the choice, I'd take physical pain over emotional any day of the week and twice on Sundays.

"I see death," I said flatly before scurrying away, tucking myself in the loneliness of my bedroom.

I sank to the ground with my back against the four-panel mahogany, trying desperately to understand Ridge's motivations. He hadn't told Adam, but he thought it was okay to tell Bridget? What did that say?

I felt a clutch of envy for Bridget, her ability to live a regular life in Cascade Hills, to be connected to Ridge by a beautiful little boy. I shook it away. I'd put up with enough whispers and stares over the course of my life, I didn't want any more. If I was going to change the trajectory of my life, I had to stop acting like the freak that I was. The shadows that haunted me needed to stay there–in the shadows.

30

RIDGE

"I want you to stay away from her." Ridge said from the doorway of the apartment Adam had helped line up for Bridget and Colton. It would offer a better setup than the temporary feel of a hotel and it was in his partner's complex. They'd be safe here, at least until the repairs on the house could be completed.

Bridget smiled, looking up at him through long eyelashes. She glanced over her shoulder toward the living room where Colton was playing before moving closer to Ridge, tugging at the lapels of his jacket.

"I didn't mean to upset her."

"She's got enough on her mind right now. I don't need you messing with her emotions."

Bridget slid her arms around Ridge's neck, her lips inches from his. Her scent, something floral mixed with a hint of vanilla penetrated his senses. He exhaled and pushed her away. Wishing, not for the first time, that he'd never fallen for the raven-haired beauty. Let alone married, divorced, and fathered a child with her.

Bridget took a step back, leaning against the Formica countertop.

"It's weird, don't you think?" When Ridge didn't answer, she pressed on. "Weird that she sees dead people? It's almost like she has some kind of mental illness."

"I'll admit I don't understand it, but she's far from crazy."

"I'm just saying that I'm not sure I'm entirely comfortable with her being around Colton."

Ridge stared at the woman he'd once loved. The woman who was now laying a foundation to withhold visitation if he didn't cut Liv out of his life. He'd be damned if he'd let Bridget take anything else from him.

"She'd make a better mother than you ever will. Don't screw with me, Bridget."

He slammed the door as hard as he dared with Colton just a room away. It may have taken eight years, but he was sick of her games. He suspected she'd been trying to get pregnant the night Colton was conceived. He wasn't clear on why, and through the fog of alcohol hadn't much cared, frankly. But he'd known. And he was confident drugs were still a go-to recreational activity for her. He couldn't prove it yet, but he had more than enough ammunition to fight back if she ever decided to try to keep Colton from him.

RIDGE HAD JUST MADE it to his Shelby when his phone buzzed from his jacket pocket. Megan Foster's voice filtered from the handset.

"Detective, I've got some more information about your Jane Doe."

"What is it?" Ridge asked. He was anxious to get back to the farm, back to the conversation he'd been putting off since picking Liv up at the airport. The one he might as well have now that there were hairline cracks in his cover. Liv deserved to know who he really was.

"I think it's something you'll need to see for yourself. Can you come down?" Megan's voice wavered to a higher pitch. Worry.

Ridge glanced at the clock on his dashboard, it was already after five. Liv probably thought he wasn't coming back.

"It won't take long," the M.E. assured.

"Give me ten minutes." Ridge hung up the phone and pulled out of the parking lot, heading back toward Foster's Mortuary and that odd smelling office.

He rang the buzzer outside the entrance twice but got no response. He heard shuffling inside, but the entryway loomed dark. He was about to call her when the door cracked open, just wide enough for Megan's face to appear. Her look of wide-eyed terror was enough to force him to pull his gun just as the door swung wide. Two men jumped at him from either side, jerking him inside and shoving the door closed. They twisted the .45 out of his grip and slammed him to the floor.

It took a moment for his eyes to adjust to the semi-darkness. He could hear Megan whimper as a man in black clutched a hand over her mouth, silencing any intended scream.

"Well, well, well...if it isn't Special Agent Ridge McCaffrey in the flesh." A gravelly voice from the rear of the room pulled Ridge's attention from Megan. "You can imagine my surprise when Miss Foster here claimed that a Detective McCaffrey was working a very interesting case for the Cascade Hills Police Department. I didn't believe her of course. Lucky for her you showed up."

"What are you doing here, O'Malley?" Ridge swallowed as he recognized his former roommate.

"One could ask you the same thing."

Ridge struggled upright, squinting to make out details of the three men in the room. Each was dressed in black from head to toe, black suits with black shirts underneath. The low light gave them a ghostly appearance, shadows morphing on their faces so that nothing was identifiable.

"Let me guess." The stainless barrel of O'Malley's Ruger caught a ray of light from the hallway beyond Megan's office as he waved it between them. "You've got an asset in Cascade Hills."

Ridge stayed silent, pulling himself up to a standing position.

"I'll take that as a yes."

"Let the M.E. go, Cam. She's got nothing to do with this." Ridge raised both hands in a signal of surrender. O'Malley trained with Ridge at Quantico. They'd both been angling for a job with Counterintelligence when Cam was arrested, pushing him out of the top spot in their training class. Ridge never knew where he'd gone after being dismissed. But in the last few years his name had come up more than once in Bureau briefings.

"Let her go and then we can talk."

"You're right, McCaffrey. She's just in the wrong place at the wrong time. But thanks to you, I learned early on, there's no room for witnesses."

O'Malley nodded to the man holding Megan. The suppressed gunshot punctuated O'Malley's words, echoing in Ridge's ears. He didn't need to look to know Megan was dead, slumped over in a growing puddle of blood at the feet of thug number two.

"Jesus, Cam. You don't have yourself in enough trouble?"

O'Malley took a seat on the other side of Megan's desk, propping his feet on the corner and leaning back. No matter what Ridge did here, it wasn't going to end well.

198 | ALICIA ANTHONY

"Sometimes one has to make sacrifices to get ahead in life. Don't you agree?"

"Not when it comes to taking a life," Ridge said through clenched teeth.

O'Malley motioned his goons closer to Ridge. They pressed in on either side, scenting the stale air with body odor and musky cologne.

"No, of course not," O'Malley said. "But what you did was equally as destructive. You may not have taken my life, but you ruined it, McCaffrey."

Ridge stayed silent. When he'd called the cops after the accident almost a decade ago, he had no idea Cam was behind the wheel of the other car. And he had even less knowledge of the drugs his training buddy had stashed in his trunk. Ridge shook his head. This wasn't the time or place to rehash old wrongs with O'Malley. Not with Megan Foster dead on the floor and Jessica Garrison laying unidentifiable in the room beyond.

"That's in the past, Cam. Why kill Garrison?" Ridge pressed on.

"Ah, nice..." O'Malley started, "I'm impressed."

"The gouge on the hip was a giveaway, Cam. I know she was one of ours, and I know she was drugged. The question is, with what?"

A row of crooked teeth appeared as O'Malley pulled his lips back into a smile. "Give us a minute, will you gentlemen?"

The two thugs retreated through the door leading to the morgue's examination room. Ridge watched as it swung closed behind them, the shadow of their shoes blacking out the slice of light from beyond.

"What do you want, O'Malley?"

Cam pulled his feet off their perch on the desk and leaned

over to flip on the lamp. The glow through the green glass shade illuminated his dark features. He still looked the same. Dark eyes, almost black, sunk in a lightly tanned complexion. Heavy brows gave him a menacing look, even when he smiled.

"What makes you so sure I'm the bad guy here, Ridge?"

Ridge leaned forward, placing his hands on the desk between them. "Dead assets, O'Malley. The Bureau knows you're targeting them."

Cam leaned back in his chair, cocking his head to the side as he studied Ridge. "We have history, McCaffrey, you and me. And I'll be the first to admit I haven't always played by the rules. But what reason would I have to kill Bureau assets?"

Cam waited for a response, but Ridge had none. Motive was one piece of the puzzle he'd yet to place.

"I've got no beef with any of them, including Garrison. But I know who does. And they like my work."

"Your mutilation?"

Cam smiled. "Think bigger, Ridge. There have been two main problems in the GenLink program since its inception—resources and efficacy. If the Bureau could resolve those issues, don't you think they would?"

Ridge knew they would. The program had been on the brink of collapse for the last several years. With every asset they lost, it came closer to ruin.

Cam rose and rounded Megan's desk. Standing toe to toe with Ridge, he continued. "Garrison's death was an unfortunate accident. But we learned a lot from it. She even had information that turned out to be very helpful."

Ridge tensed, swallowing a knot of anger. Shadows of the goons' shoes shifted beneath the door a few feet away.

"I always wondered what would motivate a by-the-book man like yourself to send a Bureau asset off-grid."

O'Malley's smile taunted Ridge as he spoke. "My first thought was Bureau command. But, then I did some digging. Didn't take long to discover there was more to your relationship with Olivia Sullivan than protection detail."

Ridge reached for Cam, the office door swinging open as he did. Thug number one gripped Ridge's arm, jerking backward and pulling him from O'Malley while shoving the muzzle of his gun firmly between Ridge's shoulder blades. Pain tore through Ridge's shoulder.

O'Malley put his hand up, signaling that all was well to the muscle in the room. Ridge shrugged out of the thug's grip.

"But you've had some complications of your own, right? Your little safety net in Ireland falling through, for one. Not to mention the fact that you're a family man now."

"It was you. In Ireland." Ridge's pulse throbbed in his eardrums. His face grew hot as the realization took hold. "And the IED?"

"I needed to get your attention."

Memories of the last time Ridge had seen Cam O'Malley exploded through his skull. It was bad enough this man had infiltrated the operation. But he was the sole reason the Bureau had pulled Ridge from Cascade Hills, leaving Liv to fend for herself against Lyle Hunt. O'Malley was working against the Bureau then and it took some time after Liv's indictment for the brass to prove Liv wasn't on his payroll.

"You've got it. What is it you want?"

"Well, first, let me put your mind at ease when I say that your ex-wife and son hold no interest for me. However, Olivia Sullivan is a different matter."

"I'll never let you near her."

Cam pretended not to hear the defiance in Ridge's voice.

"Come on, Ridge. You've known the op was on the way

out. Why else would you refuse to have your asset microchipped? Grace Sullivan had a good idea, but it was flawed. Genetics takes too long. The Bureau needs something more efficient. Something they can control."

"And they've chosen *you* to provide it?"

Cam glanced down at the Ruger, suspended as an extension of O'Malley's hand. His voice grew unsettlingly calm, menacing. "You've only seen what they want you to see, Ridge. Olivia is the final connection. The Bureau can't sustain this program. And right now, she's in their way."

"If they want to end the program, they can. Liv could go on to live a normal life."

"Ridge, you're naïve to think the feds would let that happen. She knows too much. Just like her mother before her. And Jessica Garrison after that. We may all have different motives but one of us will take her from you. You can't protect her forever."

Ridge cursed and lunged for Cam, the jolt to his ribcage immediate. He rolled to his side, pain searing through his torso as he reached for the leg of thug one, sending him crashing to the floor. Thug number two stood over him, waiting for his boss's okay to slam the butt of his gun into Ridge's skull. Ridge struggled to all fours, the metallic taste of blood working its way into the back of his throat.

"I thought that might be your first response." Cam held his men at bay as he kneeled on level with Ridge. "You've got forty-eight hours, Ridge. Think about it. I need an insurance policy to get the Bureau's attention. Give up Olivia and I'll leave the rest of your family in peace. She won't get hurt. I give you my word. I'm giving you the chance to do the right thing."

"Never," Ridge managed as he dove forward into Cam. Pain ricocheted through his skull. He fought the encroaching blackness, trying to maintain focus on the spinning room around him.

Cam's voice hummed, dancing in his consciousness, "You're either on the right side or the wrong side, Ridge. I gave you a chance. You chose wrong."

31

LIV

The first knock on the farmhouse door came around midnight. I'd been waiting up for Ridge after calling his cell phone no less than three times over the course of the evening, all with no answer. Brian and Adam hadn't heard from him either, so I was left to wait, and worry. As I walked from the den into the living room, I could see bits of the person standing outside. Swaths of charcoal gray morphed into jagged prisms behind the leaded glass panels of the front door.

My breath caught in my throat as I flipped on the front porch light. I swung the door inward, my heart somersaulting in my chest. A surge of adrenalin forced my hand to the doorframe, steading myself against spots of blackness that threatened my sight. I focused on my breath, pushing the darkness away with each exchange of oxygen.

The man standing on my front porch was an officer I'd never met. He faced me with his hat tucked neatly between his elbow and side, his face emotionless.

"Olivia Sullivan?"

All I could do was nod. I worked to process any good reasons why an unknown cop would be standing at my door in the middle of the night. As hard as I tried, the only scenarios I came up with involved tragedy.

"Good evening, Ma'am." He nodded, a hint of Southern gentleman filtering through a light drawl. "I'm sorry to wake you. I've been asked to inform you of an accident."

The harder I tried to coach my lungs, the more they refused function, a lump of uncertainty constricting my throat.

"Accident?" I repeated hoarsely.

He nodded, not meeting my gaze. "Detective McCaffrey, Ma'am. He's been injured and transported to Cascade Hills Memorial. I can give you a ride to the hospital, if you like."

His eyes bounced from my face into the darkened room behind me as he slid the rim of his hat anxiously through tight fingers.

Injured. The officer's words echoed in my skull. Not, killed–injured. I could deal with this. My breathing began to return to normal as I withdrew my eyes from his nervous twitch and accepted the offer. Grabbing my jacket and purse from the nearby coat rack, I followed him to the waiting cruiser.

We rode in silence for a while before the stillness became too much. My mind desperate for a distraction.

"I'm sorry. I don't think we've met." I surveyed the man sitting next to me. He was young, maybe twenty-two, with blonde hair cropped close to his scalp in a military-style cut. He was thin and lanky, solid, but lacking the muscle tone that Ridge possessed.

"Officer White, Ma'am. Ashton White."

"You can call me Liv," I responded.

He gave a short nod, his eyes drifting to the rear-view mirror as he pulled off Sullivan Road.

"So, you work with Ridge?" I asked. Small talk. Anything to

replace the possibilities roaring through my brain like a freight train.

He glanced at me then, as if he wasn't sure how much information he should provide.

"Yes, Ma'am." His voice lowered, softening from business to personal. "Liv, I mean. This is actually my first month on the job."

"Well, it's nice to meet you Ashton." I paused, gauging the sense in asking my next question, knowing he'd probably been given explicit instructions not to provide too much information.

"Is Ridge okay?" It came out as a whisper and I wasn't sure Ashton even heard me over the noise of the road.

"I'm really not at liberty to say." All business again.

I nodded and turned toward the window, watching the darkened landscape flash by.

"He talks about you." Ashton's voice broke through my thoughts. "You just got back from a trip to Ireland, right?"

I turned toward him and nodded. Knowing Ridge had talked about my trip, to a rookie even, made an ache grow in my chest.

"Detective McCaffrey is a great guy. I've learned a lot from him already."

I didn't have a response for Ashton's kind comment. And the words hung between us as we pulled into the hospital parking lot. He drove the cruiser up to the emergency department doors and came around to the passenger side to let me out. He pointed toward the double glass entryway where a hospital security officer stood guard.

The guard nodded to Officer White as the two of us passed through the automatic doors. The security presence inside the hospital was intimidating. There seemed to be a uniformed or plain-clothes officer posted at every corner. Many of them were strangers to me, and I guessed they must have been from precincts other than Cascade Hills.

"I'm here to see Ridge McCaffrey." My voice sounded deceivingly strong as I addressed the weary looking woman at the information desk.

"No visitors are allowed for that patient." Her eyes skimmed me then returned to the paperwork in front of her. I looked down. No wonder she was giving me the once over. I'd paired a ratty Cascade Hills High sweatshirt that should have been retired a decade ago with well-worn yoga pants. I wasn't exactly dressed for company. Although, it seemed likely she'd seen worse in the middle of the night.

I felt Ashton come up from behind to address the receptionist. "This is Olivia Sullivan. She's on the list."

"Then I'll need to see some proof of that." Irritation dripped from the woman's words as she looked me up and down again, as if I couldn't possibly be who I said I was.

My hands shook as I struggled through my purse to provide positive identification. It was Ashton who finally stepped in, taking over when my shaking fingers proved incapable of wrangling my wallet from the confines of the virtual black hole. After checking my license, the tired woman buzzed me through the double doorway.

"Room 116," she tossed over her shoulder as I hurried through, leaving Ashton standing in the lobby.

Two officers sat on chairs outside of room 116. Voices penetrated the hall from inside and I recognized one of them as Captain Wallace. I slowed my approach.

"Olivia Sullivan?" the taller one asked.

I nodded as his eyes scanned me, coming to rest on my jacket.

"I'll need you to remove your jacket."

I did as the officer asked and when he was satisfied, he jutted his chin toward the door. "Go ahead."

My heart thumped a marathon rhythm in my chest. The antiseptic scent of the hospital room attacked my nostrils, mingling with another smell, one I couldn't place, but something metallic and coppery. The second odor nagged at me, and my chest constricted against the scent, making breath difficult. If I didn't get some kind of information about Ridge's condition, there was a distinct possibility I'd lose my grasp on consciousness.

"Liv." Captain Wallace walked away from what looked to be a nurse standing at the bedside. "I'm sorry you had to hear about this from a stranger. I'm glad you're here."

A powder blue curtain was pulled along the side of the hospital bed so that only the last few inches of the mattress was visible. A thin mint green coverlet tented over what I assumed were Ridge's feet. I felt Captain Wallace's hand on my shoulder before he continued.

"He's going to be okay, Liv. He's beat up pretty good. A concussion, some lacerations, dislocated shoulder, and some broken ribs."

Captain Wallace's grey-blue eyes met mine. He seemed to be waiting for me to say something.

"Can I see him?"

"Why don't you wait a few minutes, Liv. The nurse is checking his bandages and—"

I didn't wait for the captain to finish. I broke free of his grasp on my shoulder and forced the jelly-like muscles in my legs to carry me around to the side of the bed the nurse was occupying.

She glanced over at me and offered a small smile, even stopping her work to pull a chair to the bedside for me. I eased myself onto the seat, unable to trust the stability of my legs. I reached my hand toward Ridge's, gently stroking his knuckles.

He was shirtless, dark red bruises spread over his midsection, and an IV stuck out of his left forearm. The beeping EKG machine relaxed my own throbbing heartbeat as I forced myself to breathe with its rhythmic pulse.

A black sling wrapped over his shoulder held his left arm stationary against his torso. I followed the nurse's gaze to his cheek, where she was treating a newly stitched gash above his left eye. His ocean eyes were closed, and the entire side of Ridge's head, from cheek to hairline was a deep shade of purple.

As she covered the wound with a bandage she hummed. Her voice melodic, exactly what I expected from someone with such a friendly face. The melody soothed some tension away.

"I'll be in every hour or so to check on the patient and redress when necessary. If you have any questions or concerns, you can get one of us by hitting that button right there."

The nurse pointed to the call button on a remote control lying next to Ridge.

"We gave him something to relax him and help with the pain while we relocated his shoulder. With the concussion it's important he not get too agitated. But he'll be coming around shortly."

"Thank you," I said as the nurse slipped silently from the room. I could feel Captain Wallace's eyes on me from the doorway.

"What happened, Captain?"

"We're not sure. The 911 call came from his cell, but it was just an open line. He was found in the M.E.'s office with Dr. Foster. It looks like a burglary. Dr. Foster didn't make it."

I swallowed the news of Megan Foster's death as Captain

Wallace nodded toward the door. "I'll be just outside if you need me."

I kept my hands on Ridge's flesh. His energy was subtle, but it was there. Gentle pulses morphed into flashes of light inside my brain. Images, glimmers of memories that weren't my own. I jerked my hand away, shocked by the pictures flooding my thoughts.

Haltingly, I pressed my fingers against Ridge's skin once more. Pictorial flares flickered through my mind like an old shadowy film. A woman's wide, terror stricken eyes, then darkness. A gunshot resulting in the shadowy figure of a woman's slumped body. A menacing smile from a darkened face. Then light. Dark eyes. Anger.

The eyes I knew. Somehow familiar, I wracked my brain for understanding. It was all I could do to keep the connection as a flash of light erupted in my skull followed by searing pain. The images stopped after that, leaving me with the peaceful, gentle pulses I'd started with.

I focused on the rhythm of his energy, and before long, Ridge's eyelids fluttered, opening just a crack before closing again. The muscles in his face contracted in what I imagined was an expression of pain. His hand turned beneath my own, palm up as he laced his fingers through mine.

"Ridge? It's just me. I'm here."

His eyes remained closed, but his tongue gently wetted his lips before he struggled to say my name.

"It's okay, you don't have to say anything." With that, his lids opened, the intensity catching me off guard. I couldn't understand how even after all this time, his eyes still had that effect on me. His gaze drifted behind me before I felt Adam's hand on my shoulder.

32

LIV

I huddled at a corner table in the hospital cafeteria. My phone still illuminated from the call I'd made to Skylar. I never wanted to have to make a call like that again. If they managed to hit the road by daybreak, that would put them in Cascade Hills by early afternoon at the latest. I had a feeling they'd make it well before then.

The room was empty except for Adam, who sidestepped along the food counter, pulling items onto the plastic tray in front of him. I wanted to be back upstairs with Ridge. He'd regained some clarity before a small pack of suited men and women descended to ask him questions.

"They didn't have a lot to choose from," Adam said as he returned from the food court, sliding a plate in front of me. I picked at what he'd chosen. What the food services staff at the hospital referred to as Stromboli, was really just crescent roll dough stretched and stuffed with pepperoni and mozzarella. Not the most appetizing dish in the first place, even less so at three o'clock in the morning when it had been sitting under a warmer for God knows how long.

"Bet you didn't think you'd be spending the night here." Adam dove into the doughy concoction on his own plate as my stomach churned. I tapped a drinking straw out of its wrapper and slid it into the Diet Coke Adam had delivered.

"No, I didn't," I said, taking a sip. "But this is better than the alternative."

Adam's hand reached out for mine. I did my best to stay out of reach without seeming too obvious. I tucked my napkin around my fingers, using it as a shield.

"It's okay, Liv. Ridge will be back to his old self in no time."

"Do you know who did this, Adam?" The image of dark angry eyes nagged at me.

"We're working on it, Liv. We've got officers on the ground right now trying to find out. Captain called in the feds on this one."

I picked up my fork and silently chewed a piece of the tasteless creation in front of me. "This has to do with the Garrison case, doesn't it?"

Adam put down his fork, clearing his palate before answering. "You know I can't tell you that." He hesitated, surveying my reaction before lowering his voice. "I don't want to say anything that could jeopardize the investigation, Liv. You understand that, right?"

I nodded. A ribbon of guilt wound through my stomach and squeezed. He was right. This wasn't Ireland. I was an outsider whose meddling would only cause problems if this case ever went to trial.

I pushed the ice around in my cup with the straw, trying not to dwell on the fact that I wasn't the only one who'd almost lost someone they loved. Ridge was like a brother to Adam, and professionally I knew he had every intention of righting the wrong that sent Ridge to the ICU. My interference would only make his job more difficult. We ate the rest of our meal in

212 | ALICIA ANTHONY

silence. A few early risers began trickling in by the time Adam cleared his tray.

"Why did Ridge want me back in Cascade Hills, Adam. And don't tell me because of the Garrison case. He doesn't want my help. That seems clear."

Adam leaned back in his chair and sighed. "I know you feel caught in the middle of this, Liv. Ridge had no business using Garrison to get you back here. But you have to understand. He would've done anything to get you home."

"Why now? Why not six months ago?"

"That's a question you're going to have to take up with Ridge. Besides, with or without you, this case is turning out to be one dead end after another."

"I could help, Adam."

Adam pushed the tray to the side and leaned toward me, his voice a quiet threat. "How? Three names in a tattered old Bible? Sorry, but I don't think that's going to cut it." Adam cursed under his breath. "I saw how you eyed Garrison's place. You think you can make a difference, Liv, but you have no idea what you're up against."

"Then fill me in," I said. Pushing my own plate away, I leaned forward, matching Adam's tone. "I'm sick of the lies, Adam. For once I'd like someone to give me the truth. I think I've earned that much."

"Liv—" Adam put his hand up to stop me, but the dam had broken. Every frustration I had since coming back to Cascade Hills poured forth.

"You think I don't know Ridge is keeping secrets? He used the Garrison case to get me back here, but every time I bring it up he gives me just enough to scratch the surface and changes the subject. He may not want me to connect the dots, but I'm a hell of a lot more perceptive than he's giving me credit for, Adam."

Adam's eyes shifted around the empty cafeteria. "No one doubts your skill, Liv. But bringing you in puts you at risk. Ridge can take care of himself, but neither one of us wants to see you get hurt." Adam hesitated. "Not again."

I pushed against the memory of Lyle's attack, Adam had set up the surveillance that cleared my name. And he'd pulled the madman off me when the wire went quiet, kept him down until backup arrived. I owed him.

"I know the body in the M.E.'s office is Garrison's." That got Adam's attention. "I know she never worked for any pharmaceutical company. And I know she wanted out. She trusted them, Adam, but it was too late. She knew too much."

I tried to read Adam's expression as he piled all our trash in the middle of the plastic tray. His face was drawn, emotionless.

"Have you told Ridge all this?" he asked.

I fought the threat of tears before admitting I hadn't.

"You should keep it that way," Adam said. "Ridge needs time away from this case, time to heal. At least give him that."

Adam left the table, dropping our trash in a nearby receptacle as he strode away. He was right. Ridge needed time. I just wasn't sure time was something I had a lot of right now. I dropped my head into my hands as the automatic doors slid closed behind Adam.

THE NURSE WAS in Ridge's room when I returned. Her lips turned up into a knowing smile when she saw me.

"He was asking for you after the investigators left. I told him you'd just stepped out for a bite to eat."

"I'm sorry," I whispered, more for Ridge than the nurse.

"He fought sleep for a few minutes, but the pain meds won in the end." Her words ended in a jolly chuckle.

The bruising on Ridge's sleeping form was as angry-looking as ever, but his lips relaxed into a perfect bow. Stubble had taken over his jawline and his long eyelashes tipped up over closed eyes. He looked younger than his thirty years and I couldn't help but wonder if we'd ever be in a place where worry didn't crease his brow.

The nurse studied me, and I cleared my throat, blinking to keep the tears at bay.

"The bench by the window doesn't make a bad bed. And it may not look like it, but the chair's remarkably comfortable." She headed for the door. "You let me know if you need anything, dear."

I thanked her, settling into the chair at Ridge's bedside. It was heavily padded, with a high back, designed for visitors to catch a nap when necessary. I fought to keep my eyes open in case Ridge woke again, scolding myself for being gone when he was asking for me. I vowed, as my eyelids lost the battle with exhaustion, never to let that happen again.

A MUTED GROAN of pain woke me. I sensed movement on the mattress, but sleepiness wasn't giving up easily. Ridge exhaled my name. His voice dug into my consciousness, pulling me back into reality. Ridge struggled to sit.

"Stay still." I reached forward and slid my hand down his forearm, clearing the sleep from my throat and pulling away just before the first jab of memory could invade.

He lay back on the mattress and closed his eyes, chest heaving from exertion and pain. I found the adjustment remote in the covers and edged the head of the bed up slowly. Ridge's jaw ticked as he struggled for comfort. Satisfied, he opened his eyes on me.

"I called your dad and Skylar. They should be here later today." Ridge closed his eyes again and nodded. His breath jagged.

"Do you want me to get the nurse?" At that, the crease between his brows formed and he shook his head.

"Are you okay?" He asked, staring at me. It was an honest question. An odd one, I thought, considering the circumstances, but honest just the same.

I smiled. "Of course I'm okay." He reached his hand over to my arm, thankfully covered by my sweatshirt. The soothing heat of his hand replaced the flashes of memory that rattled around in my mind. He closed his eyes and relaxed his head onto the pillow.

We sat in silence. Ridge's breathing leveled out and grew deeper, signaling the return of sleep. He was still asleep when George and Skylar arrived about thirty minutes before noon. Both wore looks of shocked panic as they pressed through the door of Ridge's hospital room.

The commotion of their arrival was enough to wake Ridge, and I vacated my chair so that George and Skylar could talk to him and calm their own frayed nerves. The nurse found me in the lounge a while later to let me know they'd be releasing Ridge later that afternoon.

I took Skylar's car back to the farm to pick up some supplies for Ridge. The clothes he'd been wearing the day before had been confiscated by the department as part of the investigation, so he needed something to wear home from the hospital.

The time in the car gave me a few moments to breathe, to try to piece together what had happened in the span of the last 48 hours. Something wasn't right. I could feel it. And no matter how I tried to shake the tumble of fear that took root in my belly, it wasn't releasing its grip without a fight.

I parked Skylar's Cavalier beside my Mustang and headed

toward the front porch, pulling my keys from my pocket. I'd made it to the first step before I felt it, a cool breeze just over my left shoulder, lifting the tiny hairs at the nape of my neck. I'd felt the same breeze just once before–at St. Mary's.

I glanced around the yard. From the lake to the porch, nothing looked out of place. I listened for footsteps but heard only the gentle rustle of leaves in nearby trees, accompanied by late season birds calling to each other. My eyes were still raking over the property when I put the key in the lock of the front door.

I'd opened the door a crack when an unexpected flash of light assaulted me. Images of Grandma and Grandpa Sullivan smiling and laughing as they entered and left through the mahogany door were clear in my subconscious. The buffer I'd spent months working to perfect, was beyond my reach.

I heard my own jagged breath as happy images faded to sad. Grandpa's death. Grandma's illness. This wasn't supposed to happen. I was fully conscious. I hadn't opened myself up, hadn't asked for it. Why couldn't I block it? *Herman, why is this happening?* There was no one here to ask.

Sun shone through the front window of the house. I swallowed a knot of fear and took the stairs two at a time to the second floor, my room, to the dresser where Ridge stashed clothes when he stayed overnight.

I tugged the well-worn drawer pulls as fast as possible, trying not to give the metal time to collide with heightened receptors. I puffed a breath of relief as the drawer opened to reveal three neat stacks: jeans, t-shirts, and button-downs.

Digging to the bottom of the drawer, I grabbed a pair of jeans, moving on to the pile of shirts. But when I reached in to grab the shirt, something cold and hard brushed against my fingertips.

I pulled the leather-bound notebook from the drawer as

another flash of light erupted in my skull, forcing me backward like a jolt of electricity. Even after I'd dropped the notebook, the image of Ridge hung on, emblazoned in my memory.

I moved forward on all fours, sitting cross-legged on the hardwood floor as I reached for the dropped journal. It was small, four by six inches at most. I tucked my hands inside my sweatshirt to protect myself from the energy that pulsed from the leather. As I opened it, I saw Ridge's handwriting, all angles and hard stops.

I skimmed page after page. What started as notes outlining my grandmother's daily habits shifted to records of conversations she'd had with Ridge. Written in a shorthand I couldn't fully understand, I worked to decode what it meant. As the dated pages progressed, those notations grew shorter, coinciding with the admittance of my grandmother to the nursing home and eventually, her death.

A dark line, hard pressed into the thin pages signified a change in topic, and recognizable words: Olivia Grace Sullivan, Asset #32, GenLink. After that, dates were about the only understandable scratches on the page. I flipped to the last page and read the date. Exactly one week before I saw Ridge for the last time. Before he disappeared and left me to face the man hell-bent on taking my grandmother's inheritance for himself.

Rising tears hiccupped through jagged breath. The pressure of half-truths, the proof of betrayal, and a glut of information I couldn't comprehend was almost too much to bear. I shoved the notebook back into the bottom drawer and left the room, leaving Ridge's clothes behind. I raced down the stairs as fast as my feet would carry me, slamming the front door of the farmhouse so hard the entire porch shook.

I drove away from that place as if ghosts were chasing me. And in a sense, I guess they were. I couldn't make sense of what I'd seen. An image of Ridge being passed paperwork, my photograph, along with my birthmother's, secured to pages within the file. Proof of conversations Ridge had with my grandmother that centered around me. GenLink scrawled under my own name. I'd heard the name once before, as a whisper when I lost contact with reality in Jessica Garrison's apartment, but I'd had no context for it. Is that what she'd been trying to outrun?

Desperate, I pulled my phone from my pocket and dialed the one person who could help me make sense of what was happening, but more importantly, help me get it under control.

As soon as the line clicked open, the words rushed out. "Herman, it's Liv. I'm sorry to call at this hour, but I need your help."

"Herman has no interest in helping any more of your kind." The voice from the other end of the line dripped with hatred.

"Rose?"

"It wasn't bad enough that your mother ruined everything we had, you had to come and finish the job." A choked sob filtered through the headset. "Stay out of our lives, Olivia."

"Rose, please, is Herman okay?"

The line clicked dead. My heart thumped like a kick drum against my sternum. And panic rose from within, sending pinpricks over my back and scalp, forcing my foot down harder on the accelerator.

33

RIDGE

Captain Wallace entered Ridge's room just as the nurse finished helping him back from the restroom to the bed. Ridge sat on the edge of the mattress, the rough fabric of the sling tight against his midsection. They'd adjusted the dosage of pain medication, and the discomfort was bearable now, but getting comfortable in this contraption was going to be a challenge.

"Glad to see you up and about," Wallace said. "You gave us all a scare."

Ridge grunted in response as he hoisted his legs back onto the bed, the muscles over his ribcage screaming in protest.

Wallace helped Ridge arrange the coverlet and adjust the head of the bed before speaking again.

"I've got every officer on this case, Ridge. The Bureau has sent in a team. If there's anything you haven't told me, now's the time. Do I need to call someone specific?"

Ridge didn't answer right away. He knew he should say no, but the fact remained that if O'Malley was cornered by one of

Wallace's uniforms, it wouldn't end well. He already had Megan Foster on his conscience, he couldn't take anymore.

"I'll send you the number of my supervisor," Ridge said. His temple throbbed. He checked his watch as Skylar poked her head through the door. Liv had been gone for over two hours. It only took fifteen minutes to get to the farm from the hospital, ten more to grab some clothes. She'd been gone twice as long as she should have been.

He waved Skylar in, relieved to be out from under Wallace's scrutiny, at least for a while.

"I'll get with Adam if anything else comes to mind, Captain."

Wallace nodded, vacating the chair and heading out. "You call if you need anything, McCaffrey. I know what I said the other day, but you're family. I mean that."

"Yes, sir." Ridge nodded, plastering a smile on his face as his sister took a seat next to him.

"The doctors are signing the paperwork now. As soon as Liv gets back we can go."

"Have you heard from her?"

Skylar held up her phone. "Just hung up. She's on her way."

Ridge tried to muffle the spontaneous exhalation of relief but was unsuccessful. How could he protect her when he couldn't even protect himself?

"What happened in that office, Ridge?" Skylar reached out for her brother's hand.

Ridge looked at his sister. She had her whole life ahead of her. She'd always been the outgoing one, the first in their family to try new things, take a chance. But right now, all her optimism had been replaced with worry.

"It's nothing, Sky. Part of the job. I was just in the wrong place at the wrong time."

She smiled at him, leaning over to plant a kiss on his cheek just as Liv walked through the door.

"You can burn this if you want once we get home, but I figured comfort was the rule of the day, right?" Liv's voice was tight, strained.

Ridge eyed the sweatsuit she pulled from a plastic sack. He held back the chuckle to save his ribs, but Skylar's laugh replaced his.

"Where'd you find that?" Ridge asked. He knew it hadn't come from the farm.

Liv hesitated, her grin tipping down a bit at the corners before she recovered.

"Walmart," she admitted. Coming closer, Liv tossed the plastic store bag into the wastebasket beside his bed and began pulling the tags from the seam. "It should fit, I hope."

Skylar giggled as she headed toward the door. "I can't wait to see this. That looks about as stylish as Uncle Rob's hand-me-down track suit you had to wear home from Christmas dinner when Riley puked all over you in the backseat of Dad's station wagon."

The memory drew a chuckle from Ridge as Skylar disappeared through the doorway. He unfolded the Army green sweatpants in his lap. Pain seized his sides, scolding him for poking fun. It took him a minute to notice Liv's eyes.

They were puffy, the whites a telltale pink, proof she'd been crying.

"What happened?" he whispered, a spike of anxiety joining the pain in his gut. O'Malley was here, in Cascade Hills. It was only a matter of time before he came after Liv. Why he hadn't already was a question Ridge found himself wondering more than once.

She shrugged, refusing to answer. "Come on, let's see if

these will work. Doc says you can leave whenever you're ready."

As Liv helped Ridge dress, he noticed she kept her hands tucked inside the sleeves of her sweatshirt. She'd just finished refastening Ridge's sling over the sweatshirt when he pulled her close.

He sensed her hesitation, her rigid posture, heels digging into the tiles as she tried to keep space between them. He leaned forward to meet her, covering her lips with his, tilting his head to coax her mouth open.

A breath escaped from her lips, almost a sob, as she gave in. Her body relaxed into his embrace. The taste of her—warm sweetness, mixing with the saltiness of the tears that slid down her cheeks—was intoxicating. He pulled away, wiping the trails of moisture from her face with his thumb.

"Come on," he said, refusing to force her to open up to him here. "Let's go home."

34

LIV

I helped Ridge get situated in George's Mercury and watched the three of them pull away from the curb before heading to my own car to follow them home. Tears welled in my eyes as I wracked my brain for a way to get a handle on the energy that surrounded the farm. I blew away the display of weakness, wiping at my eyes with my fists. I didn't have a choice. Herman or not, I'd have to figure out a way to cope.

My world was crumbling, everything I'd accepted as truth called into question, especially the motives of the man in the car ahead of me. But even so, I longed to be there, listening to George and Skylar banter back and forth while Ridge interspersed their conversation with amusing anecdotes. I figured the story about Uncle Rob's track suit would be on the playlist. Having them at the farm could be my only saving grace.

THE SUN WAS JUST SETTING over the lake when we pulled into the drive at Sullivan Farm. I parked near the barn and walked cautiously to the house. Hyperaware of every stray emotion that hung in the air. But somehow, with Ridge back, the farm felt benign, friendly, like the home it always had been. Every trace of the unsettling vibe from that afternoon had dissipated into the breeze.

For the next couple days, I resolved to ignore the flashes of what I'd found in the bottom dresser drawer. Thoughts of the time he'd spent with my grandmother, the conversations they'd had, everything–complete with the worry I harbored for Herman's welfare–I relegated to a status of non-issue. Instead, I took Adam's advice and did what good girlfriends do. I allowed Ridge time to settle in and heal.

As Skylar and George fawned over Ridge, I immersed myself in the dynamics of a family. Ridge was a good patient. Although it was hard to tell since he never needed to do anything for himself. One of them was always there, ready to do it for him.

The next days were warm and the four of us spent a lot of time lounging on the screened in porch behind the kitchen. On the third day, George took Colton out on the lake in the boat, enjoying one last fishing trip before he headed back to his own life. Skylar had just brought Ridge a glass of tea and his afternoon dose of pain meds when he started pushing himself up from the glider.

"Wait, where are you going?" Skylar looked panicked.

"I'm not an invalid, Sky."

"Ridge, just sit, what do you need? I'll get it for you."

Skylar blocked Ridge's exit from the porch. I had a feeling she would have shoved him back down onto the glider if she hadn't been afraid to hurt him. Ridge walked up to his sister, his height easily overpowering her frame.

"You've brought me three glasses of tea since lunch. Let me through, Skylar. I'm positive I can take care of this issue on my own."

"Oh," Skylar slinked to the side, letting Ridge pass as I did my best to hide laughter in the quilt I'd tugged tight around my shoulders, serving a dual purpose as it shielded me from the cooling October air and thickening pulses of energy. Skylar let out a breath as she flounced onto the glider next to me. "I need to get it together, don't I?"

"It's cute. He's lucky to have the two of you. Besides, it saves me from waiting on him hand and foot."

Her blue eyes latched on mine, humor coloring her features. "Thanks Liv, for opening your home to us. I know it's not easy for you to pretend everything is okay between you two. But Dad and I are really grateful. It feels good to be together like this."

I smiled as she squeezed my hand through the barrier of the quilt. When Ridge returned she stood and focused her gaze on him.

"Okay, I'm off the clock. I've got to go pack. Then I'll swing Colton back to Bridget's on my way out of town. He's all yours, Liv."

I tracked Skylar as she headed off through the kitchen toward the hallway.

"How did you manage that? I thought she'd never leave." Ridge's lips were turned up into a slight smile as he settled onto the glider with a groan, running his hand down my thigh.

"Give them a break. Your dad's heading back to Bishop's Hollow and Skylar has to get back to Charlottesville for classes tomorrow. She just wants to make sure you're okay before she leaves," I said, willing his hand away.

Ridge's grin didn't reach his eyes as he pushed the quilt

from around my shoulders, dragging it from the glider and onto the floor, leaving my hands exposed.

"Okay, then. Now that it's just us. What happened, Liv? Why won't you touch me?"

"It's not you, Ridge, it's everything. Everything in this house has a story. Even the air has changed. I can't explain it."

My eyes drifted to my fingers in my lap, but I could feel him staring at me. He wanted more. But so did I.

"The psychometry is getting worse?" he asked.

Worse was an interesting word choice. I'd learned to live with the unwelcome pulses of energy. I'd even figured out how to block them when I wasn't interested in what they had to say. But this–these flashes of memory were different. I'd traced it back.

The vision in Jessica's apartment had been the first of its kind. I'd attributed it to the fear I'd felt at the footsteps outside the door, but it was more than that. Before that night, I'd only had access to the images when I invited them in, like at the children's home. Now they buzzed around me anytime my fingers made even the slightest contact.

I sucked in a breath as Ridge slid his hand toward mine. Every muscle in my body tensed with apprehension. I closed my eyes, praying that he'd stop as his fingers slid from my wrist over the back of my hand. I wasn't ready. I couldn't control it, and I was terrified of what I was going to see. Terrified that I'd find out what GenLink truly was. How it involved my grandmother–me. I clenched my jaw, preparing for whatever came when our digits made contact.

A vibration from the table saved me.

"Phone," I said, reaching toward the coffee table for Ridge's cell, using the cuff of my sweatshirt as a shield. I passed the handset to Ridge, who glanced at the screen before answering. The crease between his brows making an appearance.

I grabbed a couple glasses from the side tables and disappeared into the kitchen, giving Ridge some privacy.

"When did it happen?"

He'd lowered his voice, but the wall between the kitchen and porch wasn't particularly well-insulated, and my ears hadn't given up hope of finding a nugget of truth hiding somewhere.

"You have Dublin involved?... No, of course not...It's not a problem...Everything here is under control...Keep me in the loop, okay?"

I felt myself sink. Somehow, I knew. I think I'd known since Rose answered the phone in Herman's apartment three days ago. I just didn't want to admit it.

I heard Ridge get up from the glider. He hesitated a moment before stepping into the kitchen.

"Liv?" I glanced over at him. He was still holding the phone in his hand. An irrational seed of hope took root in my belly as I shook my head, refusing to hear the words that slid from his lips. "It's Herman—"

"Please don't say it," I pleaded. Knowing was one thing. But hearing the words made it real. The first tears came as I slid down the cabinets in front of the sink. I sat, twisting a dishtowel in my hands as I hugged my knees to my chest.

Ridge came closer, kneeling in front of me and pulling me close. His hand palmed the back of my head, my cheek tight against his chest as he held me. "It was a heart attack, Liv. Herman's gone. I'm sorry. So very sorry."

35

RIDGE

"Take care of her, son. She's had a lot thrown at her since coming home," George said as Ridge walked him to the front door.

"Tell her to call if she needs anything," Skylar added, lifting onto her tiptoes to plant a kiss on Ridge's cheek. "You, too. Take care of yourself, okay?"

Ridge smiled at his sister. He brushed wispy blonde curls from Colton's forehead, promising to see him tomorrow. He ushered George and Skylar out the door and to their cars, trying to ignore the sense of relief he had at their departure.

It had been great while it lasted, but he needed a break, and time alone with Liv. Their tires crunched on the gravel as they turned out of the driveway and onto Sullivan Road, first his father, then Skylar.

Ridge stood in the late afternoon air. The old barn loomed in front of him, a grim reminder of failed responsibilities. He turned back toward the house, catching a glimpse of Liv through the office window. She was perched on the window seat, her knees tucked under her chin as she looked out through gauzy sheers to the field beyond.

He gritted against the plummeting sensation in his gut. She knew something. He didn't know what, but he needed to find out. He'd have to offer her some information if he wanted to move forward. Herman's death had been a blow. But her attempt to call him had come after he'd passed. Ridge knew Herman couldn't have been the one to tip Liv off.

A few minutes later, Ridge was cracking open the door to the old office. He'd managed to tuck a bottle of Moscato and two glasses under his good arm, so it was all he could do to coerce the knob to turn enough to release the latch. He pushed into the room, waiting for Liv to shoo him away. Except, she didn't.

She stared out the bay window at a combine harvesting corn in the field that bordered Sullivan Farm. With each pass, tall weathered stalks were cut and stripped of nourishing kernels, replaced by spiky foot-tall leftovers that would garnish the landscape until spring. Only the cows turned out after harvest appreciated the scraps left by the high-tech machinery.

Ridge used the desk as a table, unloading the bottle and glasses in a slow feat of balance that resulted in one of the glasses landing on its side. He righted the glass. The slosh of pouring liquid filling the silent space between them. She still hadn't acknowledged him.

He finished pouring and held one of the wine glasses out to Liv. She accepted the Moscato, but her eyes stayed low, never meeting Ridge's gaze. Explanations he was incapable of giving swam in his mind. *Tell her the truth,* the devil on his shoulder said. *What's the worst that could happen?* Or was that the angel? He was past the point of being able to tell the difference.

Ridge sucked in a breath, readying himself for battle, but the words wouldn't come. He pulled the glass of wine to his lips and sucked it down to half in three quick swallows. He was going to need something stronger than dessert wine.

"We need to talk," he managed, pulling a wingback office chair closer to the window seat before settling in. He fought a grimace of pain as he sunk into the chair, his ribs firing rounds at nerve endings every time he changed position. "I haven't exactly been honest with you, Liv."

"I know," she said. Her eyes skimmed over him once before she turned away.

A slice of fear joined the pain he was learning to live with, ramping his heart rate up a notch. *She could already know everything,* the voice in his head asserted.

"You do?" The words slipped out before he could censor them.

"I know you have history with the man that attacked you at the M.E.'s office. He was a friend."

Liv faced him. Ridge could feel her gauging his response. He cleared his throat and painted on the disjointed expression he'd been taught to wear.

"You knew Jessica Garrison was dead before I told you." Her voice slid over him.

An apology caught in his throat.

"You never brought me here to help with that case. And I think you know more about what happened to Herman than you've told me."

"I don't want to hurt you. Whatever you take away from this, please know that I never intended for any of this to happen." He couldn't look at her when he said it. It was hard enough to imagine her expression. Those emerald eyes shining hurt and betrayal at him.

"He was found in his flat." Ridge said, bringing his gaze up slowly, working his way from her feet to her face. She'd found the combine again and he followed it with her as it turned, slashing down the next row of dried stalks.

"There was no trauma. It was–" he hesitated, fighting every instinct they'd drilled into him over the last ten years. "It was set up to look like a heart attack."

It took a minute for his words to sink in, and he forced himself to look her in the eye when she swiveled toward him, lowering her feet to the floor.

"Set up?" she asked, blinking against the tears that threatened the backs of her eyes. "Set up by who?"

"O'Malley." Ridge kept his eyes on Liv. He needed her to see his honesty. "The man who assaulted me in Megan's office."

"What would he want with Herman?" Liv asked, her voice not much more than a whisper.

Ridge shrugged. That was one question he didn't have an answer for. He pulled the wine glass back to his lips. The liquid sloshed back and forth, threatening to spill until he steadied the trembling glass on the arm of the chair.

"How do you know O'Malley?" Liv asked.

Ridge remained silent. The urge to tell her everything nagged at him.

"Why can't you talk to me?" Her plea was like a knife to the gut.

"Don't make this harder than it already is," Ridge said, catching the blaze of resentment in Liv's eyes as he realized his mistake.

Liv blew through a jagged breath, bending down from the window seat to tie one sneaker as Ridge braced himself for the fallout.

"What's GenLink?" she asked.

Breath caught in Ridge's chest. Panic bubbled hot in his gut. He stood, sliding a hand through his hair before muttering, "How the hell–"

"How the hell did I know?" Liv shot back, pulling her own frame up as tall as she could. "It certainly wasn't through you, was it?" She paused, giving the realization a moment to sink in. "I found your notebook. Olivia Grace Sullivan, asset number thirty-two." Her voice grew louder, angrier, but tears had broken free, sliding down her cheeks in streams. "What about O'Malley? He knew Jessica was psychic, didn't he? Does he know about me?"

She paused. The barrage of questions in a momentary cease fire. Her eyes searched his for a beat before the guilt overloaded him. He turned away, shaking his head and scratching day-old stubble.

"Who did Jessica work for, Ridge? GenLink? You brought me back to help, right? Or was that another lie?" Venom dripped from Liv's words.

"You don't understand," Ridge said as he turned to meet Liv's accusations. The repercussions of the angry clench in his jaw worked its way into his temple, throbbing as he reached for Liv.

His fingers grazed her arm as she pushed him away, igniting a flare of pain through his shoulder.

"You're wrong. I do understand." Liv stepped away from Ridge, working her way toward the office door. "I understand what I should have realized last spring–that you've done nothing but lie to me since we met."

"It hasn't all been a lie–" Ridge started.

"Oh no, that's right. The bit about living with your ex-wife and son, that part was real." Liv's cynicism was palpable.

"Liv–" Ridge tried again, but she put her hand up to stop him.

"You never intended for me to be involved in the Garrison case."

"Everything I did, I did to protect you."

"Bullshit," Liv spat back. "I don't need your brand of protection, Ridge McCaffrey. What I need is the truth."

Ridge gritted against the pain as Liv pushed past him, grabbing her camera off the secretary desk in the entryway before slamming the front door behind her.

He called after her, the tension in his own voice echoing off the trees in the woods. She ignored him. He'd pushed her to her limit, had played out the charade past the point of no return. He could only hope the damage wasn't irreparable.

Ridge trudged up the path after Liv. O'Malley's threats loomed in his mind as he scanned the forest for signs of life. His ribcage pulsed with every step he took, a thousand tiny knives pricking him from the inside out. He wasn't sure he could protect her if O'Malley chose now to attack. As the gravel path gave way to less-traveled dirt, Liv was nowhere in sight. He scanned the cluster of woods ahead, hoping she hadn't ventured too far. He was in no shape to battle rogue foliage.

He focused on the crunch of leaves under his feet. A few bends later, after several stops to catch his breath and push away the pain, he found her. She aimed her camera toward a pin oak. The setting sun glittered through the yellow of a few remaining leaves, illuminating the natural red-gold highlights in Liv's hair.

36

LIV

I clicked the shutter of my Nikon three times in rapid succession. When I turned from the tree, there he was, standing at the edge of the path just looking at me as if I'd grown a horn in the middle of my head.

"I needed a way to get you back to the States. But I didn't want you any more involved in the Garrison case than you already are." His words floated on the breeze.

My heart gave a little leap, the adrenalin fueled kind that happens when you know you're about to find out something that will change you forever.

I turned my back to Ridge, walking toward another large oak not far from the edge of the woods. Ridge and I had made this walk before. I snapped a couple frames, capturing the tree we'd carved our initials into. He kept his distance, but I could feel his eyes tracking me as I stooped and contorted my body to capture different angles of the giant gnarled trunk.

"I'm sorry," he said as I slipped around to the other side, shooting one final image before backing away.

My heel caught, an apparent log peeking through the layer

of leaves on the ground. And I stumbled back, flailing my arms in an attempt to right myself.

Ridge lunged forward through the brush before I hit the ground. The pain of a rock jabbing into the flesh between my shoulder blades forced the air out of my lungs with a swift guttural sound. I lay sprawled on the damp vegetation of the forest floor when Ridge reached me, extending his hand to help me up.

"Are you okay?"

Completely inappropriate nervous giggles started up through my chest as I formulated an answer. He scanned me from head to toe and heat rushed to my cheeks as I pictured myself prone on the ground. What a gigantic klutz. I pushed up onto one elbow to catch my breath, noticing Ridge's eyes fixed on the area near my foot.

"Olivia, don't move."

He hardly ever called me by my full name.

"Not a muscle, Liv. I mean it. I'm going to let go of your hand and I want you to slowly rest it on the ground beside you."

Ridge stood motionless above me, releasing my hand so that I could do as he asked. Fear crawled into my chest, clawing at my lungs, as my heart pounded out a percussive rhythm. I followed Ridge's gaze downward to the wire caught on the heel of my tennis shoe. My grandparents had raised livestock. It was probably an old piece of baling wire. Thinner, though. Still, I could easily free myself.

"I'm not stuck," I whispered as if my voice was going to shatter some veil of secrecy that surrounded us. "I can move my foot."

"No," Ridge commanded. "The wire's attached to something." He already had his phone out and was making a call. He stepped away for the duration of the conversation, but he kept his eyes on me. I followed his gaze to the ground just to the right of my stuck heel. He was right.

A glint of metal poked out from under a layer of leaves. The piece of wire attached to my shoe was firmly secured to a metallic case still partially obscured by the forest floor. My eyes caught Ridge as he stared at his phone a moment before coming back to kneel beside me.

"It's a bomb, isn't it?" I was still using my whisper voice as images of Ridge's kitchen being blown to bits danced in my subconscious.

He sucked in a breath and blew it out through tight lips before answering. "I think so."

An involuntary gasp lurched from my throat, causing a shudder to rock my body.

"Liv, listen to me. You need to breathe, baby. Slow and easy." He took a few breaths with me. "Help's on the way."

Ridge removed some of the leaves that disguised the explosive device. A box of nails, wrapped tight with black electrical tape and two thin sticks of what looked to me like dynamite were attached to a silver electrical box. Thin red and black wires protruded from the main part of the bomb, and a long silver wire extended from the device across the ground toward the oak. It was that wire, not a log, that caught the back of my shoe.

The minutes it took for someone to show up seemed like hours. I couldn't see anything from where I lay, and Ridge kept pacing, from me to the edge of the clearing. Watching him made me nervous, so I focused on the leftover leaves quivering in the trees above and gave myself a pep talk.

This was no big deal, they'd figure out a way to disarm the bomb, or whatever it is they do, and then I'd be free. Everything would go back to normal. I could finish taking my pictures, block out our argument, or stay angry with Ridge for as long as I wanted. My choice.

Pictures. It was the first time my camera had even crossed my mind. I glanced around for it and saw it resting in fallen leaves about five feet from my left shoulder. It was still in one piece. That was a plus.

Crunching footsteps through the brush refocused my attention to the edge of the clearing. Four individuals stood with Ridge. I could hear them talking and as one of them turned I noticed the large letters on the back of his jacket, FBI. I was still stuck on the fact that the FBI was on my property getting ready to disarm a bomb when Ridge's shadow fell over me.

A fifth man approached from behind Ridge, decked out in what I assumed was a protective bomb suit, although it looked more like a get-up an astronaut might wear to the moon.

"Liv, this is Brett Chadwick, he's going to see what he can do, okay. Just stay still. You're doing great."

I nodded. No one needed to tell me to stay still. I was scared senseless. Every muscle in my body tense, rigid enough to control the slightest movement.

"Clear the area!" A gruff voice said from somewhere beyond my field of vision. "You too, McCaffrey."

Ridge's eyes locked on mine. That little line between his brows was back, and the muscle in his jaw twitched as he ran his hand through his dark hair.

"It's okay," I said quietly. "I'll be fine."

"McCaffrey, now!" The voice sounded angry.

Ridge cursed as he backed toward the group at the edge of the clearing. There was no room between the tree and me for the suited man to kneel, so he was forced to straddle my legs to get a good look at the bomb. I watched the heavy fabric of the suit twist and contort as his arms moved.

He lifted off my legs and turned to face the group, making signals with his hands that I didn't understand. Then he focused on me and lowered the shield of his helmet. Light hazel eyes peered at me. The ends of golden brown hair framed his face.

He was young, no more than twenty-five. I wondered how a person would choose this occupation over all his other options. I pictured career day at his high school, this kid being the only one standing at the booth marked FBI Bomb Unit. Crazy. How does that happen?

"I've detached the box of nails to eliminate the danger of injury from shrapnel." His smooth voice broke into my thoughts. "It's a trip line, Ma'am. Looks like it runs from here to the lake. Could be multiple explosives along the line. Please make sure to keep still. I'll be back." Something about his heavy Southern accent soothed me, even though I cringed at the "ma'am."

The wetness of the ground seeped through my jeans and sweatshirt. It took everything I had not to shiver against the cold. I tilted my head back and looked up through the trees. The dwindling leaves painted a kaleidoscope of color in the canopy above me. The rays of the setting sun filtered down through the branches as if offering beams of salvation.

I closed my eyes tight, tears escaping from the corners. I hadn't even realized they were there. I could hear Ridge arguing with the gruff voice from earlier. And I strained to hear what they were saying, but the wind picked up, muting their voices with the rustle of leaves as they blew along the ground and in the trees. I focused on nature's whisper as the cool breeze dried the tears on my cheeks.

"Liv?" Ridge knelt over me, his voice soft and breathy. I opened my eyes, shocked again by the depth of emotion in his.

"Chadwick will be back in a minute. He's going to try to deactivate the device." I nodded my understanding.

"Clear the area!" The angry voice grated like sandpaper on my raw nerves.

Ridge squeezed my hand and leaned down. The heat of his lips on mine a stark contrast to the damp chill that leached into my bones. "I love you, Liv. Whatever happens, I've always loved you."

I knew he was telling the truth, but the choke in my throat kept me from returning the sentiment. This was it. If deactivation was successful, then my life would go on like nothing had ever happened. Ridge and I could continue sparring about truth and honesty and the role of our past in our future. But if the plan failed, well–I guessed I wouldn't have to worry about the after.

Chadwick returned, covering me up to my chin with a heavy pad before straddling my legs the way he had before. I watched the folds of thick fabric again, pulsing as he worked. The thought that I might be taking him with me if he couldn't disarm the device suddenly occurred to me, sending a spike of panic through my chest. He turned toward me a minute or so after he'd started, pulling the mask back to speak.

"I'm going to count down from five with my left hand. When I get to two, cover your head with the blanket. Okay?"

I nodded.

"And if you feel me push, you run. Understand?"

Again, I nodded, dumbly. Wondering if I'd be able to force my legs into motion should the need arise. He replaced his mask and turned around. The rest of the woods seemed to fade to black. Silence engulfed the space as I watched his left hand. My breath hung heavy in my chest while I counted.

Five...four...three...two...I threw the blanket over my head, closing my eyes to the darkness...one...

C hadwick's weight lifted off my legs and I felt his shove. I scrambled to shrug the heavy blanket off my shoulders, turning over to gain footing, the damp undergrowth pulled me twice to my knees.

Weighted arms gripped my waist and drove me forward several strides before the blast hit. I saw the flash before hearing the *Boom*. Dirt and pebbles rained down on us, but otherwise the world around me was silent. When the hailstorm ended, I felt Chadwick stir on top of me.

He helped me up and led me out of the woods and into the clearing. I wasn't sure when the EMT unit arrived, but there they were, waiting. I sat on the gurney inside the truck as Chadwick removed his armor.

One of the paramedics gave him a once over before he waved them away. His choice of profession started to make some sense when I saw the bottom half of a US Marine Corps tattoo on his upper arm. Ridge had one just like it.

Ridge and the FBI officials emerged from a dark van, Ridge making short work of the distance between the van and the ambulance. He caught Chadwick on the way and slapped him on the shoulder, pulling him into a quick hug. I could hear the medics talking, but their voices were muffled, miles away. One of them touched my arm to get my attention, mouthing what looked like the words, "Are you hurt?"

I pointed to my ears. A high-pitched ringing had replaced the cotton-like silence. The EMT leaned over with a scope and peered into each ear, first the right, then the left. Afterward he scribbled a note. "From the blast. Should improve. Pain?"

I shook my head as Ridge stepped into the unit, pulling me from the stretcher and clutching me tightly to his chest. His sling pressed firmly under my cheek, but the pressure of our embrace didn't seem to bother him. I wrapped my arms around his torso, clutching at the back of his shirt and releasing the emotion I'd buried deep inside all afternoon.

The gruff voice that forced Ridge away from me earlier came between us again. At least this time it was muffled by the peal of bells in my eardrums.

"McCaffrey, come with us."

I watched as two men led Ridge toward the house, one on either side, guiding him as if he was some kind of criminal. I followed several steps behind. The fact that I had only one shoe slowed my pace considerably over the uneven ground.

By the time I got to the house, Brian was there, along with my mom and several news vans. Brian nodded to Ridge before running to meet me, shielding me from reporters who were all too eager to sensationalize the past couple hours of my life.

The door to the office was closed, but I could hear the murmur of voices even through my healing ears. I wasn't sure how many were in the room, but none of them sounded happy about what I considered an ideal outcome.

Mom pulled the blinds and turned on the television in my bedroom, well away from the prying eyes of the news media.

She and Brian stayed glued to the breaking news reports while I sealed myself in the adjoining bathroom. I ran the hottest bath I could stand, hoping to warm my chilled bones and forget about the reality playing out in my grandfather's old office downstairs.

I stepped down into the claw foot tub, relishing the warmth against my skin as the sudsy water enveloped my body. I exhaled a sigh and sunk deeper, gnashing my teeth as water consumed the gash between my shoulder blades, savoring the fact I was still alive to feel the sting of pain. I pulled my hair into a bun and closed my eyes, allowing only my head and neck to protrude from the bubbles.

It wasn't long before Mom was tapping on the bathroom door.

"Liv, honey, I think you need to see this."

"DVR it Mom. I'll watch when I'm done."

Submerged to my chin, I pushed the fear and anger of the last few hours as far away as possible. Sleep called, but confusion spiraled through my brain, creating unwelcome scenarios. I tried to relax into the bubbles, but the water cooled too quickly, an unwelcome reminder of the damp earth on which I'd laid most of the evening.

I listened for the indecipherable drone of the TV from the next room. It provided a good gauge for my steadily improving auditory abilities. Even through the slight ring of hearing damage I could make out an exclamation of surprise from my mom or a curse from Brian as they watched the news broadcast.

I stayed in the cooling bath until the ringing in my ears ceased. By then, my fingers were pruny and my skin chilled into goose bumps. I took my time drying off and getting dressed for bed. I wrapped up in my favorite robe before opening the bathroom door, punctuating my arrival with a cloud of steam.

There was no need to rewind the DVR. They'd managed to

find a news station with ongoing footage. Live shots of reporters standing outside Sullivan Farm mixed with aerial shots of the woods, complete with men and women in FBI jackets searching through the foliage like ants.

"Listen," Mom said as the reporter came back on air.

"A Cascade Hills resident was nearly blown to bits today by what law enforcement officers are calling an improvised explosive device."

"Nice," I interrupted, grabbing the remote from Mom's hand and hitting pause. "There's an image for you."

My head throbbed and the last thing I wanted was to spend what was left of the night listening to sensationalized reports of what could have happened. I was all too aware of the alternative scenario. Within an hour, I'd managed to send each of them on their way with promises to call if I needed anything.

The office door was still closed when I walked them to the front door, a thin sliver of light filtering from underneath. The voices inside sounded angry to my tender ears, but I couldn't pick out Ridge's baritone from the cacophony of others.

When I got back to the bedroom I flipped the news station back on. I listened as the reporter identified Ridge as Special Agent Ridge McCaffrey and cringed when they noted his recent injuries. One reporter went so far as to hint at either his complicity in the act or his incompetence. Questioning how the device could have been planted in an area that was supposed to have been secured by McCaffrey himself.

The reporter ended his account by declaring that the FBI planned to take "swift and appropriate disciplinary action to ensure the safety of its agents and civilian operatives." Whatever that meant.

38

RIDGE

"Y ou want to tell me what the hell is going on with this operation, McCaffrey?"

Special Agent in Charge, Marcus Sowards, was furious. He had every right to be, but it didn't soothe any of Ridge's irritation at being reprimanded. And in front of two other agents, no less. What should he have done? Watch Liv die?

"Two weeks ago, you call me to tell me the asset we thought was tucked safely away was being tailed in Dublin. Last week I get word that you've been outed at a crime scene to your CHPD Captain. Tonight, you out the entire undercover operation because that same asset is about to be scattered over the one property you're charged with securing. Explain that to me."

Ridge sucked in a deep breath and focused his gaze on the framed map of Ireland behind Sowards' head. He never should have brought Liv back.

"I never intended to jeopardize the operation, Sir. But it is my job to protect the asset, to give her the best possible chance of survival. There's no one better than Chadwick, sir, and your explosives team. After my run-in with O'Malley, I knew he'd come after her next. The choices I made were based on fulfilling my duty to protect an innocent civilian."

"You and I both know that Olivia Sullivan is no civilian." Sowards crossed his arms, staring Ridge down.

Heat rose in Ridge's cheeks as he shifted his gaze away from the wall behind Sowards and onto the man himself. Steely grey hair with coordinating eyes and a personality cold enough to match. He wasn't going to let this one go easily.

"I'm relieving you of your duties, Special Agent McCaffrey. I need you to surrender your firearm pending an investigation into your improper handling of a Bureau asset."

Ridge glanced at the junior agents still flanking him.

"I did my job," he countered, pulling his sidearm out of its holster and releasing the cartridge onto the desk in front of Sowards. "I performed every assignment handed down to me with precision. I followed orders last spring when you thought the operation was compromised. That order nearly resulted in the death of your asset, in case you forgot. Today, I did what I had to do."

Sowards excused the other agents with a nod of his head, collecting Ridge's Sig while he waited for the office door to click closed.

"Now that we're alone–" Sowards sighed. "You've always been an effective agent, McCaffrey. So enough with the hard ass act. Once this all blows over you'll be reinstated. But the Bureau wants to make some changes to GenLink."

Sowards' large, lined hands were spread in front of him on top of the mahogany desk that once belonged to Liv's grandfather. The steely demeanor had melted away, leaving a tired-looking man in his place.

"Funding is being cut. We need a more cost-effective way

to gather intel. The Bureau has too much tied up in training and protection details. Research and Development is onto other ways to create and sustain similar effects for use in counterintelligence. It's promising, and not nearly as labor and time intensive as GenLink is currently. Minimal training and more assets. It's a win win."

"Drugs," Ridge guessed. O'Malley's drug. "They're trying to use drugs to create psycho-intellectual abilities."

"Preliminary trials are promising. We can gather the same type of intel we get from our genetic assets, but with a fraction of the overhead."

"They tried this back in the eighties. It didn't work then. What makes the Bureau think it will work now?" Ridge had read the reports. Unsuspecting victims had been subjected to high doses of modified LSD to create manufactured psychic abilities at will. Lack of safety and inconsistency in the results doomed the program, and that branch of GenLink was shut down completely by the early nineties.

"The advances in pharmaceuticals have been huge, Ridge. We're light years ahead of LSD. Safer, more effective. Think about the possibilities. Take Olivia for example. She's been on our active roster since Grace gave her up but has yet to be assigned an op. Her abilities are there. Some of the strongest we've seen. But training comes at a price."

"Who's the supplier?" Ridge's chest ached from the anger seething inside. Liv's lack of participation had less to do with the shortcomings of the genetic program and more to do with his own unwillingness to force her into a life she didn't want. And as far as the drugs were concerned, the image of Jessica Garrison on Megan's exam table had an unrelenting grip on his mind. *Safe, my ass,* he thought.

Sowards' hardened persona returned. He glared at Ridge,

eyes locked on his subordinate, jaw set. "You know I couldn't give you that information even if I had it."

Ridge was well aware of the official documentation against O'Malley. The man had been like a brother to him throughout his FBI training, until the night he'd been caught trading drugs for favors from known Bureau subversives. Since then, he'd been blacklisted. But Ridge also knew O'Malley had skill, and skill bought favors.

"The point is, until we find a more efficient way to run the op, GenLink has officially been suspended. The Bureau's made their decision, Ridge. Unless we can find a way to make this work, we're done."

Ridge's heart thrummed in his chest, his respirations increased as he fought to maintain control.

"What happens to the assets?"

Ridge wasn't sure what he wanted to hear. That they'd be released? That Liv would be free to live whatever life she imagined for herself? But deep down, he knew the future would never be that cut and dry. O'Malley made himself clear. He'd always be a threat.

"Any assets in active duty will be debriefed. Some will be reassigned, others, let go."

"And Liv?" Ridge asked.

"She's never seen action. But she's valuable to the next generation of counterintelligence in her own way."

"You can't force her into service, Marc. She's a woman, not a slave."

Sowards eyes softened as he lowered himself into the leather desk chair. "That's what I'd like to talk to you about. In order to make this pharmaceutical route viable, we need her– and you."

Sowards gaze locked on Ridge.

"Tell me what O'Malley said at the M.E.'s office."

Ridge hesitated before laying out the details. He wondered how much of it Sowards already knew, and how much would be used against him. His inability to take O'Malley down when he'd had the chance would make a glistening jewel on Ridge's internal investigation file.

"You're lucky to be alive." Sowards exhaled, rubbing his palm down the back of his scalp.

"If he didn't want me to be, I wouldn't be. Cam O'Malley doesn't make mistakes, remember?"

"No, he doesn't. He's a maniac, Ridge. You know it, I know it, and the Bureau knows it. But he's our only shot. We need him."

"He's your supplier." Ridge didn't need confirmation.

"We've dedicated too much of our lives to make GenLink viable," Sowards said. "Help me put this op back together, Ridge. Give yourself a chance to get out of the field—a promotion—a normal life."

Ridge studied Marcus Sowards. They'd worked together in some capacity or another for the better part of ten years, and Ridge could tell the man was up to something. Whatever it was wasn't authorized, yet another "unofficial" dealing of the Federal Bureau of Investigation.

"If that life includes Liv, I'm listening."

"Officially, you'd be off the case. GenLink would cease to exist. The remaining assets would be released, including Olivia. You could remain here while we hold you in queue for reassignment, open an investigation into your conduct. Whatever we have to do to make sure O'Malley takes the bait."

"What bait?" Ridge knew there was more to this than an internal investigation. A slow snake of anger started up through his core.

"We'd wait for O'Malley to do what he's been itching to do since he figured out who Olivia really is."

"No." Ridge could hardly believe what he was hearing. "You can't do this to her again." The sound of his heart hammering in his ears distorted his own voice. "You're going to dangle her out in front of O'Malley, just like you did Lyle Hunt. Except this man launched an all-out attack against this program, has blood on his hands from at least one asset, not to mention the M.E. he killed less than a week ago."

"We'd be waiting for him, Ridge. He'd only have her long enough to lead us to his compound."

"Like Garrison?" Ridge voiced the theory he'd harbored since finding out O'Malley's hands were the ones responsible for snuffing the life out of Garrison. "You couldn't protect her. What makes you think you can protect Liv?"

Sowards rubbed the back of his neck. His eyes darkened. "He won't risk it. He needs Olivia. More than he ever needed Garrison."

"Why?"

"Because for O'Malley this isn't about GenLink, Ridge. This is about getting back what he feels he's owed. And right now, that means taking his revenge out on *you*."

Ridge worked to process Sowards' words.

"He knows if he takes Liv, we'll come after her. And he wants an audience. He's managed to create a drug that answers our issues of efficacy."

"His drug fried Garrison's brain, Marc. And you're willing to give him the chance to do the same thing to Olivia?" Ridge's eyes blazed at his superior. "My answer is no."

"Listen to me, Ridge. Hunt told us O'Malley was working for Grace in Ireland. Together they were working on this drug, some way to enhance already heightened abilities, without the need for training. The fact that he's back means he's ready to prove that what he's created is viable. He knows that without Liv our hopes of keeping GenLink alive are gone. By taking her, he gets our full attention. That's what he wants. He doesn't want to hurt her any more than we want him to."

"He just tried to scatter her over the woods, Marc. I'm not sure I'm following the logic here."

Sowards sighed. "I've talked with Chadwick. He said the trigger was hard. Would've taken quite a punch before it detonated. O'Malley knows you've got eyes on Liv. He knows you wouldn't let that happen. The device was meant to get our attention, to force the op into the open. It's O'Malley's way of pushing us into action."

"But you said he's doing this because of me. What does risking Liv's life have to do with getting back at me?"

Sowards didn't answer right away. Instead he leaned back in the leather chair, skimmed a hand over the back of his neck. His voice was calm, matter-of-fact. "Once upon a time, you took what belonged to him. Now he's doing the same to you. I'm offering you a chance to put an end to it. To help put him away for good."

"No," Ridge said. "Not at Liv's expense." His eyes locked on Sowards.

"If that's your answer, then I should let you know, the alternative isn't better. You'd be brought back to D.C. while the Bureau investigates your conduct. With GenLink disbanded I'd have no control over the actions of our superiors. Best case scenario is discharge, but that could be followed by prosecution for the mishandling of government assets."

It almost sounded like a threat, but Ridge knew better. Rule number one of his position as an undercover agent was to never get personally involved. It was too risky. Risky for himself, the team, and the Bureau. He wouldn't be in this position if he'd just done his job. Kept his distance. But the damage had been done. There was no going back now.

"And Liv?"

"Like you said, we can't force her into service. She'd be cut loose."

"What about protection?" Ridge knew the answer, but he wanted to hear Sowards admit it.

Sowards shrugged. "She's got friends on the force. But, regardless of the decision you make, you know as well as I do O'Malley won't give up."

Ridge slid into the chair opposite his supervisor. It was the admission he'd wanted to hear since he opened that case folder and found Liv's eyes staring back at him. He'd made an enemy in O'Malley. And Sowards was finally ready to admit it. But now, no matter what he chose, Liv's freedom came with a price.

Sowards gave him a once over, his gaze resting on Ridge's sling and the yellowing bruise on the side of his face. "You've given up a lot for this case, already. You know as well as I do O'Malley put himself in a vulnerable spot by coming to Cascade Hills. The man hasn't been a blip on a radar for over a year and he shows himself to you. There's only one reason for that. He wants Olivia—access to the mutation responsible for making her the way she is. One way or another, he'll get her. I'm offering you the chance to put yourself in a position to be able to help her."

"And if the operation goes bad?"

Sowards walked around the oversized desk, planting himself in front of Ridge before leaning back against the wood with a sigh.

"I can't guarantee her safety. You know that. But you have my word, I'll do everything in my power to keep her safe. It's no secret how much she means to you."

Ridge lifted his eyes to meet Sowards. "I don't think you have any idea, Marc. If you did, you wouldn't be asking me to use her as a sacrificial lamb."

"Her DNA makes her a sacrificial lamb no matter what you decide, Ridge."

The gentle tick of the antique clock on the nearby mantle marked excruciating seconds. A reminder that so much time had already been wasted. Time he should have spent taking care of Liv, loving her, finding a way to create a life without the meddling of the Bureau.

"I'm sorry, Ridge. It's the best I can offer under the circumstances. It's been a long day. Take the night and think about it. Whatever you decide, I'll need a call tomorrow morning."

Sowards gathered his jacket and exited, leaving the door ajar.

Ridge rested his good hand on the corner of the wide antique desk, ribbing his fingers along the edge. It wouldn't take O'Malley long to realize Liv was unguarded, and even less time to celebrate the fact that the genetic operation had been terminated, giving him free rein to manufacture whatever drug-based replacement program he wanted for sale to the highest bidder.

Letting Liv go meant walking away, turning his back as she became the number one target of a man with motives he didn't fully understand. But roping her into a Bureau scheme meant taking away her free will, putting her directly in the line of fire for a cause he wasn't sure he endorsed, guaranteeing she'd come face to face with O'Malley. Either way, Liv's life was at stake no matter what decision he made.

39

LIV

The Tonight Show's closing credits were rolling on my bedroom TV before I decided to creep back downstairs. I hadn't seen Ridge since he'd disappeared into the den with Agent Angry. So, when I slunk down the hall toward the landing I expected the door of the office to be shut tight. But instead, Ridge was sitting on the living room sofa, his legs extended toward the fireplace. The glow of flames, the only light in the room, illuminated his chiseled face. His right hand balanced on the arm of the couch twirling a glass of scotch.

"Ridge?" I trailed my hand along the back of the couch as I approached, tucking my leg under to sit on the cushion next to him. His eyes darted away from the fire, over to the glass of alcohol before lighting again on the flickering flames. His only response amounted to nothing more than a grunt.

"What went on in there?" My question was met with silence. I chomped the inside of my cheek to keep the hurt at bay. Anger I'd felt earlier had morphed into betrayal, solidifying the aching rock in my chest. Coupled with the fear and panic that still crawled through my veins, I didn't trust myself not to cry. I twisted two fingers in the belt of my robe to give myself something to focus on other than rejection.

"The FBI people were here for a long time."

His eyes went back to the glass in his hand. He twirled it, the amber liquid reflecting the reds and oranges of the fire. His response was a simple, "Yes."

"Is there anything you want to tell me?" I held my breath, the pain of loss taking root inside. I needed some response, anything that would indicate he cared enough to tell me what transpired in that room. I wanted the truth. I deserved it. All of it. But Ridge said nothing.

"I thought you were saving this for a special occasion." I said, reaching across Ridge to the side table and the bottle of Macallan single malt I'd brought home from the duty-free shop at Dublin airport.

"You're still alive. Seemed as good a time as any," he said, handing me a glass and watching me pour.

I sniffed the oaky aroma before venturing a taste. My preferences leaned more toward Guinness or wine. Hard liquor had never been my forte. I forced myself not to make a face as the liquid slid like lava down my throat. The corner of Ridge's mouth tilted into an amused grin as he took the bottle from me.

"It's an acquired taste," he said, pouring a bit more into his own glass before placing the bottle back on the table.

"Like you," I said. His grin faded from view. "Beautiful on the outside, smooth even. But too much, too fast will make you wish you'd never opened the bottle."

I let the silence stretch between us, biting back the urge to apologize. After this afternoon, I was beginning to wonder how different my life would be had I never laid eyes on Ridge McCaffrey.

INHERENT LIES | 255

"The first time I drank scotch was after my sister died," Ridge started, rescuing me from the what ifs. "Dad had us holed up in the best hotel he could afford. I had my own room, with a mini-bar. I found out pretty quick that when there's something you want to forget, whisky will get the job done."

Ridge knocked back what was left of the liquid in his glass, pouring a refill.

"What is it you're trying to forget now?" I asked.

Ridge didn't speak right away. He twirled the glass once more. "This. You."

Hurt slammed into my chest, sucking the air from my lungs. I blinked against the tears that threatened the back of my eyes.

"Okay," I whispered, pulling the leather bound notebook I'd found in his dresser drawer out of my robe pocket. "I'll let you. As soon as you explain this. And tell me why the blue bar under your picture in the news reports reads, 'Special Agent Ridge McCaffrey, Counterintelligence, Washington, D.C.'"

Ridge stopped swirling the glass, cocking his head slightly in my direction. His lips parted as if he was going to say something, but nothing came. I sat a moment longer before tossing the journal onto the sofa between us. Patience had never been my strong suit, but for this I was willing to wait him out. Herman had been right. I was too idealistic. And I'd been running from a reality I was afraid to face for far too long.

I chewed the inside of my lip, twisting my grandmother's ring as the air between Ridge and I thickened, charges of energy building, prodding me as we sat in silence.

"You don't deserve this, Olivia. I should have stayed away. None of this would be happening if I had just let you go."

The volume of his voice increased as he spoke, fueled by an anger that hung heavy in the air between us.

"Tell me what's happening," I whispered, biting my lip against the surge of electric energy in the air.

"I wouldn't be sitting here in a sling, trying to stay one step ahead of a delusional psychopath, while justifying myself to the Bureau for trying to save you. Not to mention the fact that I've had to text Bridget sixteen times a day to make sure she and Colton are okay because you two can't be in the same room together."

It hit me then. Life was no longer just about Ridge and me. Maybe it never had been. He had a son, a family, one who needed protecting just as much as I did, maybe more. Whether or not I wanted to admit it, I was in the way.

"Shit." The word escaped Ridge's lips in a breath as he leaned forward, hanging his head. "That's not what I meant."

"No." I jumped in to save him from his struggling apology. "You're right. I know how much they mean to you. I'm not sure what I expected when I decided to come back to Cascade Hills. I think seeing you after so long, finding Saoirse's Bible, the connection with Garrison, and then the fire at Cohen's... coming back seemed like my only option. I told myself maybe I could make a difference. Help Jessica before it was too late. But looking back, I did what I do best, Ridge. I ran."

Ridge studied me. Flames reflected in his eyes. I thought I noticed a flare of pity before I pulled my gaze away, reciting the only thing that felt right at the moment.

"I don't blame you for any of this, Ridge. If you hadn't come after me today–" I couldn't choke out the alternative.

Ridge was silent a moment. He picked the notebook up off the couch and flipped through it. The pages made a soft crinkling sound. The charges in the air between us thinned. "You should blame me. You were right. I lied to get you back here. I'm the reason today happened."

I slid off the couch, kneeling in front of him with my hands on his knees, forcing him to look at me. I took the notebook from his hand, grazing my fingertips along his, checking for the wall that I usually found. Gone. If I wanted to know anything, now was the time. But I needed him to tell me. I had to give him that chance.

"I'm the reason you got hurt." His voice wasn't much more than a whisper.

"I'm not hurt, Ridge."

"Last spring. Lyle had information the Bureau wanted. Information about O'Malley. So they pulled me from Cascade Hills. I let them use you."

I sat back on my heels, letting my hands drop into my lap. The rolling ache in my chest solidified into a hard knot.

"How could you know that I'd confront him? You weren't around."

Ridge glanced over at the Macallan. The alcohol was getting to him. His eyes were dark, enlarged pupils mirroring the flickers in the fireplace.

"It was all a set up. Brian to plant the idea, Adam with the wire. Everything. They did exactly what the Bureau asked them to do. They needed to know whose side you were on. My job was to stay out of the way, give you a reason to meet with Lyle."

"You knew I had nothing to do with the drugs—with Jason. That I had nothing to do with Grandma's death."

Ridge nodded. "Deep down, I knew. But to the Bureau you were volatile. They thought you could be involved with O'Malley somehow. The only way to prove you weren't was for you to confront Lyle."

I stared at Ridge for a moment. Breathing through waves of mounting anger and betrayal as flashes of O'Malley's smile superimposed on Lyle's satisfied smirk haunted my memory.

"So, you dangled me like a piece of meat to get what you wanted."

"It had nothing to do with what *I* wanted, Liv. *I* wanted *you*. I wanted the Bureau out of your life, but this is my job. I don't have the option of saying no."

Ridge leaned toward me, twisting a section of my hair around his forefinger.

"You think O'Malley is responsible for tonight?" I asked.

Ridge nodded. "He's not going to stop until–"

Ridge sank back against the couch with a shake of his head. Whether to revise what he was about to say or to whisk away the effects of the scotch, I wasn't sure.

"Until what?"

"Jesus, Liv, I can't do this. Not tonight." The note of irritation in his voice set me off.

"If not tonight, when?" I stood and stepped out of his reach. "I could have left the farm today in a body bag and you can't even be honest with me. Tell me who you are Ridge. Why are you working for the FBI and what's it got to do with me?"

"Don't make me do this," Ridge said, reaching for the belt of my robe and pulling me forward.

I lowered my voice as his hand grasped my waist. His head bowed. "I just found out the man I fell in love with doesn't exist. I don't even know who you are."

"I'm still the same person," Ridge said. "Only the details are different."

I slid to my knees, forcing him to look at me. "I need the truth, Ridge. All of it."

His eyes searched mine, his fingers skimming my jawline.

"Please," I breathed, battling the urge to cover his lips with mine.

His voice was low, hesitant. "The Bureau has been tracking your family for years." The eerie shadows of flames licked at his face as he spoke. "Everything started with your grandmother. Grace was the one who found the connection. The one who realized that the senses you have could be enhanced, that with the proper training you could become–"

I stared at Ridge as he struggled with what to say. My own breath caught in my throat as I finished the sentence for him, "–a government asset."

The image of Ridge's run-in with O'Malley flooded back. Memories of my grandmother's trips to Ireland. My own sister asking me to join her in Dublin, pushing me to work with the Garda. The months I'd spent with Michael and Herman learning to manipulate the visions.

"This isn't about missing girls here, right? You're talking about high profile government intelligence."

"People with your abilities are rare, Liv. You're a valuable asset in counterintelligence. Think of all the information you could provide through just a touch. Information that would take the Bureau weeks or months to obtain otherwise."

"So, they want me to work for them?"

"Technically, you already do. But the program could never be successful if they didn't have a way to replicate your abilities in others. That's where your grandmother came in. She discovered a way to genetically enhance your abilities."

Ridge twisted a curl around his fingertip. His eyes were glossy. I stared at the man in front of me. This was beginning to sound like the plot of some sci-fi movie. "So, the FBI wants what, then–my DNA? What are they going to do, clone an army of psychic freaks?"

Ridge pulled me closer. Too close. His fingertips slid down my arm and onto my hand. He laced his fingers through mine as spikes of electricity probed my skin, knifing the air between us. *Pull away,* my inner critic demanded, but Ridge's energy slid through my veins like alcohol and carried the same inebriating effect. *Just this,* I compromised, losing myself in the pulses of truth emanating from his flesh. *No farther.*

"It's not your DNA they want, Liv. It's your genetic code. Whatever mutation is responsible for your abilities–that's what they were after. It's what O'Malley is after now."

40

RIDGE

Ridge should have been relieved. Liv made it out of the woods alive. GenLink no longer existed. He was drinking eighteen-year-old scotch. And somehow he'd stopped Liv from hating him. By all accounts he should be a happy man. But being forced into a decision that he knew wouldn't end well sucked the optimism out of his body.

"Jessica Garrison was part of the same program?" Liv asked.

Ridge nodded. "The government is always on the lookout for more effective ways of gaining intel. Anything they can use to eliminate threats to the US, is fair game ... including psychics and genetics."

"So why didn't they ever ask me to help?"

Liv was curled beside him. He wanted to turn and pull her toward him. Kiss the lips hovering within millimeters of his neck, sending a throb of longing through him with every light puff of her breath. His eyes drifted to their hands, intertwined. Flesh on flesh. He should never have allowed it. The alcohol was making him fuzzy. Focus, he told himself, sliding his fingers out of their embrace.

"Because the operation was compromised," Ridge answered. He watched Liv shift away, rubbing the palm of her hand.

She cleared her throat and sat up. "Compromised, how? You mean O'Malley?"

Ridge nodded. "The Bureau started losing assets. They linked the disappearances to him but could never track him down."

Liv sat for a moment. "Saoirse and Jessica?"

Ridge nodded. "And Aimee."

"How long have I been your assignment?"

He sucked in a breath. *Now or never, McCaffrey.*

"I was posted here six years ago. At first, my role was to debrief your grandmother. Find out what she knew before she retired from the agency. That's how I learned about you. You were her pet project, but she'd never told the Bureau. Said she wanted you to be able to choose a life for yourself." Regret pounded Ridge, like waves on a rocky beach. It was his fault they were here. His fault the Bureau had the upper hand. *God, if only I'd known.* "It was my job to report what I learned. That's what I did. And when you returned for Grace's funeral, they reassigned me to you."

"So, I've been your project since the night we met."

His heart clenched. Liv's jaw tightened as she picked at the cuff of her robe. Her eyes firmly focused on her lap. She swallowed. Since the moment he'd met Liv, there'd been a connection. Words couldn't explain it. And it wasn't his style to fall so hard so fast. Bridget cured him of that a long time ago. But even now, Liv's presence overpowered him. *You've got one more night,* the thought came unbidden. He needed to reach out and touch her, take her in his arms. Run away.

He considered that last thought longer than he should have. They could–run away. But then what? The Bureau or O'Malley would find them. Neither scenario would end with the happily ever after he craved.

"Your grandmother spent much of her life working to build reliability into the program. She gave me names that I passed on to Sowards, my supervisor. Those individuals were then tagged and trained."

"Tagged?" Liv asked, finally looking at him through glazed eyes. *Tagged?* He cringed at his stupidity. Now he was as bad as the Bureau, treating the assets like animals.

"Each individual, when they became a part of the program was microchipped. The Bureau could track their whereabouts that way. If something went wrong, one scan would show who they were, what op they were a part of. Only other federal agencies knew about the chips, though."

"So they were marked like Jews at a Nazi concentration camp?" Her voice was soft, hurt.

"No, not–" *Shit.* He regrouped. "The program was voluntary. The microchips were simply an identification tool."

"Did Jessica Garrison have one?"

Ridge nodded.

"Then why couldn't they identify her?" Liv asked.

"Someone removed the chip."

Liv's silence closed in on him. He was glad when she left the details of Jessica's identification unspoken.

"What happened after my grandma died?"

Ridge set his glass on the side table and ran a hand through his hair. He looked at Liv. Those emerald eyes dug into his soul.

"My job was to watch you. Get close to you. Protect you." Ridge reached to tuck a curl behind Liv's ear. "You were Grace's magnum opus, Liv–her life's work. Which made you the Bureau's special project. And by extension, O'Malley's most wanted target."

Liv's brow crinkled as she worked to process what he said.

"What made me so special?"

"Grace found a way to do what the Bureau had never been able to. They knew psycho-intelligence was passed down through the female line. But Grace had contacts, both here and in Ireland. She found a way to produce heightened abilities through genetic refinement."

"You're saying my grandmother worked with the FBI to breed psychics for counterintelligence work?"

Liv's eyes shone the fire that he both loved and feared. She was still having trouble processing it all. He heard the anxiety in her voice. The tone heightened, syllables clipped.

"Grace funded the scholarship that brought your birthmother to the States. She hand-picked Aimee Callaghan. Your father's affair was no accident, Liv. Grace knew it was only a matter of time before Aimee and Stephen fell for each other. Before a child with abilities passed through both lines was born."

"Both lines...but..."

"You didn't know?"

Liv shook her head. "I was never sure. Grandma used to tell me stories when my visions would scare me. But I thought that's all they were–stories."

Ridge's heart ached for Liv. Her entire life was cracking open like an egg, the insides spilling into a mess at her feet. And it was his fault. His fault for carrying on a ruse he knew would only end in pain.

Ridge shifted on the couch. He didn't know how to tell her everything. There was too much. No matter how much he revealed about what the operation had been. He couldn't tell her what Sowards was asking him to do. He didn't have the words.

"I promised Grace I wouldn't let them use you. After Grace died, with the operation compromised, it became more personal. I didn't want to see you get hurt. That's why I never let them chip you."

Ridge emptied the last of the Macallan into his glass and downed it. The antique clock on the mantle ticked loudly in the silence. Liv left the sofa, crouching in front of the fire to throw on another log. The flames reflected onto her face, illuminating her profile as she stood.

Ridge leaned forward, pulling her to his lap. She relaxed, relenting as he clasped his fingers through hers once more. He may not have the words to tell her what Sowards wanted, but he could try to make her feel it, help her know what was in store, provide what she'd never had—the ability to choose.

Liv pulled away just once, but Ridge persisted, giving her nowhere to hide. He inhaled her scent as he kissed her, knowing it would be the last time. His lips gently pulled and sucked as he moved from her lips to her neck.

The room spun his thoughts into a tangled web. He didn't deserve her. Never had. That much he understood. But his body ached for her. Throbbing with every beat of his heart. He wanted her to feel how much she meant to him, just once more. He needed her to understand how much he loved her before he was forced to say good-bye for good. But his eyes were heavy, his movements slow. The scotch had taken hold.

41

LIV

T he remnants of singeing heat from Ridge's skin on mine still stung the palms of my hands. The image of Sowards asking Ridge to set me up, use me as he had with Lyle, twisted a spiral of fear through my stomach. Tears streamed down my face in uncontrollable waves as I gunned the engine of my Mustang. Throwing gravel, I turned out of the driveway onto Sullivan Road and toward Mom's house.

For most of the past year, I'd been angry with Ridge for leaving me alone after my confrontation with Lyle. But he'd done more than that. He'd set the whole thing up. And now, Ridge was entertaining the idea of doing it all again, but this time with a known killer. The whole revelation was more than I could process.

Mom swung the door open before I'd even knocked, grasping me so tightly in her arms that the overnight bag I carried dropped to the cement with a loud thud. She smoothed my hair against my scalp, telling me everything would be okay. I clutched her, my head buried against her shoulder, sobbing like a frightened child.

My mother and I sat on the couch in her living room, my feet folded under me and a box of tissues between us. We'd never had moments like this. As a young girl, my father had been my confidant. My mother was always a bit too remote to trust with the inner workings of my heart.

But tonight, I told her everything. Swearing her to secrecy only because I figured it could jeopardize Ridge if word got out about the operation. Relief that he'd finally told me warred with the wounds left by his lies. But the idea of him being hurt because of something I'd done wasn't a cross I was prepared to bear.

We sat in silence as she processed everything I'd told her. It was odd. The tears that flowed in rivers had dried into desert streaks. After I'd put a voice to everything, Ridge's faults didn't seem so bad. We weren't so different, after all. I'd done enough running in my day. I understood his decision to leave Cascade Hills. To leave me. In fact, considering Sowards' proposal, it seemed the lesser of two evils.

"He's just trying to protect you the only way he knows how, by pushing you away."

I glanced at my mother. Her lips tipped into a sad smile. "I've had practice at that myself, remember?"

"When do I get a say in any of this?" I asked. "I don't want to be pushed away. And I don't want to be used as a pawn."

"I know. And he doesn't really want to do it, but he thinks it will keep you safe. In his mind, sacrificing what he has with you will give you a chance to live your life, be who you're meant to be without interference from some government program. He's punishing himself for past transgressions, Liv. Your father tried the same thing after I found out about Aimee. It's what men do."

My mother and I had spent very little time talking about my birthmother and the relationship she'd had with my father.

"How'd you get so smart?" I teased, spinning my grandmother's Claddagh ring on my finger.

My mother smiled.

"Why'd you stay when you found out about Aimee?" I asked.

Mom laughed a high-pitched, airy laugh. I'd struck a nerve with that one.

"Tell me, Liv. After everything Ridge has done, are you ready to say goodbye?" She looked at me pointedly, making sure she had my full attention. "Even after the affair, I still loved your father. I wasn't ready to give up on what we had together. He made promises to me after Aimee left. And as far as I know, he kept those promises. Your father was a good man. Ridge is a good man, too. But no one is perfect."

"What if it's too late? What if he's already made up his mind?"

"You won't know if you don't open the dialogue, Olivia." She patted my knee and rose from the sofa. "You've had a long day. Try to get some sleep. Come at it tomorrow with a fresh mind."

I agreed as Mom walked away. Hesitating at the foot of the stairs, she said, "You know, Liv, lies or not, there's no question in my mind that he'd do anything to protect you. He's being forced to make an impossible decision. But one thing is clear. He loves you."

42

RIDGE

R idge woke up on the floor in front of the fireplace, his legs tangled in a patchwork quilt. An empty bottle of Macallan lay on its side on the end table, which would account for the stabbing headache. Not to mention the fact that he had very little memory of what happened last night.

He remembered Sowards leaving and Liv coming downstairs. He could recall talking to her, telling her he wanted to forget her. Nice. After that he was drawing a blank. A friendly reminder of why he rarely drank scotch anymore.

He hollered for Liv a couple times before stumbling into the kitchen and finding her note stuck to a bottle of Tylenol on the table. It was short. She needed time to process, she'd written. She'd be at Beth's. Ridge sank into the kitchen chair and ran his hand through his hair. He was running out of time.

Sowards was expecting his call. He had to make the choice between his personal and professional life. And right now, they were tangled like a ball of Christmas lights. As soon as he leaned one way the other side came roaring back into play.

Regardless, this was his last day in Cascade Hills. And he refused to leave without a proper good-bye.

BETH MET him at the front door when Ridge arrived at her house around noon.

"I figured I'd see you today." Liv's mom smiled at him as she invited him in. "She's in the shower. I'll send her down in a few."

"Is she okay?" Ridge asked as he followed Beth from the foyer into the kitchen.

Beth Sullivan shrugged before picking a coffee cup up off the counter and turning to face him. "She's hurt. But you already knew that. Maybe scared. But too stubborn to admit it."

"I don't know what I'm doing," Ridge admitted as he scrubbed a hand over his jaw, scratching at yesterday's stubble.

A bubble of laughter erupted from Beth as she answered, "Most men don't, Ridge. But here's my piece of advice as far as my daughter is concerned. Stick with the truth. She's tougher than she looks. More perceptive than you're giving her credit for. And if this relationship has run its course, then so be it. But don't push her away because it makes you feel like a better man."

Ridge nodded as Beth excused herself. He hadn't had many opportunities to talk with Liv's mom, but he could see she was just as discerning as he'd predicted. He wracked his brain. Is that what he was prepared to do here today? Push Liv away just so he could feel better about himself?

He stared out the window into the backyard. Remnants of hangover pounded against the inside of his skull as he ran over the options again. He didn't hear Liv come in from behind.

"Morning. How are you feeling?" she asked.

Her hair hung in damp ringlets, creating dark splotches along the shoulders of her sweatshirt. She looked younger. More innocent, somehow.

"I'm fine. Got your note. Good call, taping it to the Tylenol bottle."

"I wanted to make sure you found it."

Ridge detected a hint of a smile, but it was fleeting. He cleared his throat and launched into his prepared speech. "As you might expect, I don't remember everything that happened last night. But what I do remember makes me think I owe you an apology."

"You should never apologize for the truth." Liv turned her back to him and poured a cup of coffee before offering him one.

"I shouldn't have said I wanted to forget you. That was cruel. And untrue." He caught her looking at him, but as their eyes met, she looked away. "The rest, about GenLink, your grandma, Lyle–that was the scotch talking. I could have been more tactful. And for that, I'm sorry. I never intended to dump all that on you."

"I'm not upset that you told me, Ridge. The truth is, as hard as it was to hear, it's what I've wanted. What I've asked for since you came to Dublin. Michael was right. I've been living in this shroud of secrets for so long I don't know the truth when I see it. Would it have been easier if you hadn't waited so long to tell me? Maybe, but I doubt it."

"You talked to Michael?"

Liv shrugged. "I needed an outside perspective."

Ridge swallowed. The knot in his throat swelling.

"I guess the part I'm struggling with the most is that I'm just a means to an end for you–for the Bureau."

"You getting hurt has never been part of the plan."

"I know. You keep telling me that."

Ridge struggled to stay focused. He took another swig of

the steaming coffee, ignoring the burn as it slid down the back of his throat. He rubbed at his face, pushing at the remnants of hangover that clouded his brain.

"I'm due back in D.C. this evening. They're dismantling the program."

Liv sat in the chair opposite him staring into the mug she'd tucked between her hands. "So that's your choice, then? This is good-bye?"

"You deserve a life, Liv. An opportunity to make your own decisions. You're more than a means to an end for the Bureau. This is what your grandmother would have wanted."

Liv didn't have a chance to respond. Ridge's cell buzzed through his jacket pocket. *Jesus*, he thought. *Perfect timing.* He glanced at the display. It was his dad. The phone continued its vibration in the palm of his hand for a moment before Liv waved him away. Taking her coffee, she retreated onto the nearby sun porch while Ridge answered the call.

"Dad?" Ridge managed, clearing his throat as he watched Liv through the picture window. His heart seized as the reality of a life without her hammered through him. The knowledge that she was still the number one target on O'Malley's list. He should ask her to help. Do what Sowards wanted. At least then he could pretend she was protected. *What had he done?*

His father's words shoved the pulverizing notions aside. "It's your sister, son. She never made it to her apartment yesterday. I was hoping maybe you'd heard from her. Maybe she decided to stay with Brian?"

The barely contained panic in his father's voice refocused him. His dad's usually stoic tone lifted at hopeful questions. Ridge turned away from the kitchen window. Adrenalin spiked through his veins, painful thumps ricocheting through his skull.

He collected the most pertinent information. Had George called the police? Yes. Were they doing anything? No. In fact, they'd referred him to the U of V campus police department since Skylar's apartment was within the campus jurisdiction.

"I'm leaving right now. I'll meet you at her place by 4:00. Don't touch anything in the apartment, okay? I'll call in some favors." He hesitated. Lying, "Everything will be fine, Dad. See if you can get a list of her friends with their phone numbers and start calling. She probably stopped at a friends' house on the way back."

When he turned around, Liv was watching him from the doorway.

"Skylar?" she asked, quietly.

Ridge nodded. "I've gotta go."

Five minutes, two more Tylenol, and a glass of orange juice later, Ridge was heading toward the front door of Beth Sullivan's house with Liv trailing behind.

Wide emerald eyes watched his every move. He had to say something.

"We'll finish this. You know that, right?" he said, motioning between them.

"It's fine, Ridge. Go find Skylar. Let me know if I can help." He pulled her in close, breathing in the beachy scent of her freshly washed hair. His chest trembled with his exhale as Liv pushed out of his embrace, shoving him toward the front walk. He glanced back at the house once as he opened the driver's door of his Shelby. Liv stood in the front picture window, the fingers of her right hand pressed against the glass as he drove away.

He waited until he was out of Beth's cul-de-sac before letting out a growl of frustration. His fist rocked the steering wheel, driven by biting hatred at himself and the job he was required to do, and propelled by a deep-seated fear that Skylar's disappearance was no coincidence.

43

LIV

There was an unfamiliar black MKZ idling in the driveway of Sullivan Farm when I got back home from Mom's house. By the time I silenced my engine and opened the door of my Mustang, an older, steely haired man was standing by the Lincoln, waiting for me.

"Miss Sullivan." He extended a hand, but I declined, stepping to the side and closing my car door instead.

"Agent Sowards," I guessed, recognizing my visitor as the angry man locked in intense conversation with Ridge after yesterday's bomb unit rescue. Was that really only yesterday? It seemed like a lifetime ago.

"I'm sorry we were never properly introduced," Sowards said. The apology sounded strained, and instinct pushed me away from the pulsating energy that surrounded him. I forced myself to stay rooted, study him more closely. Tall, muscular, and tan, he had the qualities of a man in a position of authority. He was used to getting his way. I wondered if Ridge had told me everything there was to know about the FBI's program. If I was going to be compelled to have a conversation with this man, I wanted all the cards on the table.

"Ridge isn't here. He's on his way to Virginia for a family emergency."

"Yes. He called me about his sister. I'm on my way there myself after this, to see what I can do to help. Regardless of the impression I may have left yesterday, Ridge is family to me. We'll do everything we can to make sure Skylar is found soon. But before I head down, I wanted to tie up a few loose ends. Do you have a minute?"

I nodded and led him to the porch. I doubted Ridge had cleaned up from his Macallan binge the night before. And there was no way I was going to let Sowards get a glimpse into my private life. I had a sneaking suspicion he already knew more about what happened between Ridge and I than I wanted him to. And I refused to provide more ammunition, no matter how much brotherly love Sowards claimed to have.

"I don't know how much Agent McCaffrey told you before his departure, but he's facing suspension, possible discharge. The Bureau will launch an investigation into his conduct. Of course, part of that includes you, so I'd like to get your take on some things if you don't mind. The sooner we can conclude the enquiry, the sooner Ridge can be cleared of any wrongdoing and get back to work. I'm sure you understand."

I nodded at Agent Sowards. "Of course."

He popped the locks on his briefcase and pulled out a legal pad, situating himself in the porch rocker. I felt the heat of his stare on my face as he spoke. "Miss Sullivan, were you aware that Agent McCaffrey's assignment was to help you transition into the line of duty for the FBI's Counterintelligence Unit?"

"He told me last night. But before that I didn't know."

"And were you aware he filed paperwork with the Bureau indicating you were unfit for that duty?"

Instinct forced me to make eye contact with Agent Sowards. He watched intently, his line of sight running from my eyes down to my neck and back again. I'd been around law enforcement long enough to know he was watching for an elevated heart rate. Signs of deceit. I shrugged and shook my head in answer.

Sowards pulled some paperwork from his briefcase. Glancing at it before holding it out toward me.

I skimmed the lines of text. Ridge's official report that I was unfit for duty, negating the need for tagging. The document was proof that what Ridge had said was true. He'd tried to protect me, shield me from the program even when the storm of Grandma's death and Jason's lies swirled around us.

"Why show me this?"

Sowards didn't answer, just cocked his head to the side, reading the expression on my face. I couldn't help but wonder what he saw. I cleared my throat and looked away.

"Just a few more questions, Miss Sullivan." He ruffled some paperwork, replacing the letter in his briefcase. "At any time, did Agent McCaffrey make inappropriate advances toward you?"

This question I was ready for. "He was nothing but a gentleman, Agent Sowards. We're both consenting adults."

"I see." Sowards scribbled something on the legal pad and shuffled his stack of papers, pulling another from the pile.

"Agent Sowards, if Ridge believed I was unfit for duty why send me to Ireland? Wouldn't it have made more sense to cut me loose entirely? Remove me from the program?"

"It would have, if the Bureau hadn't understood your true value to this operation. Your genetic make up made you worth the risk. Once we realized you weren't connected to Lyle Hunt, we agreed with Ridge that keeping you off the grid was in everyone's best interest. Our contacts overseas came in handy."

"You mean, my sister?" I asked, watching for a reaction of my own.

Sowards eyes stayed flat, unimpressed.

"What about the others? Jessica Garrison? What happened to her? How many lives has this program ruined?"

Sowards straightened in his seat. Surprise flickered over his features. "I assure you, the promise of this program to create a safety net for our nation and our communities is worth the small number of unfortunate casualties we've incurred."

He leaned back in his chair, folding his arms across his chest. "I'm here because we need your help, Olivia. Ridge needs your help."

A finger of icy dread threaded up my back, raising the tiny hairs on the nape of my neck.

"Ridge said the program is being dismantled. I'll be free to go, right?"

"Officially, yes."

"But?" I was waiting for him to verbalize what I already knew.

"You were born into this. Your safety remains a concern."

"You're talking about O'Malley."

"Ridge has always done his best to protect you. From everyone."

His comment caught me off guard.

Sowards stood and buttoned his jacket. His movements were slow and deliberate. He was considering something. The weight of his decision sparked in the air between us.

"Miss Sullivan, off the record, are you in love with Agent McCaffrey?"

Sowards hesitated with the last button and examined my reaction. Silence filled the space as his eyes narrowed.

"Look," Sowards returned to the edge of the rocker. "Ridge

has put your grandmother's entire operation at risk to keep you safe. It's your turn to return the favor, Miss Sullivan."

"I thought it was the Bureau's inability to protect disappearing assets that jeopardized GenLink."

I'd struck a nerve with that one. Sowards sat back, rubbing the back of his neck with large, lined hands.

"I wondered how much Ridge would tell you. Did he also tell you that the man responsible for destroying the lives of our assets would have stopped if he could've got his hands on you?"

I sucked in a breath. The idea that I was responsible for the death of Jessica, maybe even Saoirse, hit hard.

"I didn't think so." Frustration brewed beneath Sowards' stony façade. "O'Malley and Ridge have history. And O'Malley will do whatever it takes to exact revenge. That includes taking his aggression out on Ridge's family."

"You think O'Malley has Skylar?" A plunge of panic sucked at my chest.

Sowards' silence confirmed what I already suspected.

"Where?"

"We're not certain, but with your help, we can find out." He turned to face me, his eyes probing.

My breath hung tight in my lungs. "I'm not sure I understand what you're asking."

The thought of Skylar out there, powerless against O'Malley, tugged at my conscience.

"I'm asking you how far you'd be willing to go to guarantee the safety of Ridge's sister. To take O'Malley out of the equation for good. We need you, Olivia. GenLink aside. You could be Skylar's only hope."

Sparks of tension leapt from Sowards toward me, pricking as they worked their way into my neck.

"We'd do what we could to protect you. But the risk is

clear. He wants you. And he'll do whatever it takes to make that happen."

"Bait." The word slid out almost imperceptible, even to me.

"Say again?" Sowards asked.

I shook my head. "O'Malley gets me, and Skylar gets to go back home. That's it, isn't it?"

"Skylar's abduction changed things, Miss Sullivan. Ridge and O'Malley's history changes the dynamics here. What was once business, is now personal. And I don't have to tell you how urgent this is."

Fire filtered through my veins. Purging away lurking tendrils of fear.

"If I say yes, what happens next?" Waves of relief cascaded from Agent Sowards.

"We set you up at a meeting point. Let O'Malley know where you are. And then we wait. I want to make this clear Olivia, you'll be on your own. We'll have surveillance teams on the ground, but what happens once O'Malley enters the picture is an unknown."

"And Skylar goes home." I needed confirmation that another life wouldn't be ruined.

"If all goes well."

"If it doesn't?"

"I won't lie to you, Olivia. There's a chance we'll lose both of you. But we know what O'Malley wants. Once he has you he has no need for Skylar. The Bureau's had a lot of dealings with him. The man's a maniac, but he's not a monster."

I allowed my eyes to skim from the farmhouse porch out onto Cascade Lake. This inheritance had been built on nothing but lies. Lies constructed from reasons that I would never fully understand. But for the first time I could do something to stop the fallout. For the first time, I wouldn't be part of the cleanup crew.

"Ridge lost one sister, Agent Sowards. I won't let him lose another. But I have one request."

"What is it?" Sowards asked, eyes lit with hope.

"Ridge can't know. He made his decision to walk away–to give me a choice in how to live my life. This conversation never happened. No matter how this turns out, he needs to be able to go on with his life. Be there for his family. This is *my* choice."

"Understood." Sowards nodded somberly.

"Good. Then tell me what you want from me."

44

LIV

I spent the afternoon searching the internet for anything I could find about the government using psychics for issues of national security. If I was going to enter willingly into a government plan, I wanted to know what I was getting myself into. As suspected, I found nothing.

Sowards had given me my orders, told me exactly where the surveillance team would be along the route, which hotel I should check into as I drove from Cascade Hills to Charlottesville. They'd thought of everything. Now I was just waiting for his signal.

I closed my laptop and dialed Ridge's number. He was supposed to know I was on my way down. *"For moral support,"* Sowards had said. *"We need him focused on Skylar. Which means we need him to know you're safe."* But since I didn't get an answer, I guessed he was too busy for the support I'd been assigned to offer.

Ridge's voicemail picked up, the baritone of his greeting causing pinpricks of tears to threaten the back of my eyes.

You're being stupid, my inner critic chided. *This will all be over soon enough and you can go back to living your regular life.*

I wanted to believe that could be true. But I wasn't sure I had a regular life to go back to. The little I'd pieced together created doubt that there'd be any such thing now that I'd sold my soul to the devil disguised as the FBI.

I hung up without leaving a message.

As Sowards instructed, I hit the road around 8:00 P.M., map to Charlottesville loaded on my phone. I was somewhere in the middle of West Virginia when the hum of my tires on the freeway began lulling my eyes closed.

I cracked the window. Hoping the cool fall breeze would wake me up, thankful for the momentary reprieve. But the blast of a car horn punctuating my near miss with a mile marker a few minutes later told me it was time to pull over for the night.

I squinted at the next mile marker, two more miles and I'd make the meetup point. I could do this. I *had* to do this.

The hotel was the only one off the exit ramp, a run down three story structure with a strangely tropical name. I checked the parking lot for vehicles that could harbor a surveillance team, but the sprinkling of older model cars with out of state plates seemed typical for a West Virginian hotel named Hotel Del Ray. I shrugged it off. If I could see them, they wouldn't be doing their job, right?

I started the next day by following Sowards' instructions—eating breakfast at the McDonald's across the street from the hotel. It had been over a year since I'd ordered a greasy breakfast sandwich and the thought of Ridge's opinion of my meal choice brought an undeserved smile to my face. His aversion to fast food was almost comical. The rest of the day I spent in the hotel room, waiting for Sowards to text me my next move. Daytime talk shows and cheesy soap operas entertained me until the text finally came.

Contact confirmed.

I looked at the words, reading them over and over again as if trying to decipher another language. This was it.

I slipped down to the lounge and ordered a glass of wine. Adrenalin coursed through my veins, dulling the effects of the alcohol until I was well into my third glass.

By that time, I'd stopped glancing over my shoulder, instead, playing with my phone, scrolling through Instagram and Facebook feeds to keep my mind off the scenarios attacking my imagination. *"You've got to stay calm. No matter what happens, stay calm. And just remember, we're watching."* With help from the wine, Sowards' words started to take hold.

"Are you waiting for someone?"

The husky voice from behind caused the pleasant fuzziness of the wine to fall away for a split second.

"Can I buy you a drink?"

"No, thank you. I've got one," I said, the jagged timbre of raw nerves coloring my response. I turned toward the man standing over my left shoulder.

"You here alone?" he asked, glancing around the near empty bar. A pulse of anxiety slid through my stomach. He wasn't familiar. For some reason, I'd expected O'Malley's dark eyes. Instead, I got hazel irises set in a well-tanned face.

Say no, my inner critic instructed, operating on instinct. "No, he's just...he ran to the room for something." I noticed a bit of a slur as I fought to string the simple sentence together.

The stranger waved the bartender over and bought me

another White Zin. My glass was almost empty, after all. I sat a moment, staring at the glass and wondering how I'd lost time between asking for my third glass of wine and being approached by this stranger. I hadn't spilled any. Had I? I shrugged as fuzziness won and drained what was left in my glass, starting in on the gift from the stranger.

His tanned arm supported his weight on the bar next to me. I didn't catch his name. He was an archaeology student at Virginia Commonwealth University. We talked for a while before he offered to help me to my room. Logic disappeared along with Sowards' plan as I slid from the barstool. Giggling, I grabbed the seat back for support. All my focus went toward keeping one foot in front of the other. It felt completely normal when the stranger strung his arm around my waist.

I pulled my keycard from my back pocket and he swiped it to let us in. He loosened his grip on my waist as we entered and I pressed my palms against the wall for support. Unexpected vibrations sunk into my skin and I jerked away, busting my chin on the bedside table on my way to the floor.

Blood trickled from the gash in my mouth, coloring my memory with the metallic aftertaste as strange arms lifted me onto the bed. The room spun. I squinted against the vertigo until I heard another voice. Familiar this time.

"Relax, love. You'll just feel a pinch." Cool air skimmed across my shoulder as the neck of my shirt stretched wide. The sting was followed by a gentle rub as heat expanded through me. I opened my eyes on the man hovering over me as the world darkened and fell away.

45

RIDGE

B y the time Ridge pulled into Skylar's apartment complex in Charlottesville, his shoulder ached. A reminder that he wasn't supposed to be driving. He'd called in a few favors on the way and the local police department had opened a case. Within the first hour they'd turned it over to the feds, no doubt due to his FBI connections.

An agency detective was interviewing Skylar's roommate when Ridge arrived. But as he expected, she didn't know anything, and there was nothing out of the ordinary in his sister's apartment. The roommate had been home all weekend and swore up and down that Skylar never came back. Ridge hadn't called Brian yet. George had already talked to him, and Ridge knew he'd be next on the detective's list, but Ridge couldn't bring himself to make the call. Fielding Brian's concern would make it personal, and so far, he'd managed to stay detached.

Until Liv came into his life, Ridge had been a pro at distancing himself from the cases he worked. And he'd spent the drive to Charlottesville preparing himself for whatever might turn up at Skylar's. He'd be better off if he could think of her as just another case, but the penetrating knowledge that he might lose his last sister was doing a damn good job worming its way through his thickened skin just the same.

RIDGE PURPOSEFULLY IGNORED the calls from Liv that sprinkled in throughout the day. She'd left a message once, just checking in to see if there'd been any word on Skylar. There hadn't been, and he was too preoccupied scrutinizing every move of the detectives on scene to call her back. Besides, what would he say?

But that night, as he stood in the shower at the Holiday Inn, quiet thoughts crept in. What if Liv needed him, just like Megan Foster had that day she'd called from her office? Not that he'd been able to do her any good. In moments like this he wondered if Megan would still be alive if he'd never shown up, if he'd never given O'Malley a reason to show off.

He finished his shower and towel dried his hair. He glanced at the shoulder brace strung over the back of a hotel chair before deciding to go without. The pain from earlier had subsided, and the brace did nothing but make him feel like an incompetent invalid. That was the last thing he needed right now.

He slid into a worn pair of jeans, leaving the fly unbuttoned as he sat on the edge of the bed. Snatching his phone from the nightstand, he checked his voicemail—one more message from Liv—as a knock came on the door. He opened it without checking, his eyes still on the phone display, ready to hit Liv's name to return her call.

"Sorry I didn't call first, Ridge. I drove down as soon as I heard."

Bridget's voice drove him back a step.

"What are you doing here?" He pocketed his cell as his ex-wife pushed through into his room.

"Thought you might need someone to talk to." She said, looking up at him through long lashes. "And I brought some liquid courage." She held up a paper bag, withdrawing a bottle of Jack Daniels and stationing it carefully on the beverage center near the muted television.

"You know I don't drink that stuff anymore." He glanced both directions down the hotel hall before closing the door. "Where's Colton?"

"Relax, Ridge. I left him with Brian's sister. He's in good hands."

Ridge watched the woman he'd once loved crack open the black plastic seal around the neck of the bottle of Jack. *Don't do this*, his conscience whispered as she poured him a glass. But then she asked about Skylar.

"Have they found anything so far? Your dad said there was no sign of a struggle. That's a good thing, right?"

"It is," he said. The knot of pain he'd shoved aside loosened in his gut, traveling into his chest as he gave voice to the fact that his little sister was gone. Problem was, they hadn't found any signs of her, period. All calls to her cell were going unanswered, straight to a full voicemail box.

Highway Patrol across three states hadn't turned up any sign of her car. And at this point there'd been no hint of anyone who'd seen her since she left Cascade Hills. Ridge knew the statistics. With every hour that passed, she was less likely to be found. He pushed against his subconscious which finished the thought for him—at least found alive.

Ridge took the glass. Jack had been his nemesis, but it had also been his partner in crime on more than one occasion. He needed the release, the pleasant fog that suppressed emotion long enough for him to feel human again. He gulped the contents of the glass and held it out to Bridget for a refill. He'd been told in no uncertain terms that he needed to stay out of the way, let the feds do their job. So, what was wrong with a little escape?

Ridge exhaled a sigh of relief when he woke the next morning–alone. For once he'd managed to stave off the liberating effects Jack Daniels had on him, at least he hoped he had. He scrubbed a hand down his face and headed to the bathroom. There was a lot to do today. If there was still no sign of Skylar, he was going out himself. He'd drive her route, see if there was any evidence the other agencies had been unable to piece together.

He checked his phone again. He'd never returned Liv's calls. *Nice, McCaffrey*, he scolded himself, wondering if it was better this way. *Make it a clean break. Talking to her will only make it worse.* He tossed what was left of the Jack in the trash before getting dressed and heading out the door.

The corner table of the hotel restaurant had been taken over by familiar faces. George sat in the corner, staring into a cooling coffee, while two detectives flanked him. Bridget sat off to the side, which gave Ridge's gut a jolt that he promptly shook away. He didn't have time for that now.

He grabbed a coffee from the breakfast bar and headed their way, only noticing Sowards as he turned the corner, in full view of the table.

George saw Ridge first, glancing up at him and then across the table toward Agent Sowards, who took the hint and stood, facing Ridge.

"What are you doing here?" Ridge asked, glaring at his

superior. "You couldn't wait until we find my sister before carting me off to D.C.?"

George stood, both arms braced on the table for support as he spoke.

"Son, you need to have a seat. Agent Sowards has some–"

Ridge watched his father's jaw clench. The lines between his eyebrows deepened. He swallowed hard.

"He has some news," George finished before lowering himself back into his chair, picking up his coffee with a shaky hand.

Ridge scanned every face at the table, even Bridget's, who seemed to be the only one not seriously concerned by whatever Sowards had to say.

"There's been an incident," Sowards started, "involving Olivia."

Anger, like lava, surged through him. His hands balled into fists at his sides. This was a miscommunication. She'd left a message just yesterday.

"Son, she was on her way down. It's my fault for telling her to come." His dad glanced at Sowards. "I thought she'd be good for you. I thought she'd–" George's voice cracked as he broke down, turning away from the group as a series of choked sobs racked his chest.

"What happened?" Ridge stared at the white tablecloth, his fingers spread wide, waiting.

"Her vehicle was found at a hotel in Eastern West Virginia. Along I-64 near the National Park. Close to the state line." Sowards' voice lowered. "She's missing, Ridge. Right now that's all we know. I'm sorry."

The men at the table remained silent as Ridge processed the information. First his sister. Now Liv. He looked down. His fingers wrapped around the thick ceramic coffee mug in front of him. In one sudden movement, Ridge stood and launched the mug at the wall behind their group, smashing it into shards as coffee painted a stain on cream-colored wallpaper. He regretted the impulse as pain tore through his side and shoulder.

"Let him go," Sowards said as Ridge stormed out, his father calling his name.

AFTER A FRUITLESS TRIP to his sister's apartment, and a two hour drive out US64 to the Hotel Del Ray where Liv was last seen, Ridge drove back to Charlottesville and spent the rest of the afternoon in the hotel bar. George had taken Bridget to the airport, telling her that if she wanted to do something for Ridge, she needed to take care of Colton. At least that was one worry he had off his plate. If O'Malley had Liv, he was unlikely to come after Bridget or Colton.

Guilt bubbled in his chest, reminders of how he was supposed to be helping his dad through his sister's disappearance, and here he was drowning his sorrows in old friends. *But she's gone*, his subconscious said. *Not only Skylar, but Liv. O'Malley's taking everything that matters.*

Sowards found him at the bar around eight o'clock that evening. Ridge was already three sheets to the wind. His superior studied him. With bloodshot eyes and two-days' worth of stubble, Ridge's exterior was beginning to match that of the guilt-ridden fraud he felt like on the inside. Sowards settled onto the stool next to him as Ridge lifted his near empty glass to the bartender, who came around with the bottle of Macallan.

"How many of those have you had?" Sowards asked.

Ridge shrugged. "Eight, ten. Who knows?"

Sowards put his hand up to the bartender just as he began to pour.

"You can hold your liquor better than most. I'll give you that."

"I've had some practice," Ridge said. "Just one more." The bartender waited, eyes gleaming for the tip an evening of top shelf scotch might bring in.

Sowards nodded at the barkeep who topped off Ridge's glass with a smile.

"This was the last drink I had with Liv."

"And bathing in it will bring her back?"

"No. But it'll make the guilt go away. At least for a while." Ridge paused. "How could you let this happen? You knew O'Malley was going to come after her. You should have been ready."

"We'll find her," Sowards said. But he didn't sound sure.

"She tried to call yesterday, but I missed it. Look." Ridge pulled his cell from his pocket, Liv's name stood out in red lettering on his call log. His words slurred. His voice too loud. He tried to stand, but his legs wobbled beneath him.

"Okay, I get it," Sowards said, helping Ridge back onto the stool. "But there's something you should know." Sowards waved the bartender over and waited while he poured a Macallan of his own. "I met with her yesterday afternoon about the investigation."

"You saw Liv?" Ridge interrupted, alcohol fogging his brain.

Sowards nodded. "You were right, Ridge. She's not like the others. And she sure as hell cares about you. I don't fault you for falling for her. Hell, if I was ten years younger I might go after her myself."

"Twenty," Ridge interjected. "You'd have to be twenty years younger."

Sowards laughed. "Yeah. Okay. Twenty. I just wanted to let you know that I'm working some intel. But I need your help.

You're going to need to sober up and stay that way if you want to bring her back."

Ridge studied the man sitting next to him. It might have been the first worthwhile piece of advice he'd gotten all day.

"Tell me you're going to bring her back," Ridge said, his voice unsteady.

"We'll do everything within our power. You have my word."

It was the first time in twenty-four hours Ridge had felt a ribbon of relief wind through his gut. He nodded, sliding his half-empty glass of Macallan onto the bar.

46

LIV

P ain tore at my body as I fought away the remnants of sleep. Every muscle was tender, as if a thousand tiny ants were devouring me from the inside out. Even my lungs burned, the way they do with too much exertion.

I wanted to stretch, walk around, relieve some of the tension, but I couldn't. Thin plastic encircled my wrists, pinning them tightly behind my back. Zip-ties, maybe. They cut into my skin when I tried to pull my wrists free.

"Awake, are we?" A voice, familiar for reasons I didn't fully understand, tugged me into consciousness.

I jerked upright, blinking rapidly to clear my eyesight. The sudden movement sent throbbing pulses through my skull. I clenched my jaw against the pain and scanned my surroundings.

The room was small. Four walls patterned in broad stripes. A wide dark stripe, then a thinner light stripe, dark, then light, alternating from floor to ceiling. Above me, beams crisscrossed the peaked roof. As my eyes adjusted to the low light, I realized that the stripes were hewn logs, sandwiched between thick slabs of a mortar-like substance. A cabin.

My brain told me to run, but my legs were still a victim of whatever drug induced last night's loss of consciousness. I squinted away the remaining blurriness, focusing on the man sitting in the chair across from me. He had hazel eyes and sandy hair cut short and straight. A nondescript haircut that looked self-inflicted, made by electric clippers of some kind. His skin was a deep tan, a trait likely passed down to him through Latin American genealogy.

"Who are you?" I asked, willing my legs into motion when I noticed nothing was keeping me from running.

"Oh, Olivia, I'm crushed. After last night I thought you'd remember." He paused. "But it doesn't matter."

Clarity of the situation, and recognition of my captor as the man from the hotel bar, ignited a surge of panic. The heat shot through me, winning my legs over with a rush of adrenalin.

I was off the couch and to the door before he even got up from his chair, but it didn't take long for him to catch me. The door was closed. My bound wrists no match for an unfamiliar knob. Besides, my muscles just weren't working like they should.

I stumbled against a nearby table, the edge of it forcing me to my knees. A jagged piece of wood pierced the skin on my knee, even through the barrier of my jeans.

A dark circle of blood began to spread from the rip in the denim just as he grabbed me. With one arm around my waist and the other firmly securing my mouth, he dragged me away from the door.

I screamed as he let go of my mouth to chuck me onto the sofa. He grabbed a roll of duct tape from the peninsula in the corner of the room. Ripping a piece off with his teeth, he straddled me and pushed it hard onto my lips. My head sank into the sofa cushion with each thrust.

The zip-ties came next. Biting into the flesh above my tennis shoes as he jerked them tight.

When he was done, he stood back and looked at me. Prone on the sofa, my arms pinned behind me and my ankles secured together, causing my knees to lay off to the side. A slight smile spread across his thin lips. I could feel it in the air. Pleasure. The more I squirmed, the more he liked it. I closed my eyes and fought for calm.

As the sun was setting, waning rays peeking through the one window in the space, he left the cabin. The noisy exhaust from a pick-up truck got farther away from where I sat. I urged my one remaining tennis shoe loose on the edge of the couch cushion. Working my foot back and forth, I ignored the stabbing pain of a layer of skin sloughing off my ankle as I pulled free from the noose of plastic. I searched the tiny room for something sharp enough to cut through the zip-tie at my wrists.

The kitchen seemed the most likely place. I backed up to each drawer, pulling them open and turning to look inside, but every one was empty of utensils. Small specks of mouse droppings dotted yellowed shelf paper instead.

My heart thumped in panic, wondering when Sowards and his team would find me. I chomped the lining of my cheek, reopening the gash from the tumble I'd taken at the hotel. I fought the building pressure behind my eyes. *If Skylar was home, it didn't matter,* I told myself, intent on keeping emotion at bay.

That's when I saw it. An old-fashioned bottle opener

screwed to the wall near the kitchen sink. I maneuvered onto the countertop to get my hands close enough to reach it. Positioning my arms on either side of the antique, I forced the plastic against the metal teeth for as long as I dared, giving up only after the trickle of blood from the scuffs in the skin around the zip-ties, became too sticky.

I was almost back to the couch when I heard voices outside the cabin. I froze. The exhaust of the truck hadn't come back, but maybe I hadn't been paying attention.

Hazel-eyed man's harsh voice mingled with another tone. One I was sure I'd heard before but couldn't place. I returned to the couch where he'd left me, hoping he wouldn't notice the dislodged zip-tie on my ankle, or the splotches of blood on the kitchen countertop, and waited.

The voices grew closer while I tackled task number two on my list, finding my phone. I spotted it under a chair. Sliding my foot over, I guided the phone toward me, pressing the home button with my toe, hoping for a notification on the lock screen. Only the time, superimposed over the photograph I'd taken of Ha'Penny Bridge was visible. I shoved the phone under the sofa just behind my feet.

"It's all set. You just have to take her to O'Malley tomorrow. There's nothing to worry about."

"When do I get my cut?" My captor's voice cut in.

"Not until the job is done. O'Malley gets what he wants, we get what we want. Got it?"

The door clicked and an engine growled, growing softer as it pulled away. The air in the room charged as he entered, anxiety mixed with excitement. A dangerous combination.

"Just where I left you, what a good girl." His palm started down my hair as he stepped in front of me. A finger spiraled through a curl and he leaned over, breathing in my scent. Disgust tumbled in my gut as self-preservation took over. I heaved my legs upward as hard as I could, catching him in his lower belly.

He doubled over, groaning as I stumbled toward the door. I pulled at my hands, trying to break them free without the use of the bottle opener, but the zip-ties wouldn't budge. I turned around backward to grip the handle of the door. But the man in front of me lunged, knocking me down and pinning me to the floor.

"I don't know who you think you are, but you're going to pay for that, you little bitch."

He removed the belt from his cargo pants, striking me hard across the face with it. Tears spilled from the affected eye, and I closed them as he jerked me from the floor and bent me over the arm of the couch.

I spent the next twenty-four hours in a pain-induced fog. Raw patches of skin where my attacker had used the belt on me throbbed, but the harshest damage had been inflicted on my psyche.

The time I'd spent with his hands on me, violent energy coursing through my flesh was worse than any physical assault. I lay quietly on the couch, staring at the crisscrossed beams of the ceiling, wondering if this had always been part of the plan, and reminding myself why I'd agreed to offer myself as bait in the first place.

Around mid-afternoon, Alex–he'd eventually given me a name–blindfolded me and loaded me into a pick-up truck. I lay curled in the fetal position in the passenger seat as country music blared through staticky radio speakers. We drove for about twenty minutes, never leaving the shade of the forest's canopy.

We arrived at our destination in a squeak of brakes overdue for replacement. I could hear the rustle of leaves and the gurgle of a nearby creek. Still in the woods.

He jerked me from the cab of the truck. The smell of pine and rotting leaves overpowered my senses. He ushered me into a building, another cabin judging by the unmistakable pine scent, but bigger this time.

Down a hall, and into another room, he shoved me to the floor with his knee, reigniting a streak of fresh agony across the middle of my back. I fell forward against the hardwood unable to contain the whimper of pain.

Someone grabbed me by my hair and hoisted me up into a kneeling position, holding me upright with a firm grip on my shoulder. Another set of hands removed my blindfold. I blinked against the onslaught of light. O'Malley stood in front of me with the blindfold in his hand. The man from the hotel stayed to my right, clutching me as O'Malley looked me over. He walked a circle around me. His jaw set, eyes dark and angry.

The room was quiet. There was no conversation between the men as O'Malley set a video recorder on a tripod, swinging it one way then another before checking the angle in the viewfinder.

"Well, well, well, Olivia Sullivan. You have no idea how long I've waited for this day. Your reputation precedes you, you know?"

He cocked his head, watching me. Waiting.

"I thought it might be nice if we made a video for your boyfriend. I think he'd like to see that you're okay, don't you?"

I didn't answer. My mind spun. Was there anything I could do to help Ridge find me? Had Sowards already rescued Skylar? I scanned the room. Two windows were boarded from the inside. The little information I had was useless.

I edged away from my captor. His energy burning against my bare flesh. His attack on me left him feeling invincible, and his memories from the assault tumbled in my brain. His fingers tightened against my shoulder, letting loose a force that scorched against my skin. I jerked my arm from his grip, twisting to take in the entire room, scanning for exits.

My insubordination was quickly met by the back of my captor's hand to my face, toppling me to the hardwood floor with no way to right myself.

"Easy, Olsen." O'Malley reached to pull me upward, smoothing my hair as he waited for me to regain focus. "You've already done quite enough damage, don't you think?" Rage radiated through O'Malley's fingertips, but it wasn't directed at me. "We don't want her too scuffed up for her television debut, now do we?"

47

RIDGE

Ridge figured he was entitled to look as shitty as he felt the next morning when he walked into the hotel conference room that had become a makeshift field station. The tumbler of strong black coffee was barely penetrating the throbbing hangover. But, fortunately for him, thoughts of the missing women in his life broke through the wall of pain and spurred him into action.

Ridge sat his coffee on the table and took a seat, scanning the whiteboard Sowards had set up in the corner. His eyes held on the photo of Liv before moving downward toward crime scene photos of her hotel room.

"You didn't tell me you found blood," Ridge said. A cocktail of fear and anger heated his veins, intensifying the throbbing in his skull.

"You were hardly in a state to discuss evidence last night. But it's not much. Trace at best. Nothing to worry about at this point. We found a shoe, too." Sowards slid another photo toward Ridge. "Do you recognize this?"

Ridge nodded. He swallowed a knot of frustration as large

as Liv's size seven Converse sneaker. Sowards slid the pic to the side and continued to talk.

"We've traced the GPS on both Skylar and Liv's phones. Here's what we've found."

Sowards slid a laptop toward Ridge, pointing out map coordinates on the screen.

"Skylar's coordinates put her just outside Ohio, at the West Virginia line, and they haven't moved. Chances are she's been separated from her phone. I've got a team on the ground searching that location. Liv's, on the other hand, has her not far from here, in the Park."

Ridge pinched the bridge of his nose, trying to relieve the mounting pressure.

"But you think they're together." Ridge fought the conclusions that rushed at him. He needed to see this from every angle.

"Look, Ridge, we both know this is O'Malley's work. He knows what he has and he won't be afraid to use it to his advantage."

"Her," Ridge said quietly.

"Pardon?" Sowards responded.

"He won't be afraid to use *her* to his advantage. This isn't some random asset, Sowards. This is Liv we're talking about."

Sowards nodded his understanding.

"What do we know about O'Malley's associates? He had two men with him at the M.E.'s office. He can't be working this alone. Can we trace him that way?"

"He usually uses Irish imports. Possibly relatives. O'Malley has a brother. We've got Donaghey and his team in Ireland working to track him down as we speak. But so far, it's not clear."

"So now what? We just sit around and wait?" That mode of operation did not sit well with Ridge.

Sowards studied him for a beat. "We've got agents on the ground tracing Liv's phone coordinates."

Ridge leaned back in his chair. It was the first positive news he'd had in two days.

"How involved in this do you want to be, Ridge?"

"I'd say I'm already pretty damn well involved, wouldn't you?" The combination of hangover and headache was dulling his patience.

Sowards sat back against his chair. "We had a surveillance team at the hotel when Liv disappeared. I gave her my word I wouldn't tell you."

"Tell me what, exactly?"

Sowards brought his steel grey eyes up to meet Ridge's. "She wanted to help. O'Malley made contact. Offered Skylar in exchange for Olivia."

"Son of a bitch," Ridge scrubbed a hand through his hair. "You did this."

"The plan was to track her. Whoever took her knew what to look for. We found her tracking device on the bed in her hotel room."

"Of course you did. This is O'Malley we're dealing with here. He knows how we operate. Did you really think he'd just give up my sister and whisk Liv away with a trail of breadcrumbs to some hideout? You're out of your mind!"

"McCaffrey, you're the best agent I have for this, but I need you to stay objective. If you don't think you'll be able to handle this, I need to know."

"I'd say the bigger worry is your incompetence." Ridge's superior let the remark go. "I'll be fine. I just want them home."

Sowards nodded, his eyes scrutinizing the agent in front of him. "He's made contact again." Sowards started slowly, picking his words carefully. "We got a hit early this morning, sent through a secure web link."

He swiveled the laptop again to face Ridge. The black box of a cued-up video clip filled the screen.

"It's a segment of surveillance video. I think they're using it as a test, to make sure we're watching." Sowards pushed play.

Ridge sucked in a breath as an image of Liv materialized on the screen. The quality was good, better than the grainy security footage most businesses used. He watched as she worked to free her feet from tethers. A ribbon of relief slithered through him as she found success and headed toward the kitchen. She scoured drawers and cabinets, before disappearing from the frame, reappearing moments later and returning to the sofa. She glanced toward the door several times before a man entered.

Ridge leaned closer to the screen. Pausing the video as the stranger's face became fully visible.

"We're already running him through the database," Sowards said, one step ahead. Ridge pushed play again.

His muscles jerked as the man in the frame yanked Liv to the ground, removing his belt. Sowards reached over Ridge's shoulder and closed the laptop.

"You should stop there."

Ridge laid his hands on the hard shell of the computer, spreading his fingers wide and fighting the anger that seethed inside.

"I'll give you a minute." Sowards left the room, the door clicking closed as Ridge struggled for control. His body vibrated. It was all he could do to keep from throwing the laptop against the wall, but after yesterday morning's outburst he figured he'd better resist the urge.

His mind spun through possible scenarios. Each one more brutal than the last. He had to find Liv. Had to find Skylar. Before both of them ended up broken and scarred, or dead.

Ridge scooted his chair away from the table and retreated

to the other side of the room. He ran his hand up the back of his head, rubbing at the ropes of tension in his neck.

Sowards knocked before reentering, apologizing to Ridge as he gathered his things. "I'll keep you posted. We've got IT working on getting us an IP address. We're searching every cabin in the park. If they're there, we'll find them."

"If I'm going to be part of this, we need to do it my way. I want people I can trust. Put Adam Miller in charge of surveillance."

"Done," Sowards agreed. "And Ridge, I am sorry. I never thought our team would miss them like that."

Ridge turned the knob on the door and exited. No apology would ever be enough.

GEORGE SLID into the booth opposite Ridge after dinner. He sat in silence for a moment, watching Ridge twirl a glass of water in front of him.

"I know how hard this is on you, son. I heard about the video."

Ridge took a gulp of the water and leaned back against the booth. "I haven't felt this powerless since Riley died." The image of his older sister being pulled from their burning home haunted his memory. "They're being punished for my sins, Dad. How am I supposed to live with that?"

George reached inside his coat pocket and slid an envelope toward Ridge.

"What's this?" Ridge pulled a hotel reservation out of the enclosure.

"I knew you wouldn't want to stay with Bridget. And I figured the farm would be too hard. But, you need to go back to

Cascade Hills. Be with Colton. One of these days you'll wish you'd had more time with him."

Ridge knew his dad was trying to ease his own demons.

"What about you?"

"I'm going home, too," George answered. "There's no reason to stay holed up in this hotel. Sowards said he'd move the operation to his field station in D.C. or wherever. He said you could decide. Between the FBI and the police, I think the investigation is under control. It's just a couple hours' drive either way. We'll meet up when the team finds them."

That was his dad. The eternal optimist.

"Right," Ridge said, choking back the *"What if they don't?"* that hovered on the tip of his tongue. He reached his hand across the table to cover George's. No matter what happened, they were going to need each other when all this was over. And no one knew that more than him.

48

LIV

My knee throbbed as I kneeled on the floor in front of O'Malley. The other man's fingers dug into the flesh under my arm. There wasn't a part of my body that didn't scream with pain.

"Get rid of the tape," O'Malley ordered as he pushed a button on the camera, prompting steady illumination from a backlit screen. "I need her to talk."

Alex ripped the duct tape from my lips. I stifled the gasp that rose in my throat. I wouldn't give him the pleasure of seeing me in pain. My lips burned, raw and sore. Memories of Jason's attack at the Marriott, not all that long ago, prodded from the recesses of my brain. I had a feeling things wouldn't end quite the same way tonight.

"This transmission is intended for Special Agent Ridge McCaffrey of the Counterintelligence Task Force." O'Malley's voice launched my heart into an erratic rhythm.

Ridge would see this. I glanced back and forth between the man who'd already abused me and the man who likely would, fixing my gaze on the camera lens. On Ridge.

"Agent McCaffrey, I want to remind you that I gave you every opportunity to prevent this. To ensure Miss Sullivan was taken care of properly, under your supervision. But you declined. So now, she's mine. To use as I see fit."

I felt a tear spill down my cheek, burning as it crossed a gash left by my abuser's belt. O'Malley approached, wiping the moisture away with his thumb before sliding his hand over my head, through my hair, grasping a handful and jerking backward. The scream was instinctual as he held me there, twisting slightly so that the side of my neck was fully exposed.

"No worries, love," he said, leaning in. The same voice I'd heard in the hotel–and in Jessica Garrison's apartment. I shivered against his breath along the length of my neck. Adrenaline spiked through my veins with the *shink* of a blade being unsheathed. O'Malley breathed, "Just relax."

I tried to push myself from the floor, fought against the two men as a hand grew tighter on my shoulder. O'Malley's fist tangled to the point of pain in my hair, eliciting an instinctive yelp. He pulled harder, keeping me still, as the prick of a needle plunged into the side of my neck.

"Your girl here has a lot of fight, McCaffrey. I'll give her that," O'Malley said as he emptied the syringe in a slow drip. I immediately felt why. The liquid was thick, slogging through my veins like lead as it began its course through my system. I moved my lips to scream, but no sound came.

I clenched my jaw against the coursing wave of pain, needles stabbing my muscles from the inside, through my neck down into my chest and out to my fingertips. I focused on the cold of the blade against my throat as O'Malley released my hair and pulled away, leaving his accomplice in control.

Each breath proved more difficult than the last as the liquid crawled through my system. My lungs smoldered in an oxygen-deprived fire. Cold steel against my neck juxtaposed the heat in my veins with every gasp.

O'Malley addressed the camera as tiny stars danced in my vision. "You might remember that we spoke about this briefly at the medical examiner's office. But since you didn't believe me then, I thought it only fair that I show you firsthand what we're up against. This is what your government is asking for."

A surge of bright white light seared through my skull, as Alex's grip tightened, fingers like a vise on my collarbone. My muscles liquefied, rendered useless, and I fell, enveloped by an abyss of darkness.

"Olivia," O'Malley called for me. Once, twice, three times as the room spun, fuzzy, out of focus. I wished for the return of the pleasant paralysis of the night before, but it never came. This drug was different, toxic. O'Malley knelt in front of me, pulling me from the floor into a seated position. His firm grip on my shoulders steadied me as I swayed.

"We need to help him understand, Olivia. Tell us what you know about Saoirse Quinn."

A dagger of light split through my brain at the mention of her name. Piercing pain followed. I curled into a ball on the floor, slowly shaking my head. Moaning. I focused on the vibration from my own throat. Anything to prevent the slicing ache in my skull. But her eyes came, imploring, resentful.

I slid in and out of consciousness. Blackness dissolving into an electrical storm of information pounding over me. Each scene tearing through as if I'd lived it myself.

Fuzzy half-memories of a toddler gave way to the solidity of Saoirse's recent years. Growing up at the children's home. Watching in tears as friends left St. Mary's. Signing her name below Jessica's and my mother's in her Bible. Vowing to reunite someday. Black suits. O'Malley's eyes. Glad opportunity morphing into loneliness, pain. Her face crumbling into one emotion. Fear.

A lull in the snippets of Saoirse's life gave way to O'Malley's voice. He coached me as the images jackhammered into my consciousness. Asking for information, probing deeper, forcing me to tell him what I saw. Directing me toward the facts he was looking for.

"Tell me what happened to her."

I don't know if I answered. I think so. But I'd lost myself. Each vignette struck like a bolt of lightning. Melting the real world away with a surge of pain. No longer tickles of emotion against my skin, Saoirse's emotions meshed with my own, taking over. I felt her fear as she woke in a strange place—sterile and white. Her anxiety clenched in my chest as a drug was delivered. The slog of it through her veins suffocating as she gasped for breath.

The young girl's drug-induced vignettes cut into my own. She'd woken in pain. Abused. Her heart thumped as my own as she escaped a tiny room. Trying not to breathe as she hid in darkness. Footsteps pounded nearby as he looked for her.

"He's coming," I heard myself whisper as she hid in the brush at the foot of the hills. I'd been there before. Dublin. Strong arms, like steel. A scream. I wasn't sure if it was hers or my own. Maybe both. I struggled against the force of the vision, as real as if I was experiencing it myself. Hard hands around my neck. Choking. Gasping.

"Who?" O'Malley pushed for more.

One last reel of images thrust into my mind. One I'd already seen in my own dreams. Crying. Begging for her life. Scratching against the hands at her throat. Squeezing. Pushing. Fear-widened eyes. Burning lungs. Steel grey eyes. A Bureau directive.

I breathed his name. A final exhale into blackness.

I woke on the couch in O'Malley's office. My mind sluggish, taking longer to process my surroundings. I scanned the room three times before I understood where I was. I attempted to sit, but my body was limp, trembling with the drug's side effects and remnants of emotion that pulsed through my system.

I fought through the haze, finding O'Malley sitting across from me, watching.

"That was quite a performance, Olivia." He leaned forward and stroked my head, pulling strands of hair out of my face and tucking them behind my ear. "You're the first that's been able to name him. Thank you."

My chest was heavy, like my lungs were full of lead. It took all my focus to push air in and out. My mind swirled with images of Saoirse. The circumstances surrounding her death pummeling my memory. Familiar eyes I'd seen at my own farm danced in and out of my periphery.

"Take a sip of water," O'Malley encouraged as my brain flitted on the verge of unconsciousness. "You need to stay hydrated."

My head sank back onto the pillow. Every muscle ached. Burning and screaming in protest to each tiny movement.

"I hoped I'd never have to use this on you," O'Malley started, still caressing the side of my head. "But you were the only one strong enough. They needed to see. They need to know what's really happening."

O'Malley tended to the gash on my cheek. He pressed a gauze pad lightly over it, my cheek throbbing with the pressure as he removed caked blood from my face and hairline.

"I should apologize for our friend's behavior. Alex? If that's truly his name."

O'Malley saturated a square of gauze with hydrogen

peroxide. The slosh of the bottle echoed against my overly sensitive eardrums. I turned my head away as he brought the pad to my face, but he gently repositioned me, forcing me to surrender to the coolness against my flesh.

"You'll be pleased to know I've relieved him of his duties."

Confusion permeated my skull. Comprehension of what had happened still out of reach. O'Malley finished his first aid duties by smoothing a bandage over the cut.

"Get some rest, Olivia. Tomorrow will be a big day." He pulled a blanket from the back of the couch, sliding it over me as I whispered, "Where's Skylar?"

O'Malley's brows pinched together, a glimmer of understanding colored his eyes as I lost the fight for consciousness.

49

RIDGE

It took some talking, but Sowards finally relented to Ridge's request to house the investigation in Cascade Hills. It gave him time with Colton he wouldn't otherwise have. And somehow made him feel closer to Liv.

Ridge drove each morning from his hotel to the makeshift station in Murphy's back room, going through the details of the case in his mind. Trying to wrap his head around the fact that the Bureau, with the best investigative tools in the country, was no closer to finding Skylar and Liv than they'd been the day they'd gone missing was a mounting challenge.

He never made the ten-minute drive without replaying his run-in with O'Malley. Questioning whether Skylar and Liv would be missing at all if he'd agreed to help his former roommate. He shook off the nagging guilt as he pulled into Murphy's parking lot, slamming the car door harder than necessary.

Sowards slid a bag across the table toward Ridge as soon as he entered. He caught it just before it made it to the edge.

"They just brought it in. Miller and Chadwick are in the pub getting coffee. I'll let them tell you what they found."

Ridge lowered himself into a chair slowly, his fingers sliding over the rectangular device in his hand. He heard the two agents come in, even say hello, but when Ridge didn't engage in small talk, Adam launched right in.

"Teams found the cabin last night. The one on the surveillance video. Can you identify the phone, Ridge?"

Ridge nodded, clearing his throat of the emotion gripping his vocal cords. "It's Liv's."

Adam slid into the chair beside Ridge as he and Chadwick relayed the team's findings. The conversation moved in slow-motion. Trace amounts of blood, the signs of a struggle, boot prints and tire tracks in the mud outside. Probably a full size pick-up. They'd found some hair, some fingerprints. Everything was being processed. But no Liv. No Skylar. No perp.

"I told Sowards you might know the passcode. If you do we can send it up to tech, put a rush in to see if there's anything that can help us."

"It used to be 7667," Ridge said. "The address of the farm."

Adam nodded, clapping Ridge on the shoulder before sliding the phone out of his grasp.

"I'll let you know if we find anything, Ridge."

Chadwick was already halfway through the door as Ridge asked one last question. "Where is it? The cabin?"

"Not far from US64. It's nothing more than a hunting shack. One room. No running water."

The men hesitated before Sowards waved them away. The door swung closed behind them with a thump.

"Why don't you take some time, Ridge. Stay away for a few days, at least until forensics on the cabin come back."

"The best investigative team in the country and we can't

find two missing women? Hell, we've got prints, DNA, tire tracks. Where'd the truck go, Sowards?"

Sowards ignored Ridge's question. "I've been weighing whether or not to show you this. I didn't want to make the investigation any worse for you."

He slid a paper across the table to Ridge. A report from the federal lab. Ridge checked the name, Jessica Garrison.

"Our lab confirmed your Jane Doe is Garrison. Her DNA was in our ghost database. It's why Cascade Hills couldn't ID her. Anyway, those are the findings."

Ridge read the report from the federal lab twice before giving voice to the words. "Irreparable damage to areas of the cerebral cortex. Particularly the parietal and temporal lobes." He looked at Sowards. "You're giving up on Liv."

Ridge stared at his supervisor. Grey eyes held firm. Ridge knew Sowards was doing his job, what he himself would do if the situation weren't as screwed up as it was.

"I'm calling it like I see it. We know O'Malley wants something from us. And just like Garrison, he'll use her until she's all used up. Even if we find her in time, she won't be the Liv you knew."

In that moment, Ridge couldn't breathe. His jaw clenched as he struggled for calm that refused to come.

"Garrison was dumped six days after her abduction," Sowards continued. "This is Liv's sixth day. You need to prepare yourself for the worst."

"You don't know her like I do," Ridge said as he shoved the lab report across the table and stood.

"Ridge, be realistic."

Ridge slammed the back room door open, bouncing it off the hallway wall as he strode out.

"Go to hell, Sowards."

Adam tracked down Ridge in Murphy's Pub after dinner. Ridge was tucked in the farthest booth from the door, poring over research he'd found on drug induced brain injury. It wasn't good news.

"Up for some company?" Adam asked as he approached.

Ridge waved him into the booth, pulling the paperwork into a pile before taking a swig of the Guinness in front of him. Adam eyed the beverage with suspicion.

"Give me a break, Adam. I'm just having the one," Ridge defended as Adam slid into the other side, holding up both hands in surrender. Ever since he'd fallen off the deep end with the Macallan, he'd been getting scrutiny from everyone.

"I found something," Adam started. "On Liv's phone."

Ridge stayed silent, gauging what was to come.

"It's a link. Sent as a message from a burner cell. I'm working on a trace to the closest cell tower, but it's bounced all over the place. I haven't been able to pinpoint it yet."

Adam slid the phone to Ridge, a set of earbuds already attached. "The link opens a video in a new window."

Ridge searched his partner's face. Where there was usually a smile, Adam's lips pressed into a hard, thin line. Ridge took his time with the earbuds, checking the sound before tapping the link with a shaky finger.

He sucked in a breath when he saw her. Bound and gagged on her knees, blood dried down the side of her face. He recognized O'Malley as he stepped into frame, ordering the tape from her mouth. Ridge flinched as the second man ripped it free.

By the time O'Malley plunged the needle into Liv's neck, Ridge was seething. His heart pounded against his sternum and throbbed in his ears. Liv's screams silenced with the onslaught of O'Malley's drug. By the time it was over, Ridge tore the earbuds from his ears and launched himself from the booth, pacing the empty corner until Adam spoke.

"You need to come clean, Ridge. What happened in the M.E.'s office? What does O'Malley want?"

"I got the shit beat out of me, that's what happened," Ridge answered.

"If you know something we don't, you jeopardize this entire operation. You might never get them back."

Ridge returned to the booth. His eyes on Adam. He didn't know who to trust anymore.

"Come on, Ridge. We've been partners ever since they stranded us on this island. When are you going to start trusting me?"

"Have you shown Sowards?" Ridge asked.

"Of course not. A video that paints the Bureau as the enemy? Him as a murderer? He'd go straight to the director. We need to know what O'Malley wants first. How he's planting these ideas."

"What if he's not planting them. What if it's the truth?"

Adam stared at Ridge. "Either way, we've got to figure out what we're up against."

"How long until you can determine where it came from?"

"I'm working on it. Could be hours, could be never. Whoever sent it knew how to bounce the signal."

Ridge eyed Adam over his drink. He'd always been one to keep his cards close, but he couldn't do this on his own. Trust was hard. But living without Skylar and Liv was worse. He swallowed the knot in his throat.

"O'Malley said he wanted Liv as an insurance policy. Sowards admitted Cam's making some drug that will replace GenLink. I think that's what the Bureau's after. But if what Liv says in that video holds any truth, O'Malley wanted Liv for one reason–to clear his name." Ridge slid a hand through his hair.

Adam's voice was low. "If O'Malley's found a way to manufacture lies about Bureau brass, then the viability of GenLink is the least of our worries."

Ridge considered the accusations being made against the very agency he worked for, the men at the helm. "But why, Adam? Why have a blacklisted ex-agent create a drug that could pull the entire agency down with it? It doesn't make sense."

"Agreed. But it explains why the Bureau has gone out of their way to shield Liv. And it explains why O'Malley would want her. But what about Skylar?"

"I don't know. Cam never mentioned Skylar. Sowards was the one who–" Ridge's stomach took a dive.

"Jesus, Ridge, you can't believe what's on that tape. You have no idea what O'Malley did to get Liv to say that shit. Sowards isn't involved in this. That's ridiculous. O'Malley's crazy. He could have planted that."

"Sowards is the one who pulled Liv in after Skylar disappeared. I don't know what he said to her, what he promised, but what if the Bureau has had Skylar all along? What if O'Malley's right? What if the real enemy is us?"

Adam's face fell. "You need to listen to yourself, Ridge. I get how stressful this is for you, but that video is the work of a known lunatic. You're spouting a conspiracy theory spawned by a psychopath, and the dots don't connect. You'll get yourself suspended for shit like this."

"What have I got to lose?"

50

LIV

T he faint glow from a small brass lamp on O'Malley's desk was the only light in the room when I woke. The air hung still and quiet. I could feel him watching me from behind the lamplight.

I sucked in a breath, trying to fill my lungs, but I couldn't get enough in. I lurched forward in a series of coughs. My body's way of trying to break up the heaviness weighing down my chest.

"Take small breaths." I heard as O'Malley came closer. His silhouette blocked the little light as he crossed the room toward me.

He handed me a cup of water, supporting my head as the coughs subsided.

I had no concrete memories of the last days. My body was retaliating against the drugs. Deep breaths were a chore, every muscle ached, and keeping food down was a luxury I no longer possessed. Besides the constant state of physical exhaustion, my brain remained scrambled by the combination of powerful drugs and haunting images.

"What is it you want from me?" I asked, my eyes closed as I fought for some semblance of clarity.

"You've already provided it. I needed proof, Olivia. Proof that the Bureau ruined my sister's life."

"Saoirse was your sister," I whispered, barely able to force the words through my lips. The images still spinning through my head confirmed it. A brother and sister separated after a tragic accident. The love I'd felt at the children's home, magnified by whatever drug O'Malley had injected into my veins. A brother desperate for answers after his sister's disappearance.

Cool moisture slid against my forehead. A washcloth. I opened my eyes on O'Malley's concerned stare.

"GenLink was Saoirse's way out. Her happiness meant everything to me. Your grandmother created the program for the right reasons, Olivia. But at some point, government greed stepped in. It's time for the truth to come out. My sister didn't need to die in vain."

O'Malley's words sounded far away, teetering on the ledge of an abyss of despair. Understanding slammed into me. My heart lurched, thrumming erratically.

"It's what you tried to get from Jessica, isn't it?"

"Jessica's death was an accident, Olivia. I didn't know he'd been there before me, that she'd already had too much." Sadness crept from O'Malley's fingers as he brushed hair from the side of my face.

"Who was there?" I asked, forcing my eyes open.

"Sowards," O'Malley said.

I closed my eyes, tears leaking from the corner as realization hit me.

"The fire at the children's home? My mother was right, wasn't she?"

O'Malley nodded. "And the fire at Cohen's," he added.

"They knew you were one who could bring them down, Olivia. What's the saying? Keep your friends close and your enemies closer?"

Something warm and soothing seeped from the cool of O'Malley's hands on either side of my face. I focused my eyes on his. Dark pools of chocolate stared back.

"I'll let you go. I've already made that promise. But I need you tonight. He wants the drug. He's coming here to get it. You represent the truth, Olivia. And you are everything he hates. Everything he's trying to destroy."

"But, why?" I asked. "What have I done?"

O'Malley ignored my questions, lost in a world of his own. "It was bad enough when they separated us after our parents died. But the Bureau promised to protect her. Just like they were supposed to protect you."

Flashes of Saoirse's past filtered through my memory. The black suits offering her a better life. Her optimism, followed by abuse, rejection. And finally, death. O'Malley's energy set off a moment of clarity that had been absent since the first round of drugs slogged through my veins.

"But if she was an asset, part of GenLink, why kill her? I don't understand." Fingers of haze started creeping back in. I pushed myself higher on the couch to shove it away.

"The same reason they started the fire at Cohen's. They have no interest in a genetic program, Liv. Not now that they've realized the very assets they've sworn to protect have become their own worst enemies. They can't hide the truth from you. But you do have a weakness—timing. Your abilities work on your schedule, no one else's. Until I created this."

O'Malley held up a vial of the heavy yellow liquid that had been burning through my veins.

"They can find out what you know and put an end to you. All in one fell swoop."

I sucked in another unsteady breath. My lungs burned with the exhale. A tear trailed down my cheek, but my arms ached too much to wipe it away. *Why?* The word wound itself around my consciousness, but I couldn't force it free.

"They know exactly where you are. And they left you here." The pad of O'Malley's thumb crossed gently over my cheek. "You've felt it. You know I'm not lying."

I closed my eyes, swallowing the sob that gripped my chest with a whimper. I had felt it. Each time O'Malley's fingers slid down my neck as he administered the drug I'd seen flashes of it. His anger at the Bureau, his need to avenge his sister and the girls at St. Mary's. The line between good and evil blurred beyond recognition.

"I can't do this anymore," I whispered as the tears came. Tears for Saoirse, for Jessica, for my birthmother. For Skylar, still lost to her family.

"You won't need to," O'Malley said. "I promised him an effective product. That's what I plan to deliver."

"You can't do this to anyone else. They won't know how to deal with it." A fit of coughs erupted as I struggled to sit up. I pushed at O'Malley with weakened arms, fighting for breath.

"Calm down, Olivia." He settled me back onto the couch, coaching me through tiny breaths that left me lightheaded. "I don't plan to let them get that far."

He stroked my head as my breath returned. "Don't worry. I gave Herman my word I'd take you just far enough to uncover the truth. The rest will be a gift."

I jerked forward at the mention of Herman's name. Air caught in my lungs as they seized, unable to function.

"Your truth will set all of us free, Olivia."

51

RIDGE

The next morning, Ridge picked up Colton and they headed out of town, past Murphy's, toward the open countryside. It was a welcome reprieve from Murphy's back room and Sowards' bad news.

"Where we going, Daddy?" Colton asked as Ridge drove.

Ridge glanced in the rear-view mirror, smiling at his son, poised with a matchbox car in each hand, riding cheerfully in the back seat.

"I thought we'd go check on Livvie's house today, bud. What do you think?"

"Is Livvie home?" His son's eyes brightened.

"Not yet, bud. Soon, maybe."

"Okay," Colton said agreeably.

They rode in silence until they got to the farm, Ridge hoisted his mini-me out of the back of the two-door car and up into the air. Colton squealed with delight, taking off at a run across the frost-crunchy grass of the side yard.

When he was able to wrangle Colton inside, his heart sank. The house was just as it had been the day she'd left. The

Macallan bottle and glasses still sat on the side table in front of the fireplace. The quilt bunched and wrinkled on the floor. Disjointed memories of their last night together tumbled through his brain. The final time he'd held her and he couldn't even remember.

He deserved this pain. Every ounce of it, he knew. But she didn't. The people who loved her, who missed her, didn't deserve it. Nothing she'd done justified the treatment she was enduring. Images from the video Adam showed him kept him up most of the night. The recording had been time stamped. That was just one incident of many he assumed were taking place in O'Malley's hideout. If O'Malley had wanted a glaring affront against the Bureau, he'd found it with Liv's relay of Saoirse's final days. But he still couldn't process why the FBI would go to such lengths. Without motive, he had nothing more than a hunch and the recorded ramblings of a drugged psychic. Neither of which would hold up in court.

Ridge spent the afternoon tidying the farmhouse. It was obvious the Bureau techs had been there, searching for some clue to Liv's disappearance. But they didn't know her like he did. Liv's computer was missing from its usual station on the table in the dining room. Probably taken in the search.

He washed some dishes and cleaned up the mess in the living room, brought in more firewood...just in case. *Just in case you have to hold her memorial service here?* He shook the unwelcome thought away.

Other than the imaginative mumblings of an inventive toddler, the house remained quiet until his phone buzzed around two P.M. "Are you sitting down?" The excitement in Adam's voice caught Ridge's attention.

"Yes," Ridge lied as he scoured the upstairs bathroom sink. He'd already bagged Liv's dingy clothes from the blast. They'd still been sitting on the edge of the countertop, dusting the white porcelain with a thin layer of grime that Ridge felt inclined to remove.

"They found O'Malley. He's holed up in a cabin in George Washington National Park. We're prepping to go in as we speak."

Adam was waiting for a response. Ridge braced himself on the sink. White foam from the sponge leaked between his fingers.

"Ridge. This is it. We're gonna bring them home. The rest we can worry about later."

52

LIV

"What time is it?" I asked when I woke that evening. O'Malley pulled me from the bed in the spare room and ushered me down the hall ahead of him. The cabin was quiet. Drops of rain on the metal roof pelted out an eerie soundtrack.

"Late," O'Malley finally answered, gripping my wrists more tightly than necessary as he stopped in front of his office, the room I'd spent far too much time in already. Anxiety slid from his skin into mine.

"Best behavior," he reminded me as his breath grazed the top of my ear. The fingers of his left hand pushed into the pocket of my jeans, and I squirmed against him.

"Shh," he soothed, withdrawing his hand and leaving a hardened wedge poking my skin between layers of denim.

"What is it?" I whispered, twisting my body in an effort to make out the expression on his face. But he jerked me forward.

"We're both after the same thing here." The words sent a shiver down my spine. Now I'd been lumped into O'Malley's reign of vengeance. Except, I realized. He wasn't wrong.

He turned the handle and pushed the door inward, jerking me along in front of him as he entered the room. It took a few moments for my vision to adjust to the brightness of Cam's office. Every lamp was lit. Can lights in the ceiling I hadn't known existed shone beams of white down into the room. As I blinked through the ache behind my eyes, a familiar voice said my name. Instinct forced the reality of the moment to slam into me. With my name on his lips I was back at the farm, laying on a carpet of damp vegetation.

"No," I said. Cam heaved me forward and forced me down to my knees in front of the visitor, an act which hadn't occurred since my original captor had been relieved of his duties. I cast my eyes on the man's shoes. Afraid to look up into the face I knew I'd see. Rich mahogany lace ups. The leather so shiny, I could see my reflection, dark circled eyes and all.

"It's nice to see you again, Olivia. Please, have a seat." He gestured to the leather armchair next to him.

O'Malley was still holding my wrists behind my back. I could feel the nervousness jittering off of him in waves. With the visitor's request, he jerked upward, sending a shooting pain through my shoulder blades. I teetered backward as I rose, fighting the urge to cough as the tearing pain subsided.

"There's no need to be rough, O'Malley. Release her hands. Olivia and I have an understanding, don't we?"

O'Malley freed my wrists. I rubbed them gently as I sat in the armchair, still avoiding a look at the man across from me. For the casual observer this may have looked like a friendly gathering. O'Malley in the armchair to my left, Special Agent in Charge Marcus Sowards immediately in front of me.

"You look surprised to see me, Olivia. I hope you aren't too disappointed that Agent McCaffrey isn't here."

Sowards pulled a book of matches and a cigar from his pocket. I watched him clip the tip off, letting it fall to the floor, before he puffed the cigar to life. Three quick draws before he was satisfied. Replacing the book of matches, he glanced at the lit end and settled back into his chair. The stench of smoke wafted my direction, and I turned my head to avoid the assault on my lungs.

"I promised you we'd take care of you, didn't I?"

I chomped on the inside of my cheek, refusing to show the building emotion. As we sat, Sowards' energy surged, filtering through the fog of my brain. Money changing hands, innocent young women dying, agents placed in the line of fire, and the man I loved part of it all.

"Is Skylar home?" I breathed the words, hope building in my polluted chest.

Sowards didn't answer. Instead, he reached for me, skimming his fingers from my shoulder to my wrist. Heat from his fingertips singed my skin and his eyes burnt into me as he spoke to O'Malley.

"I must say, Cam. I've been impressed with your commitment. You seem to have worked out the dosing issues."

"I've done what you asked."

"Yes," Sowards said, squinting his eyes as he pulled on his cigar. "Perhaps more than I've asked, is that right?"

Sowards turned, blowing a stream of smoke in my direction. My lungs seized, erupting into a fit of coughs that doubled me over. He gripped my shoulder and jerked me off the chair. I sucked in as much oxygen as I could, wheezing as I crawled toward the protection of O'Malley's desk.

Cam thrust himself between us. Holding his hand out to stop Sowards' advance. In the light, the tattooed cross caught my attention, a surging ribbon of doubt winding through me.

"She's already lasted days longer than the last asset. Do you really need another Garrison on your hands?"

Sowards hesitated, as if he was considering O'Malley's

objection. He screwed his face into a grimace. "Care to explain your little videos, Cam? Personal messages to Agent McCaffrey?"

He laid his cigar in the ashtray on Cam's desk. "It seems to me an unfortunate accident is exactly what this situation calls for." A flash of metal caught the light as Sowards drew his weapon, pointing it at Cam as my coughs subsided.

"Open the door," Sowards ordered.

A thump in the hall stopped Cam cold. "You said you were coming alone."

"We all say things we don't mean sometimes." Sowards gripped my upper arm, his fingers digging into sensitive flesh. O'Malley walked to the door and disengaged the lock.

The door sprung inward with force, knocking O'Malley back a few steps. A bound body fell into the room, somersaulting over the floor. I sucked in a lungful of air, my eyes focused on a mass of dark matted hair.

"Skylar," I wheezed, pulling against Sowards to get closer to Ridge's sister. He let me go, and I lurched forward, dropping to the ground as a single gunshot exploded in the room. I lifted my head from the floor, watching in horror as fingers of blood leaked from a head wound on O'Malley's lifeless body.

Sowards dragged Skylar past me, toward O'Malley's desk in the center of the room. She was bound and gagged, blindfolded, but she was fighting. Her body writhing against Sowards' grip. A tendril of relief filtered through me.

"Now that the hard part's done," Sowards started, leaning down. Stale, cigar-scented breath puffed across the back of my neck and along my jaw. "Why don't we have a little fun?"

I felt him shift behind me. Exchanging his grip for a knee against my spine as he pulled Skylar closer, face down on the hardwood. I saw her wince against the bite of a too tight zip tie.

"It's okay, Sky," I offered, reaching my hand toward her as

Sowards pulled me upright into a sitting position, kneeling in front of us both as he spoke.

"So, what is it about the two of you that has Special Agent McCaffrey so willing to give up everything to bring you home?" He brushed a hand over the side of my face, smoothing unruly curls. "Do you know he's already concocting some crazy conspiracy theory about your disappearance?"

I didn't answer. What did he want me to say? One corner of his lips tipped into a smile.

"It's unfortunate the two of you will miss out on your happily ever afters." Sowards paused, nodding toward the exterior wall of the office. "McCaffrey's out there now you know. Waiting."

My heart leapt in my chest as I sucked in a breath. Too fast. A series of coughs followed.

Sowards' half smile morphed into a full grin. "Ah, there it is. Hopefulness. Just the reaction I was looking for. However, that was never part of the plan. O'Malley made his mistakes. Now it's time for you to pay for them."

He took my chin between his thumb and forefinger, turning my head first one way and then the other.

"You do bear a striking resemblance to your mother, Olivia. Remarkable."

Loud voices, indecipherable shouts, sounded from outside as Sowards pulled a syringe from his pocket. He rummaged in O'Malley's desk until he came up with three vials of the familiar yellowish fluid. He pocketed two before filling the syringe.

I focused on my breath. Skylar lay motionless, face down on the floor beside me. Ragged sobs wracked her back in a jagged rise and fall. I couldn't let him hurt Skylar. I climbed my fingers toward the top of the desk, watching Sowards' smirk as he fixated on the emptying vial.

"Since Cam insists this would be too much for you, Olivia. I think the only option we have is to try a fresh source. Don't you?"

I wrapped my fingers around the only weapon I could find as Skylar lifted her head. Sowards twisted her arm in search of an accessible vein. She squirmed against him. He unpocketed a folding knife, flicking it open with one hand before slitting through the zip ties at Skylar's wrist. He grabbed her arms and thrust her to the floor as I lunged, plunging the lit cigar into the back of his neck, the only flesh I could find.

Sowards yelled, the syringe and knife clattered to the floor. His hands flew to his neck scraping away the remnants of burning ash. Skylar screamed through her gag as Ridge's superior turned on me, knocking me to the floor and wrapping his hands around my neck. Flashes of light danced in my vision. His thumbs thrust upward with precision, cutting off airflow.

The squeak of the door, followed by footsteps over hardwood thrummed in my ears. My pulse echoed the percussion as I clutched at Sowards' hands, scratching, aware that Saoirse's last moments were becoming my own.

"Thirty seconds, Sowards." The voice sounded far away.

"Take that one out the back. I'll be right there," Sowards responded through clenched teeth. He jerked me upward before slamming me against the floor one last time. My head ricocheted off the hardwood.

The frenzy in the room thinned. Retreating footsteps. Cool air against my neck where Sowards' hands had been. Pain radiated through the back of my skull as I struggled to move–to breathe. Silence settled. The tinny taps of raindrops on the roof quieted–thinned. My eyes fixed on the crossbeams above as one last huff of air escaped immobile lungs.

53

RIDGE

R ain slid down Ridge's windshield in sheets, making it hard to see the overgrown driveway around the corner ahead of him. He'd promised Adam he'd stay out of the way, let the unit do their job, but that didn't mean he couldn't be close by. Just in case.

He pulled a pack of gum from his console and unwrapped it, folding the stick into his mouth without taking his eyes off the scene in front of him. Unmarked cars, positioned strategically around the woods, blocked the access roads to and from O'Malley's cabin. No one could come in or out without being seen.

Ridge glanced at his watch. 6:45. He'd driven like a bat out of hell to get here in time to see the team move in about fifteen minutes ago, and every minute that ticked by signified one more thing that could go wrong. The radio had been silent. In and out. It should be quick and there should be more communication.

Sowards' voice broke the radio silence at 7:07, crackling out a command. "Get me a bus at point A. We've got visuals on O'Malley."

The commotion was immediate. Cars streamed around Ridge's Shelby, heading toward the lane designated as point A. He gave them their space. Adam's request still rang in his mind. "You're not supposed to be here Ridge. So, whatever you see, whenever the team starts pulling out, give us five before you move in." Ridge intended to keep his promise.

After five more minutes of excruciating radio silence, Ridge followed, popping open the door of the Shelby and stepping into the pelting rain. The cabin was barely visible from where he stood, hidden from the road by thick brush and a steep embankment. He itched to go down himself. Find out what was taking the team so damn long.

His heart pounded in his chest, thumping in his ears and drowning out the hiss of the rain on the gravel road. As he rounded the bend, two agents stood at the back of an open medical unit. A glimpse of long raven hair between them sent him into a sprint.

"You've got to go back," Skylar screamed at the agents. "She's still in there! She's in there with him!" She swung her head back and forth between the men. Her eyes wild with rage. Ridge had never seen his sister so hysterical.

"We're taking care of it, Miss McCaffrey," one of the agents said. They glanced at each other and then toward Ridge. One of them jogged back down the hill while the other helped Skylar into the waiting medical unit.

Ridge stood back a few feet, letting the rain slide over him, through his hair and down his face. Sowards approached from behind. A hand on his shoulder before Ridge met his eyes, dark and serious. Ridge readied to explain himself, but it wasn't necessary.

"Go." Sowards nodded him forward. Fear Ridge didn't

fully understand constricted his lungs. He'd seen her. She was fine. *Skylar is coming home*, he allowed the thought to wash over him, cool the heat of anger.

"Will she be okay?" Ridge asked the medic. The continued presence of Sowards following close behind sent a ribbon of panic through him.

"Agent McCaffrey is the patient's brother," Sowards explained to the tech.

"She's stable," the EMT said. "Worked up. Dehydrated. Some bumps and bruises. We're taking her to County Memorial. You can follow us if you like."

The rain Ridge had barely noticed before now grew cold. His wet clothes sucked and pulled at his skin. He shivered against the discomfort as Sowards pulled him to the side.

"Go be with your sister, Ridge. She needs you more than we do right now."

"I'm not leaving until they find Liv. Sky said she was in there."

Sowards shook his head. "Your sister's been through a lot. She was hysterical, Ridge. You've been in this position before. Until we've got a confirmed report of her in that cabin, we've got nothing." Sowards walked away from Ridge as the radio in his hand crackled to life.

Ridge strained to hear, but rain overpowered the words. Sowards' order, though, was loud and clear. "Pull out. Disengage and clear the area. I repeat, clear the area."

Ridge launched himself past Sowards and down the hillside. Sowards reached for him, fingers slipping from sopping clothes as Ridge fought through the small army of agents in the process of climbing their way up.

"Clear the area," a few of them yelled as Ridge continued toward O'Malley's cabin.

"It's too late," Sowards yelled over the increasing rain. But

Ridge ignored him, turning back toward the cabin just as a flash of light spread through the front windows. The earth rocked with the blast, the cabin erupting in a ball of flame and smoke.

The thrust of heat knocked Ridge backward, mud from the slope seeping through already drenched clothes. Ridge dug his fingers into the earth around him, inching toward the inferno. Heat singed his face. Sowards' words fell on deaf ears as Ridge pushed toward the cabin. But his superior persisted, wrapping his arms around Ridge's chest and dragging him the rest of the way up the incline as the second and third explosions shook the woods around them.

RIDGE SAT in his sister's hospital room, her hand sandwiched between his palms as she drifted in and out of sleep. The doctors hadn't found any evidence of abuse, drugs or otherwise, which was the only thing keeping him from falling off the deep end right now.

"Ridge?" Skylar's sleepy voice was music to his ears. "Did they find her?"

He looked at his sister for a beat before shaking his head, not trusting his voice to answer.

Skylar's eyes grew large, panicked. "She was in there. With him. You have to go back and find her." Tears leaked from the sides of his sister's eyes, falling in moist puddles on her pillow.

"It's okay, Sky," Ridge said, kissing the back of Skylar's hand before pulling it against his cheek. His hair was still damp from the shower, but the rancid odor of smoke was imprinted on his senses. On his skin. In his memory. He'd live with that stench for the rest of his days, he was sure.

Skylar closed her eyes. "She attacked him, Ridge. I couldn't see him. Don't know what he was doing. But I heard him shuffling. Felt him coming closer. He shoved me to the floor. Held me there. Liv pulled him off." Soft sobs rose in Skylar's throat.

"Shhh..." Ridge leaned over his sister, brushing her hair off her forehead. He wanted to ask her who it was. Could she identify the voice? Did he have an accent? But it seemed pointless. Instead, he whispered, "You're here, Sky. That's all that matters right now."

54

RIDGE

A week later, Ridge trudged through blackened ash surrounded by the trunks of partially charred trees. Sowards' invitation for a last look at O'Malley's cabin before Ridge left the Bureau had been an unexpected severance gift.

Sowards must have known he needed closure, but Ridge hadn't agreed right away. The wreckage of Liv's home for the last ten days of her life was already haunting his dreams. Seeing it not only cemented her death, but gave rise to the what ifs.

What if the Bureau hadn't dropped in such high numbers? Would O'Malley have taken the measures he took to ensure there'd be no evidence? What if Ridge had been there instead? Would O'Malley have negotiated? Could he have talked him into letting Liv go? Or would he have been forced to choose between the life of his sister and Liv?

He'd never know the answers to those questions, but the weight of them caused him to surrender his badge the day after Skylar got home. His dad and sister pestered him regularly to come back to Virginia, but right now his biggest accomplishment was getting through each day. And spending time with Colton was a big part of his therapy.

He couldn't bring himself to consider leaving Cascade Hills, at least, not yet. There was still a part of him that hoped he might visit the farm one day and find her there. Taking pictures in the woods. Sitting on the porch in her bathrobe, glitter nail polish sparkling from soft toes. The memories pressed a hard knot into his chest.

The crime scene team had found the remnants of O'Malley's lab. But the blasts had been well-executed. Three blasts, meant to destroy everything in their path. And they had, down to the scattered human remains still being sifted from the ash beneath his feet. The fire had burned hot for three days. The drugs acting as an accelerant and incinerating everything in the cabin.

It would be months before Liv's remains could be identified, but the agents on the scene reported seeing her, laying on the floor in O'Malley's office moments before the blast went off. He hoped she had already been dead by then.

Autumn sunlight filtered through cloud cover overhead as Ridge headed back toward Sowards' car. He wasn't sure why he'd come. He'd seen photographs. Read the reports. Adam had even been stationed outside the cabin during the raid. But Ridge wanted to walk where Liv had walked. Breathe the air she breathed. Anything to be close to her one last time.

As he stepped over what was left of the foundation, he felt it. The imperceptible jolt you feel when you kick a tiny stone. He looked down. Glinting up at him was a gold band, blackened and misshapen from the fire, but unmistakable. Her ring, the one she twisted when she was nervous, lay in the ash by the toe of his boot. He picked it up and dusted it off. Two hands, clasping a heart, topped by a crown. Grace Sullivan's

Claddagh ring, inherited by Liv, and worn every day that Ridge could remember.

"THIS IS THE LAST OF IT," Brian said a couple weeks later, as he slid the final moving box across the living room floor of Ridge's new apartment. He stood up and stretched the kinks out of his back as Ridge thanked him.

"So, I, uh...have something I need to run by you."

"Okay, shoot," Ridge said as he unpacked a box of dishes in the kitchen. Brian came closer, pulling up a barstool to sit on the other side of the Formica breakfast bar.

"With your dad and Skylar coming up for Christmas, and with everything that's happened lately–"

Ridge glanced over at his friend, shoving at the familiar squeeze in his chest that accompanied the mention of recent events. He slipped another dish into the cupboard with the satisfying *shink* of ceramic against ceramic.

Brian fiddled with his jacket that was laying across the bar, pulling something from the pocket and sliding it across the surface between them.

"I'm going to ask Skylar to marry me."

Ridge's heart thumped, his pulse loud in his ears as another dish hit the back of the cabinet with a *thunk*. He stared at the white box between them. Forcing a smile, he picked it up and opened it. A glittering solitaire winked up at him.

He pushed the box back toward Brian, conjuring up as much excitement as he could muster.

"Congratulations, Bri. The two of you are great together."

The knot in Ridge's throat returned with those last words and he turned around, starting on a stack of bowls.

Brian didn't move. "I could wait," he said quietly. "You're my best friend, Ridge. If it's too soon–"

"No," Ridge shot back, too forcefully. He took a moment to collect himself before turning toward Brian. "I'm happy for you, Brian. Really. Don't postpone your life because of mine. It's fine. I'm fine."

"Thanks," Brian finally said, tucking the box into his jacket pocket as Ridge went back to work.

"Now I know why I got a full day's work out of you, today." Ridge smiled at Brian, cutting the tension as Brian opened another cardboard box and began emptying the contents onto the island for Ridge to put away.

RIDGE SAT on the balcony of his new apartment that night, twisting the small gold ring around his pinkie finger as he looked out over Cascade Lake. He'd chosen this apartment for one reason, its proximity to Cascade Lake and the view it provided of Sullivan Farm. From his third floor flat, the back side of the farm was unobstructed. The old house loomed like an eerie fixture on a horror movie set, black in the wake of the setting sun.

As the sun made its final descent, an orangey glow glittered across the darkened windows of Sullivan Farm. Ridge sucked in a breath of the late November air, holding it in his lungs until it hurt.

He almost didn't hear Beth Sullivan knock on his door a few moments later. He pushed the ring into his pocket and waded through unpacked boxes to the front door. Liv's mom was dressed in jeans and a button down blouse, her shoulder length hair hung in soft curls framing her face. But when he looked closely he saw it. The repercussions of losing someone you love more than life. He'd recognized similar etchings on his own face in recent weeks.

"Can I get you something to drink?" He offered, holding up what was left in his own glass. She accepted and he popped open a second can of Guinness, pouring it into a pint glass before handing it to her. "To what do I owe the pleasure?"

"I wanted to talk to you about a few things. About Liv."

Ridge nodded and unloaded a box from the recliner before sitting, leaving plenty of space between himself and the perch Beth had taken on the couch. He'd been avoiding this conversation. Although he'd known it was coming.

Ridge took a gulp of Guinness as Beth fumbled in her purse. She pulled out a keyring and slid it across the coffee table between them.

"What's this?" Ridge asked.

"The keys to Sullivan Farm," Beth said, struggling to keep her composure. "I should have said something before you got this place, but–" She looked away, tucking her bottom lip under her top teeth. *Just like Liv*, Ridge thought.

"Liv would want it this way. She would want you to live there. To raise Colton there."

Ridge pushed the keys back across the table.

"You know I can't do that, Beth."

Silence expanded like a bubble in the room.

"Ridge, please listen to me. When I think about everything that has gone on in this family over the course of the past year, you were a part of it. I know you and Liv had some things you needed to work through. But–" Beth sucked in a jagged breath. "You're the only part of this family that's left."

Ridge looked away, rubbing at the coils of tension in the back of his neck.

"Liv's not here to ask," she continued. "So, I have to do

what I know in my heart my daughter would want. And I know she'd want you to have the farm."

"I can't be there without her." Ridge admitted. "I'm not ready. I don't think I'll ever be."

Beth nodded. "You don't have to decide right away. Take some time. I just wanted you to know you have my blessing."

Liv's mother left the keys on the table and headed for the door. Hesitating, she turned the handle.

"She and I had a nice talk after you left for Charlottesville that last morning."

Ridge clenched his jaw against the accusation that wasn't. Beth turned from the door to face him. "She only had one regret."

"Just one, huh?" He almost chuckled at the thought. "What was that?"

"She wished she'd said, 'yes'."

Ridge's chest seized as he staved off the hot threat of emotion. He could still see the look on Liv's face when he'd proposed on the beach after her run in with Bridget. Hurt. Betrayal.

"She loved you, Ridge. Find comfort in that."

55

LIV

My grandmother's old cottage sat on a hill overlooking Lough Dan, in County Wicklow, about an hour south of Dublin. I'd avoided it as much as possible before, choosing to take care of repairs and paperwork from a safe distance while I worked in Dublin. But for the past three months it had been my recovery center and makeshift prison, chosen by Michael and Ashlyn. Far enough from the nearest town to isolate me, yet not so far from Dublin to inconvenience them.

"So, tomorrow, then?" the taxi driver asked as he pulled up to the cobbled path in front of the house.

"Actually, I'll need a ride into Dublin tomorrow. I've got a plane to catch. Is that too far?"

"Never too far for you." He winked a twinkling powder blue eye at me as I handed him his fare. I smiled in return. Perhaps the first true grin I'd mustered since waking up, dazed and confused, under the interwoven pattern of my grandmother's Celtic knot quilt.

I waved as the cab pulled away from the front walk, a

bubble of excitement rising in my chest. The cabbie, Colum, had proven to be a willing accomplice in my quest for answers over the past several weeks. Picking me up and driving me to the nearest town where I spent my days in the back room of McGill's Pub, using an unreliable internet connection to research the official record of my last days in O'Malley's cabin. But it wasn't until I pulled a discolored list of names from the pocket of dingy jeans hidden at the bottom of my grandmother's cedar chest that I knew I'd found my key to escape.

From that back room I sent my first email to Michelle Rogers, a lawyer in the prosecuting attorney's office at the US Department of Justice. And where, today, I'd picked up a passport and plane ticket that would get me back to the United States.

The red door of the cottage creaked as I pushed it open, swollen from the morning drizzle that had given way to a grey-blue sky. I exchanged ill-fitting jeans and a sweater for running pants and an oversized Trinity College sweatshirt, all hand-me-downs from Ashlyn, I assumed.

Pulling a wad of cash out of the pocket of the jeans, I tucked them in the bottom dresser drawer. What was left of my grandmother's mad money, I stashed in the lock box she'd hidden decades ago. Adding my plane ticket and passport, I slid the box into position under the loose floorboard at the foot of the bed.

I sucked in a lungful of fresh Irish air as I headed out the back door. Stretching and taking off at a jog down the path toward the lake. When Ashlyn and Michael had first brought me here, I could barely walk. My lungs scorched, my legs weak and unstable. My mind a jumbled mess of foggy memories. And at first, I was just happy to be alive.

Frustration set in when my growing questions were met

with sideways glances and silence. Michael and Ashlyn did their best to seclude me. I had no phone, no transportation. The nearest town was too far a walk for the girl with singed lungs. It took three weeks for them to finally admit that the whole escape had been planned from the moment O'Malley got his hands on me. But to this day, they wouldn't tell me who was in on it.

After a few weeks with no answers, I tucked a handwritten note inside the cottage mailbox and hoped for a response. In typical Irish style, the mail carrier went above and beyond, sending Colum out to the cottage the following morning instead of giving me written walking directions as I'd asked. The first words out of Colum's mouth when he knocked on the door were, "Sam brings the mail, said to tell you it's too far to walk."

Weeks later, the thing that shocked me most wasn't the pre-planned escape from Sowards, but the fact that Michael and Ashlyn believed I'd just let it all go. They'd let down their guard. Settled into a predictable routine that made my trips to town possible.

"Will you ever tell me everything?" I'd asked when anger boiled over into a heated screaming match with Ashlyn, fueled by the frustration of a block of blank memory and her refusal to let me call home.

Ashlyn had shrugged and said, "You run the path around Lough Dan without walking, I'll tell you anything you want to know."

I'd been able to do that for the last two weeks. But I needed more time. Time for Ms. Rogers to corroborate the information I'd sent her. Time for her to tell me they'd presented the evidence against Sowards and that he'd been suspended. Time for her to arrange a way to get me back to the US so I could testify, do something to untangle the inescapable knot of secrets that Sowards assumed died with Liv Sullivan.

My feet landed in even strides against the hard-packed dirt path as my thoughts wandered. Ridge, Mom, Skylar—I'd read the reports. Google searches in the back room of McGill's and an email from Ms. Rogers confirmed what I'd found. Everyone back home thought I was dead. The explosion leading to a determination of death in absentia. An issue I'd yet to bring up with Ms. Rogers.

I could deal with fragmented memories, with the fact that Ashlyn and Michael had fulfilled a promise to Herman by getting me away from the Bureau. But I couldn't understand why my family, why Ridge, had to be told I was dead.

The only thing that made me feel any better was the local Cascade Hills news clip I'd found of Skylar standing beside Brian during my funeral service. Seeing her face gave me the first breath of relief I'd managed since waking up in my grandmother's cottage.

My chest ached as I puffed toward the three-quarter mark. The cold March air bit at my tender lungs. In just a few moments, the cottage, now hidden behind a tree line, would return to sight. I powered through burning muscle, waiting for the pain in my lungs and squeeze of my chest to rival the loss I felt. It never did.

Ashlyn and Michael stood on the flagstones behind the cottage as I started up the hill toward them. I glanced at my watch. Four o'clock. Right on time. Ashlyn was smiling and clapping, hopping up and down like an excited child. While Michael just watched, arms crossed across his chest.

Ashlyn grabbed me and hugged hard as I doubled over to catch my breath. "You did it!" she cried over and over until her excitement unleashed my own, a fit of giggles taking over recovery breaths.

I showered while Ashlyn made our afternoon tea. She tugged the whistling teapot off the antique stove as I entered the kitchen, still towel drying the ends of curls that hung well past my shoulders. I pulled a chair out from the table as she handed me a cup of Barry's Tea.

"You made me a promise," I said, stirring honey into the porcelain teacup. Waiting out their silence.

"Herman knew you'd never be safe with the Bureau. After Cohen's burned, he made me vow to never let anything happen to you," Michael started, pulling another chair out before sinking into it.

"But he had no proof the Cohen's fire was meant for me."

"Aye. He didn't. But your mother trusted him, Liv. She knew Grace had hand-picked her to create you. She knew the Bureau was using girls from the home for their program. And she knew why. They were expendable."

"No one's expendable." I said, considering Michael's admission. Had he known the whole time about Saoirse? Jessica? Their names had been on the list, along with my own. So many truths had been left unspoken.

"Aimee knew Grace's creation had become corrupt. The more she learned about GenLink, the less she wanted you involved."

I chewed the inside of my bottom lip. I almost felt sorry then. Sorry for sneaking around, for pretending to be oblivious. Michael's eyes darkened as I studied him.

"So, the whole time–Saoirse, the girls from the home–you knew who they were?"

Michael nodded and stared into his tea. A flicker of anger surged in my chest, squeezing my lungs. He could have ended this before O'Malley, before the explosion.

"And O'Malley? He was just a pawn, wasn't he? It was the Bureau that wanted me out of the picture." I ran my hands down the top of my thighs, pushing away the seething heat of anger. Reminding myself that tomorrow I'd get to start over.

"O'Malley was a man with a score to settle. His taste for retaliation and Sowards' need for power were our strokes of luck." Michael cocked his head to the side. "'Twasn't the whole of the Bureau against us, Liv. But determining who to trust was not an easy feat."

I swallowed my first sip of tea, the liquid burning as it slid down my throat. "Did you know when we found Saoirse's remains what was about to happen?"

Michael shrugged, leaning back in his chair with a sigh. "Nah. But when Agent McCaffrey arrived in Dublin, I knew the Bureau was ready to finish what they'd started."

Michael paused. His voice softened. "Your mother dedicated most of her adult life trying to do what was best for those girls, to make sure they were treated fairly. And they were, until Sowards came along. 'Twasn't long before she realized they'd become throw away operatives to your Bureau."

"Sowards ran her off the road that night. Killed her." I already knew it was the truth. Ms. Rogers had found a record of his visit to Ireland coinciding with the time of my mother's death.

Michael stayed silent.

"Why didn't you tell me before I left? Why didn't you tell Ridge?"

"Would you have believed me? I knew Agent McCaffrey wouldn't. Lyle Hunt confessed to Aimee's death, remember? 'Tis hard to overturn a confession with circumstantial evidence."

I considered his answer, puzzle pieces clicking into place. "That's why they let Lyle off with just five years. His false admission protected Sowards." I hesitated, grim understanding threatened to take over as I forced the next question through my lips. "Did Ridge know?"

Michael shook his head. "No. Agent McCaffrey was just as much a victim as you were, Liv. His past made him vulnerable and Sowards used that against him. He did everything within his power to protect you. Kept you from being chipped like the rest of them." Michael hesitated, the weight of his words deepening the creases around his eyes. "Falling in love with you worked in our favor. It opened his eyes."

Michael's words twisted like a knife in my stomach. "He lied, Michael. Our relationship was based on nothing but a lie."

"Do you really believe that?" Ashlyn cut in.

I didn't. And I knew I couldn't just go back–start over as if nothing had happened. Ridge would never understand.

"Ridge never saw the big picture, Liv," Michael said. "Even now, I don't think he fully understands."

"He still thinks Sowards is innocent?"

"He has his suspicions, but asking him to believe Sowards would jeopardize the integrity of an entire program at the expense of the reputation of the FBI is–" Michael shook his head, the statement drifting off.

"What about the remaining assets? Sowards slid a vial into his pocket that night. What's keeping the Bureau from using it? Couldn't they use it to destroy whatever assets are left?"

Michael fiddled with his teacup, flicking a finger against the fine porcelain handle as he looked out the window, Lough Dan in the distance.

"They may try. But, O'Malley's drug was special, Liv. He built it to avenge Saoirse. You were the only one with a strong enough connection to her. It's side effect had purpose. It was meant to destroy your usefulness to the Bureau–to set you free." Michael looked from Ashlyn to me.

My heart pounded, pulsing in my ears. "It's why the dreams are gone?" I asked.

It was the first time I'd admitted aloud that everything had changed since I'd woken up in my grandmother's cottage. There'd been no visions. No pulses of remnant energy. All of it, gone, disintegrated into a void that was, at times, just as hard to live with. Life was–for lack of a better word–normal.

"Your mother wanted to give you the opportunity to live the life she never could. Herman's dying wish was that we keep that promise."

"And Jessica? Was she O'Malley's accident?"

"Not exactly. Jessica started with O'Malley. But her life ended because of the Bureau–on Sowards' order."

I shook my head. "But I saw O'Malley's hands–his tattoo. When I was in her apartment, his hands were at her throat."

"There was a struggle at the end. O'Malley tried to revive her. It's likely Jessica didn't know who killed her. The effects of the drug were too strong. You would have seen the only memories onto which she was able to hold." Michael sighed. "It's like O'Malley said, people like you knew too much. Sowards got paranoid when Jessica got suspicious."

"So he killed her."

Silence stretched between us. I skimmed my finger around the rim of the teacup. The pull of regret seeped into my chest. I should have told them what I'd been up to. I clenched my jaw against the pang of guilt.

"What about the cabin? How did you get me out without Sowards knowing?"

Michael and Ashlyn looked at each other. Another moment, since the ability had been stripped, that I longed to feel the energy between them.

Ashlyn moved from her perch against the doorframe to the table, sliding into the chair next to mine.

"Liv, listen to me. None of the decisions we made were easy. We knew they'd leave scars, have repercussions that would be difficult for you to understand. But we had to get you out. For Herman, for Mom–for you."

"How did you get me out?" I demanded.

She glanced at Michael who had left the table and stood hunched at the kitchen sink.

"The only way to make this work was with Agent Miller's help," Michael said, his voice low, careful.

"Adam?" I jumped from the table, the wooden chair clattering to the floor behind me. None of my research prepared me for this. "Adam knows I'm here?"

Ashlyn shook her head, pulling the chair from the floor. I ignored her gesture for me to sit.

"He only knows he helped get you out of that cabin and into a safe house. We took it from there," she explained.

"And Ridge?" My breath caught in my throat. Tears stung like hot irons against the backs of my eyes. Ashlyn took my hand. "What was the plan, Ashlyn? Keep me locked up in this cabin for the rest of my life?"

"I'm sorry, Liv. He can't know. It's too dangerous. If Sowards finds out you're alive he'll–"

"What? Kill me?" I interrupted, my heart pounding in my chest. "I'm already dead, remember?"

DEAR
READER

Thank you for taking the time to read Inherent Lies, the second installment in the Blood Secrets Saga. If you're ready to find out what else life has in store for Liv and Ridge, pick up INHERENT FATE, Blood Secrets Book 3, today.

Liv and Ridge have been through a lot, and there are sure to be more trials to come. But at its heart this is a story about love, faith, and the ability of those qualities to overcome even the most dire circumstances. I hope you're enjoying the ride.

Before you go, please consider leaving a review at your retailer of choice. Even if it is only a line or two, it truly is the best gift a writer can receive, and makes all the difference in helping Blood Secrets find fans.

Want to stay up to date with new releases, appearances, and exclusive reader extras? Subscribe to my newsletter.

Or visit me at

www.AliciaAnthonyBooks.com

I hope to hear from you soon!

To find out what happens next in the
Blood Secrets Saga

Join my Readers Club
for updates

and

keep reading for a sneak peek

of

INHERENT FATE

Blood Secrets

Book 3

ALICIA ANTHONY

BLOOD SECRETS ✚ BOOK 3

INHERENT FATE

CHAPTER 1
INHERENT FATE

Liv

Something about death makes invisibility easy. After all the years I spent trying to disappear, who knew all I needed was a death certificate issued by the very government who did everything within their power to bury me?

I gripped the porcelain around the pedestal sink, my knuckles white. The gray-toned walls of the law office bathroom squeezed in on me. *Breathe*, I coached myself. *You can do this, Olivia Sullivan. You made it this far. He can't hurt you anymore.* That was a lie.

A soft knock sounded on the ladies' room door.

"Miss Allyn?" A man's voice broke the silence, the same man who'd waited for me outside Arrivals at Dulles International less than two hours before.

Tony Medici, as he'd introduced himself, was a tall, muscular brick wall of a man. His eyes were a muted hazel, almost gold, and he was close-shaven, his nose just a bit

358 | *Chapter 1*

crooked. The result of an injury, I was sure, but too intimidated to ask.

His broad back and shoulders strained the seams of his dark suit. And he looked less like a go-fer for the US Attorney's Office and more like a mob boss. When I closed my eyes now, I could picture the sign clutched in one of his meaty paws, my new pseudonym printed in bold black letters–Olivia Allyn.

Tony cleared his throat from the other side of the door. "Ms. Rogers is waiting."

I swallowed hard and stared at the reflection in the mirror, wondering why the unaffected gaze of the woman in the mirror didn't match the rabbit race of my heart.

"Thanks, Tony. Be right out." I pushed the door open just enough for him to see a slice of my face, ensure I hadn't ducked out the window and ran. Not that the possibility hadn't crossed my mind in the five minutes I'd been holed up here, but it was dark. I wasn't familiar with D.C., and everyone I'd once known on this side of the Atlantic thought I was dead. In short, I had nowhere else to go. Besides, how far could I get before the USAO tracked me down?

I washed my hands under lukewarm water and jerked a couple paper towels from the metal dispenser on the wall. Glancing back at the reflection, I wiped away the glaze of moisture on my palms. *You deserve a fresh start*, I reminded myself. *Fresh doesn't mean forgotten*, my inner critic chattered at me, the black-lettered sign surging back full-force.

Two months ago I was sitting in the back room of McGill's Pub, two miles from my grandmother's cottage on the shores of Lough Dan, fighting my way through dial-up internet to find an attorney willing to listen to my story. A story that implicated a high-ranking Bureau official in conspiracy against his own department, his abuse of power and misuse of government assets–namely me.

Assistant US Attorney, Michelle Rogers, wasn't even on my list, but somehow, she'd found me–intercepted the email intended for one of the other prosecutors in her office. She was young, driven, and had an obvious hatred for men who used women as rungs on the ladder of power. And if Marcus Sowards' conduct over the course of the GenLink operation didn't fit that description perfectly, I didn't know what did.

She'd launched an investigation into his handling of the Skylar McCaffrey rescue and by extension, the GenLink operation. The evidence I turned over, coupled with the dirt she turned up on her own, was enough to convince Bureau Director, Cristophe Hamlin, to put Sowards on administrative leave pending further investigation.

Now, she was knee deep in building a criminal case against Sowards, while the Bureau itself launched its own inquiry. And for that, she needed Liv Sullivan in the flesh. There was just one problem. Liv Sullivan no longer existed. It was up to Michelle Rogers to bring me back to life.

The door to the bathroom breezed inward with a *thwap*, heels clicking across the tile floor. I tossed the paper towel in the trash between the sinks, catching the reflection of Michelle Rogers in the mirror. Blonde hair hung at shoulder length, streaks of well-placed lowlights proof it wasn't her natural color. Pale blue eyes locked on mine as she extended her hand in greeting.

"Michelle Rogers," she offered. "It's nice to finally see you in person."

I cleared my throat and smoothed travel wrinkles from my purple button-down, pulling myself up as tall as my 5'3" frame would allow before facing the lawyer and shaking her hand. "I apologize for keeping you waiting, Ms. Rogers."

Michelle smiled and shrugged, less like a lawyer and more like a friend–an observation that spiked an unanticipated blade of unease. "Please. It's Michelle. And I expected it." She retreated to the door and propped it open with the toe of her pump. "Come. We've got a lot to cover before Sowards' firing squad moves in."

ACKNOWLEDGEMENTS

It's been said that authors always have that one person that helped them have faith in themselves at a crucial turning point in their career. This is the person who somehow made the author believe that what they produced was worthy of an audience, helped stoke that spark of inner confidence into a flame bright enough that they could trudge on. For this manuscript, that person was Sarah Morganthaler. We met by chance, both finalists the same year in the RWA Golden Heart® contest. But without that chance meeting and her kind words, I may have given up on this manuscript, and writing as a whole. So Sarah, thank you for being my one.

I'd also like to thank the guidance I received along the way as this manuscript was being written. A portion of this book originally began as my MFA thesis project, then titled *Inheritance*, and would not have been possible without the insistent, character-driven eye of Leslie Daniels, who pushed me to edge of my comfort zone to make me a better writer. I thank you from the bottom of my heart.

Of course, the guidance of fellow students and staff at Spalding University's School of Creative and Professional Writing will always rank high on this list, particularly Diana Wilson and Mackenzie Jervis, for making our Ireland experience one I'll not soon forget. Diana, I'm still waiting on your book about Irish cabbies.

A book is not a book without the eye of critical editors. So, to Manufixers, Sam and Cristina, thank you for your gentle guidance as this manuscript found legs. Your support and thoughtful insight was just what I needed. And to Holly Ingraham, the editor who somehow helps me feel like anything is possible, you are the reason book 3 will exist. I can't thank you enough.

My Persister and Omega sisters, you will always be a source of unending inspiration. Thank you for your continued support and gracious words of wisdom. And to Kandy Williams, thank you for always being there for a kind word or a well-timed piece of advice. I'll always be in your debt.

Finally, to Doug and Jillian, without whom none of this is possible. Thank you for sharing Ireland with me, for taking an interest in a culture I claim as my own even if that DNA test says you're more Irish than me. I can't wait for our next adventure together.

ABOUT THE AUTHOR

Alicia Anthony's first novels were illegible scribbles on the back of her truck driver father's logbook trip tickets. Having graduated from scribbles to laptop, she now pens novels of psychological suspense in the quiet of the wee morning hours. A full-time elementary school Literacy Specialist, Alicia hopes to pass on her passion for books and writing to the students she teaches.

A two time Golden Heart® finalist and Silver Quill Award winner, Alicia finds her inspiration in exploring the dark, dusty corners of the human experience. Alicia is a graduate of Spalding University's School of Creative & Professional Writing (MFA), Ashland University (M.Ed.) and THE Ohio State University (BA). Go Bucks! She lives in rural south-central Ohio with her amazingly patient and supportive husband, incredibly understanding teenage daughter, two dogs, three horses, a plethora of both visiting and resident barn cats, and some feral raccoons who have worn out their welcome.

When she's not writing or teaching, Alicia loves to travel and experience new places. Connect with her online at www. AliciaAnthonyBooks.com. She'd love to hear from you!

Made in the USA
Coppell, TX
17 January 2024

27799278R00215